T0033289

HOLDING the LINE

Books by Jennifer Delamere
from Bethany House Publishers

LOVE ALONG THE WIRES

Line by Line
Crossed Lines
Holding the Line

LONDON BEGINNINGS

The Captain's Daughter
The Heart's Appeal
The Artful Match

HOLDING *the* LINE

JENNIFER DELAMERE

BETHANYHOUSE
a division of Baker Publishing Group
Minneapolis, Minnesota

Published by Bethany House Publishers
Minneapolis, Minnesota 55438
www.bethanyhouse.com

Bethany House Publishers is a division of
Baker Publishing Group, Grand Rapids, Michigan

Printed in the United States of America

Library of Congress Cataloging-in-Publication Data
Names: Delamere, Jennifer, author.
Title: Holding the line / Jennifer Delamere.
Description: Minneapolis, Minnesota : Bethany House, a division of Baker
    Publishing Group, [2022] | Series: Love along the Wires ; 3
Identifiers: LCCN 2022029123 | ISBN 9780764234941 (trade paper) | ISBN
    9780764240812 (casebound) | ISBN 9781493439034 (ebook)
Classification: LCC PS3604.E4225 H65 2022 | DDC 813/.6—dc23
LC record available at https://lccn.loc.gov/2022029123

Scripture quotations are from the King James Version of the Bible.

This is a work of historical reconstruction; the appearances of certain historical figures are therefore inevitable. All other characters, however, are products of the author's imagination, and any resemblance to actual persons, living or dead, is coincidental.

Cover design by Create Design Publish LLC, Minneapolis, Minnesota/Jon Godfredson

Author is represented by BookEnds.

22   23   24   25   26   27   28   7   6   5   4   3   2   1

I am my beloved's, and my beloved is mine.
—Song of Solomon 6:3

PROLOGUE

London
Late September 1881

There wasn't too much in life that seriously chafed Rose Finlay, unless it was someone trying to overlay their brand of happiness onto hers. She knew her own mind well enough not to be taken in by such attempts, not even when they stemmed from the best intentions.

She supposed she could forgive her dear friend Emma for this infraction today, given that the lady was newly married, blissfully in love, and had just this hour departed on her honeymoon.

Nonetheless, Emma's admonition about a certain book continued to jangle in Rose's head: *"Definitely don't read the section for widows!"*

The way Emma had said it made clear she was goading Rose to do just the opposite. But how could her friend honestly think any part of that book would hold the least bit of interest for her?

Rose had seen the newlyweds off, standing on the steps of their newly acquired house and waving as their carriage left for the railway station. Now as she walked home, she found

Emma's words growing increasingly heavier, as did the book to which she had been referring. Rose held it close, with the title facing toward her so no passerby would know that she, of all people, was carrying *The Spinster's Guide to Love and Romance*.

It was an absurd title, with equally absurd content to match. It was stuffed with balderdash, designed to feed the romantic longings of lonely and impressionable females. Rose gave a snort of derision. She was neither lonely nor impressionable, thank you very much. The ship *Impressionable* had long since sailed, and Rose was comfortable with her own company.

She'd been tasked by Emma to return the book to the home of its rightful owner, their friend Alice Shaw. Alice and her husband, Douglas, were traveling overseas, but Emma and Rose had been looking in on their flat every week and watering the plants. Rose was determined to return the book at her next opportunity. When the Shaws returned, she would encourage Alice to get rid of it once and for all. Both Alice and Emma had tried their hand at applying the "advice" contained in it, sometimes with disastrous results. Both ladies had found husbands, but in Rose's view the book had been more of a harmful distraction than a helpful guide.

Rose arrived at her lodgings hot and disgruntled. She tossed the spinster book onto a table and made a face at it. She tugged off her gloves and dropped them onto the book, along with her hat. After opening a window to let in some air, she sank onto the sofa. It felt good to get off her aching feet. She fanned herself with a copy of her favorite literary journal, happy to be home after a tiring day.

She lived in a nice set of rooms, although the place felt rather large now that Emma had moved out. Rose sighed. She'd lost her two best friends to marriage. That wasn't entirely true, of course. Alice and Emma were still her friends. Rose was sure the three of them would find time to get together once the ladies returned from their travels. They might even share tea on Sunday afternoons sometimes, as they used to do when they were all single. However, Rose had no illusions that things would be the same. Her friends' lives would be centered around their husbands and homes. Perhaps soon there would be children. In Emma's case, it seemed certain. She was eager to start a family. Rose could easily picture the kind and compassionate Emma with a little brood of laughing, towheaded children hanging about her neck. It would be the hearth and home Emma had longed for. Rose was genuinely happy for her.

She laid a hand on her stomach, feeling a dull ache in her midsection. Her body was healed now, at least as far as the doctors were concerned. Perhaps the source of the ache was closer to her heart. This sensation came over her from time to time, when she was in an especially sentimental mood. Today, as usual, it was followed by the sting of tears. Rose blinked them back. There was no use crying over a past that could not be changed. She was not destined for motherhood and never had been. Rose was sure of this, and not simply because she'd made a disastrous choice by marrying Peter Finlay. No. Her own body had betrayed her first, and then Peter had.

He had betrayed her twice, if she counted the early death he'd brought upon himself, leaving Rose with the bitter task of cleaning up the mess he'd made of his life. But then, Peter had always been a master at shirking responsibility. Any remnants of Rose's fancies regarding marriage and a happily-ever-after had vanished permanently on the day he had died.

She had found a new life, though, Rose stoutly reminded herself. She had replaced a foolish dream with a more practical and satisfying goal—one she could attain on her own. Thanks to hard work and dedication, she was succeeding. Truth be told, dying had been the best thing Peter could have done for her. Rose supposed she ought to feel shocked by such a thought, but anyone who knew Peter would certainly understand. Except for

Peter's mother, of course. Old Mrs. Finlay had been completely blind to every one of her son's faults.

Rose looked down at the mourning ring on her left hand. Gold and black, with a ring of seed pearls and *In Memory of* inscribed on the band, it was elegant enough, if somewhat morbid. Much as she preferred *not* to remember Peter, she didn't mind wearing the ring. It conferred upon her a status for which she was grateful. A widow was generally accorded more deference than a mere spinster. She had more freedom to manage her affairs without the condescending attitudes of men or their oppressive oversight. That had been an advantage, and she'd made full use of it. However, she didn't wear the ring solely to advertise her widow status. Nor did it signify, as her mother-in-law wrongly believed, that Rose was heartbroken over losing her husband. It had a more important purpose.

The ring remained on Rose's hand as a reminder to never again allow a man to dominate her life—and most importantly, her heart.

CHAPTER

One

Two weeks later

Rose sat in the tea shop next door to the post office where she worked. Dusk was approaching, but Rose was in no hurry to leave. After a busy day dealing with an endless parade of needy customers, she had come here for a bit of a rest before walking home. The shop was one of many owned by the Aerated Bread Company. Known as ABC depots, they were welcoming places that offered tea and inexpensive meals. This was one of Rose's favorite places to go after work.

A bright autumn was now taking a sour turn toward winter. Dark clouds brought cold rain almost daily. Rose had taken a table away from the large windows and the chill seeping through their edges. Nevertheless, she still had a view of the outside. She noticed the lamplighters had begun their tasks early to ward off the advancing gloom.

The pot of tea and a ham sandwich, a tiny luxury she occasionally allowed herself, were giving her the fortification she needed to tackle several errands on her way home. She pulled out a list of tasks from the book she'd brought with her. As she read over it, Rose began to consider whether some of these could be put off until tomorrow. Given her tiredness and the inhospitable weather, it was an appealing option.

"Will there be anything else, miss?" Rose heard the waitress ask. She looked up, about to answer, but then she realized the waitress was addressing a young lady two tables away.

Rose was surprised to see the lady seated by herself, without a family member or chaperone of some kind. She couldn't be more than eighteen years old. In fact, she and the waitress appeared nearly the same age. The difference in their circumstances could not be plainer, however. The waitress wore a black frock and a plain white cap, whereas her customer looked like she'd stepped off a fashion plate. Her gown was a rich shade of blue with white ruffles along a V-shaped collar that highlighted her delicate neck. Her hair was swept up and arranged with pretty tortoiseshell combs. It was clearly the work of an expert ladies' maid. Her hat was small and elegantly simple, allowing her hairstyle to do the work of framing fresh features that were lovely with or without embellishment.

What was this girl doing in a tea shop on her own? It was highly unusual, not to mention potentially harmful to her reputation. She clearly came from a good family that would likely care about such things.

The young lady seemed to hesitate and throw a glance out the window before answering the waitress. "Yes . . . I believe I'll have a currant bun, please."

"And more tea?"

"No, thank you."

"Very good, miss," the waitress answered smoothly, although Rose noticed the look of surprise in her eyes as she turned away from her customer. It was odd—why get bread without tea?

When the waitress had gone, the girl surreptitiously pulled

12

a few coins from her reticule and counted them. Perhaps she was calculating how much she could spend and still have cab fare to get home. This was the hallmark of someone who had a rich father to buy her fine things but not a lot of her own money to spend. At the post office, Rose had waited on women who were dressed in clothing that would cost the yearly wage of many workers, yet they could barely find coins for a few penny stamps. It always made her thankful that she was able to earn her own money and had the power to spend or steward it as she pleased.

After placing the coins back in her reticule, the girl turned her attention once more toward the window. She watched the pedestrians as they bustled by the shop, even after the waitress had returned with her order. She seemed to be waiting for someone. But whom? When the girl's face lit up in a radiant smile, Rose could easily guess the answer.

The bell over the shop door jangled as a man strode in. He was tall and lean, handsome in the way that only men of the upper classes could be—which was to say, he was wearing the very best clothes and carrying himself with the proud stance of someone born into wealth and privilege.

Rose recognized him. He was Sanderson Deveaux, the younger son of the Earl of Ormond, widely known by his nickname of Sandy. He was a frequent customer at her post office. He rented a private box there for receiving mail, although much of his correspondence was done by wire. Incoming telegraph messages were dispatched to Sandy's lodgings at the Albany, an exclusive block of residences for well-to-do bachelors. He wasn't the only resident of the Albany to come to her post office, but he was the best known to Rose because her cousin Abby was the head cook at his father's estate in Sussex.

Rose grew concerned when Sandy made a beeline for the young lady by the window. In the glittering society world Sandy inhabited, he was known as a bon vivant whose personal charm and aristocratic lineage made him a sought-after guest for parties and a favorite of many ladies. Rose knew from her work that many women were among his frequent correspondents.

According to Abby, there were occasional whispers that Sandy had been the downfall of several naïve females who'd been led astray by mistaking his lavish attentions for genuine affection. If so, his powerful father had been able to prevent any scandal from becoming public, thereby maintaining the good family name. There was something about Sandy meeting up with this pretty, unchaperoned girl in an out-of-the-way place that increased Rose's worry.

"Miss Sophie Cochrane, as I live and breathe," Sandy said with playful astonishment as he reached her table. He removed his hat and gave her an elegant bow. "What a wonderful surprise to see you."

Rose snorted in disgust at this obvious pretense, but Sophie beamed up at him. "Sandy! I'm so glad you're here. I was afraid you might not come."

Heavens, they were pretty far along if Sophie was addressing him so casually.

"I would jump at any chance to be with you, dear girl." Sandy indicated the chair opposite her. "May I?"

Sophie nodded eagerly.

He sat down and began plucking off his fine leather gloves. "I was out for much of the day, but when I returned home, I found your telegram waiting for me." He draped his gloves over his hat. "I knew if I hastened over, I could make it before you left." His voice was a smooth, rich baritone, the kind that could draw females like flies to honey. He took her hand and kissed it with a flourish. "How glad I am to have caught you."

From her position, Rose could see both their faces, albeit in profile. Sandy released the girl's hand, but he kept her rapt attention with his charming smile and quite possibly a wink. Sophie was starry-eyed with happiness.

Their subsequent conversation was held in muted tones, but Rose was able to catch enough words to follow the gist. She opened her book and pretended to read, covering the fact that she was straining to listen. From time to time, she managed a surreptitious glance in their direction.

Sandy looked down at the currant bun on Sophie's plate. "You've already been served, I see."

"I was afraid if I didn't order something, they might ask me to leave. I'm sure the waitress will be back soon to ask for your order."

"Excellent. I'm famished." He leaned forward. "Now, my dear Sophie, you must tell me what you've been up to. How on earth did you manage to escape your velvet cage?"

"I told my mother I was going shopping on Regent Street with Mrs. Drayton and her daughters, which we did. Then they went home, and I came here." Sophie looked pleased with herself as she related this information.

"The redoubtable Mrs. Drayton simply allowed you to wander off on your own?" Sandy made a tsking sound. "I am deeply disappointed in her lack of oversight."

This brought a giggle from Sophie. "It wasn't quite so easy as that. I told them I had an appointment for a fitting at the dressmaker's shop on the same street, and that my mother was going to meet me there." Sophie's mouth widened in a sly smile. "So everyone is happy."

Sandy grinned in return. "I knew from the moment I met you that you were a clever girl."

"It isn't that I enjoy subterfuge," Sophie insisted coyly. "It's just that life can be so very dull if one adheres to the rules *all* the time." As she spoke, she picked up a teaspoon and scraped some glaze from her currant bun. She placed the spoon into her mouth and took a delicate taste of the glaze, all the while holding Sandy's gaze. "Don't you agree?"

This girl was a flirt of the first water. Rose could only marvel.

How did one so young learn about such things? Perhaps she had an older sister, or—heaven forbid—was taking advice from a more questionable source. Rose thought about the spinster book. It was bad enough that Emma, who at least had some experience out in the world, had been influenced by it. What if such a book got into the hands of a very young person like this?

The object of her seductive playfulness responded in a manner that was no doubt what she was hoping for. "My dear Sophie, you are a girl after my own heart." He covered her free hand with his own and gave it a little squeeze.

Sophie gave a tiny movement, as though a shiver of delight ran down her spine.

Rose didn't like this scenario at all. Sandy was at least ten years older than Sophie—decades more than that, if one counted life experience. He could easily crush her heart and walk away without thinking twice about it.

No one else in the shop seemed to be paying attention to the lovebirds by the window, aside from a few admiring glances sent toward Sandy by some of the female patrons. The ABC depots were known to be safe and respectable places for women to take tea or enjoy a light supper. Sandy could sweep this girl off her feet and out the door, and no one would suspect anything was amiss.

The waitress approached their table, looking as impressed by Sandy as the other ladies in the shop. "May I get you something, sir?"

Removing his hand from Sophie's, he took a more relaxed position and glanced up at the waitress. "What's good here?" He was clearly out of place in these humble surroundings. He had probably never entered an ABC depot in his life. "I'll need something substantial."

"We've beef rissoles, sir. They're very good."

"That sounds fine. And some ginger beer, too, if you please.

I suppose that's the most bracing beverage one can get at this establishment."

"Yes, sir. Right away, sir." The waitress hurried off.

Sandy's hand returned to Sophie's, which had remained conveniently placed on the table. He traced a little pattern on the back of her hand with his forefinger, although he was gazing into her eyes. "I can't tell you how much I've been thinking of you, ever since that delightful conversation we had at Mrs. Dover's home."

Sophie blinked. "At Mrs. Houghton's home, do you mean?"

"Ah yes, forgive me for getting those ladies mixed up. It's understandable, seeing as how it's *you* I remember most about that visit. Those stuffy matrons are all rather interchangeable, aren't they? Promise me you'll never become like them."

Sophie tittered. "Oh, there's no chance of that!"

"Good. Stay as fresh and enchanting as you are now."

This eavesdropping was becoming painful. Rose knew very well there was no chance of that girl staying fresh and enchanting if she continued to welcome a man's attentions in this way.

"I don't believe my mother and aunt are stuffy old matrons," Sophie said. "It's true my mother hardly ever attends parties anymore. But it's because they wear her out so easily. She's got a weak heart, you see. But she's perfectly happy to let me go out. My aunt Marjorie has been taking me with her on social calls to introduce me to people."

Sandy nodded. "Your aunt was that charming lady you accompanied to Mrs. Houghton's home, was she not?"

"Yes, and she was completely taken with you." Sophie smiled. "She told my mother all about meeting you in the most glowing terms."

Rose blew out a breath. No wonder this girl was wading so eagerly into deep water. Her mother was absent, for all intents and purposes. Her aunt was apparently a dolt, if her head had been turned by Sandy's wily charms. Being from an aristocratic family would only add to his appeal. There were many women who could be swayed by such things, abandoning their better judgment as easily as checking a coat at the theater.

"In fact . . ." Sophie paused, then finished her sentence with the air of someone imparting the most delicious information. "My aunt is trying to persuade my mother to come with us to Miss Lester's recital at Lady Bromley's home, so that she can meet you."

"So you received the invitation?"

"Yes, and my mother has agreed to let me go." Sophie appeared to be nearly bubbling over with anticipation.

Sandy rubbed his hands together, nodding in satisfaction. "I knew Lady Bromley could be counted on."

"I just had to see you today, so I could thank you," Sophie exclaimed. "I'm sure we never would have been invited to such an exclusive event if you hadn't put in a good word for us. The Draytons barely secured invitations, but only because Lady Bromley's cousin has his eye on Jane."

Sandy smiled indulgently. "I merely informed Lady Bromley you were the most charming and accomplished young lady I'd ever met, destined to go places in society, and that you would be a sparkling addition to the guest list."

"You didn't!" Sophie protested, blushing at his praise. "How shall I ever live up to such high expectations?"

"But you shall, my girl. And once we have won over Lady Bromley, it will be a simple thing to get you an invitation to the autumn ball at Lord and Lady Randolph's home. That's the highlight of the Season. Loads of people come back to town just to attend it."

"I can't wait to meet them all!" Sophie said, looking enthralled as she envisioned the scene.

"What I like most about Lady Bromley's home is the charming garden out back." He resumed his gentle caress of Sophie's hand. "It's the perfect place to escape to if the room gets too hot. . . ."

Rose wasn't able to hear the rest. Irritatingly, the waitress chose this precise moment to return to her table.

"Will there be anything else, ma'am?" she asked.

Rose could hardly take her eyes from the scene playing out a few tables away. She was sure they were planning a tryst in that garden of Lady Bromley's. She felt like a terrible busybody, and yet, she also had an undeniable urge to protect this girl, if possible. She had no idea how she could do so. She only knew she wasn't ready to leave the shop. "Yes, I believe I'll have a slice of gingerbread," Rose told the waitress. "And more tea." That would give her a reason to linger a while longer.

The waitress left to fill the order, and Rose trained her ear once more on the conversation between Sophie and Sandy.

By now, the subject must have moved to something else, because Sophie's expression had grown serious. "There is one thing I should warn you about. My mother insists on speaking to my uncle John about this event. She wants him to go with us. He's very likely to object to the whole plan. He's such a stuffy old man. He's always telling me to slow down, be cautious, that I'm too young to be out in society. But I'm eighteen years old!"

Sophie said this last bit as if it completely negated her uncle's fears. It sounded to Rose as though this uncle was the only one in the family with any sense.

Sandy tilted his head in surprise. "Did you say *uncle*? I was under the impression your aunt Marjorie was a widow."

"She is. Uncle John is my mother's brother. He's been looking out for all of us since my father died."

"I see." Sandy shrugged. "I have found that men are not always as intractable as they seem. Doesn't your uncle want you to rise in the world?"

"He does. That was the fervent wish of my father as well."

"Then you keep working on him and get him to agree to the party. If he comes along, I'll find a way to set him at his ease."

"Yes, I will! He simply must allow me to go, once my mother and I explain how important this is."

The waitress brought Sandy's food. He exclaimed over it, using such glowing terms that one would think he was at a fine restaurant. The waitress stammered out a happy reply and practically curtsied before moving away.

Rose made the gingerbread last as long as she could, still pretending to read while trying to listen in on the tête-à-tête. While Sandy ate his rissoles, he continued to build up Sophie's excitement for Lady Randolph's ball. He described the lavish food, fine music, and dancing. He went on to talk about the people who would be there. It sounded like an impressive list.

Once he'd finished eating and the waitress had taken away their plates, their conversation shifted to a more personal tone. Their voices dropped to low murmurs as they leaned close in an almost conspiratorial air. At this point, Rose could only catch bits and pieces, enough to know Sandy was playing up the romantic aspects of the ball. She heard mention of the waltzes, of their getting away for a private moment alone. Sophie hung on every word, her eyes shining.

Rose couldn't help but think back to the first time she'd danced with Peter. He had made her feel like the most special woman in the world. He'd wooed her with expert precision, capturing her heart, weaving a romantic spell just as Sandy was doing with Sophie. Even at a young age Rose had prided herself on her good sense, and yet she had not seen past the dashing exterior Peter had presented. Poor Sophie, from what Rose had seen of her, stood even less of a chance against Sandy.

Finally, though, Sophie seemed to take note of the gathering dusk. "I really must be going," she said reluctantly. "Mama will start to worry if I don't get home soon."

"You're right, it wouldn't do to raise her concerns. It's growing too dark for you to be out on the streets alone. Allow me to get you delivered safely to a cab. Where's that waitress, so I can pay the bill?" He looked around and spotted the waitress at a table near the back. "There she is. Wait here. I'll be back in a moment."

Sophie's face was alight with pleasure. It wasn't too surprising. Sandy was acting every inch a gentleman, despite adding a nauseating helping of flirting into the mix. Even if Rose hadn't known about that man's dubious reputation, she would never have fallen for his pretend concern about keeping a lady safe. Unfortunately, Sophie was exactly the sort of girl who would succumb to it.

As she waited, Sophie looked absently out the window, watching the people who passed by. Suddenly, her eyes grew wide, and she started up from her chair. Rose saw that a man had stopped and was staring in the window. He was looking directly at Sophie with a displeased expression.

Sandy was still at the counter at the back of the shop, settling the bill with the waitress. Sophie didn't even glance in his direction. She hurried to the door and went out just in time to meet the other man and stop him from coming inside.

It was easy to guess what was happening. This man knew Sophie, and Sophie did not want him to know about Sandy. Did Sophie have multiple men on a string? Rose could hardly believe it, except that she had seen how the girl knowingly flirted with Sandy.

Sophie and the other man were standing in front of the shop window, clearly visible from where Rose was sitting. Sophie took the man's arm in a familiar gesture and smiled artlessly up at him. By contrast, he was frowning down at her. If this was a beau, he wasn't a happy one. He began speaking to her in a way that suggested he was asking her pointed questions. She kept her cheerful countenance as she replied, clearly looking to assuage his irritation.

The man was handsome and well-dressed—two things Rose had gleaned by now were sure to get Sophie's admiration.

However, she wasn't looking at the man in the same way she had Sandy. Her smile seemed easy and friendly, not coy and flirtatious. Was this a family member, perhaps? Considering the guilty way Sophie had fled the shop, Rose thought it was possible. This was surely not her uncle, though. Sophie had described him as a stuffy old man. This man looked to be in his midthirties.

Rose sent a glance over to Sandy. He watched, brow furrowed, as the pair outside continued their conversation. Instead of trying to join them, he lingered at the back of the shop, striking up a conversation with two ladies who were seated at a nearby table. Rose couldn't hear what was being said, but it was clear he was chatting with them like old acquaintances. Obviously flattered, they responded to him warmly.

By now, Sophie and the gentleman were in animated conversation. Given that Sophie presented an attitude of cajoling deference toward him, Rose leaned more toward the belief this was a family member of some kind. He certainly hadn't lost his stern expression.

She was so busy watching them without any pretense of doing otherwise that she was taken by surprise when the gentleman suddenly turned to look inside the shop. Their eyes met. He lifted his eyebrow, silently asking her, as he had Sophie, just what she'd been doing. Mortified, Rose looked hastily down at her book, trying to appear wholly absorbed in it. She doubted she fooled him. She suspected that none of Sophie's excuses—for that was surely what she'd been giving him—had fooled this man either.

After a few more moments, Rose hazarded a look back at them. She caught sight of the pair walking off together. Sandy continued his conversation with the two ladies for another few minutes, then said a polite good-bye and exited the shop. He went up the street in the opposite direction Sophie and the other man had taken.

Sophie was apparently safe from Sandy—at least for today. Rose was still worried for her, though. She ought not to be so invested in what happened to the girl, given that she didn't even know her, but she couldn't help it. Perhaps it was because she saw something of herself at the same age. She'd been so young when she'd met Peter, and his flattering pursuit of her had completely swept her off her feet.

It was easy, at that age, to think that one knew better than one's "stuffy" relatives what was best for one's life. Hadn't Rose thought the same thing? Yet the steps she had so confidently taken had led only to disaster. It made her heart ache to think of it, now more than ever.

CHAPTER

Two

John Milburn walked along the busy avenue, so intent on his thoughts that he barely noticed the bustle of people and traffic surrounding him. He glanced idly into shop windows as he passed them, but he was still ruminating on the meeting he'd just had with his solicitor. The man had provided little help, despite the absurdly high fees John was paying him. After two years of sorting through piles of documents since his brother-in-law had died, John found his sister's financial affairs were still in a tangle. The money set aside for his niece's dowry seemed to still be intact, but extracting it from other obligations had proven to be complicated. They needed to resolve this soon. Sophie was on the verge of her debut and had clearly stated her desire to enter the marriage market.

John gave a little grunt at the thought. Life was complicated enough, without adding the strings and burdens of tying oneself to another person. And if that person should die before setting their affairs in proper order? His sister and his sister-in-law, both with children at home and no idea how to manage their affairs, were examples of that sort of catastrophe. It was a good thing they had John to help them, or heaven knows what they would have done.

Not that John begrudged them even a minute of all the work he'd done on their behalf. He loved them and his nieces and nephews dearly. Yet these troubles had shown him he'd be better off to steer clear of such entanglements for himself, which he was more than happy to do. He enjoyed his quiet home in Mayfair and the small staff who kept it running like a well-oiled machine. Given that his days were filled with the frenetic pace of work and the constant needs of his family, going to his own home at night was like returning to a veritable haven.

He paused at a street corner to pull his coat collar tighter against the chill. As he did so, he happened to look inside the window of the tea shop that he was standing beside. He blinked in surprise to see his niece Sophie staring back at him. At first, he wondered if he'd somehow conjured her up because he'd been thinking about her. But that was a foolish notion. She appeared to be alone. That couldn't be right, could it? He quickly rounded the building to get to the door.

He was just reaching for the handle when the door opened, and Sophie walked out. She closed the door behind her and stepped away from it.

"Why, Uncle John, it *is* you!" she exclaimed, wrapping her arm through his. "I thought I saw you through the window. What are you doing here?"

Her question sounded more like an accusation, as though she'd caught him doing something wrong. John wasn't sure whether to be irritated or amused. "I've just come from the solicitor's office, working on behalf of your mother, as it happens. And pray tell, why are *you* here? You're not alone, are you?"

John turned to peer through the window of the shop, fully expecting to see Sophie's maid or some other suitable chaperone hurrying to catch up with her.

He had no time to get a good look before Sophie tugged his

arm, drawing his attention back to her. "I am alone, I confess." She pouted in a way that was supposed to appear contrite. "However, it's only because of a silly mix-up. I was shopping on Regent Street with the Draytons. But then they went home, and I went to the dressmaker's shop. I thought I was supposed to meet Mama there, but the dressmaker said no, the appointment is for tomorrow."

John took a moment to consider this information. Even if it was true, she'd given him only a partial explanation. "Therefore you took advantage of this lapse to take a stroll around London?"

Sophie smiled up at him, as though to neutralize the censure in his words. "I am on my way home," she insisted. "But I needed some stamps, so I stopped in at the post office next door to buy them."

"Wouldn't it have made more sense to go to the post office closer to home?"

Sophie gave a little shrug. "I felt like walking. Besides, I was desperate for a cup of tea, and I like coming to this tea shop."

John knew something was amiss. The weather had been gloomy all day, the sun blocked by gray clouds. It was hardly ideal for walking. In addition, London was littered with ABC depots, all of which had similar furnishings and character. This one could not differ in any material way from the others. He eyed her intently. "You decided to come here all by yourself?"

She drew back defensively. "The tea shop is perfectly respectable. Ladies come here all the time."

"How many young ladies go there alone, I wonder, without the protection of a chaperone?"

"I am not the only one," Sophie replied, giving a good impression of the exasperation so often present in her mother's tone whenever she quibbled with John over something she deemed important. "I assure you, it's perfectly safe."

"No one tried to bother you?" John pressed, turning to look

once more through the shop window. This time, he scrutinized it more carefully despite Sophie's tugs on his arm.

Among the shop patrons he saw several men. Two were seated at a table, deep in conversation. A third was standing, leaning with his hands casually on the back of an empty chair as he chatted with two ladies seated at a table. The ladies were smiling up at him and replying cheerfully to whatever he was saying.

The only lone customer was a woman. She was seated with a book in front of her, but she was staring straight at John.

Surprised, John stared back.

The lady broke eye contact first. She dropped her gaze to her book. In another moment, she looked quite absorbed in it, as though her glance up had been merely a momentary break from her reading. John couldn't shake the feeling, though, that she'd been studying him.

It would appear Sophie was correct in her insistence that she was not the only lady to come here alone. But there was no comparison, really. This woman was older than Sophie. She was probably married or a dedicated spinster. John thought the first possibility was more likely. She was pleasant to look at, even if she was not what many would consider a classic beauty. She had a certain poise that increased her attractiveness even more. Her clothing, though modest, was neither drab nor unflattering. The overall effect was appealing, drawing his attention and making his gaze linger. A foolish thought passed through his mind that he would probably enjoy knowing her. He shook it off, amused by the odd bit of fancy. It wasn't a completely farfetched notion, however. It was likely prompted by the fact that she was reading a substantial-looking book.

"I assure you I was not accosted," Sophie said, her words finally drawing John's attention away from the window. "I simply wanted a cup of tea to warm myself before walking home. But now that you're here, perhaps we can take a cab together?"

John hadn't planned on stopping by his sister's house today, but he wasn't going to leave Sophie here on her own. Easily guessing she wasn't going to escape his oversight, Sophie must have decided to make it seem as though being hauled home by her uncle was her own idea. The girl acted too independently for her own good. "Sophie, I can't stress enough how improper it is for you to be wandering around the city on your own."

His niece scrunched her nose. "You may spare me your lectures. I'm quite able to look after myself."

"I've no doubt you think so, but you are too young to understand these things. I shall have to talk to your mother about this."

Sophie huffed out a breath. "Really, Uncle John, you worry too much."

"I don't think so. I find it's better to be safe than sorry."

"Yes, you would say such a thing."

John ought to have rebuked her for offering such cheekiness to him. Just today, however, he didn't have the energy for it. Perhaps he *was* getting old—in outlook, if not in physical years. After all, he was in the prime of life. But his eighteen-year-old niece could not comprehend the weight of the responsibilities that had been placed on him.

He sighed and concentrated on finding a cab.

Once they were in the cab and underway, Sophie began to chatter. She went on at some length about the details of the day's shopping trip. John did his best to seem interested as she detailed the agony of finding just the right color of gloves for her new gown, but he wasn't really paying attention. His thoughts had strayed back to the tea shop and the lady who'd been seated alone there. He wondered what book she'd been reading. He couldn't decide if she seemed the sort of person who preferred novels or nonfiction. Eventually, he smiled at himself for even pondering the question. Why should it matter to him what a random stranger was reading?

"Sophie, is that you?" her mother called out from the parlor, evidently hearing them enter via the front door.

"Yes, Mama. Uncle John is with me."

They entered the parlor. As John expected, they found Pearl seated in a large chair with her feet propped up on a footstool.

Sophie gave her mother a kiss on the cheek. "Hello, Mama. Have my packages arrived yet?"

"Yes, and I was wondering when you might do the same."

"I did stay out longer than planned." Sophie sent a brief glance at John but kept speaking—probably to prevent him from breaking in. "I had a lovely time with the Draytons. But then I stayed at Regent Street while they went home. I was sure you and I had planned to meet at the dressmaker's shop this afternoon."

Pearl shook her head. "No, dear, that's tomorrow. You know this is my resting day. It always takes me a full day to recover from our at-home day, and we had so many visitors yesterday."

"We had four."

John was about to remind Sophie not to contradict her mother, but Pearl gave her daughter a look that said quite the same thing and with even greater emphasis. She wagged a finger at her. "Yes, four—including that old windbag Mrs. Hendricks, who quite wore me out with her endless chatter."

Sophie pretended to look chastised. "I'm sorry, Mama. How are you feeling today?"

"I've had better days. It's impossible to find my breath." Pearl gave a deep sigh, which dissolved into a cough.

Looking alarmed, Sophie picked up a nearby glass of water and pressed it into her mother's hand. Pearl gave her a grateful smile and sipped from the glass. Placing a hand to her chest, she closed her eyes and breathed deeply, as though willing her heart to do its job.

Sophie continued to stare anxiously at her. "I was hoping you would say you are feeling better. I do so want you to get stronger."

Pearl's expression softened. "Don't fret, my dear. I promise you, I'll survive. Now run along and get ready for dinner. I'm in no mood for cold soup."

This assurance, followed by Pearl's motherly command, seemed to reassure the girl. She brightened. "Yes, Mama."

Sophie left the room with a light step, probably anticipating a joyful review of the shopping treasures that were now awaiting her upstairs. She gave John a sunny smile as she passed him. He tried not to think how far this family's finances might be set back by Sophie's shopping expedition.

Pearl held out her hand to John. "How nice to see you. I thought you were still in Birmingham."

"I returned yesterday." He strode over and gave her hand a gentle squeeze. "I hope I shan't wear you out if I stay another minute or two?"

Pearl sat up straighter, rearranging the pillow behind her. "I'm never too weak to spend time with my brother."

John took a seat in a nearby chair. He always felt guilty whenever he had to discuss heavy topics with her, but sometimes it couldn't be avoided. "Do you remember that conversation we had last month—about how important it is to explain to Sophie the limits to her allowance?"

Pearl let out another sigh, the kind she always gave whenever they had to discuss money. "Of course I remember. And yes, I did talk to her." She said this with a tone of voice that tried to imply it had been a firm talking-to, but upon seeing John's skeptical look, she waved a hand wanly in defeat. "You know how I hate to deny the girl anything. We have certain standards to keep up, after all."

"And I've got the bank account to look after."

"I know we've been spending more money on clothes for Sophie lately, but think of it as an investment."

30

John lifted an eyebrow. "How so?"

"We must get her properly outfitted for her entrance into society. If we give her every advantage now, Sophie is bound to make a good marriage. And soon, too, I'll wager. She's mature for her age and so pretty. She can easily catch the eye of any man."

"That's precisely what I'm worried about." John thought back to that tea shop and the men he'd seen there. Sophie had insisted that no one had bothered her today, but that was no guarantee for the future. "Sophie neglected to tell you what she did after she discovered she'd been mistaken about the dress fitting," John said, although he was still entertaining doubts about Sophie's truthfulness on that point.

"Oh?" Pearl looked as though the suspicion hadn't even arisen in her mind. But then, Sophie had a way of turning the conversation to keep her mother from straying to inconvenient tracks of inquiry. "What did she do?"

"Apparently, she decided to walk all the way to Piccadilly to buy stamps. After that, she went to an ABC depot to have a cup of tea." He added pointedly, "She did all of this *on her own.*"

"I suppose she must have been alone, given that she'd already parted from the Draytons." Pearl shrugged. "It sounds to me like she made the best of an odd situation."

His sister's untroubled response only increased his agitation. "The best thing she could have done was come straight home. Do you understand how dangerous it is for a young lady to walk around London alone? I'm speaking of her physical safety as well as her reputation. She'd be an easy target for all sorts of unscrupulous people."

"Surely you're overexaggerating. She was on busy public streets in broad daylight."

"Unsavory people don't work only at night, and what would be the damage to her reputation if she'd been spotted by someone we know? If Sophie had at least been accompanied by her maid, the worst aspects of this situation could have been avoided. Why did you allow her to go out without Aileen?"

"I didn't see the need, since she was with the Draytons. We couldn't have foreseen Sophie's mistake about the dress fitting. Clearly there was no harm done as she obviously ran into you at some point."

"I happened to see her at the tea shop. I'd been in the neighborhood for a meeting with Mr. Sadler."

Upon hearing this, Pearl leaned forward eagerly. "Are we any closer to settling the estate? With Sophie coming out soon, we must ensure her dowry is secure."

"We're planning to open a new line of inquiry in the courts. But about Sophie's actions today—"

Pearl held up a hand. "Please, John, let's not argue over it. If Sophie says nothing happened, then I believe her. She is quite capable. She's been such a help to me. I don't know how I shall manage when she's married and gone. I'm sure I'll be depending more on Louisa's help after that, but it will be difficult nonetheless. Louisa is a dear child, but she seems more interested in her books than running a household."

Louisa was indeed a great lover of reading. Although she was just fifteen years old, she'd already devoured the books in this house and was beginning to make inroads into John's collection. His thoughts returned to the lady in the tea shop. Would Louisa end up like her someday—a spinster who ate supper on her own, with only a book for a companion?

But then, he didn't know whether the lady in the tea shop was a spinster. She might well be married. Louisa would likely get married one day too. As much as she loved books, she also shared Sophie's fascination with handsome young men. The two of them were probably inspecting Sophie's new purchases right now, despite Pearl's admonition not to dawdle.

"I'm sure Louisa will rise to the occasion," John said. "As for help with household matters, I daresay she has more common sense than her sister."

Pearl's mouth dropped to a pout. "You always look down your nose at Sophie. I can't think why."

"I love her dearly, as you know. I love you all, but sometimes love requires telling the truth, even if it's uncomfortable to hear. Sophie will not make a good marriage if she continues to go about London unescorted. She might even end up harming Louisa's chances, if a scandal should ensue."

"You needn't elaborate on your visions of doom. I'll have another talk with her. Let us just be grateful everything turned out all right today. Sophie has shown she is able to look after herself when need be."

"So she told me"—John grimaced and shook his head—"several times."

Pearl gave a tiny smile of pleasure. There was no denying she was proud of her daughter. "John, I do believe you have our best interests at heart. But if we are to speak seriously for another moment, perhaps you ought to be less concerned about my daughters and more worried about Eddie."

John gave a start of surprise. Edward, the eldest son of his sister-in-law, Marjorie, was safely away at boarding school. Or so he'd thought. "Why should I be worried about Eddie? Is something the matter with him?"

"He's healthy enough, thank God. But Marjorie tells me he's having problems at school."

"How can that be? Eddie's one of the cleverest boys I know. He could easily be top in his class."

"The problem isn't with academics. It's his unruly behavior. Marjorie received a sternly worded letter from the headmaster. It sounds as if the boy is close to being expelled."

John grimaced. Why were his eldest niece and nephew so determined to get into trouble, when both were so intelligent and had every advantage? He couldn't understand it. "That is terrible news. However, I don't know what I can do about it."

"Don't you? You have such a winning way with him. The boy looks up to you. If you could go see him and have a good talk with him, I believe that would go a long way." Pearl shook her head. "Poor lad. A young man really does need a father. I believe he looks at you that way already."

Already? John bristled. There was an assumption in her words that John had tried time and again to put to rest. "Pearl, may I remind you *yet again* that I harbor no romantic inclinations toward Marjorie?"

"But why not? I wish you would at least consider the idea."

"There is nothing to consider, given that it would be illegal for me to marry the wife of my deceased brother."

Pearl blew out a breath. "Such a petty law. Loads of people have simply ignored it. No one's been thrown in prison. If I were in love and in that situation, I certainly would not let it stop me."

"It's comforting, I must say, to know my sister would break the law if it suited her." John was beginning to think no one in his family cared about keeping within society's boundaries, even the ones designed to preserve their well-being.

Pearl smirked back at him. "Honestly, John, you can be such a stick-in-the-mud sometimes."

"You should be glad of that," John returned, unwilling to be cast as a villain for doing the right thing. Even if he were to feel romantic love for his sister-in-law—which he most certainly did not—he would never act on it. "Perhaps marrying Marjorie would not lead to jail, but it would lead to scandal. Didn't you just tell me you were concerned about keeping up standards? How far do you think your daughters would advance in society if we became embroiled in such a controversy?"

Finally, John had found an argument that could put this matter to rest. He could see it in Pearl's expression. She knew he was right. She wanted above all for her daughters to make good marriages and for the family to continue its rise in status. They were solidly middle class, but Pearl aspired to more. John had made his point, at least for now.

Unwilling to admit outright that she'd lost, Pearl simply said, "I can see why you're such a good businessman. You're so persuasive—who can resist your logic?"

"It is no doubt the reason why I'm so immensely successful," he agreed, managing a wry smile. "And which allows me to help you and Marjorie and your children keep living in the manner to which you are accustomed."

"And we are grateful for it," Pearl said. "Truly we are."

John could hear the sincerity in her words. It was gratifying to think they had some measure of thankfulness for all the ways he was putting himself out for them. "I'll speak to Marjorie tomorrow. I'm going up to Leeds next week. Perhaps I can stop by Eddie's school on my way and have a chat with the boy."

Pearl beamed. "That will be a great comfort to Marjorie, I'm sure."

John stood up. "I'll drop by here tomorrow after I see her. Mr. Sadler is drawing up a petition to the courts that you will need to sign."

Pearl's smile faded. "More paperwork." She gave another of her trademark heavy sighs.

It alarmed John to see his sister withdrawing from her responsibilities. Despite her earlier assurances to her daughter, she was growing weaker, and John did not know how to prevent it. He covered his worry with an exaggerated roll of his eyes. "It is a great burden to put your signature on it, I know."

She batted his arm playfully. "You are invaluable, dear brother, even if you are insufferable. Won't you stay for dinner?"

"No, thank you." In truth, John was looking forward to a quiet evening in his own home. He'd spent three weeks traveling for business, and his personal affairs needed tending.

35

"Then I shall have the carriage brought round for you." She tugged on the call bell next to her chair before he could object.

In the end, John was glad for the ride home, and not only because the thick clouds had let loose a cold rain. He was tired. He closed his eyes, mentally reviewing the many things he had yet to do this evening. Yet somehow, the image of the lady in the tea shop kept returning to him. She really was quite striking in a quiet sort of way. Perhaps not the kind of woman who turned the head of every man she passed—only the ones who were looking for something a little deeper. Maybe it was that indefinable quality often lauded by the etiquette books as *poise*.

John shook his head, trying to dislodge the foolish notion that he might have learned so much about a lady from just one look. It was true that he had allowed his glance to linger . . . until Sophie had interrupted him. John pushed his thoughts back to the problems at hand. His niece was just one example of how he had too many women taking up his energies already.

CHAPTER
Three

Rose turned the key in the lock, then tapped on the door before letting herself in. "It's me," she called, seeing no one in the sitting room.

Mother Finlay emerged from her bedroom with a thick woolen shawl in her hands. "Poke that fire, will you, dear? The chill has gotten quite through to my bones."

Rose did as requested while her mother-in-law made herself comfortable in a chair, murmuring, "This damp cold is going to be the death of me, I just know it."

Rose set aside the poker. "Nonsense, you'll outlive us all."

She immediately regretted her little pleasantry. Mother Finlay emitted a deep sigh—the kind reserved for only one subject.

"I wish I hadn't outlived my son, I can tell you that," Mother Finlay said, pulling out a handkerchief and dabbing her eyes. "Oh, if he were alive today . . ."

Rose said nothing as Mother Finlay continued on. Inwardly, she tamped down painful feelings of her own. She dutifully waited for her mother-in-law's ramblings to run their course, as they always did.

Mother Finlay clasped a hand to her heart. "How I should

love to see my dear, sweet boy bounding into the room once more, and to hear him say, 'Cheers, Mother!' just as he always did."

Rose never quite knew which version of Peter her mother-in-law was envisioning during these times when she waxed eloquent about her lost son. Was it the impish, eight-year-old Peter, the little boy she'd adored and spoiled? Or was it the grown man, whom she'd idolized—the man who could charm and bamboozle anyone, most especially his doting mother?

There was only one version of Peter that Rose remembered: the two-timing schemer who would do or say anything to get what he wanted, and yet somehow everyone still loved him. Rose had loved him once too. But that love had died on the day she'd made the trip up to York after Peter's fatal accident to bring his body back to London for burial. More precisely, it had died the moment she'd arrived at the undertaker's premises and found another woman sobbing over Peter's lifeless body. A woman who thought she was Peter's wife.

"I'm such a silly old woman, to indulge myself in my sorrows," Mother Finlay said, interrupting Rose's dark thoughts. "But how can I help it? The love of a mother for her child is fathomless and unchangeable. Yet I know how much you suffer, too, in your loss." She reached out to take Rose's hand, the one with the mourning ring on it. "The holy bond between husband and wife is a sacred one that can never be broken. Not even by death." She caressed the ring with a rapturous expression, almost as though she saw Peter's face somewhere in that ring of seed pearls. "What a wonderful day awaits us, when we shall all be united once more."

Rose's stomach turned at the thought of being with that man for all eternity. She could not imagine a worse fate.

Normally, she bore these maudlin episodes with patience, but today she couldn't bear to spend even a moment pretending she was still heartbroken over Peter. Especially not after what she'd witnessed in the tea shop today. Seeing the way Sandy's flattery had won over Sophie had brought back afresh her own pain at having been manipulated by an unscrupulous man.

She pulled her hand away, using the excuse of walking over to the bag she'd brought with her. "I brought you a fresh bun from the tea shop. I know how much you like them." She pulled the wrapped bun from her bag and extended it toward Mother Finlay. "Shall I get you some butter to go with it?"

Mother Finlay waved away the proffered treat. "Thank you, dear, but I've already had my tea. I didn't expect to see you."

Rose looked at her in surprise. "You knew I planned to pop round to see how you're doing."

"Yes, but when there was no sign of you by six o'clock, I decided you must not be coming. I know you have so many more important things to tend to than looking after an old woman."

"I'm sorry I was delayed." Rose had no intention of elaborating. Whether Rose was late by one minute or an hour, her mother-in-law would attempt to make her feel guilty about it. Keeping her voice chipper, she said, "I'll just take this to the kitchen and wrap it in a moist towel. It should still be delicious for your breakfast tomorrow."

"You are so kind," Mother Finlay answered, but she wasn't really listening. She was reaching over to pick up the framed photograph of Peter that was on the little table next to her chair.

Not wanting to be forced to contemplate that hateful face tonight, Rose hurried to the kitchen. She wrapped the bun and set it where her mother-in-law would be sure to see it in the morning. The kitchen was in disarray, with dirty dishes scattered about. Rose took a few minutes to wash them and put them away. She did this not only from kindness but also to distance herself while her mother-in-law was in one of her moods.

By the time she returned to the sitting room, the photograph was back in its place, and Mother Finlay was sitting quietly with her eyes closed. She opened her eyes as Rose reentered the room. "As you can see, I'm quite worn out. I went to the meeting of the Ladies' Temperance Society this afternoon. Walking in the cold took a lot out of me."

"Be careful not to fall asleep in your chair," Rose admonished. "I don't want to have to be summoning a doctor when your back pains flare up again."

"I won't." She gave Rose a grateful smile. "You are a good and dutiful daughter."

Mother Finlay always called her *daughter*. Never the more accurate *daughter-in-law*. She had effectively adopted Rose, but this was not so much out of love for Rose herself. She had no interest in Rose's personal life. She never asked for details about her work. She had no curiosity about Rose's involvement in the wider world, what books she was reading or what friends she had. Mostly, she wanted Rose around to help her cherish the memory of her son. She assumed Rose shared her grief at his passing.

For many years after Peter's death, Rose had been able to keep Mother Finlay at arm's length, visiting her only once a month or so. But the woman was growing frail. Unlike Rose, she had no other family. She'd begun pressing Rose for more of her time and help. Rose had complied. She would feel guilty otherwise. Her tasks were made all the more onerous by the impression her mother-in-law was deliberately stoking those feelings of guilt.

The best Rose could do was draw the line in any area she could, not allowing Mother Finlay to consume all her time. "I'm leaving now," Rose said, reaching for her coat. "It's been a long day for me too."

"Yes, of course," the lady said magnanimously. "Good night, my dear."

It was a relief to get outside. Even a walk in the rain was preferable to the stuffy confines of her mother-in-law's flat.

As she opened her umbrella and strode up the short lane to her own lodgings, Rose found her thoughts returning to the events she'd seen at the tea shop. She remembered how much she valued her freedom at that age, yet she also knew from painful experience that serious calamities could befall a naïve girl who was not gently reined in and given proper guidance. She hoped whoever had intercepted Sophie today was alert and able to give the girl the oversight she clearly needed.

Upon reaching her flat, Rose was pleased to find a letter waiting for her from Emma. While on their honeymoon trip in Scotland, Emma and Mitchell had made the acquaintance of a wealthy shipbuilder and his wife who turned out to be avid theatergoers. Given that this was also a passion of Mitchell's, they had struck up a warm conversation, which had blossomed into friendship. The couple had even invited them to visit their estate in northern England. It was an offer Emma and Mitchell had been thrilled to accept.

Feeling an immediate lift to her spirits, for she enjoyed Emma's lighthearted letters, Rose removed her coat and gloves and sat down to read.

My dear Rose,

As you know from my previous letter, we've been having a wonderful time here at the Clarkwells' estate. Their home is charming, and the gardens are extensive. The gardens are largely dormant at this time of year, but they are still lovely. I spent several hours walking around with the gardener, gathering wonderful ideas and information.

Here is some exciting news: it appears our honeymoon trip may not be over yet! Yesterday we were packing for home when Mitchell received a telegram. He had sent a letter to Mr. Fawcett, asking whether he might go directly from here to Lincoln, rather than returning to London.

He was scheduled to go to Lincoln later in the month anyway to get started on the work the postmaster general wants him to do—collecting information from the larger towns about their processes, their complaints, and how they might improve. (He is going to be wonderful at this task, I know! You should see how easy it is for him to talk to people, and how they warm to him so quickly because he is so personable. But then, I could go on endlessly about my wonderful husband, so I had better not bend your ear any longer on that subject!)

As I was saying, Mitchell thought, why not go to Lincoln now, while we were still in this part of the country? Yesterday he got a wire back from Mr. Fawcett saying that it is all arranged. So Mitchell is going to Lincoln, and I am going with him.

I know you must think it strange that a homebody like me has been gallivanting all over the country. I find it strange myself! But I don't feel homesick in the least because I am with my dear husband. Although I am excited to return to London and settle into our new home, I don't mind waiting a few more weeks. We'll have the rest of our lives for that. And besides, I can't get a proper start on our garden until spring.

Mitchell is tugging at my sleeve, telling me we shall miss our train if I don't end this letter and post it. Good-bye for now. Enclosed is the address of our hotel in Lincoln. Please write to tell me what you've been up to. You know how much I love hearing from you!

Ever your friend,
Emma Harris

Rose set down the letter with a sigh. She was thrilled for all the successes Emma and Mitchell were having. Just now, though, Rose was feeling a little bereft. She longed for a personal chat with a dear friend. Loneliness was an unusual sensation for her even though she'd been on her own for many years.

Setting the letter aside, Rose reminded herself she still had the luxury of losing herself in a good book for an hour or so before going to bed. Tomorrow would bring plenty of challenges and rewards, all of which would be gratifying enough. That was what she would focus on.

John went down to the kitchen at Pearl's home, intending to speak to the cook about the monthly food budget. Pearl had consented for him to do this since it meant one less task she had to tackle.

As he and the cook reviewed the accounts, John happened to notice Sophie's ladies' maid quietly accepting a folded piece of paper from a man at the back door. As soon as the note changed hands, the man slunk quickly away.

"What is that?" John asked, pointing toward the maid's hand.

"It's just a note from—from my sister, sir. She, erm, works nearby." Looking flustered, she attempted to tuck the paper into her skirt pocket. John took hold of her wrist to prevent her doing so.

Meanwhile, the cook fixed the maid with a hard stare. "Now, Aileen, you know the rules. There's to be no walking out with any man while you're employed here. That's grounds for immediate dismissal."

"It's not like that, Mrs. Brown," the maid protested, although the fear brought on by the cook's threat was evident on her face.

"It's all right, Aileen," John said. He might not have thought twice about this incident, if it had not been for finding Sophie on her own at that tea shop the other day. Now he couldn't help but wonder if the passing of notes by means of a willing maid might be related to Sophie's going about London unsupervised. He tugged the paper from Aileen's unwilling hand, although she was too obedient to refuse him.

The note was short.

Marble Arch on Saturday? O

Knowing Aileen's only time off was a half day on Sundays, John surmised the note wasn't meant for her. The mark at the end of the line looked like an O, but there was a slight indent at the top, enough to suggest a heart shape. John didn't know who this O was, but he was determined to find out.

"Yes, I can see this is from your sister," John said. He returned the note to Aileen, who gaped at him in surprise. "You needn't even tell anyone I've seen this note nor asked you about it. I think that would be best, don't you?" He gave her a pleasant smile, which Aileen understood was the seal to his command.

She nodded dutifully. "Yes, sir."

John turned back to the cook. "No harm done, Mrs. Brown. I'm sure Aileen can be depended upon to follow the guidelines laid out for her."

Mrs. Brown looked unconvinced, but she wasn't going to contradict him. After another suspicious look at the maid, she gave a curt nod. "All right, then. Haven't you got work to do upstairs?"

"Yes, Mrs. Brown." Looking relieved, Aileen scurried from the room.

Mrs. Brown had unwittingly helped John's plan. It would now be a simple thing for Aileen to deliver the note to Sophie, if she was indeed the intended recipient. John had a strong suspicion she was.

He didn't want to interfere with this messaging system for now. He only hoped the maid would not reveal to Sophie that he'd seen the note. But he thought he'd made his wishes clear. She was a perceptive girl. She wasn't going to risk being put out on the streets without a reference.

John would find out soon enough, because he was going to the park on Saturday to see for himself just what was going on.

⁓⸜◌⸝⁓

It was a rare day at the post office when business was slow. This location in Piccadilly had a steady stream of customers from opening time to closing. Rose knew all aspects of the business. She could send and receive telegrams, sort mail, and wait on customers. Through diligent effort, she had risen to the position of assistant manager. Her overseer, Mr. Gordon, was trusting her more and more to help with scheduling the staff and administering the payroll. This week he'd left the office entirely in her hands while he was on holiday in the country. It was more proof that Rose was bound to be promoted to manager one day.

Despite cheerfully tackling other tasks, she was keen to remain fluent at operating the telegraph machine. She was filling in while Stan, the telegraph operator, was out for a luncheon break, when a message came across the wire that took her by surprise. She could hardly believe her eyes as she transcribed the words tapped out by the sounder.

TO: SANDERSON DEVEAUX, THE ALBANY, LONDON

FROM: SOPHIE JONES

SUCCESS. CAN MEET SATURDAY AT 3. ARCH.

Rose had done her best to forget the incident at the tea shop, telling herself that surely Sophie had relatives who were watching over her. Yet this message seemed to indicate she and Sandy were meeting again tomorrow. Sandy had addressed her at the tea shop as Sophie Cochrane, but this could well be the same person. She might have used a false name to add privacy to this communication. If so, it meant Sophie was continuing her deceptions. Surely that could only lead the girl to harm.

Rose filled out the form and wrote up the clean copy that would be taken to the recipient. Her mind was whirling in a hundred directions.

She walked to the room at the back of the post office where the messenger boys lounged about between errands. The others were out making deliveries, but Charlie was there. He was reading a tattered newspaper that had probably been discarded by its original owner. The moment he saw Rose, he stood up and tucked the paper under his arm. "Something for me, Mrs. Finlay?"

"Yes." She handed him the telegram.

He looked at the address and grinned. Rose knew the Albany was one of Charlie's favorite places to deliver messages. Like many people of scant means, he was awed by the elegance of the place, finding pleasure in having an acceptable reason to enter it, if only briefly.

"Mind you make good time," Rose admonished. "The wires are busy today."

"Yes, ma'am. I shall be quick as the wind." True to his word, he took off at a run.

Rose returned to work. She read over the original telegram one more time before filing it. Perhaps *arch* referred to the Marble Arch, located at the northeast corner of Hyde Park. It was only a guess, but Rose thought it a reasonable one. A stroll in the park would provide the perfect setting for a private conversation.

Rose found herself wishing there was some way she could intervene. She was surprised at herself for this. Never before had she wanted to insert herself into a situation that was none of her affair. Perhaps after seeing her two best friends happily married to good men, she was paradoxically more sensitive to the bad ones that were out there. Or perhaps it was because she really did see something of her younger self in the girl. If only Rose could go back in time to talk to her younger self—oh, the things she'd tell her!

She began to consider an idea that was completely outlandish, especially for her. On Saturdays she left work at noon. There was nothing to stop her from taking a walk in the park herself. It was a public place, after all. Rose had no idea what she could accomplish. Even if she saw them, she would not be able to listen in on their conversation as she had at the tea shop. But she could at least observe them. And if Sandy should do anything that seemed the least bit untoward, Rose would—

Stymied, Rose paused midthought. What would she do? What *could* she do?

She had no idea. She only knew that something was compelling her to be there.

CHAPTER
Four

It was not an inviting day for a stroll in the park. The fog was thick, swirling along the ground, at times covering the walkways. It was difficult for Rose to give the impression to any passersby that she was here for her own enjoyment. Fortunately, there were not many people about. The few she did see were generally moving quickly, intent on getting to their destinations.

The only people who *did* seem to be enjoying themselves were Sandy and Sophie. Rose had caught sight of them not long after entering the park. They were walking slowly, pausing often. Sophie's arm was wrapped tightly around the arm of her escort, and she seemed to be taking the cold weather as an excuse to get close to him, as though seeking warmth. That girl certainly knew all the ways to make flirting appear natural and easy.

Rose was following them at a good distance, pausing whenever they did and trying to look interested in the bushes lining the path. The cool weather had turned them bright red, which gave a somewhat credible reason for her to pause and admire them. She didn't worry overly much about it, since no one was paying her any attention, least of all the lovers ahead of her. Sandy had opened a wide umbrella. He'd perched it on one shoulder, effectively giving the couple a shroud to chat with a semblance of privacy. This cut them off from Rose's view from about Sandy's waist upward. Rose figured that as long as the pair was walking, there was nothing too scandalous they could be doing, although heaven knew what they might be saying. Rose had heard enough at the tea shop to believe Sophie's heart was soundly—and unwisely—in Sandy's pocket.

The couple paused again, and so did Rose. Once more, she tried to look fascinated by the red bushes, especially as a man walking in Rose's direction happened to be passing by her just as she stopped. He tipped his hat. "Good afternoon." He didn't pause for an answer but kept on going. A moment later, Rose heard him repeat the greeting. She turned her head enough to see he'd addressed someone who was coming up the path.

Rose nearly jumped in surprise when she saw who was approaching her. It was the man who had met Sophie outside the tea shop. Would he recognize her? There was no reason why he should, even though their eyes had met briefly through the shop window. But if he did, he would surely wonder what she was doing here, trailing the lovers up ahead. Rose felt warmth in her cheeks now, burning off the chill that the fog had brought to her face moments before.

He stopped two feet away from her. "Excuse me, miss."

Rose turned toward him. "Yes?"

"Do you know that couple?" He pointed toward Sandy and Sophie. He was taller than Rose had realized when she'd seen him from the tea shop. He was probably around six feet. He was scowling down at her in a way that bordered on threatening.

Rose stiffened, meeting his gaze squarely. She might be unwisely involving herself in someone else's affairs, but she wasn't going to allow any man to make her cower. "What makes you think I know them?"

"I saw you in the same tea shop where that young lady was just a few days ago."

Rose didn't know whether she was more stunned that he was here, or that he had remembered her from one brief glance. Whoever he was, he had a sharp eye for details.

When she didn't answer, he added, "That is, I *believe* you were there. Were you not?"

Trying to cover her embarrassment and confusion, Rose countered, "Might I ask who you are, to feel you can approach a stranger and immediately fire off questions?"

Her words had the desired effect. The man took a step back. "My apologies. I'm anxious to sort out this situation, but that was no excuse to accost you. My name is John Milburn. The young lady on the path up there is my niece. I am worried she might be in a situation that could be harmful to her or to her reputation. I would greatly appreciate any information you might be able to offer."

He gave her a little smile that was somewhat disarming, given that he was still looking at her intently. The apology seemed sincere, however. It was difficult to believe this was the stodgy old uncle that Sophie had been describing. Then again, the girl had been speaking from the perspective of youth. There was certainly no doubt this man could be intimidating if he wanted to be. Yet he had shown by his quick apology that he could be reasonable.

"There's no harm done, Mr. Milburn. You are understandably concerned about your niece."

In fact, Rose couldn't help but wonder why he was standing here talking to her instead of chasing down the errant couple. She gave another glance toward them. They were still paused on the walkway, still partially shrouded by the umbrella and the fog. "Yes, I was at that tea shop. I happened to notice the young lady seated by herself. I thought that was curious, as I could tell she was a lady of some means."

He shook his head, looking perplexed. "She was alone?"

"The gentleman arrived a few minutes later. It soon became clear to me this had been a planned meeting." Remembering how both Sophie and Sandy had acted once Mr. Milburn had arrived on the scene, Rose added, "I don't suppose you knew about it."

"No, I came across Sophie outside the tea shop quite by accident. Would you happen to know the identity of the man she met there?"

"I do, as it happens. His name is Sanderson Deveaux. He's the younger son of the Earl of Ormond."

"An earl's son!" As he turned his gaze back toward the couple, his astonishment changed to awe. "How could Sophie possibly know such a person?"

The question was posed more to himself than to Rose. She did know the answer, however—or at least, the little bit of it that she'd overheard at the tea shop.

She was considering whether to offer that information, when she saw another change in his expression. The illicit nature of this stroll must have taken precedence in his mind because the intensity she'd seen earlier returned.

"Might I ask how you know this man's identity?" he demanded, sending his anger, whether purposely or not, toward Rose. "Are you one of those society mavens who can identify aristocrats on sight? Or perhaps you're a journalist, sent out to collect gossip for the scandal sheets, Miss, er—?"

Rose bristled. "*Mrs.* Finlay," she supplied, emphasizing the honorific, as she often did in order to be taken seriously by men. It was ironic in this case because Peter's ability to turn quickly from kind words to harsh accusations appeared to be one of Mr. Milburn's traits as well. "I am an assistant manager at the Piccadilly post office."

That got his attention. He drew his head back. "The post office?"

"It is next door to the tea shop," Rose went on, seeing she had surprised him enough to get the upper hand. "Mr. Deveaux is a frequent customer there, which is why I recognized him. Believe me, I am no scandalmonger. I don't even read the gossip rags, much less write for them."

He didn't miss the reproof in her tone. To his credit, he looked properly abashed. "I must offer you my apologies once more, Mrs. Finlay. As you have gleaned, I am heartily dismayed by this situation. To learn that Sophie has been engaging in such meetings would be trouble enough, but to learn who she has been seeing . . ." He let out an exasperated breath. "This puts me in a difficult position. I'll need to tread lightly."

Rose's first thought was that if she were him, she would be confronting the man right now, not standing here discussing the finer points of the issue. What was stopping him? Was he worried about insulting a man of Deveaux's high station? Not that John Milburn was a nobody. His top hat, fine white woolen scarf tucked into a good-quality topcoat, and polished boots were all evidence the man had garnered some wealth. Then again, those in the middle class who aspired to breach the higher echelons of society were usually more harmed by scandal than the aristocrats, who could use their power to sweep any such troubles under the rug. Sandy was proof of that.

"Was Deveaux still in the tea shop when Sophie left it?" Mr. Milburn asked.

"He was."

Mr. Milburn made a sound that might have been a grunt or a curse. "I should have known."

Now Rose felt guilty for not having done anything at the time, even though she knew there had been no expectation for her to do so. Years of handling personal messages in a confidential manner had established a solid line across which she never strayed.

Or had she? Mr. Milburn's next question, coupled with the

curious way he was looking at her, raised a point she'd been hoping to avoid.

"Might I ask what you are doing here today, Mrs. Finlay? I can't imagine you ran across them a second time by accident."

Rose had not expected she would need to explain to anyone her reasons for being here. Now she was in a tight spot. She could not admit she used information encountered at work to find Sophie and Sandy today. She would have to find some way to equivocate. That was an awful choice, but it was the lesser of two evils. "I was . . . able to overhear snippets of their conversation while they were at the tea shop."

John was still reeling from this discovery that Sophie had been seeing a man without anyone's knowledge—and that it had been an earl's son to boot. The O on that note would stand for Ormond. As a younger son, Sandy would have no title of his own. His father's title as Earl of Ormond would be the name by which the family was generally known. Why was such a man dallying with Sophie?

And why was Mrs. Finlay involved? Her face had pinched as she'd responded to his question. Something seemed off. "Do you mean to say they were speaking at the tea shop about to-day's meeting?" he prompted.

"I only overheard snatches of their conversation. They definitely planned to meet again. I made some guesses based on what I heard."

This didn't exactly fit the information John had. He was sure the details had been only recently decided upon. Apparently, the maid had done as she was told. She'd delivered the note to Sophie without saying anything about John, and Sophie had come here to meet Deveaux. John had been right in his guess about what time the pair would meet. He'd based that on a few casual questions to Pearl regarding Sophie's plans to "visit a friend."

"As you might well guess," he said, "I also learned about their meeting today. I want to end these private outings once and for all—without word getting out to anyone."

She nodded. "I certainly hope you can accomplish this."

"Might I ask why you are here?" He chose his words carefully, remembering how she'd reacted to his initial questioning.

"I hope you won't think I'm intruding where I don't belong. That certainly was not my intention. When I was about Sophie's age, I was taken advantage of by a smooth-talking charmer. It did not turn out well. I suppose I wondered if I might find a way to prevent Sophie from a similar fate."

He looked at her, arrested by this information. Although she was by no means old, he still couldn't imagine her as a naïve girl. Certainly she seemed wise and confident now. He supposed things must have turned out all right for her since she was married. "You came here today merely from a desire to help her?"

"Yes, odd as it seems."

John found his burden lifting a little. "Thank you. I greatly appreciate your kindness."

"It was a small thing," she replied. "I had no way of reaching out to the family, or I certainly would have. Now that you are aware of the situation, there's nothing more I need to do."

"Might I ask you one more question?"

"All right."

"You mentioned that Deveaux frequents your post office. I wondered if you'd seen any correspondence to him from Sophie. A telegram, perhaps?"

She drew back. "Please don't ask me such questions. My clients' correspondence is strictly confidential."

John couldn't argue that point. He tried another tack. "But you have some reason for thinking Mr. Deveaux's intentions are not honorable? You must have an idea of his character."

"I know only what I've heard through general sources. Given his position, Mr. Deveaux is practically a public figure. But any man who would draw out a young girl as he has done—" She turned to gesture toward the pair as she spoke, but then she paused and frowned.

John followed her gaze. Sophie and Deveaux were no longer in sight. The fog seemed to have swallowed them up.

"We should go after them," Mrs. Finlay urged. She looked ready to sprint down the path.

"No, I'll do it." John figured his best chance for catching them was to run. Mrs. Finlay would only slow him down, and he couldn't afford it. He was sorry for this, but he had no time to explain. "Please accept my sincerest thanks for your help, and for your interest," he said and raced off before she could reply.

Despite their earlier slow pace, the couple now seemed to have moved surprisingly fast. John reached the place where they'd been standing and peered into the fog. About twenty yards ahead, the path diverged in two directions. One led back to the road. A bend in that path, as well as the fog, kept him from seeing very far. The second path was straighter, leading deeper into the park. It was also obscured by fog, yet John felt sure they had not gone that way.

He hurried down the path leading out of the park. At last, he rounded the corner and was able to see the road ahead. In the swirling mist, he could just make out a closed carriage pulling away from the curb. He could not read the markings on the carriage door, but the vehicle was large and well-appointed and clearly belonged to a person of means. John ran, calling out for the carriage to stop, but he was too late. It took off at a brisk pace and was quickly out of sight.

John let out a curse, even though he was breathless from running. It was anger at himself as well as them. He had spent too long talking with Mrs. Finlay. They'd both wanted to help, but perhaps they had thwarted each other. And now the pair had escaped in a closed carriage. An unscrupulous gentleman could get far with a willing lady in such circumstances. It was too horrifying to envision, to imagine that Sophie could throw away all her opportunities for a good marriage and a respectable life so easily.

He had to admit he could not be sure they had been in that carriage, despite his suspicions. He decided to go back and try the other path, just in case. He practically ran, despite the fog hampering his vision, and covered a lot of ground. He did pass a few people, but he saw no sign of Sophie and Deveaux. Finally, he reached a point where he felt satisfied he would have found them if they'd come this way.

He began to walk back the way he'd come. He thought of Mrs. Finlay. Was she still there, waiting for news, perhaps? Speeding up once more, John retraced his steps to the spot where they'd met. No one was there. A stiff breeze had picked up, stinging his cheeks and blowing dead leaves across the grass. Given the miserable weather, John wasn't surprised that she'd gone home. Still, he was disappointed. She had come here with the intent to help, and for a few brief minutes, it had felt as though he had an ally of sorts. Now he was on his own once more.

His next task was clear. He set off at a brisk pace out of the park.

CHAPTER

Five

R eally, John, you're going to wear a hole in the carpet,"
Marjorie said. "Why don't you sit down?"

John paused to look over at his sister-in-law. She was
sitting placidly on the sofa. He knew she'd been watching him,
even as she and Pearl had been chatting about some party that
was going to be the "highlight of the winter Season."

"She's right," Pearl said. "What has you so agitated?"

"I told you—"

"Yes, yes," she said dismissively. "You wish to speak to Sophie. Why is it so urgent?"

"And why won't you tell us what it's about?" Marjorie added.
"We have no secrets in this family."

"Don't we?" He fixed her with a stare. Marjorie was too le-
nient with Sophie, and both were intent on securing her a good
match. He wouldn't be surprised to discover she was somehow
mixed up in this business.

It was like staring down a cat. She quickly looked away and
murmured, "My goodness, someone is testy today."

John checked the time on his pocket watch once more. "Isn't this rather late for her to be out?"

Pearl leaned her head back against the pillows. "She often stays long at Miss Drayton's house. Those two have been friends forever, as you know. They get to talking and quite forget about the time."

John had no doubt Pearl was correct about what happened when those two were together. Although only seven months older than Sophie, Jane had been old enough to have her debut last spring. Since then, she'd regaled Sophie with endless stories about the soirees and outings and the excitement of being courted by handsome young men—although to John's knowledge, Jane had not yet snared any of them. She'd been feeding Sophie's desires to join that scintillating world. Had her enthusiastic descriptions led Sophie to take a step too far?

With each passing minute, John grew more worried that Sophie might not come home. He sent another glance out the window. There was no sign of a carriage. Dusk was drawing on. It was probably time to level with the women. "All right," he said, walking back to them. "I had hoped to wait until Sophie returned to broach the subject. However, it appears we need to get this out in the open now, especially as we might need to go and search for her."

"Search for her?" Pearl repeated. "Don't be so melodramatic. You know where she is."

"I know that's what she told you."

"And you have reason to doubt her?" She grew serious. Perhaps John's anxiety had finally stirred up her motherly instincts. "John, what's this about?"

"Sophie has not been honest with you. Nor with any of us."

Hearing the sound of a carriage in the street, he went again to the window. This time, he was relieved to see Sophie alighting from a cab. She was not alone. Aileen trailed in her wake as Sophie tripped gaily up the steps, smiling broadly.

"At last!" John burst out.

Behind him, Marjorie said smugly, "I knew there was nothing to worry about."

John didn't try to contradict her. He didn't speak until Sophie entered the parlor. John fairly stalked across the length of it, reaching her as she walked in. "Sophie, where have you been?"

John could see Aileen crossing the entrance hall behind her. Hearing John's furious tone, and no doubt guessing what was coming, she skittered away like a mouse and disappeared through the door to the servants' stairs. He returned his hard gaze to his niece. "Where have you been?" he repeated sternly.

"I was at Jane Drayton's house. Didn't Mama tell you?" She tried to peer around his shoulder to get a look at her mother.

"You went nowhere else?" John pressed.

Sophie dropped her eyes. She was normally a good and honest girl. This Deveaux fellow had obviously turned her head. John could see her struggling to avoid telling an outright lie. "Jane and I were looking over fashion magazines, and I suppose we lost track of the time. We've done that often, as Mama will attest." Sidestepping John, she managed to send an apologetic look at Pearl. "I'm terribly sorry, Mama. I'll be ready in time for dinner, I promise. In fact, I shall go upstairs straightaway—"

"Not so fast, if you please." John stepped between her and the door. He motioned for her to move into the parlor. "We have something to discuss."

Uncertain at this turn of events, Sophie looked to her mother for confirmation. Pearl waved her toward a chair, and the girl reluctantly obeyed. Pearl said, "Now will you tell us what this is about, John?"

"I happen to know Sophie was not at Jane Drayton's house today. Not all afternoon, at any rate. Tell me, Sophie, is Miss Drayton in on this with you or only Aileen?"

"I . . . she . . . that is . . ." Sophie looked up at him with wide eyes, fear and worry stamped on her features.

"Go on," John said, uncompromising. "Where were you?"

"You are frightening the girl," Marjorie said, trying to wave John away from Sophie's chair. "If you would stop looming over her, perhaps she could answer you properly."

"She's right," Pearl said. "Please sit down, John."

John compromised by stepping back several paces. Meanwhile, Marjorie poured a cup of tea from the tea service set out on the low table in front of her. "Have some tea, dear. It's frightfully cold out today."

Sophie gratefully accepted the tea and took a sip, perhaps to buy some time.

Pearl looked over at John. "I don't suppose *you* know where Sophie was—if she wasn't at the Draytons' home?" she challenged.

"She was walking with a man in Hyde Park."

Pearl gasped. She turned a disbelieving gaze on her daughter. "Sophie, is this true?"

Now that the truth was out Sophie's demeanor changed. She answered her mother with a defiant look. "I was with Mr. Sanderson Deveaux."

"Mr. Deveaux?" Marjorie exclaimed in delighted surprise.

"We walked in the park, just for an hour. It was all very proper."

"Oh my heavens!" Pearl exclaimed. "How can you possibly think such a thing was proper?"

"I don't believe it's cause for alarm," Marjorie assured her. "Mr. Deveaux comes from one of England's best families. Besides, Sophie was chaperoned. She had her maid with her."

"No, she didn't," John said. "Aileen must have been cooling her heels somewhere else. Sophie was alone with Deveaux, just as she had been on the day that I found her at the tea shop."

"And how would you know?" Sophie said angrily. "Did you follow me? Are you spying on me? How dare you!"

"Don't use that tone of voice on your uncle, young lady." Pearl sat up with an energy she rarely exhibited these days. "Never mind how he knows. Tell us the truth."

Sophie replied with a mute glare at all of them. Now that her secret was out in the open, her earlier chagrin had turned to full-blown belligerence.

"Sophie and Mr. Deveaux were introduced recently at Mrs. Houghton's home," Marjorie said, smoothly speaking up for the girl. "He is a perfect gentleman. Since you know Mr. Deveaux's name, John, I presume you are aware his father is the Earl of Ormond. Such an old and distinguished family. They are wealthy, too, and you cannot say that about all titled families nowadays. If Mr. Deveaux has taken an interest in our Sophie, surely that is a good thing. Think of all the doors this could open for us."

"Aristocrat or not, I hardly believe a *perfect gentleman* would entice an innocent young girl to meet him on the sly."

"It isn't like that at all!" Sophie protested. "I'm no longer a girl. I'm quite grown up now. Yes, I've met him twice, but all we've done is talk."

"I believe we ought to give Mr. Deveaux the benefit of the doubt," Marjorie said. "He and Sophie were meeting in a public place, and Sophie has arrived home unharmed."

"And he's procured invitations for us to attend a concert next week at Lady Bromley's home," Sophie added. "He's going to introduce us to all sorts of important people."

"There you have it," Marjorie said with a note of triumph. "If his intentions were less than honorable, he certainly would not be going out of his way to present her to the broader world."

"But how can Sophie attend such an event? She's not out yet. Her debut isn't until next spring."

"That doesn't matter," Sophie said eagerly. "We're going to—"

"It's only a concert, John," Marjorie broke in, sending a warning look at Sophie to stop her talking. "It's a small, private gathering to hear an accomplished pianist and a young soprano—barely Sophie's age herself—who I understand is immensely talented and will one day be a great sensation."

John shook his head. "Even so. Are you sure it's acceptable to take Sophie along?"

"Yes, Marjorie, are you *sure*?" Pearl echoed. "You know I depend upon your knowledge in such matters."

"It's perfectly acceptable, trust me."

John always felt a prickly sensation on the back of his neck when Marjorie used that tone of supreme confidence about a questionable topic. "I still don't like the idea."

"But, Uncle John, I must go," Sophie pleaded. "I promise I won't see Mr. Deveaux on my own again."

"See that you don't. I'll know if you break that promise."

"So I can go to the concert?" Sophie said, hope on her face.

John blew out a breath. "I don't know. I think we should consider this further."

Pearl understood what he meant. "Sophie, go to your room."

"But you can't let him talk you out of it!" she insisted.

"Go. I'll see you at dinner." Pearl spoke with a force and authority that were so unusual the command could not be denied, much as Sophie clearly wanted to.

Sophie sent a pleading look to Marjorie before leaving the room. It was clear she expected her aunt to be her advocate.

When she was gone, John finally sat down. "Marjorie, explain this to me from the beginning. Why does Deveaux suddenly have so much sway over my niece, and why is this concert acceptable—and so critical? Aside from Sophie's desire to go."

"Yes, I want to know too," Pearl said. "We want to be sure we do the right thing."

"I'm more than happy to explain," Marjorie said. "Two weeks ago, Sophie and I went out for an afternoon of social calls. It's not unusual, as you know, for young ladies to accompany their elders on such calls."

John nodded. This much he'd gleaned over the years. "Go on."

"We called on Mrs. Houghton, who is very well connected, given that her cousin's daughter married a viscount. While we were there, Mr. Deveaux also paid her a call. He is handsome as well as personable, and he made an excellent impression on all of us."

"Why was an earl's son paying a call on a banker's wife? Does it have something to do with this viscount you mentioned?" John tried to follow the logic of Marjorie's story.

Marjorie shrugged. "It's possible he had his eye on the Houghtons' daughter, Francine, although I can't fathom why. She's the same age as Sophie but not nearly as pretty or gifted. Mr. Deveaux must have seen that, too, because his attention was riveted on Sophie from the moment he saw her. I believe he is quite enamored of her. Just imagine, Sophie marrying into the aristocracy!"

"Marriage!" Pearl exclaimed.

"That's quite a leap, Marjorie," John agreed.

"Perhaps," Marjorie conceded. "But such a happy outcome is not inconceivable. That's why we must attend that concert. We should do all we can to encourage the match. Mr. Deveaux is the younger son and will never have a title, but even so, just think of the rise in status for Sophie, and for the rest of us as well. Not even our dear, departed Roger expected his daughter would achieve such heights. He was hoping to see her rise in society, though, wasn't he, Pearl? As are you?"

Pearl nodded, looking more than ready to follow Marjorie's reasoning. "Roger would be awfully proud if Sophie were to make such a connection."

"It's settled, then," Marjorie said. "We shall attend the concert."

John still couldn't shake his unease about Deveaux. The man

had been meeting secretly with Sophie outside of the approved channels. That would seem to confirm Mrs. Finlay's insinuations that he was not to be trusted. Marjorie might think she was being clear-eyed about Deveaux, but she could be easily blinded by dreams of wealth and privilege. She obviously had seen only his better attributes. Maybe Pearl would be more perceptive. "I'd feel better about this if you could go as well, Pearl. Do you think you could manage it?"

"I'm quite capable of looking after the girl," Marjorie insisted.

"No one doubts that," Pearl said. "Nevertheless, I believe I should go. What kind of mother would I be if I didn't meet Sophie's prospective suitor? I'll be sure to rest beforehand so that I'll have the strength to make it through the evening."

"It would be good for you to meet Mr. Deveaux," Marjorie agreed. "Then you can see for yourself that this idea for a match is not out of the realm of possibility."

"Why don't you go along too, John?" Pearl suggested. "Marjorie, do you think we could secure him an invitation?"

John shook his head. "Don't bother. I have a meeting with a potential client in Leeds. It took months to arrange; I can't cancel it now."

"That's too bad," Marjorie said with a playful pout. "I wish you didn't have to travel so much."

"So do I, but it pays for the fine clothes you ladies like to wear to these elegant soirees."

His dry remark only drew a look of adoration from Marjorie. "I don't know what we'd do without you to take care of us."

John disliked when her voice got treacly. He stood up, more than willing to bring this meeting to an end. As for their attending the concert, he still didn't like it, but he had to accept Pearl's decision. He wished he wasn't committed to going to Leeds. Otherwise, he probably would have joined them, if only to ensure there was at least one adult present who could truly watch over Sophie with the care she deserved.

⁓·⊙⊙·⁓

He was still mulling over the issue on Monday, and he decided he could accomplish several important tasks by going to Piccadilly. His first stop was the post office where Mrs. Finlay had said she worked. He saw her the moment he stepped inside. She was standing at the sales counter, helping a woman who was purchasing stamps. When the lady's transaction had been completed and she moved away, John approached the counter.

Mrs. Finlay's eyes widened when she saw him. She gave him a smile that was wary but not unfriendly. "Mr. Milburn, I must admit I was wondering how things worked out. Did you catch up to Sophie and Mr. Deveaux?"

"I did not. However, Sophie returned home before dinner, seemingly unscathed."

Her smile warmed. "That's a relief, isn't it?"

"Yes, although I understandably caused an uproar when I confronted her about Deveaux. We'll be watching her more carefully now."

Mrs. Finlay nodded but looked unconvinced. "That will only work if she truly understands the problem."

"Believe me, I did my best to impress it upon her."

His gaze dropped to her left hand. She'd been wearing gloves at the park, but her hands were uncovered now. On her ring finger was a widow's mourning ring. That made everything much clearer. The ring was a marker of the woman's bereavement, yet it also signaled why she was free to work here and move about London as she chose. She was, presumably, unattached. It was going to make his next question much easier.

He turned his eyes from the ring before she could notice him staring at it. "Would you, by any chance, be willing to continue the conversation we began in the park?"

She appeared genuinely taken aback by this request. "Just for a friendly sort of chat," John added, lest she get the wrong idea about his intentions. "You've shown a desire to help, so I was hoping I might ask you a few more questions."

Instead of answering, Mrs. Finlay sent a concerned glance beyond him.

John turned to see that two men had entered the post office and were waiting to be served. In addition, a clerk had approached and was now hovering at her elbow. "I wouldn't dream of interrupting your work," John said to Mrs. Finlay. "Perhaps we might arrange to meet later?"

She gave him an appraising look. She was probably weighing the pros and cons of accepting an invitation from a man she barely knew. John held his breath, suddenly surprised at himself for just how badly he wanted her to say yes.

"Excuse me, Mrs. Finlay—" the clerk began.

She held up a hand to stop his talking, although her gaze never left John. The clerk obeyed, but his urgent need to speak to her was palpable. "How about the tea shop next door at five o'clock?" she said to John.

"Yes, thank you," he answered without hesitation, grateful she hadn't turned him away. He tipped his hat. "Until then."

Five o'clock was two hours off, but John's other tasks would easily fill the time. He planned to visit Mr. Sadler's office and badger him further about getting those documents before the judge. Then he would investigate a warehouse space nearby that he'd noticed was to let. He was looking for a new place to store his inventory.

He paused at the door before going out. Looking back, he could see Mrs. Finlay had been immediately besieged by the clerk, who was speaking intently and pointing toward the recessed area that housed the telegraph machine. Meanwhile, the first of the two men who'd been in line behind John had set a package on the counter and appeared anxious to post it. Mrs. Finlay seemed to be doing a good job of handling both men at the same time, as though she was used to carrying out numerous tasks at once.

A lad of about twelve came in through the door. Spotting the satchel slung over the boy's arm, John asked, "Are you one of the messenger boys who works here?"

The boy paused and looked up at him. "Yes, sir."

"Is the post office always this busy?"

The boy gave a quick look around. There were by now two more people in line, plus another man filling out a telegram form. "This is slow for us. We get lots of people here to send mail. And telegrams, of course. Keeps us hopping."

"The lady at the counter seems quite efficient," John said.

The boy grinned. "That's Mrs. Finlay, the assistant manager. She keeps a tight rein on things. We've four boys here, and she's got an uncanny way of knowing where we are at all times. In fact, I'd better dash. Mrs. Finlay gets annoyed when we don't keep to our time."

John made a movement to stop him. "Would you happen to know her given name?"

The boy's eyebrows raised, and John felt the heat of embarrassment. He realized the question was imprudent as well as unnecessary. Why had he been so curious to know her name? The boy continued to smile. John had had many interactions with messenger boys over the years. He knew what the glint in this one's eyes signified. He quietly offered a coin, which the boy pocketed in a heartbeat. "It's Rose." He grinned. "And she's a thorny one, for sure."

John nodded. He'd seen a glimpse of her prickly nature during their conversation in the park. "Thank you."

The boy gave a nod and loped off toward a door that led to a back room.

John left the post office, feeling elated. Or perhaps it was relief. Perhaps he'd found someone capable and sensible with whom he could discuss the situation with Sophie. Perhaps she could provide the wisdom and insight he needed. He would be glad to have such a friend.

It was highly unusual to reach out like this to someone he barely knew, but he decided to trust his instincts. He had liked Rose Finlay from the moment he'd set eyes on her.

CHAPTER

Six

Rose was still reconsidering her decision to meet Mr. Milburn as she approached the tea shop. Was he truly interested only in talking more about Sophie, or did he have some other motive? Despite his friendly tone earlier, he might want to warn her to stay away, or even threaten her against spreading the information she knew.

"Rose, you are such a worrywart." She could almost hear Emma's admonition ringing in her ears. Well, perhaps she was. She had good reason to be. Even if it seemed Mr. Milburn was being aboveboard, Rose knew she would do well to keep a wary distance. She knew nothing about this man, other than he had a wayward niece who enjoyed flirting with danger.

Still, Rose couldn't deny she was curious to learn more about the situation. An odd sense of anticipation had filled her from the moment John Milburn had invited her to chat with him.

She'd had to constantly push aside that feeling as she'd tackled numerous problems at work. It hadn't been enough that Miss Palmer, her postal clerk, had been out sick today with a bad case of the grippe. If that had been brought on by the recent freezing rain, so too had been the problem with the telegraph machine. The exterior wires had been damaged, making the reception spotty and unreliable. There wasn't anyone who could come and repair them until tomorrow. These issues had placed even more work on Rose's shoulders than the extra tasks she was already doing while her manager, Mr. Gordon, was away.

Normally, such challenges invigorated her. With every problem she surmounted, she was proving she could be more than an assistant manager. Mr. Gordon was planning to retire soon. Rose was certain she was qualified to fill the position he'd be leaving. Today, however, instead of being absorbed by work, she'd been counting the minutes until she could close up shop. That alone was a sign she ought not to be here. She didn't need this sort of distraction. Her life was full enough already.

However, it was too late to turn back now. Rose had given her word that she would come. She decided to keep the meeting as brief as possible. Sophie's family was aware of the trouble, and they would have to be the ones to address it.

Setting her shoulders in firm resolve, Rose pulled open the door of the shop.

Her eyes were drawn to the man immediately. He sat facing the door, clearly alert for her arrival. He stood up the moment she entered and smiled as she approached him.

Rose was slightly taken aback to realize he was more handsome than she'd first thought. He'd removed his hat, and she could see he had jet black hair that set off his blue eyes. His bearing was affable but also self-assured. It was a pleasing combination. He was at the same table where she'd been on the day she'd seen Sandy and Sophie together. She couldn't help but think he'd chosen it on purpose. After all, he had spotted her through the window that day. Rose wasn't entirely sure how she felt about that idea.

This uncertainty was heightened by his friendly greeting and the smooth way he helped her into a chair. Everything felt oddly comfortable, as though she'd known him for years instead of mere minutes. Was he the sort of man who could easily draw in women? None of the men she'd known with that defining trait had been good for her. The memory of Peter rose up, turning her ease into discomfort.

Rose tried to cover the swing in her emotions by dropping her gaze to the table, on which was laid out a tray of sandwiches, two teacups, and a teapot. "You appear to be hungry today, Mr. Milburn."

His smile widened at her jest. "This is for you, too, of course. Katie told me you are partial to ham sandwiches and bergamot tea." He indicated the waitress, who was approaching their table. "And gingerbread," he added as the waitress set down a plate with several generous slices of the spicy treat.

Rose was impressed at this thoughtfulness. She was also more than a little chagrined that as often as she'd come here, she'd never once inquired as to the attendant's name. "How very kind of you," she murmured.

"It's the least I could do, to thank you for agreeing to speak with me." He spoke as if she'd done him a great honor.

This ought to have set off her alarm bells. Instead, as he regarded her with a kind, open expression, Rose felt again that odd sensation that they were old friends. She barely noticed as Katie left them to attend to other customers.

He picked up the teapot. "May I?"

Rose shook her head to clear her thoughts. He looked surprised, as though he thought she was refusing the tea. "Yes, thank you," she added quickly, smiling.

As he deftly filled their teacups, Rose realized how much she'd been longing for a cup of tea. She took a sip and sighed with contentment, feeling all kinds of warmth as the beverage went down.

John watched her with satisfaction. "I thought you could do

with some refreshment. When I was in the post office earlier, I could see you were in the midst of a very busy afternoon."

"I certainly was," Rose agreed. "My sales clerk is ill, plus we have an issue with our telegraph wires. My manager is away on holiday, so I was bearing the brunt of the customers' dissatisfaction."

He nodded. "As a business owner, I can appreciate what you've been through. I've had similarly rough days. How long have you been working there?"

"Eight years. I started as a postal clerk, although I became proficient in telegraphy as well. Two years ago, I was promoted to assistant manager." She set down her cup, and immediately Mr. Milburn refreshed it for her. He also motioned toward the food. She obliged with a murmur of genuine thanks. She hadn't eaten anything substantial since breakfast.

"What do you do, Mr. Milburn?" she asked once they had both served themselves from the sandwich tray. She was intrigued at his mention of owning a business. From what she had seen so far, she'd been unable to discern whether this family was independently wealthy or earned their money through trade. It was the latter, it seemed.

"I sell finished iron products to factories. Machine parts, gears, things of that nature."

"To factories? There must be plenty of those, given how industrialized our country has become."

"Indeed there are."

"It's a large business, then?"

He shrugged, giving a show of modesty. "We're doing well. I have a staff of about twenty—salesmen, liaisons with the various foundries who supply our parts, plus the clerks and money counters who keep everything running smoothly. We even have our own telegraph line."

Rose smiled, guessing he had added that last bit for her benefit, since she had mentioned being a telegraph operator.

It was also an indication that his company was prosperous, because leasing a telegraph line was expensive. "It sounds like a lot to manage."

"I have a manager to oversee the day-to-day things. I travel a lot to see our clients, primarily up north." He paused, frowning. "That's one reason why I have trouble keeping up with Sophie."

"How is it that her care has become your responsibility?" This was a question that had been on Rose's mind from the beginning.

"Her father is deceased, and her mother—my sister, Pearl—is practically an invalid. She has a weak heart, which saps her of energy. She doesn't leave the house much. Our sister-in-law, Marjorie, has been helping Sophie prepare for her launch into society. But her oversight is variable at best. Marjorie was married to our brother, Lionel, who is unfortunately deceased. She has three children to look after by herself, in addition to running her household."

Rose could understand the frustration in his voice as he described his family's situation. Sophie had plenty of opportunities to evade the oversight of her three guardians, and it seemed she was taking full advantage of them. Rose took a bite of her sandwich, watching him as she chewed. He had set a sandwich on his plate but seemed more interested in talking than eating.

"The situation with Sophie and Mr. Deveaux has me somewhat alarmed, as you can probably guess," he said. "I'm trying to gather as much information as I can, and I'm hoping you can help."

"Didn't you say you spoke to Sophie? I doubt I can add anything of value."

"Yes, we discussed it together with her mother and aunt. They were not aware that she'd been sneaking away to see Deveaux, but they don't seem overly concerned about it."

Rose was so surprised she nearly dropped her sandwich. "They're *not*?"

He gave a pained smile. "You may be sure I had the same reaction."

"But they can't just allow him to—to—" Rose sputtered, hardly knowing how to complete the sentence. She settled on "to risk Sophie's reputation with such improper meetings." In her heart, she was thinking of things far darker.

"I could at least get her mother to agree to that," Mr. Milburn said. "Sophie is under strict orders not to see Deveaux privately again."

"And how did Sophie react?"

"She wasn't happy about it." He shook his head. "Sophie and her aunt were strident in their insistence that no harm had been done, and that it is a good thing to have garnered the interest of someone in the aristocracy. They don't want to do anything that would impair the possibility of a formal attachment down the road."

They thought Sandy had *marriage* on his mind? Rose found that highly unlikely. He had shown no inclination for it thus far. If the rumors Abby had heard were to be believed, he'd left plenty of broken hearts in his wake.

"I don't like the situation," Mr. Milburn went on, echoing Rose's thoughts. "But I'm limited in what I can do. The final decisions belong to her mother. I can only do my best to offer help and guidance. Pearl does not like the idea of confronting Deveaux directly about the meetings he's had with Sophie."

"The *illicit* meetings, do you mean?" Rose said pointedly.

"Pearl and I agree those were ill-advised and bordering on dangerous," Mr. Milburn answered. "However, she feels the best way to avoid trouble is to attempt to quietly steer their relationship onto a more proper course. She doesn't want to risk raising an uproar and jeopardizing Sophie's prospects. I suppose I can see her point of view. This situation puts me in a bind as well. When the son of an earl is involved . . . well, there are many things to consider."

"I understand," Rose said. She certainly did. Aristocrats always enjoyed a certain deference not afforded to the average man. If provoked, they could wield their power in detrimental ways over those who occupied a lower rung on the social ladder. This knowledge irked Rose even more. "But you can't simply do nothing!"

"I will not stand idly by and allow Sophie to get hurt, I assure you. That's why I'm here today. You already had knowledge of this man when you saw him here with Sophie. The fact that you were so worried tells me a closer look is warranted."

Rose was glad he had a clear view of the situation, even if the women in his family did not.

"I wonder if you would be so good as to share with me in detail what you saw on the day Sophie and Mr. Deveaux were here. And anything you overheard as well."

"I did not intentionally plan to eavesdrop," Rose said. "It's just that our tables were close." She pointed toward the table Sophie and Sandy had occupied. "Naturally, I couldn't help but hear some of their conversation, and that's when I grew alarmed and tried to hear more."

"Trust me, I take no offense on Sophie's behalf. I'm grateful for any information you can give me. What was the tenor of their conversation? How intimate did they seem with one another?"

"Most of what I heard was the usual flirtatious banter. From what I could tell, this was only their second meeting. I thought they spoke rather too familiarly for such a short acquaintance, but I did not get the impression they had gone any further."

He let out a breath. "Thank God."

"Nevertheless, I must honestly say that Sophie seems only too willing to stray into more dangerous paths, if such opportunities should present themselves."

"We are going to make sure they do not," Mr. Milburn said with grim determination.

"You might have more trouble reining in the girl than you realize. I was surprised when I heard Mr. Deveaux say that he'd received a telegram from Sophie, informing him she would be waiting at the tea shop. In other words, it seems she was the one who initiated that meeting."

He groaned. "She might just as well have said she was a woman for hire."

"I believe she's simply caught up in the idea of romance, her dreams fed by the idea that a handsome aristocrat has taken an interest in her."

"So you're saying that she innocently did a very unladylike thing."

"Not entirely. Although she is young, she must surely be aware that what she did was wrong. But being in love can fuel all sorts of foolish actions that a girl can justify to herself when she wants to. I've seen it happen before."

He shook his head. "I still don't understand it. But then, I have no experience in these matters."

"You've never been in the heady grip of young love?"

The question hung in the air as Rose gulped, astounded such words had slipped from her mouth.

For a moment, she thought she saw a sparkle in John Milburn's eye. He was probably wondering why she would allow the subject to drift in such a saucy direction. But then he shrugged, his expression sobering. "I certainly never tried to lead any young lady into improper actions."

Rose had the impression he was telling the truth. He was clearly trying to do the best for his family. It couldn't be easy to look after two widows and their children while running his own affairs and a busy company.

"I'm not so sure we can say the same about Mr. Deveaux," Rose said, glad to get the conversation back on track. "He's known for being flirtatious—a ladies' man, if you will. It's treated as all in good fun, and it makes him very popular. However, I have heard rumors from a credible source that he has mistreated several young ladies. If so, the family has avoided scandal because his father is powerful enough to ensure the truth doesn't get out." Rose was sorry to have to share such information, but she knew she had to be as honest with him as possible.

His face pinched with worry. "Did you hear them speak of any future plans?"

"Yes, they were discussing an upcoming soiree. Sophie is keen to go, although she said her uncle would probably not approve of the idea."

"She's correct on that point. And that walk in the park the other day? You mentioned they were planning that as well. What did they say, exactly?"

Rose finished the last bite of her sandwich before answering. She ought to have known he might probe deeper into how Rose knew about that meeting in the park. She did not want to lie, but neither could she divulge the whole truth. "It was only bits and pieces that I overheard, as I told you before."

"Yet somehow you were aware they would be meeting," he persisted. "You said Sophie had sent a telegram to Mr. Deveaux to arrange their meeting here. I don't suppose she sent one confirming the meeting at the park, and that you happened to see it? Is that how you knew the time and place?"

"I said I had overheard—while at the tea shop—Mr. Deveaux's mention of a telegram to meet that day. That is all. I said nothing about any additional telegrams."

"But I'm asking whether you saw—"

She held up a hand. "Might I ask how *you* knew about that meeting in the park?" It wasn't her right to ask that question, but she was desperate to change tack.

He paused, studying her intently. Rose had the feeling he knew exactly what she was doing. But he seemed willing to oblige her. "A few days after that meeting here at the tea shop,

I intercepted a note Deveaux had sent to Sophie via her ladies' maid. The note suggested a day and a location, but asked Sophie to confirm it, presumably with a time. That's why I believe there must have been further correspondence of some kind."

"I'm afraid I can't help you there," Rose said firmly. She picked up her gloves and began to put them on. "I've told you as much as I can. I'm glad to know you're doing your best to prevent Sophie from lurching into disaster. I certainly hope you will be successful in that endeavor."

She pushed back her chair, regretting that she had involved herself in this business at all.

"Wait." Mr. Milburn stretched out his hand in an imploring gesture before she could stand up. "I do have one more thing to ask, if you would be so good as to stay a moment longer."

Rose paused, even though she could not imagine she could be of any further help.

He cleared his throat. "I am so very grateful for all you've done. You went out of your way to look after Sophie, when you didn't even know her. I can see you are still concerned for her well-being. Might I ask if you would contact me, if you should happen to see any more correspondence between Sophie and Deveaux?"

"You said you were going to put a stop to that," Rose hedged.

"Yes, but we've also established that Sophie has ways of eluding our best efforts. I'm trying to plan for any eventualities."

Rose shook her head. "Confidentiality rules prevent me from telling you the contents of any telegrams I process in the course of my duties."

He leaned forward. "Mrs. Finlay, I am trying to protect my niece. She is a naïve and headstrong girl who is being drawn toward a man who, by your own admission, has a questionable reputation. Surely the rules might be bent a little if they protect an innocent young woman from harm?"

Rose had been having the same struggle within herself. In

a way, she'd breached the confidentiality rule simply by acting on the information she had seen and going to the park with the intent of following the pair. And hadn't she told herself at the time it was for a worthy cause? Yes, she had. But acting on such information was not the same as sharing it with third parties. That was a step she was not willing to take. Aside from the ethics of doing such a thing, there was also the very real danger of losing her job at the post office. She could not risk such a devastating blow. She resented being placed in this position, even though she knew her own faulty judgment had led her here. "No, I cannot do it."

It wasn't easy to watch him struggle with his disappointment. Rose could see how badly he wanted to press her further. She replied to his searching look with a hard stare that telegraphed he would get nowhere if he tried.

"Understood," he said at last. "It was wrong of me to ask you to go against rules and conscience."

He sat back in his chair, and Rose breathed a sigh of relief.

"I hope I might at least prevail upon you to accept this," he added, reaching into his coat pocket. He pulled out a card and handed it to Rose. It had his name and place of business printed on it. "If you should hear of anything or see anything—outside of your workplace and not part of your official duties—would you be so good as to contact me?"

"That's unlikely to happen," Rose said, trying to hand back the card.

He pushed it toward her. "Please keep it just in case. For Sophie's sake."

Relenting, Rose tucked the card into her reticule. She rose from her chair, extending her hand to him as he followed her up. "Good-bye, Mr. Milburn. I do wish your family all the best. It seems unlikely we shall meet again."

He took her hand, shaking it lightly as he looked into her eyes. "My thanks, once again, for all your help."

Rose didn't move, even after their handshake had ended. Why should she suddenly not want to leave, when she'd been so desperate to do so only moments before? It felt like there was something here that was unfinished. "Thank you for the meal," Rose said, thinking perhaps that was it.

He smiled and dipped his chin. "It was my pleasure."

Once more Rose tried to leave but found her feet not budging. Instead, she kept looking at him like someone who had lost their wits.

"I did have one more question," he said, taking advantage of her inaction. "It's unrelated to what we've been talking about, and you may think it impertinent."

Rose lifted a brow. "What's that?"

"I believe you were reading a book when I first saw you. I was just wondering what it was."

Rose blinked in surprise. It was such an odd and unexpected question, but she didn't mind. After what they'd been discussing, it was a reprieve to move to a more pleasant topic. "I was reading *David Copperfield* by Charles Dickens."

"Were you really?" He looked genuinely delighted. "I love his work. Is this your first time reading it?"

Rose shook her head. "I first read it some years ago, but I like to revisit it from time to time. I find it inspiring somehow."

"Is it because a destitute orphan boy ultimately finds success, happiness, and love?" he suggested, still smiling.

Rose hadn't thought about it that way at all. Certainly not the part about finding love. That was the farthest thing from her mind. "Let's just say I find it inspiring whenever anyone triumphs over long odds. I've heard the book is somewhat autobiographical, and that Mr. Dickens retained a great deal of bitterness over his early life, even until his death. Yet I like how the character of David can let go of that and dwell instead on his hard-won successes."

"That's very astute. You make me want to read it again."

"Do you have a favorite Dickens work?" Rose asked, marveling that their conversation had taken such an interesting turn.

He thought for a moment. "I'd have to say I greatly enjoy his early work, *The Pickwick Papers*. Each chapter is like a fresh vignette of a different part of the country. Perhaps I like it because I travel so much. I often run into characters and places as oddly humorous as the ones he describes."

Rose wanted to ask him for more details. Perhaps he had truly interesting anecdotes to tell. But that was not why they had met today. Was this foray into one of her favorite topics a way of trying to win her over? That idea immediately put a damper on the pleasant feelings she'd been having.

"I never quite finished reading that one. Perhaps I shall give it another go." Rose said this to be polite, although she had personally found the episodic nature of the book to be unappealing. She was surprised he chose that as his favorite. "Well, I must be off. Good-bye again."

"And my thanks to you again." His blue eyes seemed to smile into hers.

Finally, Rose pushed herself into action and left the shop.

She had held her ground, and Sophie was taken care of. Or at least, Sophie had an overseer who was working diligently to protect her. Why, then, did Rose feel so unsettled? She refused to feel guilty for turning down a request to do something unethical. She was right to leave things as they stood. Shaking off any lingering doubt, she set off down the street for home.

CHAPTER

Seven

U ncle John, I'm glad to see you!"

John was surprised by the cheerful greeting. He'd expected his nephew to meet him with a guilty air, given that there was a serious cloud over his head. Or that the lad would present the surly expression that the headmaster had complained was his way of interacting with everyone, from students to teachers.

At the moment, the only frown was on the face of the headmaster, who had just ushered the boy into the room where John was waiting. "Mind you behave," the man admonished Edward. "Don't give your uncle any grief. Give strict heed to what he tells you."

Edward dropped his chin obediently. "Yes, sir."

However, the second the headmaster left the room, Edward threw a malevolent look at the door. John was glad that murderous glance couldn't pierce wood.

He was here to keep his promise that he would visit Edward and get him to stop his troublemaking. At the very least, he wanted to see if he could understand why the boy had become so unruly. Surely there had to be some underlying reason for it. Edward had never been overly studious, but he'd generally been well behaved, at least as much as one could expect from a child with so much energy. John had always enjoyed spending time with his nephew. He only wished that for today's visit he didn't have to play the part of the chastising adult.

They were in a small sitting room located in the building that housed the offices of the school. It offered a hospitable spot to welcome visitors, such as family members of students. John was grateful the headmaster was giving them an opportunity to meet privately.

Rising from his chair, he extended a hand. "How are you, Edward?"

The boy smiled as he shook John's hand. "Better, sir, now that you're here."

Although John spoke of him as Eddie to his mother and aunt, he knew the young man now preferred the more formal version of his name. At age fifteen, Edward was on the cusp of manhood. He looked it too. He was already as tall as his father had been. His once-lanky frame was filling out into more adult proportions. Edward's shoulders looked broader than the last time John had seen him. John also thought he detected a hint of hair on the boy's chin.

John motioned him to a chair. Edward complied, looking at him with pleased expectancy.

When they were both seated, John said, "It seems you've been having a difficult time here lately." He figured there was no point in beating around the bush. "I'm told you've had to be disciplined a number of times, and that your schoolwork is suffering. The headmaster describes your behavior as obstinate and unacceptable."

"Naturally, they paint me as the monster," Edward replied, his expression souring.

"Would you care to tell me what's bothering you?"

"I don't like it here." He gave John a defiant look. "I want to leave."

The boy certainly had changed, and not just physically. He'd always gotten on well at this school, ever since his father had brought him here at the age of ten. And why shouldn't he? This was one of the finer boys' schools for families who were rising in the middle class. It wasn't an elite school such as Harrow or Eton, but the majority of its students went on to university, so as far as John was concerned, the end result was the same. The school was located on a large tract of land near a picturesque little village. It attracted top-notch teachers. The dormitories were clean and airy, and the food was plentiful. There was nothing at all to complain about. Edward didn't realize just how lucky he was.

Attending a school like this was a privilege that had never been afforded John or his siblings. They had attended local schools and had teachers of middling quality. If their parents hadn't pressed them to work extra hard on their studies, and to fill their free time by improving themselves, they could not have advanced in life with as much success as they'd had. Yet there were times, even now, when John felt at a disadvantage due to his lack of a quality education. It had been a tough road, and his brother, Lionel, had been determined to save his own children from the same fate.

"Is there a specific problem?" John pressed. "Are they mistreating you in some way? We haven't heard any complaints from Rupert."

Edward made a scoffing noise. "He's twelve. He doesn't understand anything."

This clear dismissal of his younger brother's opinion took John back to his own childhood. "I remember your father thinking the same thing about me once upon a time. Of course, there was a bigger age gap between us than between you and Rupert. One thing was the same, though. Lionel was definitely the more intelligent one. He was smart as a whip. Always seemed to know the right thing to do."

Edward straightened in his chair, his expression warming again. "I should like to think some of that has rubbed off on me. I know what I want to do in life, and I'm tired of these old schoolmasters holding me back."

He truly was becoming more like his father. Lionel was always one hundred percent sure of any decision he made.

John didn't want to crush the boy's spirit, only to ensure he channeled his ambitions sensibly. "I do believe you have inherited many of your father's good traits. You learn quickly, and you're anxious to make your way in the world. But as I just said, your father always seemed to know the right thing to do—and he was positively adamant that you should have the very best education. He knew it was critical to getting ahead in life."

"My father was a successful man, and he left school at age fifteen—just like me."

"No, Edward. You *aren't* leaving school at age fifteen. You're going to remain here and finish the year. If you stay focused on your studies, the time will pass before you know it, especially since you are now behind. You will need to work extra hard to prepare for university. That entrance examination is no walk in the park."

"No!" Edward fairly shouted the word.

John frowned, taken aback by the outburst. "I beg your pardon?"

"I don't want to go to university." Edward sat forward, his stance so adamant that he nearly lifted off his chair. "I'm going to leave school. It's time for me to get out in the world."

"Would you go against your father's wishes? Would you toss aside everything he worked so hard to give you?"

This challenge made Edward pause. John could see him struggling between his father's directive and his own desires.

He answered John's question quietly but with no less resolve. "Rupert can go to university. He wants nothing more. Surely that's enough. Father would be perfectly happy with this arrangement. Everything has changed because of his death. He'd understand what I want to do."

"And what is that, exactly? If you left school, what would you do?"

"I'd return to London."

"And then?"

"I don't know yet." Edward was beginning to look annoyed by John's badgering. "What I do know is that my mother and sister need me. I can't just leave them to fend for themselves."

For a moment, the lad sounded as grown up as he was beginning to look. Did Edward truly want to come home because of a desire to help his family? It was admirable, no doubt. Yet ultimately, it didn't matter what Edward's motivations were. Nor were his concerns warranted.

"Your mother is perfectly capable of looking after herself and Ellie," John pointed out. "Besides, they aren't alone. Your aunt Pearl and I are helping them in every way we can."

Edward shook his head. "Mother says she hardly ever sees you. And Louisa says—" He cut himself off.

"Louisa?" John said in surprise. "Are you two corresponding?" He supposed it wasn't too unusual for cousins to write to one another, and these two were the same age. Even so, he hadn't been aware they were so close.

"She writes to me every week," Edward confirmed. "I'm glad of it. She tells me everything that's going on in the family. No one else will. Mother sends me letters, but she censors things she doesn't want me to know."

"That's very insightful," John said. "And yet she tells you she never sees me? That's not true. I see her all the time."

"Only if she's at Aunt Pearl's house. Louisa thinks you avoid coming to our home."

"Does she?" John didn't like that accusation. Then again, the way Marjorie fawned over him when he did visit her was making him increasingly uncomfortable, so perhaps there was some truth to it. He preferred to meet with her when Pearl was present. It didn't mean he cared any less for Marjorie or her children. It wasn't right for the children to make judgments about their elders' decisions. "What else does Louisa tell you?" John prompted, sensing there was more the boy wasn't saying.

"She says my mother is always complaining about how unhappy she is without a man in the house. It's hard for her to run the household and take care of Ellie, in addition to all she is doing for Sophie."

"And you think you can help her by going home?"

"I can be the man around the house. I can help with lots of things."

"I'm sorry your mother feels overtaxed. I will do more to ensure she gets the support she needs."

This clearly wasn't the answer Edward was looking for. In fact, he looked affronted. "Don't you understand? She hates to ask you for anything because you always act so put upon and give her the sense that she is a burden."

John stared at him. After all the ways he'd willingly extended himself for his sister-in-law, this felt like a harsh and unfair assessment. "Did she say this to you directly, or is this something Louisa wrote to you?"

Edward gave a shrug. "Anyone in our family will tell you."

John supposed he shouldn't be surprised that Marjorie's constant harping on her widowhood would have filtered down to Edward this way. Unfortunately, despite the lad's good intentions, what Marjorie wanted was not something Edward could supply. She wanted a husband. John had no way of solving that problem.

"I promise I will do more to help your mother. Let me assure you, it is not an imposition at all, despite what she may think. I

87

will simply have to make that clearer to her." It wasn't a prospect he was looking forward to, but he'd faced worse tasks.

"But I can help too," Edward insisted.

"No, Edward. You are going to stay here." Not wanting to delve into the quandary of Marjorie's desire for a husband, he kept to his initial reasons. "Your father and I never had this kind of opportunity growing up. He wanted you to have every advantage."

"But you both did just fine without it, didn't you? Even now, you are running his company successfully. Why should I languish here when I could be out doing something?" He looked all but ready to jump out of his chair and get started.

He certainly had inherited the fire that had been resident in his father. John could admire the boy's tenacity, although it didn't change the circumstances. "There are times when we have to do things we don't want to do. That is part of being an adult as well. Don't you want to honor your father's wishes?"

"He didn't know he was going to die so young," Edward persisted. "That changes everything."

"Not in the ways you think. His legacy for you has not changed. You need to accept this and act accordingly." John rose from his chair. "I must go, or I'll miss my train."

Edward bounded up. "Let me go with you."

"I'm sorry, Edward. This is a time when you've simply got to believe we know what's best for you. Will you promise me you'll apply yourself to your studies and set aside the idea of leaving school?"

Edward stood ramrod straight, staring John in the eye. "No, sir, I won't."

John had no idea what to do in the face of such an unflinching refusal. Clearly the lad wasn't going to be reasoned with. Much as he hated it, John supposed he had no choice but to fall back on stern commands. "Edward, you will stay at this school, and you will apply yourself, just as your parents have directed.

You're still underage, and you must live by their rules. I shall direct the headmaster to use whatever disciplinary tactics are necessary to ensure you stay the course."

John strode for the door, intending to leave it at that. However, something inside him knew he couldn't live with himself if he did. He paused, turned back to Edward, and said more gently, "However, I hope a heavy hand won't be necessary. Please think over what I said."

"I had thought I could talk to you. I thought that you, at least, would understand."

Clearly the boy was wrong on that count. John did not understand. Not at all. From his point of view, it was his job to make his nephew realize what was good for him. "Edward, I admire your energy and your drive. I also believe you are an intelligent fellow, wise enough to perceive when good advice is being given to you, able to accept it in the spirit with which it was given, and to act on it as being in your own best interests. You simply must stay in school. It's the only way to make the most of your talents."

This order, thinly veiled as a compliment of sorts, had no effect. Edward merely looked at him with cold, flat eyes. John could see disappointment in them as well. Why should he feel as though he had let the boy down? He was doing the very best for him. Most importantly, he was steering Edward exactly where his father had wanted him to go.

But Edward couldn't see that. They had reached an impasse. John left the room, knowing the boy was probably staring daggers after him the way he had done earlier with the headmaster. It troubled him to be leaving the situation unresolved, but what more could he do? How should he know the best way to handle such matters? No reasonable person would expect him to. That didn't stop him from feeling like he'd failed in this critical task.

Why had everything become so complicated? As he rode the

train, John kept turning the situation over in his mind. He stared out the window, watching the landscape that was so familiar and yet constantly changing. A metaphor for his life, perhaps.

In the distance, he could make out a steeple rising above a modest village. His traveling often interfered with regular churchgoing, but he carried a Bible in his valise and did his best to remain diligent in daily prayers. If ever they were needed, it was surely now. He spent several minutes praying silently, asking God for wisdom on how to best help his family.

The train began approaching the outskirts of Leeds. John had lived for six years in this city. He'd been building a good life for himself here, but then Lionel's death had changed the course of the entire family and taken John back to London.

He had attended a church here that he liked very much. John could still remember one Sunday vividly. The minister was teaching energetically from Jeremiah, highlighting one verse in particular: "Behold, I am the Lord, the God of all flesh: is there any thing too hard for me?"

That teaching had stayed with John, taking on greater significance when his brother died a few months later. The verse became a mainstay for him through all the upheavals and hard decisions that had followed. Stepping into an entirely new life had tested him nearly to his limits, but God had sustained him.

John reminded himself now that its truth had not lessened. If God had given him the task of managing two young people who were determined to plunge into adulthood when they might have enjoyed their youth a little longer, then surely He would give John the strength and help he needed to carry it out.

John didn't doubt this. He didn't even begrudge the time and effort required. And yet, even with many people to care for, he felt lonely.

His thoughts kept returning to Rose Finlay. They'd met because of Sophie. Rose's interest in the girl and the information she'd provided at a critical juncture could be taken as evidence of how God was providing help for him along the way. But for John personally, she had done more.

Spending time with her had reminded him there was a wider world beyond the constant needs of work and family. She had seemed like a breath of fresh air. He could appreciate a practical, down-to-earth woman who seemed to have a solid grasp of her place in the world. To cultivate an acquaintance, or even a friendship, with such a woman was highly appealing. John was surprised at himself for thinking this, but there it was.

In the week that had passed since their conversation in the tea shop, she had made no effort to contact him. Who could blame her? He'd overstepped in asking her to reveal confidential information. He was sorry for that now. Was there any way he might approach her again without causing offense?

After mulling that over for a while, he came up with an idea: there was an upcoming lecture in London, to be given by two critics who had known Dickens personally. Did Rose know about it? Perhaps she'd be interested in attending. What would be the harm in dropping by the post office to mention it to her? The more he thought about the idea, the more he liked it.

The prospect filled him with such happy anticipation that when he reached Leeds, not even the leaky cab ride through the cold rain to his hotel could dampen it.

⁂

Normally on a Saturday afternoon, Rose was out and about doing errands, catching up on many things she could not do during the week. Today, however, she'd decided to come straight home from her half day at work and concentrate on indoor tasks.

She was pleased to find a letter had arrived from Abby. She was eagerly anticipating seeing her cousin next week. It was a rare occasion when Abby managed to arrange time away from her work and come to London. Rose eagerly opened the letter and began to read.

My dear Rose,

I'm sorry to report I cannot come to London as planned. I was so looking forward to visiting some proper shops, for I am in desperate need of a new Sunday frock. Mostly, I was excited to see you! It seems such a long time since we've been together, and there is so much to catch up on.

Our reunion will have to wait, however. The Ormonds have decided to throw a large house party next week. The Prince and Princess of Wales have just returned from a month in Scotland, and they will spend a week here before departing for Paris. There will be twenty other guests in addition, so the entire staff has been working night and day to prepare. I'm rather proud to know His Royal Highness will be enjoying my turtle soup, turbot a l'anglaise, and of course a variety of fresh fowl and beef. One unfortunate wrinkle is that a new pastry chef has been brought in for this occasion. He's rather a pushy fellow and seems to look down on all of us in the kitchen. Miranda, my most valuable assistant who always handles the desserts and sweets so admirably, has been vexed to no end by his demands.

But we shall get through this challenge, as we always do. Our reward may well be an easy time at Christmas, because Lord and Lady Ormond are considering spending the winter in southern France. I confess I would be happy for this, as I've already been invited to a holiday party that sounds quite appealing, but I shall write more on that subject later!

I shall write again as soon as we have recovered from this momentous event. Dear cousin, it seems like ages since you and I have spent a day together. The seasons are turning rapidly—perhaps bringing winds of change in our own lives? But we'll find time soon for a long, comfortable chat. I promise to bring your favorite lemon cakes for the occasion.

With all my love,
Abby

Rose let out a long sigh as she reached the end of Abby's letter. She felt in need of her cousin's companionship just now. Abby was the one person with whom she could always be completely honest about anything in her life. Not to mention that Rose was teeming with questions about Sandy. They were questions that Abby, who was well attuned to all the gossip in that household, might well have the answers to. However, they could never be posed—nor answered—via letter. That would be too risky. Rose would simply have to wait.

Perhaps it was just as well. Rose had decided not to involve herself any further in the saga of Sandy and Sophie. Therefore, the private life of a certain aristocrat should be no concern of hers.

As Rose reread the letter, new questions arose in her mind. Did Abby have something specific in mind when she mentioned the seasons of life turning? It wasn't like her to use such fanciful language. It was also unusual for her to be so happily nonchalant about getting an "easy time" at Christmas. Lord and Lady Ormond were famous for their elaborate Christmas parties, which generally extended from Christmas Day to Twelfth Night. Abby had always reveled in the work and taken pride in her culinary masterpieces.

As for her own life, Rose didn't see it shifting too much. If she was promoted to manager, that might count, she supposed. Yet to her it was merely a sign that things were proceeding along a steady course. She had resisted the pull into the affairs of Sophie's family. That was surely for the best. She was sorry to have been so brusque with John Milburn, but she was glad to have made her point. In the end, she couldn't fault him for pressing so hard for information. She rather liked him, in fact. He was simply trying to do the best for his niece. Perhaps he had effectively managed to cut any ties between Sophie and Sandy. Rose certainly hoped that was the case.

She was still pondering these things when she was surprised by a knock at the door. She opened it to discover two cheerful faces on the other side.

"We're back!" exclaimed Alice Shaw, who immediately embraced Rose with an enthusiastic hug and added playfully, "Did you miss us?"

CHAPTER

Although Rose was not normally effusive in her emotions, she not only submitted gladly to Alice's hug but returned it in kind. Perhaps the vague out-of-sorts feelings she'd been having lately had been loneliness. She had missed Alice during the thirteen months the Shaws had been away.

She was so elated that she had to remind herself to let go of her friend. Alice beamed at her, looking more beautiful than Rose could remember. Wiping away a touch of mistiness in her eyes, Rose gave a welcoming smile to Alice's husband, Douglas.

Douglas tipped his hat. "Good afternoon, Mrs. Finlay." His light Scottish brogue lilted the words as he used her formal name with a teasing grin. "I do hope we're not disturbing you?"

By way of a response, Rose opened the door wide and ushered them inside. "When did you get back? I thought it would be at least another week."

"The ship made better time to Liverpool than expected due to calm weather, and then we caught the fastest possible train to London," Alice said, pulling Rose over to the sofa. "We got in late last night. I'm so glad to be home. We've been gone for an *eternity*!"

Douglas listened to Alice's report with a bemused expression, remaining standing while the two ladies made themselves comfortable on the sofa. "My apologies, my love," he said with a smile. "I didn't realize you were so miserable traveling with me. Is that why you wouldn't let me spend even one hour at the Liverpool office?"

Alice scrunched her nose at him. "You were in fact there for *two* hours, as I recall. We nearly missed our train." Despite this reproof, she motioned him over as she spoke.

He pulled forward a nearby chair so he could sit closer to her. He clasped her left hand, which was resting on the arm of the sofa, and his thumb lightly skimmed her gold wedding band. The look of love that passed between them only renewed all the odd feelings afflicting Rose earlier.

"I can see you've had quite the honeymoon," she said, using the wry remark to calm her tumbled emotions.

"It was wonderful!" Alice affirmed, too happy to notice Rose's teasing. "There is so much to tell you." Gently extracting her hand from Douglas's, she turned to give Rose her full attention. "How are you, Rose? And how is Emma?"

"Emma and Mitchell have decided to extend their honeymoon," Rose said, answering the easier question first. "She is accompanying him to Lincoln while he completes an assignment for the Royal Mail."

"How interesting! I cannot wait to meet Mitchell and offer them both my good wishes. How was the wedding?"

"Emma was radiant, and Mitchell looked as though he could not quite believe his good fortune."

"I can understand that feeling," Douglas said, giving his wife another tender glance.

"And how are you, Rose?" Alice asked again. She inspected Rose's face with a serious expression. Maybe she could discern the unsettled state of mind Rose had been in before their arrival. If so, Alice was as astute—and kind—as ever.

"I have been desperately forlorn without my dearest friends," Rose joked, growing uncomfortable under Alice's scrutiny. "However, I soldier on. My manager is on the verge of retiring, and I believe he will recommend me for his replacement."

"What great news," Alice enthused. "You've been working toward this for a long time. I'm glad to hear things are going so well."

"Yes . . ." Rose had a brief thought about Sophie and John Milburn, but she didn't feel that situation was worth bringing up.

"And how is old Mrs. Finlay?" Alice asked.

Rose shrugged. "Well enough. Her mind is not as clear as it once was, but I help her as much as I can."

"So things are well between you?" Alice was aware of the friction that often existed between Rose and her mother-in-law.

"We're never going to be fast friends, but we've made peace with that. She's grateful for my help, and I am grateful for hers. It's why I'm still here." Rose briefly lifted a hand to indicate her flat. With Emma no longer living here to share expenses, Rose would have had difficulty paying the rent if she hadn't had help from Mother Finlay. But after her promotion at the post office and the accompanying pay raise, Rose would not be dependent on the lady's money. It was a day Rose was heartily looking forward to.

"I want to hear all about your trip," Rose said, wanting to change the subject. "Your letters were informative but sporadic, and I have so many questions." The Shaws had gone to South America to solidify business for Douglas's company, which was expanding its beef imports. They had also spent time in the United States to shore up contracts for imports of cotton and grain.

"I feel certain I know just about all there is to know about the beef industry at this point," Alice said. "I confess I had a difficult time learning Spanish, but Douglas seemed to pick it up easily. He has an astounding memory for so many things."

She turned toward her husband, perhaps expecting him to make some comment. But his attention had been caught by something on the small table by the sofa. He picked it up, and Rose saw it was the card John Milburn had given her.

Douglas read the name aloud. "I believe I've met this Mr. Milburn. Are you buying iron products for the post office now?"

Despite his joke, Rose could see he was genuinely curious. "How interesting that we have a mutual acquaintance," she hedged, hesitant to answer his question. "How do you know him?"

"I met him about two years ago at Mr. Henley's club," Douglas replied, referring to the owner of the company where he worked. "We often took luncheon there. Mr. Milburn was new to the club, as I recall. He had recently taken over his brother's business after the man's unfortunate demise. I believe Lionel was his brother's name."

"I told you Douglas has quite a head for remembering details," Alice said proudly.

"I suppose I remember him because of the way he spoke about his business," Douglas answered. "We discussed challenges we'd both been facing regarding warehousing and shipping goods within England. He gave me some useful ideas. He seemed to have an excellent grasp of the business, even though he'd not been involved with it before his brother died. I recall admiring how quickly he'd taken to an entirely new occupation."

"What did he do before?" Rose asked. She knew him primarily as an iron merchant and concerned uncle. It was interesting to think there was another side of him she hadn't been aware of.

Douglas shook his head. "I'm afraid I can't recall—despite my wife's claim about my excellent memory." He winked at Alice, who gave his arm a playful nudge.

"And how did you meet Mr. Milburn?" Alice asked. "I don't suppose they allow women to join that club."

"No, they don't," Douglas put in. "That's both a blessing and a curse."

"Perhaps one day I should try to storm the gates," Rose said. "I could be their first female member."

Alice was not distracted by these asides. "But how did you meet him?"

"I suppose you could say we met by accident."

"At the post office?"

"No, at Hyde Park. We . . . er, struck up a conversation there."

"It can't have been recently, with this dreary weather. Happy as I am to be back in London, I can't say I'm enthusiastic about the cold rain and the soot that pours from all the chimneys, filling the air and soiling one's clothing."

"And the fog," Rose agreed. "I don't suppose you saw much of that in Argentina?"

"No, although there were some torrential rains. But tell me about this Mr. Milburn." Alice returned to the subject so eagerly that she reminded Rose of Emma. Ever the dreamy optimist, Emma would instantly assume there was a romance brewing as a result of this chance meeting in the park. Alice had always been a more practical sort. But after succumbing to a romance of her own, she seemed to have taken on the same annoying tendency as Emma.

Rose wanted to nip any wrong assumptions in the bud. "It was not a pleasure walk. We were trying to locate Mr. Milburn's niece, who had been lured there by a man who we felt had less-than-honorable intentions."

Alice's eyes widened. "How awful! So you are acquainted with the niece?"

"Not exactly." Rose sighed. Having been drawn into revealing the story, she supposed she might as well tell them all of it. "I first saw Mr. Milburn's niece Sophie at the tea shop next to my workplace. I happened to notice her sitting with a man I recognized named Sanderson Deveaux, and I overheard some of their conversation."

"Sanderson Deveaux?" Douglas repeated. "He's an aristocrat, isn't he?"

"That's right. He's a frequent customer at my post office. I've heard unsavory bits of gossip about him, mostly through my cousin, who works at his father's estate in Sussex."

"I understand Deveaux is quite the ladies' man," Douglas said. "Handsome and dashing and all that. He was spoken of favorably by the ladies I met during my foray into the world of the debutantes—which was brief, thankfully," he added, sending a worried glance at Alice, as though he might have offended her. Rose knew this was a vague reference to the woman he'd been courting before he met Alice.

Alice didn't even notice. Her brows were drawn together as she tried to digest the information Rose had given her. "How did all of you get from the tea shop to the park? Did you follow them there?"

Rose shook her head. "Let me start over."

In the end, Rose found it was a relief to share the story with them. She had not been able to put the situation to rest in her mind.

"Clearly he values your help to seek you out like that," Alice said as Rose finished her tale by describing her last discussion with Mr. Milburn in the tea shop.

"Perhaps, and yet there isn't any further help I can give him. As I explained to him, I can't divulge anything I might see in the course of my work, but he insisted on leaving his card with me anyway."

"*Have* you seen anything?" Alice asked.

"You know you can't ask me that question."

"Come now, we are friends. I'm curious, that's all. I won't divulge this to anyone."

Douglas gave her a skeptical look. "Alice, haven't you heard that the fastest ways to spread information are telegraph and tell-a-woman?" This joke earned him another shove from his wife.

"I have no doubt you could keep a confidence," Rose said. "However, I haven't heard nor seen any further correspondence between the two."

"That's a good sign, isn't it?"

"I was thinking the same thing. I certainly hope for Sophie's sake that Mr. Deveaux has lost interest in her and moved on."

Alice was looking at her thoughtfully again. "I don't wish to sound rude, but why did you go out of your way to enter into this affair in the first place?"

That was a difficult question to answer—not just because it meant revealing aspects of her past that Rose preferred to leave hidden. Although she thought she knew the reason, it seemed her motivations went deeper in ways she couldn't explain. "Well, I couldn't just stand idly by, letting an innocent young girl get taken in like that and allowing some man to ruin her."

"You feel this sort of thing deeply, it seems."

Rose knew Alice's statement was meant to probe. "Yes," Rose said quietly. "I was young and naïve once, though you may not believe it. I was led astray by a smooth-talking ladies' man and lured into decisions I never should have made." She met Alice's gaze squarely. "He married me, but that didn't stop him from hurting me. Sophie has so many more advantages in life than I had—she is beautiful and comes from a well-to-do family. I would hate to see her throw it away for a man who would ill-use her. I would hate for her dreams to be crushed when she could have so much more."

That was all Rose was willing to say about it.

Alice took her hand. "You have such a tender heart, despite all that has happened. You are a good woman, Rose."

It was enough to make Rose misty-eyed all over again. She definitely did not want that. Certainly not in front of Douglas.

He might begin to wonder why his steady, sensible wife had such a sentimental ninny for a friend.

Rose said briskly, "That's quite enough on that subject. I've told you all about me; now you must tell me about your travels. I have never set foot outside England, and I'm dying to live your adventures vicariously."

Alice and Douglas were happy to describe their adventures—and misadventures—as they'd learned to navigate life in Buenos Aires and the ways business was conducted there. Then there had been the voyage to America. They'd spent six weeks visiting several cities along the eastern coast.

"It all sounds lovely," Rose said, finding it hard to suppress a sigh. She was surprised at how much she envied them when she'd never been prone to wanderlust. "And how did you find the Americans?"

"They are so . . . *energetic*," Alice replied with a laugh.

Douglas nodded in agreement. "It seems they are always busy, always involved in some new project, from the wealthy business owners down to the common laborer."

"It fascinated me to see how they were thriving with this industrious outlook, as though they thought anything was possible," Alice added with a smile. "I found it very inspiring."

"Does that mean you're ready to start that business school you've been dreaming of?" Rose knew Alice had been thinking of opening a school to teach telegraphy, typewriting, and other business skills. She was an excellent telegrapher, and also very organized and ambitious. She was just the sort to succeed at building a business.

"I'm definitely excited about starting the school. But it may need to wait just a little longer." She sent a coy glance at Douglas, who beamed.

Rose looked between them for several moments, trying to understand what was being conveyed. Then understanding dawned. "You're going to have a baby!"

Alice nodded. "Sometime in March, I believe."

Rose blinked, trying to imagine Alice as a mother. It was a big change from when Rose had first met her, when Alice was a woman determined to remain single and pursue other goals. It was even a large shift from her more recent role as wife and partner in her husband's work. But the joy on Alice's face was unmistakable.

Rose's throat tightened. The hollow feeling she'd felt at times rose again, despite her joy for her friend. Casting about for something to say, she remembered how Alice came from a large and ever-expanding family that had encouraged Alice to add to the brood. "Your family must be over the moon."

Alice laughed. "No doubt they will be. We haven't told them yet. We hope to pay a visit home to Ancaster as soon as we can. I want to see the look on their faces when they find out!"

For the third time, Rose found herself fighting back tears, as she pictured the large, happy family surrounded by smiling children of all ages. For years she had kept her regrets successfully at bay, but today they seemed unwilling to be ignored.

Alice must have seen something was amiss. Her smile faded to a look of concern.

Rose didn't want to risk more questions, and she wasn't going to allow her own weakness to dampen Alice's good news. She brightened her expression. "No one will be more surprised than Emma, I'm sure. Yet no one will be more pleased. I fully anticipate that before long, you will both have little ones playing together on the carpet."

"It's a charming picture," Alice agreed with a smile. "Mind you, it doesn't mean I've given up on the idea of my school. In fact, I was going to ask your advice about a few things."

"I'd be happy to offer any help I can."

"Well, you see, I was thinking—"

Douglas cleared his throat. "Perhaps this discussion could

wait until next time, my dear? Don't forget we've a long list of errands to run before the shops close today."

"Yes, that's true," Alice said, if somewhat reluctantly. "It does remind me of one reason why we came to see you, Rose. Will you dine with us next week? Then we shall have plenty of time to talk."

Rose willingly agreed.

After they'd gone, Rose sat in the now-silent flat, thinking over what had happened. What questions had Alice wanted to ask her? Rose looked forward to finding out.

Their invitation to dinner suddenly reminded Rose that she had never returned the spinster book to the Shaws' flat. It was tucked away in a drawer where Rose had put it on the day Emma had left for her honeymoon. She'd forgotten all about it. Well, it was too late to return it now. Rose decided she'd give it to Emma and make her return it herself. If Alice noticed its absence before then, she'd just have to wait to get an answer to that mystery.

What was it about this ridiculous piece of literature that had exerted such a pull on her friends? Rose found herself walking over to the drawer and pulling out the book. Returning to the sofa, she opened the book.

She had already read a small portion of it, back when they were all still single women. They had been perusing the book together and discussing it over tea, shortly after Alice had acquired it. Rose had read a section describing a widow who "forgot" how to send a telegram just so she could rope in a nearby eligible-looking gentleman by asking for his help. How absurd was that? Rose couldn't think of anything she was *less* likely ever to do in her lifetime.

Against her better judgment, Rose flipped the pages to the chapter on widows.

A charming maid will attract admiration and love, and an honorable wife gains respect and high regard. But the widow is of

particular interest; her state elicits sympathy and protective-
ness, quite naturally drawing the care and attention of nobler
gentlemen. If she is beautiful, her fascinations are even more
powerful—for the man may say, "How happy must he have been
who called her his!"

"No word about whether *she* was happy in the arrangement,"
Rose murmured. "No one ever seems to think about that."

The black gown now covers the snowy bosom, and the mourning ring binds the heart; how could the flame of love possibly
be rekindled? Ah, but that is the fascination for the man who
would woo the widow! It is an irresistible urge for some. For he
knows, even as he carefully advances his suit, that she will set
him in comparison to the virtues and merits of her lost love.
Therefore, to win her heart is a triumph indeed.

"'Virtues and merits.'" Rose shook her head, unable to apply
those words to Peter. "Short list, in my case."

She was not helpless nor heartbroken. Yes, she had deep
regrets about her past. But surely everyone did, in one way
or another. Such was life. Rose hadn't allowed these things to
defeat her. She was successfully living her life as she saw fit.

That was the best outcome of all.

CHAPTER

Nine

When John returned to London, he took a cab directly from the railway station to Marjorie's home. There were plenty of other things he preferred to do—including visiting Rose at the post office to tell her about that lecture. However, he knew this task should be handled first.

As the cab pulled up to Marjorie's home, John noticed her carriage was standing outside at the ready. When the butler ushered him inside, he found Marjorie in the front hall, putting on her gloves.

"Have I come at a bad time?" he asked, giving her the usual perfunctory kiss on the cheek.

She smiled at him. "This is a perfect time. I'm just on my way to Pearl's house. We can ride over together."

"May I come with you, Mama?" said a young voice. John's seven-year-old niece, Ellie, padded barefoot into the hall and hugged her mother.

John was surprised to see Ellie in her dressing gown even though it was the middle of the afternoon.

Marjorie gently disengaged the girl from her skirts. "You should be in bed. Where is Lettie?"

"Here, ma'am," said the nursery maid, hurrying up to them. "I left Miss Ellie for five minutes to get her some warm milk, and when I returned, I found she had snuck away from me." She turned to the girl. "Shame on you, Miss Ellie."

John sent a worried look to his sister-in-law. "Is she not well?"

"It's her lungs," Marjorie said. "She has trouble breathing when there is too much smoke or fog."

Lettie took hold of the girl's hand and gave it a gentle tug, but Ellie didn't budge. "I want to see Uncle John." She looked up at him. "You haven't been by in ages."

"I'm sorry. I do so much traveling these days." He knelt down so his face was even with hers. He noticed her cheeks had little spots of pink. Signs of a fever? "How is my favorite niece today?"

This brought a smile that had a hint of mischief in it. "Louisa says she is your favorite."

"Does she? Shocking hubris. I'll have to take that girl down a peg when next I see her."

Ellie giggled, but the cheery sound devolved into a rough, chesty cough.

"That's enough visiting," Marjorie told the girl. "You must get back to bed."

"I promise to come back soon," John said, giving Ellie a hug before rising to his feet. He didn't know when he might keep that promise. An echo of what Edward had said, about how this family never saw him, sent a sliver of guilt through him.

After a reluctant good-bye, Ellie allowed the nursery maid to trundle her off to her room.

"Have you had a doctor come by to look at her?" John asked once the pair was out of earshot.

"Yes, he made a poultice we can apply to clear out some of

the congestion in her lungs. I expect she'll be better tomorrow." She eyed him. "Don't look so worried! It's not unusual for little ones to get phlegmy sometimes, especially when the cold weather draws on."

John didn't remember his other nieces and nephews having so many issues. But then, back when they were Ellie's age, their fathers had still been alive, and John had been living in another part of the country, pursuing his own career.

"I saw Edward."

"You can tell me all about it on the way to Pearl's house. She's expecting me for tea today, and I know she'd love to see you." She angled a look at him. "Or have you already been to visit her?" Marjorie always seemed jealous at the idea that John would want to spend more time with his own sister than with her. Perhaps he was more alert to it now, after talking with Edward.

He shook his head. "I came to you first. I was sure you'd be anxious to hear about my visit with your son."

Her expression softened to a smile. "You are so kind. Come on, then."

As they rode in the carriage, John described his visit with Edward. He did his best to repeat the conversation verbatim, feeling it was important for Marjorie to understand how things stood. The only part he glossed over was Edward's accusation that John was somehow neglecting them. As far as he was concerned, it was manifestly untrue. He wouldn't give credence to it for a moment. He'd done as much for them as his life could allow, and it was quite a lot.

Marjorie looked rightfully worried about Edward's desire to leave school so early. "I can't think what to do about him," she said, shaking her head. "It warms my heart that he feels such an obligation to take care of us. He's so like his father in that regard. But what in the world would he do without a proper education? Did you manage to persuade him how important it is that he remain in school?"

"I told him in no uncertain terms he must stay. Whether I succeeded in persuading him is another matter altogether."

"I do hope he'll listen to you. With Lionel and Roger gone, he has no man to look up to except for you."

"I've done what I could. Perhaps you might write him a strongly worded letter as well. If he knows you and Ellie are perfectly well and that you wish him to remain in school, it might have some sway. Or perhaps you might visit him to make the case in person?"

Marjorie shook her head. "I will write him a letter. I do miss him terribly, but I must be strong, for Lionel's sake. I know this is what he wanted. It will be easier for me to remain firm if I do it in a letter."

"Will you do it soon?"

"I'll send it tomorrow. I will also tell him you were right in everything you said. From what you've shared, I imagine the boy is quite put out with you."

"There's no doubt about that," John said ruefully. He didn't like being at odds with his nephew, but doing the right thing wasn't always easy.

Marjorie gave him a friendly nudge. "Cheer up. You've still got Ellie's undying admiration."

He smiled as he considered his plucky little niece. "So I have."

The carriage drew to a halt at Pearl's house. As John helped Marjorie from the carriage, she gave his hand a squeeze and sent him a demure smile—the kind that always made him uncomfortable. As usual, he did his best to shrug off the feeling.

When they entered the parlor, they found Pearl seated in her customary chair. She was listening, eyes half-closed, as Louisa read aloud to her.

Louisa caught sight of them and stopped reading. "Uncle John!" she said happily, setting her book aside and coming over to greet him.

"And your aunt Marjorie," Marjorie reminded her.

Louisa gave her a hug. "Good afternoon, Auntie. We've been waiting for you to arrive. We want to hear all about last night."

"Oh? I'd assumed Sophie would have told you about it in complete detail by now."

Pearl motioned for them to be seated. "I believe last night's events quite wore her out. She's been resting for the greater part of the day."

"I thought you were going to this soiree as well?" John asked Pearl.

"I was planning on it, but then all day I was lightheaded and having terrible palpitations. I was afraid I might end up collapsing on the floor or something."

John wasn't too surprised to hear she hadn't gone, although he was disappointed.

"It's a good thing I stayed home," Pearl insisted. "What if I'd fainted dead away in the middle of everything? Poor Sophie would have been so embarrassed. I wanted her to get off on the right foot."

"I assure you, she did," Marjorie said with a smile.

"I can confirm," Louisa added. "I went to her room this morning. She had a dreamy expression of happiness on her face, but when I asked her about it, she threw a pillow at me and told me to leave." Louisa gave a shrug, looking mystified by these contradictory pieces of information.

"She just isn't ready to talk about it, that's all. It can be like that sometimes, as you'll likely find out soon enough."

Louisa made a face. "I hope when I fall in love, I shan't turn into a silly goose."

John chuckled. He enjoyed Louisa's independent spirit.

"This is why we depend on you to give us a full report," Pearl said to Marjorie.

Looking more than happy to oblige, Marjorie took a moment to settle herself on the sofa, arranging her skirts in elegant drapes before speaking. "The entire evening was a great success, just as we'd hoped it would be."

"No issues with Mr. Deveaux?" John asked.

Marjorie frowned at him. "I don't know why you keep making a fuss about Mr. Deveaux. He was quite the gentleman all evening."

"And how do you know this?" John pressed. "You kept an eye on him and Sophie the whole time?" John found this hard to believe, given Marjorie's tendency to flit about at social events.

"It was a simple task. I sat in the back row during the recital. I prefer not to sit too close to sopranos. Those high notes can hurt my ears sometimes. Happily, Miss Lester is quite gifted and didn't screech. She is not terribly pretty, however. She can't hold a candle to Sophie. I sat with Dr. and Mrs. Greville, and we had the most delightful conversation. They agreed with me on my assessment."

"About Miss Lester or about Sophie?"

"Both, of course."

"I hope Sophie didn't hear that conversation," Pearl said with a playful roll of her eyes. "She has quite a good opinion of herself already."

"She wasn't sitting with us. She wanted to sit up front with the Draytons. What a perfect decision that turned out to be! Her chair was right in front of Mr. Deveaux's. He couldn't take his eyes off her during the entire performance. He even leaned forward to whisper to her several times during the applause between songs."

"How thrilling!" Pearl exclaimed. "I'm glad we decided on that blue gown. It's truly elegant, and the lower cut at the shoulders makes Sophie look so grown up."

Both ladies tittered, but for his part, John wasn't so delighted. It disturbed him to think of that man being forward enough to whisper in Sophie's ear. "What happened after the concert?"

"There was a bit of a crush as people stood up and began

milling about. Some went up to give their compliments to Miss Lester and the pianist."

"And Sophie?" Pearl asked eagerly. "Did she and Mr. Deveaux continue their conversation?"

"I believe that was the gentleman's intention, but he had to compete against a half dozen other men who flocked to her side. Everyone was enchanted—simply enchanted!—by her." Marjorie leaned back with a satisfied smile. "I think we may say she has been successfully launched into society."

"Launched?" Louisa repeated. "Did someone smash a champagne bottle on her?"

"Hush, girl," Pearl said primly, but there was a glint in her eyes from the joke.

John wasn't finding any of this amusing. "Marjorie, I thought you said Sophie's attendance at this event was not going to be akin to her coming out."

"Well . . ." Marjorie cleared her throat. "I believe I said it needn't *necessarily* be seen that way. But look what happened! This gave us an opportunity to test the waters, so to speak, and it was an unqualified success. Other invitations will undoubtedly arrive for Sophie now. It would be foolish for her not to accept them. It might even appear rude."

John rubbed his eyes, sighing. How effortlessly they'd gone from allowing Sophie a few forays with adults into a full-on launch into the marriage market. Marjorie had engineered it from the beginning, he realized. He turned to his sister. "Pearl, do you agree with Marjorie's assessment?"

Sensing his disapproval, Pearl looked conflicted. "It has all been unorthodox, I agree," she said, trying to strike a conciliatory tone. "That doesn't mean it can't be for the best. Not too many weeks ago, you were going on about the need to economize in preparation for the cost of Sophie's debutante activities next spring. Yet here we've accomplished virtually the same thing with minimal fuss."

"And to top it all off, she has won the attention of Mr. Deveaux," Marjorie added enthusiastically. "I tell you, John, this has been an absolute coup!"

"I'm glad to know Sophie garnered so much interest from those other fellows last night," Pearl said. "However, I hope they won't impede her chances with Mr. Deveaux."

"I don't think there's much chance of that. When next I saw her, she and Mr. Deveaux were deep in conversation and looking quite enamored with one another."

"What do you mean, 'when next you saw her'?" John asked.

"I suppose I did lose sight of her for a few minutes. I went with the Grevilles to search out a glass of punch. Sophie was with the Draytons, so I knew there was nothing to worry about."

"And was she still with the Draytons when you saw her again?"

Marjorie let out an exasperated huff. "If you will stop acting like a prosecuting attorney, I will be happy to explain it to you."

John lifted his hands in surrender. "All right, please explain it to me."

"Thank you. As I was saying, I did lose sight of her for a bit. It couldn't have been more than ten minutes. I'm sure there was no harm done. There is a lovely terrace and garden behind the Bromleys' home. Sophie and Mr. Deveaux must have gone outside to get a breath of fresh air. I saw them as they came back inside and made directly for the refreshment table. But I don't believe a single person took any notice of it."

"You don't feel there was anything untoward in their slipping outside into the dark night?"

Marjorie gave an unconcerned shrug. "For all I know there were other people outside as well."

John had no way to dispute this assertion.

"We must extend her some trust," Pearl said. "I know she's a good girl."

"But she hasn't made very good decisions on her own recently, has she?"

Marjorie opened her mouth to object, but Pearl, nodding soberly at the truth of John's statement, put up a hand to stop her.

"Ladies, listen to me. Even though Deveaux acquits himself well in society, we can't take that as the full measure of his character. You must continue to exercise caution, and see that Sophie does too."

"Yes, yes, we shall watch over our girl," Marjorie said impatiently. "Although I'm sure your suspicions will turn out to be unfounded."

Pearl clasped her hands together, smiling. "How I am looking forward to meeting Mr. Deveaux." Probably out of deference to John's concerns, she added, "For all the reasons you listed as well, naturally."

"I would like to meet him too," John said. He was going to make certain he did.

"Ah, here's our lovely debutante!" Marjorie said as the door opened and Sophie entered.

"Did you finally get enough beauty rest?" Louisa teased. "I can't tell any difference."

Sophie stuck out her tongue at her sister. It was a childlike gesture that made her look so young. Surely it was too soon for her to contemplate jumping into marriage. Evidently, John was the only person in the room who thought this. Perhaps he was wrong. He was no expert on these things. As he thought back on it, Pearl had been married at nineteen, and Marjorie at twenty. It was strange to think one of their children might soon be doing the same. It made him feel old.

"Have you all been talking about me?" Sophie said, smiling with pride as though she hoped that were true.

"We've just learned that you won over every single gentleman at Lady Bromley's party—and that you had a private tête-à-tête in the moonlight with one of them," Louisa said, finishing her statement with a suggestive waggle of her brows.

"Aunt Marjorie, you weren't supposed to tell them about that part," Sophie said.

"I couldn't help it. Your uncle dragged it out of me." She motioned Sophie over to sit next to her. "Not that you have a single thing to feel embarrassed about."

Sophie looked to her mother, who nodded her confirmation with a smile. Even so, John couldn't help but notice Sophie's cheeks coloring.

"I'm sure you won't mind telling us all about it," he said.

"Really, John," Marjorie admonished.

"We did go out to the garden," Sophie said. "The house was overstuffed with people. It felt good to get into the cool air."

"What did you do then?" Louisa prompted.

There were times when John could appreciate Louisa's unfiltered way of asking questions.

"We talked, that's all. About all sorts of things. Then we came back inside."

The way Sophie looked at her hands as she spoke, without meeting anyone's eyes, hinted more may have gone on besides talking.

"What's next?" Pearl said. "When shall I meet him? If he comes to our home, I would like some advance notice. Just to ensure everything here is at its best."

"I did mention it to him, but I don't think it will happen anytime soon. He told me he's staying at Lord Braden's country home until the end of November. At this time of year, he only comes to town for special occasions."

This was good news. If Deveaux was largely out of town, that would offer fewer temptations for Sophie to steal off on her own.

"But he will be attending the ball at Lord and Lady Randolph's home in two weeks," Sophie added. "And he's going to ensure we get an invitation. Oh, Mother, do say you'll go!" She looked pleadingly at Pearl. "I so want you to meet him."

Pearl took a deep breath, her eyes closing briefly, almost as if she were experiencing a spasm of pain. "I'll do my best, dear."

John guessed she was imagining the enormous effort it would take for her to attend a ball. It troubled him that his sister was finding it increasingly difficult to partake in functions outside her home. She had always been so energetic and vivacious. More and more, she seemed to be fading like a flower left too long in a vase.

John stayed through dinner, partly because he was still concerned over Pearl and partly because of the promise he'd made to Edward to spend more time with his family. The subject did turn to his nephew at one point, with Louisa chiming in her view that she didn't see why Edward shouldn't be allowed to come home. All of the adults were in agreement against her. Louisa didn't press her argument, but John could see she was unconvinced. Sophie had nothing to say on the subject; she spent dinner with her head in some distant cloud.

If there was one thing that kept John's spirits up throughout the evening, it was contemplating his plan to see Rose Finlay. Monday afternoon he should be able to get to the post office to tell her about that Dickens lecture. He fully intended to keep his promise not to discuss his family issues with her any further. It would be a relief, actually, to set aside this knot of problems for a few hours and engage in something enjoyable. John was quite sure spending time with Rose would fall firmly into that category.

CHAPTER

Ten

Rose entered the little recessed area where Stan Reese was busy at the telegraph machine. Stan was not even twenty years old, but he was one of their best clerks. Like Rose, he was able to work by ear, although how he could hear anything today was beyond her. The poor lad had been coughing all morning.

She set a mug of hot tea on the desk as he finished receiving a message and signed off. "I brought you some tea. I added lemon and honey to help soothe your throat."

"Thank you, ma'am. That's awfully kind." He sent her a grateful look and took a generous swallow of the tea. Then he held the mug to his chest, warming himself. Another indication he wasn't well. This area was the warmest and stuffiest part of the office.

Rose studied him with concern. "Are you sure you ought to have come in today?"

"I can't afford to stay home. Mr. Gordon will dock my wages." He took another sip of the tea, this time swallowing it as slowly as possible. "That does feel better. You're always so kind to us, Mrs. Finlay, looking after us."

"Us?" Rose repeated.

"Me and Miss Palmer. And the messenger boys. I heard you gave a woolen scarf to Charlie the other day."

It was true that Rose had gifted the youngest of their messenger boys with a scarf. The child's family was barely scraping by, and his clothes were inadequate for the bitter weather. The scarf had been among the items in a box of clothes she'd collected for charity. She'd decided Charlie had as great a need for it as anyone.

"Miss Palmer told me you gave her extra drilling on maths so she could work the till properly," Stan went on. "She was having a tough time of it." He lowered his voice. "She thinks if Mr. Gordon hadn't gone on holiday when he did, and you took over and helped her out, she very well might have been sacked. It's almost like you're mothering us."

Rose did not like for her actions to be compared to mothering. "It's all for the good of our workplace, I assure you. How can we carry out our tasks efficiently if our people are not healthy and adequately trained? I knew Mr. Gordon would berate me soundly if our finances were off, or if messages weren't delivered in a timely manner."

"If you say so, Mrs. Finlay." Stan smiled and took another sip of tea.

Rose picked up the message he'd been taking down when she came in. "I'll take care of this. And by the way, I expect that mug to be washed and clean when you return it to me." She spoke in her best managerial voice.

"Yes, Mrs. Finlay." Stan tried to give a cheeky grin, but this was stopped by another bout of coughing. He doused it with more tea, then got to work as the sounder started up again.

As Rose passed by Mr. Gordon's office on her way to the filing area, he called her inside for a meeting. "I've been reviewing the books and looking over your notes about the daily activities here during my absence. I have to say you did an excellent job—especially in regard to that emergency with the exterior telegraph wires."

"Thank you, sir." Rose spoke modestly, but inwardly she was glowing with pride.

"There's just one thing. I don't see where you got approval from the main office for the money spent on the repairs."

"There wasn't time. I was told the forms would take over a week to process. It was imperative that we get the wires up again immediately. I believe you'll find the cost was not excessive, especially considering the complicated nature of the work."

"I agree with you wholeheartedly. Even so, I need to clear this bill with the assistant superintendent."

"I don't see that he has any choice but to approve it. The work has already been done."

"Yes, but he's a stickler for keeping to the rules. He might well take it out of our operating budget. We'd have to delay hiring another clerk, which we are in great need of."

"That would be unnecessarily harsh—not to mention illogical. It would hamper our operations. It's rather like shooting oneself in the foot."

Mr. Gordon chuckled. "You are very outspoken, Mrs. Finlay. And you have a knack for going after any problem with great energy. These are all excellent qualities in a manager."

Rose leaned forward. He was hinting that he did indeed view her as a replacement for him when he retired. "I always do my best, sir. I'm sure you will agree that everything here is in tip-top shape."

"Yes, it is. Despite my two-week absence. It makes me feel somewhat redundant."

"I wasn't trying to imply that," Rose protested.

He held up a hand. "I understand you completely. But let me

give you a word of advice. It's also important for a manager to work well with those above him—or her, as the case may be. You cannot brush aside the approved policies every time something out of the ordinary occurs. I'm not saying it wasn't warranted here; I'm merely advising you that in the future, you should consider all the options carefully before deciding the usual rules don't apply. It's the only way the Royal Mail can continue to operate as an efficient, well-oiled machine."

"Thank you, sir. I will keep that in mind."

Rose thought over his words as she returned to her tasks. Mr. Gordon had given her both praise and a warning. It was good advice to heed. At times she felt hemmed in by the strict hierarchy of the post office. But these were minor inconveniences compared to her overall satisfaction in working here.

She went to the front counter to see how Miss Palmer was doing. It was true the girl did not have a good head for numbers, and she was still confused by the complicated forms for the parcel post. But she was improving.

In fact, today she seemed to be handling these tasks well. Rose observed for several minutes as Miss Palmer successfully completed a variety of transactions. Yes, the girl was going to work out all right.

Rose was about to return to her other duties when she noticed John Milburn entering the post office. It was surprising, so why did it also feel somehow inevitable? Perhaps because he had frequently come to Rose's thoughts over the past few days. The information she'd learned from Douglas Shaw had piqued her interest in him. What must it be like to give up one's own occupation for the sake of one's family? What had been his occupation before, and did he regret having to make the change? Rose had tried to mentally shrug off those questions, figuring she probably wasn't going to see him again. Yet here he was.

She battled mixed emotions as he strode up to the counter.

If he wanted more information regarding Sophie or Sandy, he was going to be disappointed. She had none, and she wouldn't have shared it if she had. But why else would he have come?

He gave her a cheery smile. "Good afternoon. I hope you are well."

"Yes, thank you. What brings you here today?" She made a movement toward the second till, in case he was here for a postal transaction.

John shook his head. "To be honest, I was hoping to have another chat with you—if it's convenient."

"What about?" she countered.

He placed a book in front of her. Its title was clearly embossed on the cover: *The Pickwick Papers*. "We talked about Dickens the last time we met. You mentioned that you might be interested in trying it again, so I brought this along, just in case you didn't have a copy."

In fact, Rose did not own a copy. She had a subscription to a circulating library, which provided most of her reading materials. That was a lot cheaper than buying books, especially given how many she devoured in a year.

He pushed it toward her. "It's just a loan, but you may keep it as long as you like. I thought it might be fun for us to discuss it sometime."

This obvious kindness only heightened her wariness. She'd learned long ago to be careful about taking any gestures from men at face value. "Thank you, but I don't think I could accept this."

"It's just a loan," he repeated. "I'd be pleased if you accepted. And I hope you'll allow me to buy you a cup of tea. There's an upcoming lecture on Dickens, and I'd like to tell you more about it. Perhaps you'd be interested in going."

He seemed to be genuinely going out of his way for her. Even so, Rose could not let go of her concerns. What she'd seen of John Milburn, and heard about him from Douglas, had been good. Yet given the situation with his niece, Rose could not ignore the fact that he might still have ulterior motives.

"My offer is coming strictly from a place of friendship," John said, almost as though he were reading her thoughts. "Do you think men and women can be friends?"

Rose couldn't help but feel an odd sense of unreality. Was this man really trying to befriend her—and with a *book*? It was such a marvelous idea that she couldn't quite bring herself to believe it. She'd always been comfortable working around men, but never had one tried to strike up a friendship with her. Certainly no man had ever wanted to make her acquaintance simply to discuss books. They usually had very different things on their minds. "You honestly just want to talk about Dickens?"

He lifted his hands. "I promise I will not broach any other subjects. Certainly nothing about my family if that's what's concerning you."

By now, there were no customers left in the post office. Rose sent a glance toward Miss Palmer and Stan Reese. Each had dutifully begun their end-of-day tasks, but it was clear they were also watching Rose and Mr. Milburn's interaction with some interest. Perhaps that was because Rose allowed no part of her private life to blend with her work. She wasn't about to begin today. It was going to be easier to relent, if only to bring this conversation to a close more quickly. "I do have a bit of time this evening, as it happens. It will take me a few minutes to close up here. If you want to wait at the tea shop, I'll be along presently."

"Thank you." He straightened and stepped back from the counter but took the book back in his hands. "I'll keep this for you until then. It will give me something interesting to read to pass the time."

The way he spoke, and the jauntiness in his step as he left, made Rose want to call out to him and cancel the whole thing.

But he was out of the shop before she could make up her mind to do it.

It took all of Rose's determined concentration to help Miss Palmer close out the till and count the money. Miss Palmer counted the coins aloud while Rose watched in order to check her work. Unfortunately, Rose's train of thought slipped to John Milburn one too many times. She lost her place and made Miss Palmer count everything again. The girl gave her a curious look, but Rose passed it off as ensuring she got more practice.

At last they got the money counted and into the large iron safe, along with a bag of valuable parcels that would be handed off to a courier tomorrow morning. Miss Palmer and Stan remained at the counter, chatting with one another while Rose and Mr. Gordon made their final reviews and everyone was dismissed.

Rose donned her coat and hat, although she didn't bother with her gloves since she was only going next door. Mr. Gordon's carriage was waiting for him. He entered it and was swiftly off. The rest of them were leaving on foot, and it didn't escape Rose that her two coworkers paused and watched as she entered the tea shop. What must they be thinking? Feeling more than a little embarrassed at having brought on such scrutiny, Rose entered the shop and closed the door behind her.

John Milburn was waiting for her at a table in the back. The place was nearly full. The table John and Rose had been seated at last time was currently occupied by a portly, balding gentleman and a stout woman with rosy cheeks and a very red nose. Mr. Milburn was reading his book, but he immediately looked up when he heard the jangle of the bell over the door.

He stood as she approached, moving around the table to help her get seated.

"I feel an odd sense of déjà vu," Rose quipped, still uncertain whether coming here had been the right thing to do.

"It is the same, only different, of course. I'm afraid the clergy-man of Dingley Dell and his wife have taken over our previous meeting place."

"Do you know them?" Rose looked back over her shoulder.

He smiled and handed her the book. "Only in these pages. Mr. Pickwick meets them in his travels."

Once more, Rose felt that sense of unreality that had over-taken her earlier. "I do that sometimes myself. I'll see a person and think, 'they are just like such-and-such a character.'"

"Do you really?" He seemed pleased by this.

"It's easy to do, with so many different kinds of people visit-ing the post office. There is a reason why Dickens's characters seem so alive to us—he was clearly drawing from life."

John nodded. "Yes! And paradoxically, the way he exagger-ated their characteristics somehow made them seem more real. How does that work, I wonder?"

"It's a wonderful mystery," Rose agreed. As they regarded one another warmly, Rose began to feel more comfortable with her decision to come here.

"Ah, here's our tea," John said, sending a glance over Rose's shoulder. "The girl must have had to go to India for it." But he said this as a jest and not a criticism.

"Beggin' your pardon for the delay, sir," said the waitress as she set down a tray with a pot and two cups. "We're awfully busy tonight." She scurried away without waiting for a reply.

John sent a smile toward Rose. "I suppose one advantage is that it's perfectly hot, just in time for your arrival."

"It seems a luxury to have hot tea ready at a moment's no-tice."

"I'm glad I could oblige." He picked up the teapot and filled their cups. "Another long day at work?"

"Not quite as hectic as on the last day we met, but we're always busy. How about you? You seem to have been able to break away early."

"I had some business in the area. I've decided to take a lease on a warehouse nearby. I signed the papers this afternoon."

"How long have you been selling finished iron products?"

"About five years. I took over my brother's company after he died."

Here was the information Douglas had told her. It provided an opening to ask the question that had been on her mind ever since. "What did you do before that?"

"I was apprenticed to a surveyor and architect."

She looked at him in surprise, her interest increasing. "Were you really?"

He nodded. "I attended the Crystal Palace School of Engineering, in the drafting section. We studied surveying as well. After that I began working with an architect in Leeds. We were in the process of designing new buildings for the city that would include the town hall and library. I had to leave before the project was completed, but later I found out it had been accepted from a number of competing bids. I'm rather proud of that."

"Are you sorry you gave it up?"

"I don't regret keeping my brother's business alive to provide for his family, but I do miss the work. I've been fascinated by architecture ever since I was a young lad. There are so many wonderful examples here in London of buildings that are both beautiful and functional. They are inspiring just to look at. The same way a person's spirit might be edified by hearing a soaring orchestral piece. In fact, the German poet Goethe once said, 'Architecture is frozen music.'"

"That's a lovely observation."

"He also said, 'Few people have the imagination for reality.' I'm still trying to puzzle that one out."

Rose smiled. "Oh dear, now you'll have me wrestling with it."

He laughed. It was a gentle laugh, followed by a diffident nod. His charm seemed so natural. Like he didn't even realize he was wielding it. "Please let me know what answers you come up with."

"I will." Her words came out easily. It felt odd to be enjoying the conversation so much, but really, what was the harm? "Do you suppose that's a good description of Dickens—having an imaginative way of taking reality to interesting and vivid extremes?"

"That's a good way of looking at it." He set down his teacup. "That reminds me . . ." He pulled a piece of paper from his pocket and handed it to Rose. "Here is the information about the lecture. These two gentlemen are literary critics, and they also met Mr. Dickens several times. I believe they will be including some personal anecdotes. It could be fascinating. We know what an interesting character Mr. Dickens was in his own right."

"That's certainly true." Rose looked down at the paper. It was a short article that John must have torn out of a newspaper. The article explained how it was going to be a fundraiser for books for a local school. Rose was thrilled at the idea of attending the lecture, but she was dismayed when she saw the date and time. "This will take place tomorrow evening?"

"Yes, I hope you don't have other plans. I'm sorry I wasn't able to tell you about it sooner. I've been traveling for work. I do hope you can go. It would be a shame for you to miss it."

Rose would have preferred a daytime event, such as a Saturday or Sunday afternoon. An evening lecture would have her rushing after work to change clothes and get to the location where it was being held. There was also the need to visit her mother-in-law. But it wasn't really critical that Rose go there so often. Mother Finlay wasn't helpless, only frail and wishing for company.

Rose made up her mind. She wasn't going to allow that woman to control her free time. It was only one day, after all. She could visit her tonight and tell her she had another engagement tomorrow. She looked up from the paper. "I believe I'll be able to go."

"Wonderful!" He looked so pleased that Rose couldn't help but feel complimented. Perhaps finding someone with a mutual interest was just what she needed to ease some of the loneliness that had been plaguing her of late.

"We're attending this event only as friends," Rose said firmly. Perhaps he might take offense, but she wanted no misunderstandings.

He nodded, not looking the least bit affronted. "Only as friends. I'd be happy to give you a ride to the lecture—unless it would make you uncomfortable to accept. If so, I understand completely."

She thought about it for a moment. "I believe it will work out better if I meet you there."

"Very well." He pointed toward the paper. "You have all the information you need there. I'll look for you in the lobby."

Rose pushed back her chair. "I should hurry home now to arrange a few things."

He came around the table to help her with her coat. He seemed a very solid presence as he stood behind her, helping her effortlessly with this gentlemanly task. Rose surprised herself by taking a moment to savor the warmth emanating from him. It felt almost comforting. It brought up a memory from the day Alice and Douglas had called at her flat, and how she'd seen him hold Alice's coat for her before they left. He'd briefly leaned toward his wife as the coat slipped onto her shoulders, smiling at their moment of closeness. The memory sent a brief, visceral bolt of feeling through Rose. She realized now that in that moment, perhaps she'd felt a touch of envy. . . .

But of course, this moment was not like that one at all. John Milburn had offered himself as a friend. Rose had no need of more, nor was she looking for it. Shaking off the unsettling feelings that threatened her usual equilibrium, she quickly buttoned her coat and pulled on her gloves.

"May I walk you to the cabs?" John offered as they left the tea shop.

"Thank you, but I believe I'll walk. I've some errands to handle on the way home."

He nodded, gave her another smile, and tipped his hat. "Until tomorrow, then."

Rose walked home, carefully holding the book John had loaned her. She still could not entirely believe what had happened. John Milburn wanted to befriend her. Not once had he spoken of Sophie, nor anyone else in his family. Perversely, this raised her curiosity. Was Sandy still pursuing Sophie? Or had John managed to end it? Rose decided she wasn't going to ask. If he never brought it up, she'd take that as proof he was sincere in everything he'd done today.

Much as she would have loved to settle in with her new book for the evening, she knew she had to visit Mother Finlay first. She smiled in anticipation of tomorrow's event being a reward for the less appealing tasks she had to undertake first. John Milburn had brought a generous portion of pleasantness to her life, and she was grateful for it.

CHAPTER
Eleven

The lecture hall was packed. Every available seat was taken. The people filling the limited space, plus the heat from many gas lamps, made the room very warm. It was a stark contrast to the cold night outside. There had been no place to leave coats or hats, so everyone had to hold these items on their laps. This seemed to intensify the stuffiness of the room.

Despite these inconveniences, John was finding the lecture as good as he'd expected. The two critics delivered valuable insights into Dickens's work. Their highly entertaining personal memories of the man added extra interest, making John very glad he'd come.

What especially heightened his pleasure was sharing this evening with Rose. When he'd asked her to come to this event, he'd done his best to keep a friendly and casual air. It had been a bit of a charade; he'd worked hard to hide just how badly he wanted her to accept the invitation. During the week he'd been traveling, she had begun to loom so large in his thoughts that he told himself he must surely be exaggerating her memory in his mind. But the moment he'd walked into the post office with the book and saw her at the counter, he'd known his memory was accurate. In her wonderfully unique way, she was as stunning as he'd remembered. He was sad their first meeting hadn't ended well, and he'd been anxious to erase any lingering bad feelings.

Happily, his approach had worked. She was here, and it was clear she was enjoying this evening as much as he was. Through subtle sideways glances, he watched her reactions to the information shared by the speakers. She was engrossed in it all. She was especially appealing when she smiled at the funnier anecdotes. He liked the way her face lightened, erasing her normally serious expression, and there was a particular lift to her brow that was enchanting. Her profile was rather nice, with a straight nose and a chin that was firm but not unfeminine. She wore a modest gown of burgundy with thin gray stripes. It was a flattering color on her.

The audience erupted into applause and laughter as one of the speakers described Dickens's antics as an amateur magician at an exuberant Twelfth Night party. John hadn't known until tonight that Dickens celebrated Twelfth Night every year, usually with many friends as well as his family. One of his magic tricks had been that he'd seemingly cooked a Christmas pudding instantly in a top hat. As Rose turned to share a smile with him over this story, he realized just how warm the room had become. As a result, he didn't entirely absorb the last few minutes of the lecture.

As the program wrapped up, there was another round of energetic applause when the amount of money that had been raised for the charity was announced.

"It seems everyone's a winner tonight," Rose said to John when the event was over and everyone began rising from their chairs. "We got that wonderfully informative talk, and the school will get new books."

"I'm glad you enjoyed it."

"I learned many new things." She said this so cheerfully that John had the impression she sought out ways to increase her knowledge and relished doing so. It made him like her all the more.

The room began to clear out, but John was in no hurry to leave. It was nearing ten o'clock, so it was too late to take Rose anywhere but home. He would not have thought twice about asking a male friend to a late supper, but with a woman such a thing would feel too intimate. There was nothing left to do but make this moment last as long as he could.

Rose made no move to put on her coat. Perhaps she was feeling the warmth of the room as well. She also looked as though she was still mulling over the lecture.

"Did something in particular strike you?" John prompted.

She nodded. "Much as I love Dickens's writing, I do agree with the first critic that he could get overly maudlin at times. I have felt that way with some of his Christmas stories—except for *A Christmas Carol*, of course. That is perfection. My father used to read that aloud to us every Christmas. He had a wonderful, booming voice that was perfect for the Ghost of Christmas Present, filling our little parlor in much the way Dickens described."

"It must have been very entertaining. Is your father still living?"

"Sadly, no. I believe one of my cousins has picked up the tradition, but I haven't been able to get back to Surrey to experience it." She gave a wistful smile and wiped a strand of hair from her forehead, as though carefully setting those memories aside. "What did you find most interesting this evening?"

"I didn't realize Dickens was so devoted to celebrating Twelfth Night. That's rather gone out of fashion in England, hasn't it? Of course, I can understand the motivation that it was also his eldest son's birthday. But it seems there was more to it."

"A touch of nostalgia, perhaps? He seemed interested in keeping a lot of the older Christmas traditions alive."

"That's a good theory."

To John's delight, they spent several more minutes discussing other points that had been raised during the lecture. Rose seemed as happy to extend this time together as he was. In John's view, she seemed even more attractive when her mind was engaged on a topic that provoked thought. John had plenty of work colleagues, a few friends, and, of course, his ever-present family. But as they continued talking, he began to realize that being with Rose filled a gap, meeting a need he hadn't consciously been aware of.

They hadn't moved from where they were standing, other than to step aside for others who were passing by them along the row of chairs. When the room was nearly cleared out, one of the ushers approached them with a smile. He thanked them warmly for coming, and for their support of this worthy charity, but John could see the man's underlying motive was to get them moving along.

"My goodness, it's getting late, isn't it?" Rose said, as though just realizing the time. "I should be going home, if I'm to have any hope of getting to work on time tomorrow."

"Will you allow me to escort you home?" John asked. "Just to ensure you get there safely."

He probably shouldn't have added that last bit. It caused her right eyebrow to arch ever so slightly. By now he could discern that she was proud of her ability to live independently and take care of herself.

But then she smiled and said with a nod, "That's very kind of you."

The cold night air was refreshing at first, but a stiff wind quickly made its way down John's collar. It was a relief to locate a cab and get inside.

Once they were underway, the topic of conversation returned

to Dickens, this time spurred on by Rose because John's mind had gone blank for several long moments after he'd handed her into the cab and then joined her there. Or rather, not blank, exactly, but oddly focused on how natural it felt to hold her hand as he helped her up, and how smooth and comfortable the action had been. As though they had done it countless times. Her movements always seemed poised, confident, and instinctive, never put on for show.

She took a moment to adjust her hat, which had been nearly knocked off in the stiff wind, then turned to look at John. He realized she had said something and was expecting a reply. Searching through the wool that had gathered in his brain, he managed to locate the question she had just directed at him and decipher it to coherent thought. "No, I wasn't too disappointed that so little time was spent on *The Pickwick Papers.* I can see why they focused on his works with more depth. . . ."

Now that he had pulled his thoughts back in line, their conversation during the ride to Rose's home went as smoothly as it had in the lecture hall. John only changed the subject when he realized they must be nearing her street, based on the directions she'd given the driver. He didn't want the evening to end before he had secured a way to see her again.

"Do you enjoy the theater?" he asked.

Looking surprised at this sudden change of topic, she answered, "It depends on the subject matter."

"I was thinking of attending the Saturday afternoon performance of *Patience,* the comic opera by Gilbert and Sullivan that has just moved over to the new Savoy Theatre. Would you be interested in going?"

She pretended to study him critically. "I would not have thought you're the sort who enjoys opera."

"I'm not, generally." John felt it was better to be honest. "However, I've heard this one is quite good, and very funny. Mostly, I'm intrigued because the Savoy is the first theater I know of that is using electric lighting instead of gaslight. I read a review in the newspaper that said it gives the performance an entirely different feel. They even had to completely change the way they paint the backdrops."

"So you're interested in going because you like the novelty of it?"

"Yes, and I thought you would too. As a telegraph operator, you understand the benefits of electricity. I imagine you've seen its potential for future applications. I'm sure there will be many we haven't yet thought of."

"That's certainly true," Rose agreed, looking as though she was warming to the idea. "Saturday afternoon, did you say?"

"That's right." He'd deliberately suggested the afternoon performance so that they might have time together afterward. Also, since Rose had stressed the friendship aspect of their time together, a daytime show would seem less formal. He hoped she did not already have plans. He had to leave town again next week, and he truly wanted to see the show—and Rose—before he left.

The carriage came to a stop, and that seemed to help Rose finalize her decision. "Thank you, I'd love to go."

Elated, John jumped down from the cab. As he helped Rose down, once again loving the feel of her hand in his, she added, "Why don't I meet you there, as we did tonight?"

John wasn't going to quibble.

They took another minute to finalize the details before bidding one another good night. John stayed on the curb until Rose had entered her building.

During the ride home, John thought back over every detail of the evening. How pleasant it was to spend time with someone like Rose. She was intelligent, perceptive, and . . . He strived to come up with a word. *Calm.* That was it. Filled with purposeful energy, and yet calm. Also, *levelheaded.* John laughed to himself as these descriptions came to him. He thought of

Marjorie and Pearl. Weren't they always on edge and in a dither about one thing or another? Or did they simply make *him* feel that way? Ultimately, he supposed it didn't matter. Something similar happened with him when he was around Rose too. The difference was that she unsettled him in good ways. The way he'd felt as he'd looked at her in the moonlight just now . . .

He wasn't going to analyze it. He was simply going to bask in the knowledge that in a few days he would be able to experience such delightful turbulence again.

～∞～

On Saturday, Rose hurried home after working all morning, intending to make the most of the brief time she had to prepare for going to the theater. After changing out of her working clothes to a prettier gown, she did her best to touch up her hair. She frowned at herself in the mirror. Her hairstyle would never look as elegant as those of the ladies who had their own maids and hours to primp. Rose had spent a few more minutes than usual fixing her hair this morning before work, though. As she studied it now, she decided the extra braiding she'd added to her bun was a nice touch. Certainly Miss Palmer had noticed it. She hadn't said anything outright, but Rose had seen her admiring glance. Rose scrunched her nose as she continued to look at herself in the mirror. Why did women always have such an intense interest in what other women were wearing or how they styled their hair? For that matter, why was Rose suddenly so concerned about her own appearance? She always took care to dress appropriately for any occasion, but she was aware she'd put in extra effort today. She didn't want to think she was growing vain. Rose moved away from the mirror. There was no time to think about it now, or she'd be late to the theater.

She had just put on her coat when she heard a knock at the

door. Blowing out a breath in exasperation at this interruption, she went to answer it. Even more annoying was that the visitor was Mother Finlay.

As she entered the flat, she took note that Rose was putting on her gloves. "Are you going out, dear?"

"Yes, and I haven't time to talk. Is there something you need?"

Her manner was too brusque. Mother Finlay gave her a hurt look. "I'm sorry you haven't time for your poor old mother-in-law. But then, you've been awfully busy these days, haven't you?"

She was getting at something, but Rose could not think what. She'd spent a few hours at the woman's flat just two nights ago.

"Where are you headed in such a hurry?" Mother Finlay asked.

"To the theater. I've been invited to a matinee by a friend."

"I wouldn't have dreamed of bothering you if I'd known, but you didn't mention it when I last saw you."

Rose took a deep breath, trying to quell her agitation. Of course she had not mentioned it. She hadn't wanted to raise questions about whom she was going with, or whether the show was the kind that was "proper" for a lady to attend.

"Have you been spending time with a gentleman?" Mother Finlay asked, adjusting her spectacles as she peered up at Rose.

"Why do you ask?"

"Mrs. Riley visited me yesterday. She mentioned that she saw a man bring you home on Tuesday evening. *Very late.*"

It was no surprise to be gossiped about by Mrs. Riley. She was Rose's landlady. On the night of the lecture, Rose thought she'd seen the curtains twitch in Mrs. Riley's front window as she and John had said good night. The old busybody was always watching her. Rose ought to have known she'd say something to her mother-in-law, since the two were friends.

"If you'll recall, I told you I was going to a lecture on Tuesday. My friend escorted me home. Would you have had me traveling the streets alone at that hour?"

She didn't expect Mother Finlay to argue that point. The woman had old-fashioned notions about how ladies ought to behave.

She gave a little sniff. "And pray tell, what are your plans for today?"

"As I just said, I'm meeting a friend at the theater." Rose gently scooted her mother-in-law out the door, following close behind her.

"The same friend as on Tuesday, or is there another?" Mother Finlay persisted as Rose locked the door to her flat.

Rose began walking down the stairs, leaving the other woman no choice but to follow. "I'm living no differently now than I have during the past seven years since Peter died. As you can see, I have come to no harm thus far." As they got to the street, she added, "Now, if you'll excuse me, I need to find a cab, or I'll be late."

"We'll talk about this later!" Mother Finlay called after her.

Rose was sure they would. This wasn't the first time she'd regretted having been drawn so close to Mother Finlay's orbit by moving here. She resolutely decided not to let the insinuations of two meddlesome ladies bother her. She was going to spend the afternoon with John Milburn and not feel one ounce of guilt about it.

⚜

Rose arrived at the Savoy Theatre with barely five minutes to spare. It had been surprisingly easy to forget her agitation over why she'd been delayed the moment she saw John.

He was waiting outside, tickets in hand. His smiling demeanor showed he wasn't the least bit disturbed by her tardiness. They were seated just in time for Rose to catch her breath as the orchestra began the overture. As the music played, Rose took in the beauty of the new theater. Painted in designs of white, yellow, and gold, it was bright and airy. It was different from other theaters Rose had seen, which were generally painted in darker hues. This felt fresh and appealing.

"It's very nice, isn't it?" John remarked.

It appeared that he, like Rose, had taken extra care with his appearance today. His hair looked freshly trimmed and his face was clean-shaven. He looked as though he'd come straight from the barber shop. He smelled that way too. The scent of his shaving soap and hair pomade reached her from time to time as they sat so close. She had always enjoyed those things about men, from her courting days to her first weeks married to Peter. They were among the few pleasant sensations that had never been ruined by Peter's subsequent bad behavior.

The audience gave a gasp of delight as the curtain rose to reveal a lovely set. The electric lighting did indeed change the very feel of theatergoing. Everything seemed brighter, cleaner, and more vivid.

"This will be good, I think," John whispered to Rose.

She turned to murmur an agreement. Their gazes met and held—in a way Rose wasn't entirely ready for. As though the electricity illuminating the theater was coursing through her as well. The odd stammering of her heart was unexpected too. That was more likely caused by the silent question that seemed to arise in John's eyes. Unwilling, or perhaps too afraid, to allow this powerful connection to continue, Rose turned away and riveted her attention on the chorus of women entering the stage. Ironically, they were singing about how miserable they were because they were all lovesick for the same man. It was meant to be exaggerated and satirical, but for Rose it hit a strangely different note.

Rose knew what the feeling she'd just experienced with John had been. Fortunately, by this stage in her life she was also wise enough to know why she'd felt it. After all, she'd just been thinking over the more pleasing aspects of being around men. As far as Rose could tell, John was turning out to be one of the better ones. Why else had she been so willing to spend time with him?

It did not follow that Rose should swoon in his presence, as the ladies in the chorus did when they saw the object of their affection. Rose forced herself to settle her thoughts, reminding herself of the many important reasons why she must never allow her friendship with John to become anything more intimate. To do so would surely ruin everything, leaving Rose worse off than before. It wouldn't do John any favors either. She wouldn't risk hurting them both. She couldn't bear to lose his friendship. It was already beginning to mean so much to her.

⁓◦⊙◦⁓

As John had hoped, Rose was amenable to joining him for tea after the show. The performance had been marvelous, but it didn't provide him the same joy as strolling down the street with Rose on his arm. She was on his arm figuratively, at any rate. They walked side by side to the nearby café, not touching. Rose seemed careful to keep daylight between them. John went along with her desire to maintain a polite distance, although he already missed sitting close to her in the confines of the theater.

Aside from setting this obvious physical boundary, Rose's interactions with John were as warm and friendly as ever. Their conversation at the café moved effortlessly from one interesting subject to another.

They'd been discussing how the opera poked fun at several popular fads in the fields of poetry and fashion when Rose said, "The satire was perfect, especially in regard to those ladies who were in love with their perception of a man, rather than the man himself. There's more than a bit of truth there."

"Are you speaking from personal experience?"

He expected her to smile, catching his obvious attempt at a joke. Yet there was a slight pause before she drew back in pretend surprise and said, "Certainly not!" It almost made him wonder if she was being entirely truthful in her answer.

"It is, however, a failing of many young ladies," Rose added more seriously. "I confess it got me thinking of Sophie. How is she? And might I ask, is she still involved in any way with Sandy Deveaux?"

John was so surprised by her question that he found it difficult to answer.

"You've kept your word and not mentioned her," Rose went on. "I respect you a great deal for doing so. I have no information to share, nor am I implying that I would do so if I had any. But I am genuinely wondering how she is doing."

"Please don't apologize for asking after my niece," John assured her. "It's very kind of you. Sophie is doing well enough. Her night at the private recital was by all accounts a smashing success and scandal free, although I did learn she and Deveaux escaped to the garden for a few minutes."

"Oh dear."

"I was assured by my sister-in-law, Marjorie, that no harm was done. He was in all other ways a perfect gentleman."

"They always are—in the beginning," Rose murmured.

This sentiment, slipping so easily from Rose's lips, took John aback. It hinted at the unhappy experiences from her past that she'd vaguely referred to when they'd first met. A tiny burst of anger lit within him at whoever had left an ugly scar on her heart, coloring her opinion of all men.

Speaking further of Deveaux would only keep her mind on the same dark track. John tried to think of a way to put the subject to rest, at least for now. "We remain cautiously optimistic but firmly on the watch."

Rose did not reply, but she looked unconvinced.

"Do you have family in London?" John asked. "I hope you won't think I'm prying. Then again, you know so much about my family that it seems only fair."

Rose nodded again, this time offering a smile. "I agree that under the circumstances, you are well within bounds to ask. I have relatives in Surrey and elsewhere, but here in London there is just my mother-in-law. She lives up the street from me. My husband was her only son. He died seven years ago, but Mother Finlay and I continue to be . . . er, close." Her face seemed to sour on the word.

Perhaps that was sorrow at the memory of her late husband? Marjorie had been widowed for five years. In many ways, her grief still seemed as fresh as the day Lionel had died. John sensed that Rose was different. Aside from the mourning ring, she'd shown no outward signs of grieving. Maybe she simply chose not to show it publicly but to keep it private. John had been wondering about this quite a lot, especially since the night of the lecture when he'd realized how much he was beginning to care for this woman.

"I'm sorry for your loss," he said, but the words felt inadequate.

She gave him a grateful smile. "Life is hard at times, but we do what we must, no matter the circumstances. I'm glad you are making such an effort to watch over Sophie. I would like to see things turn out well for her."

She was deliberately turning the discussion away from herself. John still had many questions, but he could see that now was not the time to ask them. There would be other openings later, perhaps, as they got to know one another better. It was clear he was going to have to work hard to earn her trust.

When they left the café, Rose turned down his offer to escort her home. John did not press it, although he was disappointed.

"Thank you for inviting me out this afternoon," Rose said before they parted. "I had a lovely time."

"I'll be traveling next week, but perhaps we might do something again when I return?" John offered.

After a moment, she nodded. "I'd enjoy that."

John decided to walk home. He had too much energy to sit in a cab. When he arrived, he discovered a letter waiting for him from Marjorie. His housekeeper informed him that the servant who delivered the letter said it was urgent. With his earlier happiness changing to alarm, John tore open the letter.

CHAPTER

Rose walked toward Regent's Park, puzzling over why John had asked to meet her this afternoon, and why he'd said it was urgent. The note had been hand delivered by one of his servants, who'd explained that he had instructions to wait for an answer, if she would be so kind as to provide one.

John had offered to meet somewhere near her home, but in her reply, Rose had suggested Regent's Park. That would be far away from Mrs. Riley's prying eyes. As she approached the meeting point she'd described at the southern entrance of the park across from St. Marylebone Church, she saw that John was already there. She'd find out soon enough what the trouble was. She couldn't help worrying that it had something to do with Sophie.

John quickly closed the distance between them. He looked harried, but he managed to offer up a smile. "Thank you for coming."

"It's a pleasant day for a walk," Rose replied, only half joking. It was cooler than yesterday, but the sun was out and the air was calm. As they entered the park, Rose saw that lots of other people had not allowed the chilly weather to prevent them from taking a Sunday-afternoon stroll. The trees lining the path were mostly bare of leaves, allowing plenty of sunlight to make the walk more pleasant. "Your note said this was urgent. I hope there is no trouble in your family?"

"There is, actually."

"Oh dear, Sophie?"

He shook his head. "It's nothing like what you're probably thinking, thank God. The problem is that my youngest niece, Ellie, has taken ill. She has delicate lungs, and at times she has trouble breathing properly. It's made worse in the winter by the fog. Even on clear days like this, there is always soot in the air from the chimneys. She has a fever, in addition to her struggle to breathe, which has grown quite alarming. The doctor has advised Marjorie to take her out to the country or the seaside for a few weeks—longer if she can manage it."

"I'm sorry to hear it. It seems especially awful when illness strikes the young ones." Rose was earnest in her reply, but she wondered why John would feel the need to share the information with her. "I do hope she recovers soon."

"I believe she will. The timing, however, is unfortunate. With Marjorie leaving town, it's left us without a chaperone for Sophie. Her mother can't do it. I believe I mentioned to you before that she's not able to be as active as she once was."

So this *was* about Sophie. Indirectly, anyway. "Can you get a family friend to do it? Or yourself, perhaps?"

"My need to travel hinders me from helping out as much as I'd like to. As for family friends—the only real possibility is Mrs. Drayton, the mother of Sophie's closest friend. Mrs. Drayton and her daughter are as thrilled by the idea of Sophie being courted by Deveaux as the rest of them, so I haven't much faith they'll be the most cautious of chaperones."

Rose could picture it all clearly. Here was a group of women so naïve as to think a Cinderella story was playing out in front of them. Because of this, they were encouraging a lovestruck girl to walk right into danger. What annoyed Rose most of all was that they were old enough to know better. "What does Sophie's mother have to say about all this?"

"Pearl is heartily in favor of Mrs. Drayton, especially as she feels it's critical to find someone as soon as possible. Now that Sophie has been officially launched into society, it would be considered a major misstep to pass up the invitations coming her way. Nor do they want to do so—least of all, Sophie."

"I imagine not." *Foolish, foolish girl.* Rose spent several moments ruminating over this—then suddenly asked herself why she was so invested in this story. As much as she hated to think about it, scenarios like this were played out every day. The bigger question was why John had sought her out to tell her this. Perhaps it had been a mistake to ask after Sophie yesterday.

"I have a favor to ask you," John said. "You will likely think it outlandish, and you would have good reason to think so. But I felt I had to give it a try. I wonder if you would be willing to act as a chaperone for Sophie."

Rose was so surprised that she came to a halt. "*Me?* How in the world could such a plan possibly work?"

"Please, hear me out." He motioned toward a nearby bench.

Rose complied. Although she didn't think she wanted to hear more, she felt at this point she would be unkind to refuse. John looked genuinely worried about the situation.

"Our acquaintance has been short," John began once they were seated. "Yet I already know you are a respectable and responsible woman. Plus, with your knowledge of Deveaux's background and his inclinations, you have a better understanding of this situation than anyone I know." He paused, then added more tentatively, "You've also hinted at a past that includes some experience with dishonorable men. Please forgive me if I'm too impertinent for bringing that up, but it's something I've deduced from our past conversations. I thought you might be able to share some of the wisdom you've acquired with Sophie."

His words were complimentary and, as far as Rose's past was concerned, accurate. Not that she was prepared to discuss it. "What, exactly, did you have in mind?" She pointed a warning finger at him. "I'm not saying I agree to it, mind you."

"Well, there is a ball next Thursday. That's the first and most important thing. If all goes well, we could discuss other possibilities."

"How many events are we talking about? Don't forget, I already have work. I'm not at leisure to attend an endless string of parties."

"I understand, and I've no wish to upend your life. Perhaps we could start by introducing you to Pearl? You could also meet her daughters. Her youngest, Louisa, is fifteen. She's a lovely girl, and quite precocious. She helps her mother a great deal with things around the house. And then of course there's Sophie." He gave a quirky smile. "You already know her, even if you haven't officially met her yet."

"Would we tell her about the times I was spying on her?" Rose said this with a smirk of her own, aware she was being hard on herself with this description.

"I think we should skip that part. We don't want to give her any reason to object to you. She and Pearl will both need some persuading. I'm hoping they'll come around to the idea."

"How, exactly, would you introduce me? Your sister is bound to ask what my qualifications are for acting in such a critical role."

"I can say we met at the post office. Since my work often involves visits there for sending telegrams, I don't think she'll question it. As for qualifications . . ." He thought for a moment, then gave a shrug. "I'm recommending you, and Pearl knows I'm a good judge of character."

Rose was flattered to learn John's high opinion of her, but

she suspected Pearl would need more than his mere assurances. She'd probably ask for details about Rose's background. She couldn't risk sending her daughter off with someone who might have even a whiff of anything unsavory in her past—or who didn't know how to comport herself in good society. They could afford no faux pas. Was Rose prepared to submit herself to that kind of scrutiny?

No. This was precisely why Rose should refuse this idea outright. She didn't, though. She merely studied John, pondering.

He returned her scrutiny with an affable expression. "Please. I'll gladly pay you—or if that feels insulting or demeaning, I'll give you more books."

Rose couldn't help but smile. "You'll pay me in books?"

"Whatever it takes."

He couldn't know just how attractive that sounded. Or did he? "You certainly are a very persuasive man, Mr. Milburn."

He sat up straighter and said proudly, "I have been accused of that more than once."

It was a flash of gentle humor that Rose had seen several times with him. She thought there might be some truth in his statement, given his success in business.

For whatever reason, it seemed impossible to turn him down. "All right, I'll meet your sister. But I make no promises."

"That's all I ask. Even for that, you'll have my undying gratitude."

Rose could only hope she wasn't making a huge mistake in wading into these unknown and murky waters. But the desire to help Sophie still tugged at her heart, perhaps even more than the day Rose had first seen her. If she could prevent the girl from going through the kind of pain she had known, wouldn't it be worth it? This, plus the warmth she was feeling at the way John's face had lit up from her answer, made her willing to try.

"John, I cannot understand how you could even conceive of such a thing." Pearl frowned up at him from her chair. "Worst of all, that you would give me so little time to prepare."

"I apologize for the short notice. I wanted to see if Mrs. Finlay was willing to entertain the idea before I broached it with you. If she had refused, I would not have mentioned it at all. However, she is willing to meet you and discuss the matter." John took a seat in the chair nearest her. "You should be glad for this opportunity. After all, your choices are rather limited."

"I can't think why you object to Mrs. Drayton as strenuously as you do. At least she is someone we know. What do we know about this Mrs. Finlay?"

"I've just explained this to you." John had told her what he knew about Rose, thinking he'd presented his case well. Yet Pearl was proving hard to win over.

Pearl shook her head in objection. "You've told me only about Mrs. Finlay's present circumstances. Where does she come from, and from what sort of family? Who was her husband? What was his occupation?"

John was sorry now that he hadn't pressed a little for those details during the times he and Rose had been together. "These are all things we can discuss with her. That is precisely why I invited her to call."

"On short notice," Pearl said, returning to her original complaint.

"I'm sure Louisa can help direct the staff for whatever's needed to prepare."

Pearl sighed and said wanly, "I don't know. It's such a lot of work."

John strove to curb his exasperation. He knew it would not take much effort for her to receive a guest and offer her tea and biscuits. Her staff could easily handle the details. Nowadays, however, every task felt large to his ever-weakening sister. Perhaps she also needed time to prepare mentally to make a new acquaintance. John would just have to encourage her as best he could. "We haven't much time before the ball, in case you've forgotten."

Pearl gave him her trademark look. "As if I could. Sophie has talked about it day and night." She coughed. It was a loud, rasping sound, followed by a rattling inhale of breath. It was alarming enough to tempt John to reconsider. Before he could say anything, Pearl pressed a hand to her chest and nodded. "I'll get Louisa to marshal the troops."

"Thank you," John said in relief. "Are you sure you're all right?"

"Don't give up your victory, John. I've said she can come."

That was more like the sister he knew. He stood up. It had been a long day, and he still had a stack of business papers to review before a meeting tomorrow.

Pearl held out a hand. "There's one more thing. We might allow Mrs. Finlay to meet the girls, but I don't want them present during our interview. I don't want to tell Sophie what this meeting is about unless I decide to use Mrs. Finlay's services as a chaperone."

"That's fine," John said.

"I mean it, John." Pearl spoke firmly. "You know how much I value your advice, but in this instance, if I have any qualms at all about Mrs. Finlay, I shall put my foot down and allow Sophie to go to the ball with the Draytons."

"I'm not going to argue with you over it. You are her mother and entitled to have the final say. I'm grateful you're at least willing to consider it."

By the time he left the house, his sister was mollified. There was nothing left for John to do but hope for the best.

⁓⁓⁓

Rose was helping Miss Palmer at the front counter when she noticed Sandy Deveaux strolling through the door of the post office.

She gave a little start of surprise. This was the first time she'd seen him since that afternoon in Hyde Park when he and Sophie had disappeared into the fog. He walked over to the table that held blank telegram forms. He moved with his usual air of superiority and confidence. The man always looked supremely self-satisfied, Rose thought with distaste.

Upon reaching the table, Sandy picked up a pencil and began to fill out a form. Rose transferred her attention back to the woman she was waiting on. The lady was carefully counting out the coins she needed to pay for her purchase of stamps.

By the time the transaction had been completed, Sandy was on his way to the counter. He tipped his hat to the woman as they passed one another.

"May I help you?" Rose asked. She'd spoken to Sandy a number of times before, but not since she'd seen firsthand the evidence of the unsavory side of him that her cousin Abby had described. She felt a touch of unease. Had she really agreed to discuss being a girl's chaperone with the express purpose of protecting her from this man?

Too late, she realized she ought to have stepped away from the counter as soon as he'd come in. Then he would have gone to Miss Palmer's till for service. If Rose did end up attending that ball, he'd be more likely to recognize her after talking with her today. But there was nothing to do about it now.

Sandy placed two forms on the counter. "How soon can you send these?"

"Right away, sir." She could say this with confidence, knowing that Stan had been able to keep up with the flow of messages today. He'd recovered from his cold and was back to his usual quick speed on the wires.

"Good. Put that on my account, will you? Sanderson Deveaux."

He spoke his name as though he didn't know perfectly well that Rose knew it already. It was also written on the forms he'd just given her. Rose suspected he was vain enough to enjoy the sound of his own name. She also knew his account was three months in arrears. There was nothing she could do about that either. Mr. Gordon had directed her not to say anything to him nor turn away his business. The world functioned differently for aristocrats than for ordinary people.

Rose looked over the forms. Both telegrams were of a personal nature. Rose found the second one to be the most arresting. It was addressed to the Duchess of Sunderland at a London address.

BACK IN TOWN. PLEASE KEEP MISS B AT BAY ON

THURSDAY IF YOU CAN. AM PURSUING ANOTHER

PROSPECT. EVERYONE PROFITS.

Rose gulped. Was this a reference to the ball? To Sophie? She fought to keep her expression neutral as she returned her gaze to Sandy. "Everything seems to be in order. I'll get these out right away."

"Thank you. And check my private box, too, while you're at it."

"Yes, sir." Irritated at being addressed like a servant, Rose turned away to complete the errands. She delivered the telegram forms to Stan for transmission, then went to check Sandy's postal box. There were five pieces of mail waiting for him. One had no return address on the envelope. Rose took a moment to study it. The handwriting looked like that of a female. Was it from Sophie?

It was useless to conjecture. Sandy received letters from women all the time. This could be from anyone. Even so, it ratcheted up her worries. *"Everyone profits."* If that telegram was about Sophie, then Sandy was after her primarily for her money. Even though Rose had agreed to meet Sophie's mother today, she was still undecided about whether to get more deeply involved.

She returned to the front counter and handed the letters to Sandy. After quickly perusing the envelopes, he pocketed them, gave Rose an offhand word of thanks, and turned away. He left the building, still with that stride that Rose was beginning to find aggravating.

What would he think if he knew of Rose's potential involvement in a scheme to thwart his plans with a certain young lady? Rose was going to have to tread carefully. Perhaps at the very least she could succeed where John had failed in getting Sophie's mother to understand the seriousness of the situation. She had been second-guessing her decision to get involved, but after being personally reminded of Sandy's arrogance and his self-serving tendencies, she was more than willing to do what she could.

⁓⟳⁓

Rose's earlier determination began to dissolve into misgivings once she was seated in the parlor of Mrs. Pearl Cochrane.

When she'd arrived, both mother and daughter had reacted with obvious surprise upon seeing her. She worried that she'd somehow misunderstood the day or time, but they had quickly assured her they'd been expecting her.

John hadn't arrived yet, which left the ladies to make stilted small talk while they waited for him. Louisa regarded Rose with intense interest, almost as if she were a specimen in a zoo. Perhaps this was because she'd quickly ferreted out the fact that Rose had an occupation. Rose could imagine this family mostly traveled in circles where females were pampered at every stage of their lives.

John had been correct in his description of Louisa as a right-hand aid to her mother. She had been standing at the parlor door as the butler had ushered Rose inside, waiting to greet her and offer her a seat and cup of tea, much as if she were the hostess here instead of Pearl. Rose suspected this was not solely due to the need to help her mother. She seemed quite naturally to want to be a part of this conversation among adults, as if she already saw herself as one.

Perhaps another reason Louisa was so engaged was because she was still trying to work out exactly why Rose was here. Apparently, her mother had not enlightened her. "How is it that you know Uncle John?" Louisa asked, once they'd exhausted the banal subjects of the weather, the dismal fog, and the abysmal state of the city streets.

Rose was unsure how to frame her reply. She could see Pearl didn't want to discuss anything of note without John present.

She was saved from having to answer by John's arrival. As he came through the parlor door, he was smoothing down his hair and coat lapels, as though he'd hastily given his hat and coat to the butler as he'd hurried inside.

Louisa jumped up from her chair. "It's about time you arrived," she admonished him playfully, though she also gave him a friendly peck on the cheek. "We thought you'd deserted us."

"I'm terribly sorry. I was detained at work. I got here as quickly as I could. I see you've already met Mrs. Finlay." He gave Rose an apologetic look. "I hope you will forgive my tardiness and any awkwardness it might have caused."

"It was no trouble," Louisa chirped. "We introduced ourselves."

"What an ingenious solution," John said with exaggerated astonishment. "Do you suppose such an idea will catch on?"

"It's already a trend among younger people." Louisa spoke as if the rest of them were aged.

It was clear she was simply teasing her uncle, but Rose couldn't help smiling. At times she felt quite as old as Louisa implied. Seeing the indulgent smile on John's face increased

Rose's enjoyment. The easiness with which he and his niece sparred with one another reminded her of such times she'd had with her father. She blinked, feeling a fresh wave of sorrow at his loss, even though he'd been gone for many years.

"Come and have some tea, now that you're here," Pearl said to John.

"Don't trouble yourself. I'll do it." He went to the table by Pearl's chair where a tea service had been set up.

"We were just asking Mrs. Finlay how it was that she became acquainted with you," Louisa said while John was pouring his tea.

"We met at the post office. As you know, my work often takes me there—for sending telegrams and such."

"To the one in Piccadilly? Isn't your office closer to Gray's Inn Road?"

Clever girl, Rose thought. Too clever by half, as the saying went.

Unruffled, John took a seat in a nearby chair. "I've just signed a lease on a warehouse in that area."

Louisa looked unconvinced. Rose could only put it down to her curiosity about why a postal worker had been invited to their home. To her credit, the girl was too polite to ask such a rude question outright.

The parlor door opened again, and this time Sophie breezed into the room. "Good afternoon, everyone! Uncle John, I thought I heard your voice in the front hall." She gave Louisa a quick smile that passed as a greeting, then paused as she got nearer to Rose, looking at her with evident surprise. "My apologies. I didn't know we were receiving guests today."

"This is my oldest daughter, Sophie," Pearl said to Rose. "Sophie, this is Mrs. Finlay."

"How do you do?" Sophie said, looking at Rose with the same curiosity Louisa had leveled at her, albeit not quite as friendly.

"Mrs. Finlay is an acquaintance of Uncle John's," Louisa explained.

"I'm pleased to meet you," Rose said, meeting Sophie's gaze and wondering if the girl would recognize her. She didn't think it likely. Sophie's attention had been focused on Sandy at the tea shop, and she hadn't seen Rose at all in the park. Her guess was correct. There was no glimmer of recognition in Sophie's eyes.

Rose had nearly forgotten just how pretty this girl was. Her blue eyes, soft brown hair, and smooth complexion would be an irresistible draw to most men. A large dowry would only sweeten the deal. Rose thought back to Sandy's telegram and wondered once more if he'd been referring to Sophie. Everything about this house—from its location and fine furnishings to the liveried servants—indicated the family was very well off indeed.

"They met at the post office in Piccadilly," Louisa went on.

"Really? Do you mean the one near Fortnum and Mason?"

"That's the one," Rose said.

"I've bought stamps there before." Sophie sent a sly glance at John as she said this. Had she perhaps used a visit to the post office as an excuse on the day John had found her coming from the tea shop? Redirecting her gaze to Rose, she said, "Are you a clerk there?"

"Assistant manager." Rose thought it wise not to mention that she'd also done telegraph duty there countless times. That could raise Sophie's suspicions.

"Oh, I see. I didn't think I'd seen you at the counter."

"More tea, Mrs. Finlay?" John said, rising from his chair.

"Yes, thank you."

While John was refilling her cup, Rose noticed that the sisters took this moment to exchange a brief glance. Louisa gave a little shrug.

"I'd love a cup too," Sophie said.

"I need to ask you girls to take tea down in the kitchen to-night," Pearl interjected before John could reply. "Mrs. Brown has prepared chocolate biscuits," she added, speaking brightly.

Sophie rolled her eyes. "We're not children anymore."

"Nonetheless, you still need to do as your mother says," Pearl replied tartly.

"But why—?"

Clearly seeing an argument brewing, Louisa stood up. "Come on, Sophie. It will be fun to tease Mrs. Brown like we used to do." She tugged at Sophie's sleeve. "I, for one, won't turn down a chance at warm chocolate biscuits."

Sophie rose reluctantly, seeing the elements were stacked against her. Rose was sorry to see her sent off so quickly. She would have liked more time to chat with these young ladies. But Pearl seemed determined to keep their interactions to a minimum. Rose supposed there would be less to explain later if this turned out to be her only visit to their house.

Rose was bid a polite good-bye from both the girls—even Sophie, who was still clearly annoyed about having to leave. Pearl had raised them well. They had done a good job of minding their manners, even though it was obvious they were filled with curiosity about Rose. How well they behaved when they were *not* in their mother's presence was another question. In that regard, Rose already had a good idea about Sophie. She hoped Louisa would not turn out to be so wayward.

When they were gone, Pearl turned her full attention to Rose in a way that told her it was time for the hard questions. John, too, set aside his teacup and took on a more serious expression.

This was when the real conversation would begin, and Rose was ready for it.

CHAPTER
Thirteen

There was a brief silence after his nieces left the room. Rose was looking expectantly at John, as though he should be the one to lead the conversation. But where to begin?

"Thank you for coming here today," he said. Good heavens, he sounded as though he were opening a board meeting. He couldn't think why his words sounded so wooden. He was overjoyed that Rose was here. He wanted everyone in his family to like her as much as he did.

"Now you've met Sophie," Pearl said to Rose, evidently deciding she would have to be the one to get the discussion rolling. "She's quite beautiful, is she not? We had planned to wait until spring to bring her out in society, but there are so many opportunities available for her now that we decided it would be foolish to wait. She has already collected quite a few admirers."

"Yes, I understand that's why I was invited here today," Rose said.

"My brother has this idea that Sophie needs some sort of

professional chaperone. I agree we need to do something for her, although we differ on how to solve the problem."

"I've already outlined the pertinent facts to Mrs. Finlay," John said.

"Have you?" Pearl straightened in her chair, looking affronted.

Really, though, how else did she expect he'd gotten Rose here, if he hadn't told her something of their family affairs? "She was understandably curious as to why I'd approach her about being a chaperone for Sophie," John explained.

"I haven't agreed to anything yet." Pearl directed this remark at Rose more than John.

"Nor have I," Rose said calmly. She did not appear the least bit intimidated by Pearl's excessive posturing. "I'm here at Mr. Milburn's request. I'm sure you and I both have questions as to how this would work, or even *if* it would work."

Rose seemed determined to keep herself on an equal footing with Pearl. John approved of this. After all, Rose wasn't here as a supplicant for work. She already had work, and she'd made it clear to John that it was an occupation she enjoyed.

"Well then," Pearl said, "since you know all about us, Mrs. Finlay, perhaps you'd be so kind as to tell us about yourself?"

"I'd be happy to. What would you like to know?"

"Where were you raised? How long have you been working at the post office? And—" she gave a little cough—"I understand you are a widow?"

Rose nodded. "My husband died seven years ago. He was struck down by a carriage while crossing a busy street."

So that was the reason for her bereavement. John had suspected something awful must have happened to have made her a widow at such a young age.

This information seemed to finally elicit a show of sympathy from Pearl. "How terrible to have lost your husband in such a way! I assure you, I understand your pain. My own husband died just over two years ago. And Marjorie's husband, Lionel, who was John's and my brother, died a few years before that. These losses have been devastating for us."

"That's something we have in common," Rose answered. "It would seem we are all members of the young widows' club."

She said this with a commiserating smile, and yet John detected a slightly acerbic tone in her voice.

Pearl gave a gloomy nod. "It's a sad state of affairs, let me tell you. Thank heavens for John! I don't know what we would have done without him."

Rose's brows lifted slightly.

"John is ten years younger than me," Pearl went on. "He was twelve years younger than our brother Lionel. John was what you would call a last-minute surprise. And what a good thing he came, since he has been the one to save our family."

John was glad to see Pearl warming up to Rose, but he was embarrassed at the direction of the conversation. He didn't like it when his sister became so effusive about what he'd done. As far as John was concerned, he'd done the responsible thing. Surely anyone in his position would have done the same.

"We depend on him so very much," Pearl continued. "Marjorie and I would have been quite lost without his help. We would probably have been thrown on the mercy of our solicitors to sort things out, and then who knows where we'd have ended up? John often jokes that we need a solicitor to keep an eye on our solicitor. They don't always have one's best interests at heart, do they?"

"No," Rose replied. "A few of my relatives were bled dry by members of the legal profession. Rather like those unfortunate cousins in *Bleak House*."

Pearl gasped. "How funny, that's what John said!"

Rose turned an approving glance in his direction. "Why am I not surprised?"

John grinned in return.

"You enjoy reading Dickens?" Pearl aimed this question at Rose with an arched brow. John knew it was because she didn't think a love of the great author was a good thing. It certainly wasn't going to win Rose any points with her.

"Naturally," Rose answered without hesitation. "I enjoy his marvelous descriptions and keen insights into the human condition."

"Well, I haven't the patience for such lengthy stories. Louisa can get lost in his books for hours at a time, though." Pearl shook her head. "I do worry about that girl sometimes."

John worried for Louisa, too, but not for the same reasons as Pearl. Louisa loved the idea of romance as much as she loved books, so he didn't think she would end up a spinster. He could only hope that when Louisa ultimately did get married, her husband would appreciate her intellectual gifts as well as her beauty.

"Have you any family, Mrs. Finlay?" Pearl asked.

"I have several cousins in Surrey. Most of them work at the paper mills. One is a schoolmaster—the first in our family to enter that profession, although my grandfather was a vicar, and my father helped him give reading lessons to the poorer children in the town. My mother-in-law lives near me. She has no other relatives, so I help her as much as I can."

Rose shared this information so easily that John had the impression she'd practiced it beforehand.

"I'm surprised you're not a teacher yourself," John said. "I think you'd make a good one."

"Do you?" Rose looked pleased, as though he'd offered her a compliment. "I suppose I might have enjoyed the challenge of trying to pry open young minds to the infinite wonders of great literature. And the way mathematics, too, has a certain beauty in its logic and innate perfection."

The way she nodded at John as she said this last bit made him think she was in some way referring to his work as an architect. It was true that there were plenty of mathematical calculations and physics involved in that work. How astute she was to recognize this.

"However, being a schoolteacher was never a possibility for me," Rose went on. "Most are expected to remain single, and I was married very young. After my marriage, I did eventually begin working a few hours a week as a postal clerk to help make ends meet."

"Your husband could not support you?" Pearl asked, looking aghast at the idea.

A slight flush came to Rose's cheeks. She tensed, her expression hardening, but she said evenly, "My husband was a graduate of Cambridge University. He was a physician, working mostly in east London. Then he went to York, where he'd been invited to train with an expert surgeon. I remained with my mother-in-law in London. She had been ill, and she needed help as she recuperated. I didn't mind working at the post office, especially since my husband was away. By the time of his accident, I'd begun learning telegraphy, which fascinated me. As I mentioned earlier, I am now the assistant manager."

John was finding her story very interesting. It was easy to see how she'd developed into such a resourceful and independent-minded woman.

"You have no children, Mrs. Finlay?" Pearl asked.

John saw Rose wince, as though Pearl had hit upon a tender subject. She tried to cover it up by carefully setting down her teacup, but John thought he saw her hand shake slightly.

"No," Rose answered simply.

Her reaction surprised him. She didn't seem the motherly type. And yet, given her concern for Sophie before she'd even met her, perhaps she was.

"I imagine your work keeps you busy," Pearl said. "I can't think you'd have time to shepherd a young girl all over London."

Rose met Pearl's gaze squarely. "You are correct; my work

and other commitments fill much of my time. I was under the impression this would just be for a few events. I'm happy to help out in some way, if we should decide it is the best course of action."

She was fighting to make it clear she saw herself as being on the same level as this family. She didn't need to persuade John of it. What was blinding Pearl that she could not see how Rose was a woman of quality?

"Mr. Milburn thought it worthwhile to ask me here to discuss it," Rose added. "Perhaps he might explain his reasoning to us."

Both women turned their gazes to him, expecting answers. This conversation was not moving them closer to the decision John was hoping for. He couldn't reveal to Pearl the real reason he wanted Rose as a chaperone—which was to have someone who could help Sophie evade Sandy's machinations, if it turned out the man was leading her toward harm. Pearl would never agree if she thought Rose would be a hindrance.

He cleared his throat. "I mean, it's obvious, isn't it? Mrs. Finlay is a woman of integrity. Her position as an assistant manager proves she is capable, intelligent, and dependable. She is an astute judge of character, which can be helpful in any situation. She could provide a level of detached oversight you might not get from Mrs. Drayton or the others who are in the thick of the expectations of society."

"But that's just it!" Pearl said, latching onto his last statement. "We cannot have someone purporting to chaperone my daughter who has no idea how to move about in society. We have a reputation to maintain. This will be the most important event in Sophie's life to date. We can't risk Mrs. Finlay barging into situations she doesn't understand. We might lose everything we've worked so hard for, simply because we take on someone whose actions might make us a laughingstock."

Pearl seemed to be going out of her way to belittle this woman.

His sister had never been one to be unnecessarily cruel. Why was she doing this? He could only think she'd been swayed by Marjorie's pretensions toward grandeur. John was so stunned that all attempts to rebuke his sister froze on his lips.

With deliberate actions, Rose folded her napkin and set it aside. It was clear she was about to rise and take her leave.

This is it, John thought. *We've insulted her, and she wants nothing more than to be done with the lot of us.* He had to at least try to make amends. "Mrs. Finlay, I believe my sister has misspoken. You were kind to consider my request and come here today. On behalf of the entire family, I would like to extend our respect and thanks."

Pearl seethed, clearly about to object. John sent her a sharp look to keep her quiet. He was poised on the edge of his chair, ready to rise when Rose did, ready to follow her to the door and keep on apologizing and doing his best to repair the damage Pearl had done.

To his surprise, Rose remained seated. She did not respond to John's apology; it seemed she barely heard it. She stared at Pearl with a serious, reflective kind of expression. Oddly, it made John think of a chess player considering her next move.

"There is one other family member I forgot to mention. That would be my second cousin on my mother's side, Lavinia Mowbray. Her mother and my mother were first cousins. Lavinia is married to a Scottish earl—James Mowbray, the tenth Earl of Bancroft. Perhaps you are aware that his father, the ninth Earl of Bancroft, was a favorite of Prince Albert? His Royal Highness often visited their estate whenever he was in Scotland. The prince and the earl both passed away before Lavinia's marriage to James, but she tells me the family have related to her many wonderful stories about their friendship."

This was the most marvelous piece of information John had ever heard. Rose's mouth parted in a wisp of a smile. John could see the satisfaction that had caused it. It answered the question of why she had withheld this information until the last. She had been playing chess, indeed. And who did that, unless they were determined to win? This showed him Rose wanted to help Sophie—and by extension, this family.

For several long, wonderful moments, one could have heard a pin drop in that room.

The silence was broken when Pearl finally recovered herself. She gasped, sitting up straighter to give room for her lungs to expand and find more air. "But you said your cousins work in the paper mills in Surrey!"

This remark only caused the smile playing around Rose's lips to become more defined. "My family tree has branched off in several directions, some of them quite tangled."

"Jarndyce versus Jarndyce," John murmured, remembering her comment about her family being swindled by lawyers. Why did he like her more for this? Probably because she'd met terrible setbacks head-on and not only survived but thrived.

"Lavinia and I are the same age," Rose continued. "We were inseparable during the summer we were eighteen. It was Lavinia's debutante Season, and I was invited to London to be her companion. We attended everything together—balls, dinners, the opera. Not to mention yachting at Cowes. My mother hoped I might parlay that summer Season into a 'marriage up,' as they say. But my heart lay elsewhere, with a man who had limited means but noble dreams. My marriage to him, and his untimely death, set my life on a different path."

Although she sounded sincere, John had spent enough time with Rose to suspect she might be laying it on a little thick for Pearl's sake.

"You gave up money for love," Pearl said. "That's admirable, if not very practical. Yet you remain close to your cousin, I hope?"

John felt embarrassed for his sister, that the mention of titles still turned her head. Yet he was glad if it would help in this situation.

"We write to each other often, although I haven't seen her since the birth of her third child two years ago. Her husband travels to London frequently, and they maintain a lovely home in Belgravia. Lavinia used to come here every spring for the Season, but now she prefers to stay in Scotland with her growing family."

Pearl leaned forward, her haughtiness all but gone. "I suppose you met a great deal of important people during that Season?"

"That was twelve years ago. But life changes slowly among the better class of people, does it not? I imagine that, if I were to go to a ball, I might see a number of people I know."

"Did you ever meet Lord Ormond, by any chance, or his son, Mr. Sanderson Deveaux?"

Rose took a moment, as though searching her memory, before answering. "I did not have the pleasure. The family was traveling on the Continent that summer. I believe Mr. Deveaux would have been around sixteen at the time."

"Right, I hadn't considered his age," Pearl said, smiling with amused embarrassment. "I asked because Mr. Deveaux is the most important of Sophie's suitors."

"Is he?" Rose answered in a noncommittal tone.

"Sophie is thrilled, as am I. She likes Mr. Deveaux very much. However, John is worried that Mr. Deveaux is not sincere. It's true Sophie may have done some things that made her appear too eager, and we've already spoken to her about that. But I think John wants to prevent the match altogether."

John did not reply to this accusation, either to confirm or protest. He decided it would be better to wait for Rose's response. He practically held his breath, sensing this was the question that could make or break Pearl's decision.

"A measure of caution is always advisable to protect a young lady's reputation. However, I also believe there are many ways to do this while not inhibiting the flourishing of true love."

"Exactly!" Pearl said, taking this judicious response as a full affirmation of what she thought.

John exhaled, his opinion of Rose rising even higher. She was walking a fine line and doing it beautifully.

She gave John a quick glance, one beautiful eyebrow lifting just enough to signal that she knew she'd won.

⁘

Over the years since John had stepped into his brother's role as owner of a business, he'd come to feel proud of his growing prowess in salesmanship. Yet he didn't think he could best the feat Rose had just accomplished.

By the time the conversation had ended, not only were they on equal footing but Pearl was somewhat in awe of her. John was happy for this because it would make Pearl invincible in her powers of persuasion when she explained the situation to Sophie.

"Is your second cousin truly the Countess of Bancroft?" John asked as he escorted Rose to the front door. She had allowed him to do this much for her but had insisted that she could see herself home.

She paused, turning to face him. "Everything I told her is easily verifiable."

"I can't believe you withheld that information until the end." John was still marveling at what Rose had accomplished. "If it had been me, I suppose I would have made it my opening salvo."

"That tactic might have saved me a lot of grief," Rose conceded.

"I'm sorry," John said, chagrined. "I've never seen Pearl be as rude as she was today."

"I've faced worse. But I approached this interview as I did because I prefer to stand on my own merits. To be honest, I don't think much of those whose greatest success in life is having been born into the right family. Nor was I entirely sure I wanted to take on this task of chaperone. But the more I listened to your sister, the more convinced I became that I ought to help."

"Will you also try to keep Sophie from 'marrying up'?"

"I would like to help her learn how to make the best decision, whether it be up or down. At this point, I can't think the best man for her is Sanderson Deveaux."

"We are in agreement about that," John replied.

When they reached the front hall, the butler smoothly provided Rose's coat. John walked with her down the steps to the street. He wanted his time with her to last as long as possible.

"Thank you!" He wanted to reach out, to shake her hand, anything to emphasize his gratitude. He even wanted to plant a kiss on her cheek, but that would definitely be unadvised. "I'll be traveling for the rest of the week. After I return, I'm sure I'll hear all about the ball from Pearl and Sophie. However, I hope you and I can meet up after that, perhaps at that tea shop, so I can get the unedited version?"

"I'll be glad to."

After a few final good-byes, she set off. John watched her striding purposefully up the street, looking for all the world like she owned it. The woman had a powerful combination of confidence and modesty that John found immensely appealing.

John heard a quiet cough coming from the doorway. He turned to see the butler looking at him.

"I beg your pardon, sir. Mrs. Cochrane is asking for you."

"Right." John bounded up the steps and went back to the parlor.

"There you are," Pearl said. "I was worried you'd left without saying good-bye."

"I was seeing Mrs. Finlay to the door. It's a marvel she's willing to escort Sophie after the way you treated her. It's unlike you to be so cruel."

"I know it was awful of me. I'm just so concerned that we

do the right thing. You must admit that at first blush, it appeared she had nothing of the proper background needed for the job. How was I to know she'd practically rubbed elbows with royalty?"

"Was her pedigree—or presumed lack thereof—genuinely all that was bothering you? Or is there something else?"

John could read his sister's reactions well enough to know he'd hit upon something. She gave him a stricken look and then dropped her gaze.

"Out with it, Pearl, if you please."

She plucked absently at the handkerchief she was holding. "It's just that she took me by surprise. You told me she was a widow. I had not expected someone so young. Why, she's younger than you are."

"Why should that make a difference? Were you disappointed she's not an aged woman in black, hobbling about with a cane?"

"I was worried she might have somehow caught your eye, and that was why you invited her here."

"Caught my eye?" Now he understood why she'd taken so much time to explain to Rose how John had "saved" her and Marjorie and the family. Pearl was dependent on him, and she was afraid of losing him—and his help—to another woman. In short, she was staking her claim.

It was an arresting idea to think his sister was jealous of another woman. But he could not allow her to remain needlessly in fear. "You've nothing to worry about. I have no designs in that direction."

Deep down, he wasn't sure that statement was correct. He liked Rose very much. Nevertheless, if she preferred to think of him merely as a friend, that's how things would have to stay. And if things changed? It was becoming an ever more enticing idea. Yet even then, he would never abandon his family.

"I'm so glad to hear you say it," Pearl exclaimed. "I'm sure you think me selfish for worrying about such things."

"No." He took hold of her hand, giving it a comforting squeeze. "You know I'll always be here for you."

John never doubted that helping his family had become his calling. He'd never really given much thought to the romantic side of life. Now with Sophie entering the marriage market, and Louisa following close on her heels, it was a subject he was forced to examine.

He was still thinking about it later as he walked home. He began to wonder how it had been for Rose Finlay. What had made her fall in love with the man she married? What instinct—if that was what it was—led someone toward one person and not another? Did falling in love happen as quickly as a thunderbolt, or did it grow slowly? Perhaps it was different for everyone. Was it possible to truly love someone who was an ill-suited match, or was that merely an infatuation that would resolve itself in time? These questions seemed unfathomable to John, although that last one seemed especially relevant to the current situation with his niece.

Evidently, Rose had successfully navigated these issues. So had John's siblings. Surely, together, they'd all find a way to ensure Sophie did the same. John remained firm in his belief that Rose could be instrumental in helping them. Whatever happened, he was elated she had entered his life.

CHAPTER

Fourteen

During the omnibus ride home, Rose mused over what she'd just done. Going into the interview, she had thought she might end up reluctantly accepting this mad scheme of being a chaperone to a debutante; by the end of it, she had actively embraced the idea and done all she could to overcome Pearl's objections. It had become a course of action she simply had to take. For John's sake as well as Sophie's.

She had even revealed her tenuous connection to the aristocracy to appeal to Pearl's obvious desire to mingle with the upper classes. Doing so went against Rose's principles of self-sufficiency and her determination to succeed by her own abilities. In recent years, she had told very few people about Lavinia. They always got the wrong idea, assuming Rose must therefore spend a great deal of time in that rarefied milieu of the upper classes. In truth, she'd had few personal interactions with them since that one Season, when she'd been thrown into a world she had previously known only as most ordinary people did: through books, newspapers, and hearsay.

170

It had been eye-opening, to say the least.

She'd seen how every hour of the day was strictly regulated for young women such as Lavinia. This was something Rose had never faced. She'd grown up in a modest home in a small town. When her school studies and home tasks were done, she was free to do as she pleased. She might take a walk by the river, go to the shops, or visit with friends and townsfolk. She was too independent to envy her cousin's opulent but confined life.

When it came to the entitled young men she met at those society events, Rose was even less impressed. They'd all gone to the best schools, yet rarely had any of them shown a real life of the mind. Few had any deep interest in science or literature. Most had bragged about their trips abroad or their expensive carriages or horses or hunting dogs. They had seemed shallow to her, even then.

That was precisely why Peter had stood out. He'd not been one of them. His father was a merchant who had acquired enough wealth to get his highly intelligent son into Cambridge. Once there, Peter had become friends with a student who was heir to a marquessate. His friend often secured invitations for Peter to attend society events that might otherwise have been closed to him.

Peter and Rose had met at one such event. He'd spotted her across the crowded ballroom and had made a beeline directly for her. Rose had been watching Lavinia and many others dancing an energetic quadrille. She'd been content to observe the festivities, fanning herself, for the room was stifling hot, when she'd noticed Peter looking at her. Even knowing nothing about him, she could tell he was different from the other guests. He was dressed for the occasion, but with simple elegance, not like many of the dandies there. He seemed alert to everything that was going on in that enormous space that was filled with hundreds of people.

Immediately he'd begun working his way through the crowd,

moving with purpose while also managing to appear nonchalant about it. Rose had watched his approach with growing fascination, even as she pretended not to be aware of him. Everything about him had taken her complete attention, and somehow she sensed he'd had the same reaction to her. Her heart beat rapidly as she tried to guess how he might dare to approach a woman he didn't know.

In the end, he accomplished it effortlessly. En route, he snagged two punch glasses from the tray of a passing waiter. Upon reaching Rose, he extended one toward her. Affecting an air of solicitous concern, he said, "I beg your pardon, miss, but I couldn't help noticing you appear desperate for something to drink."

Rose had laughed. "Do I?"

"I can see you are absolutely parched. As a gentleman, I felt it was my duty to save you from fainting dead away in the midst of this crowd. That kind of embarrassment would be a fate worse than death, as they say."

"Would it?" Rose's answers were short and teasing, largely because she was too breathless to say more.

"Oh yes, you'd never live it down. Your name would live in infamy, Miss . . . ?"

"Rose Trent," she'd supplied.

"The name Rose Trent would be forever associated with the mortifying moment when you hit the floor, your arms and legs askew and your skirts nearly to your knees."

"Really, sir!" Rose said, affecting a shocked expression. The picture he painted was scandalous, but something in his manner had made it all seem like a harmless pleasantry.

That's how Peter was. He could say the most outrageous things with a seductive charm that titillated without giving offense. This trick of his fooled all the ladies. Including Rose. Especially when he followed up his remarks with an irresistible look of contrition.

"In truth, Miss Trent, I merely wanted to make your acquaintance, as I'm sure you must have guessed by now, for you are an intriguing woman."

"And how do you know that I am intriguing?" Rose asked, loving every moment of their banter.

"I saw you standing here by a wall but giving no appearance of a wallflower—all by yourself, yet not looking lonely. You looked as though you were perfectly satisfied to be doing exactly what you were doing, content with your own company. I have to say, you drew me to your side like a magnet."

"So I noticed."

This admission had told Peter all he'd needed to know. After just one look at him, she, too, had wanted this encounter to occur. He smiled, as though knowing he'd snared her, while allowing her to think she had snared *him*.

As they chatted, it didn't take long for both to confess they were here merely as a result of knowing someone who was better connected. Rose had revealed that first. Over the course of the Season, she'd gotten into the habit of doing this early in an acquaintance. It saved both her and the gentleman a lot of wasted time if he was merely looking for someone with a fat dowry.

"So we are both the poor cousins at this party," Peter had summed up, once he'd told her his story. They'd bonded over that. Peter had said that a man who forged his own path to success was better than one who'd had it handed to him at birth. Rose had agreed.

By the time the evening had ended, Rose had no doubt she'd chosen the very best man there. And because she'd been so sure—and so determined to live unbound by the foolish conventions of high society—she'd willingly followed Peter into a dark corner, where he'd kissed her passionately and ignited dreams of romance she'd never once thought lived within her.

That, too, had been her downfall. She had given away her

heart too soon, to a handsome man filled with good words and fair speeches. She had not taken time to investigate the substance of the man who lay beneath those exterior qualities. She'd discovered the awful things only after it had been too late.

Why his life had ultimately taken the turn it had was still something of a mystery to her. She could guess at certain circumstances that had driven him to do what he'd done. The other woman he'd "married" was very young, fresh and beautiful, and she had idolized Peter. Much as Rose had been at the beginning, before their marriage began to sour. The woman had been ignorant of his duplicity until Rose came to York. She and her parents had been rightly horrified to learn the truth. They'd all agreed to keep the matter secret, for legal as well as moral reasons. Her parents had sent the devastated "widow" to live with relatives in another part of the country, and Rose had never heard from her again.

Rose would never know how Peter had justified his despicable actions to himself. He had taken that information with him to the grave. Her anger was kindled anew whenever she thought about it. It was a fire that could not be entirely quenched, only banked, along with the lingering pain and humiliation. Those had lessened over the years but would remain with her forever.

Many of those painful memories had resurfaced on the day she'd first seen Sophie in that tea shop, flouting convention in order to go after the man she wanted. Rose understood the girl's desires completely. Unfortunately, she'd already had enough clues to the kind of man Sandy was, and she knew Sophie was out of her depth.

Rose truly believed that Peter had set out in life with admirable goals that had been waylaid by the darker aspects of his nature: his tendency to drink too much, spend too much, and boast too much. The way he became too friendly with women, beyond the bounds of propriety, even before he'd moved to York. Whereas Rose couldn't see that Sandy had begun with much of anything that was admirable. From the things Abby had told her and what Rose had seen of his correspondence, Sandy's actions were entirely self-serving. He picked up acquaintances that could be of use to him and dropped them once he'd gained what he'd wanted. That included women.

There had been a moment today when Rose had a vivid mind picture of Sophie being thrown to the wolves—or more accurately, one aristocratic wolf. That was when Rose had decided she truly wanted to do this. Her marriage had been a disaster. What ought to have been idyllic deteriorated to something messy and heart shattering. Perhaps she could save Sophie from a similar fate.

John had been so grateful, as though she were doing a personal favor for him. He wasn't wrong. Rose had developed a wariness of men in general, but John was different. He was kind, hardworking, and loyal to his family. She was bemused at the way he loved to talk about books, at how energetically he involved himself in anything that interested him. To be with someone who ignited her mind with insights and ideas as he did was a pleasure that was new to her. From the day John had stepped into the post office holding that Dickens novel, it seemed the time they spent together was never long enough. She wanted nothing more than to get back to such hours together, once they were able to set Sophie on the right path. That would be the best reward for all her efforts.

For now, there were more pressing matters. Rose had reached her flat and was unlocking her door when a vital detail suddenly impressed itself upon her brain: she was going to need a proper gown to wear to this event. How could she possibly come up with one so quickly, even assuming she could afford it? Not even her best gown was suitable for a grand ball. Rose would *not* wear something that made her look like a poor relation. Nor did she need something so fine that she stood out in the crowd. She needed only to be well enough dressed to avoid undue notice or comment.

She pondered this as she ate her supper. Finally, the answer came to her. There were dozens of gowns in Lavinia's London house that she wore to events here but never took back with her to Scotland. She had an entirely different wardrobe up there. Lavinia had good taste and was never gaudy. It was likely Rose could find something suitable there that would need minimal alterations at best. She would send Lavinia a telegram tomorrow with her request, adding that further explanations would follow by letter.

Two days later, Rose was standing in front of Lavinia's bedroom mirror. She was trying on the third of four gowns from Lavinia's collection that she thought would work best. Lavinia's response had been immediate, insisting that Rose could take her pick of the gowns and sending instructions to her staff to help in any way they could.

The parlor maid, who'd been pressed into service as a ladies' maid for this occasion, fastened the row of buttons that went up the back. "I think this is the best one yet," the maid offered as she worked. "The color suits you."

"Yes, I think you're right." The gown was a lovely dark blue, festive but still appropriate for a widow and chaperone. "The bodice will need to be taken in, though."

"I'll pack it right up for you, ma'am. The footman and driver are ready to take you to the dressmaker for a fitting. Her ladyship has arranged everything."

This was so at odds with her usual routine. Apart from attending luncheons or dinners at Lavinia's home during the rare times she was in London, Rose had distanced herself from this world. Yet here she was. Everything had been upended by that one overheard conversation in the tea shop.

No, that wasn't exactly true. This was a temporary change only. She still had her own life, her own friends, and satisfying work where a promotion was surely imminent. There was still her mother-in-law to look after too. Rose decided she would not mention any of this to her. That would require too much explaining—after which, Mother Finlay would draw her own conclusions anyway and give Rose more grief, just as she had after Rose went to the lecture with John.

As Rose traveled to the dressmaker's shop in Lavinia's carriage with its liveried driver, she considered how astoundingly easy it was to accomplish even large tasks if one had servants at their beck and call. Rose couldn't deny it was appealing to sometimes set aside one's hearty self-sufficiency and enjoy being waited upon. It was a taste of what was to come, she supposed. At least while she was at the ball.

She had some trepidation about being among those in high society again. Would she see some of the people she'd met twelve years ago? Would they recognize her? Rose snorted. It wasn't likely. Someone "unimportant" like her had surely left their thoughts the moment the Season had ended.

A bigger unknown was how well she would get along with Sophie. The girl had eyed Rose with some suspicion. How had she taken the news that Rose would be her chaperone? Pearl had given her no clue. She'd sent only one follow-up note since their meeting, and that was to confirm the time Rose should arrive at the house on the night of the ball.

Whatever happened, it was going to be an interesting evening. Despite a certain nervousness, Rose felt up to the challenge.

After a busy day traveling around Birmingham and nearby towns to visit several clients, John had planned to spend a quiet evening at the hotel. The weather had been foul all day, and his meetings had not been as successful as he'd hoped. One factory owner kept stringing him along, apparently hoping John would lower his prices. But John had already offered the best possible deal. He generally enjoyed the bargaining process and his interactions with his customers, but there were some days when it only agitated him. This had been just such a day. He decided his best plan was to go to bed early and start the day with fresh energy tomorrow.

He sat in his room with a book open on his lap, although he wasn't really reading it. His thoughts had wandered back to London and the upcoming ball. He'd left town the day after the meeting between Rose and Pearl. He had heard no more news, so he had to assume the plans they'd made for Rose acting as a chaperone for Sophie were still going forward. He was glad of this. There was no way he could have returned in time to fulfill that role himself. He was pretty sure Rose was going to be better at it anyway.

A knock sounded at his bedroom door. Surprised, John got up to answer it.

He opened the door to find the hotel bellman standing there. "My apologies for disturbing you, sir. You've received a telegram. I thought you'd want it brought straight up." He extended it to John.

John accepted the telegram, tipped the bellman, and returned to his chair. When he opened the envelope, he was surprised to see that the telegram was from Marjorie. Per the address at the top of the form, she was still in Ramsgate, the seaside town in Kent where she'd taken Ellie. In a flash John worried there must be some further emergency with his niece, but it only took him another moment to see that was not the case.

EDWARD EXPELLED FROM SCHOOL. HE MUST LEAVE
TOMORROW. CAN YOU FETCH HIM? AM AT MY WITS'
END. MARJORIE.

John crumpled the note, expelling a long, frustrated sigh. That boy had been determined to leave school, and now he'd accomplished it. The hard way. It would leave a blot on his record that would be hard to overcome if they were to get him into university. Not surprisingly, it was going to be left to John to pick up the pieces. Marjorie was in no position to travel to Edward's school right now.

This was a huge inconvenience. He was scheduled to continue his trip north to Manchester tomorrow. Now he was going to have to make this side trip, setting all his meetings behind. And what would he do with the boy? After he'd berated him soundly, that is. That was going to be the first step in his plan.

With another sigh, he pulled out his itinerary and his copy of the railway timetable. It was a good thing he hadn't yet changed out of his clothes. He was going to have to go back out into the blustery night and send several telegrams.

CHAPTER

Fifteen

Rose and Pearl sat looking at one another, waiting for Sophie to make her entrance into the parlor. Pearl had already explained the agenda for the evening in detail. It sounded much the same as many of the balls Rose had attended during that long-ago Season. She had assured Pearl she was confident everything would go well.

There had been a pause at that point, during which Rose noticed that Pearl was once again inspecting her, as she'd done when Rose had arrived. From her hair to her gown to her shoes. Rose was sure there was nothing Pearl could find fault with.

During the silence, Rose was aware of the ticking of the clock and the crackle of flames in the fireplace. She was trying to ignore the scratchy feeling of the gown and her stays, which seemed to rub her the wrong way. It had been a long time since she'd worn anything so uncomfortable.

"There is one more thing I should like to add before Sophie comes in," Pearl said.

"Yes?"

"You'll recall that at our last meeting, we spoke about Mr.

Deveaux. Although your job is to watch over Sophie, I promised her you would not try to interfere with any opportunities they might have to be together. Within the bounds of propriety, of course. As we agreed, it's important to give love a chance to blossom."

"I will do my best not to be too overbearing," Rose said. *And not give Sandy Deveaux one lecherous inch*, she added to herself.

Pearl nodded her approval. "I have already told Lady Randolph about you. It was necessary to explain why you were going to the ball instead of Marjorie. She thinks she remembers you."

"I'm honored that she does."

Rose had spoken to Lady Randolph a few times during that Season. Most of her memories of the lady were positive. She'd always treated Rose kindly and never like the poor cousin. Perhaps she had felt magnanimous, given that her oldest daughter had been a debutante that year and had just made an excellent match.

Pearl sent an anxious glance at the clock. "What in the world is keeping that girl?" She was just reaching for the call bell when Louisa came into the parlor. "Where's Sophie?" Pearl demanded.

"She'll be down directly. Aileen had a near impossible time trying to get her hair just right. This damp weather has made it hard to keep a curl. But I think they've finally got it." She gave a friendly smile to Rose. "Good evening, Mrs. Finlay. Have you read any good books lately?"

The question took Rose pleasantly by surprise, but Louisa continued talking before she could answer. "Uncle John says you are a great reader. I'm a great reader too. He says I've read nearly half his library, but that's probably an exaggeration."

Pearl pursed her lips. "That's nothing to brag about, Louisa. You've many other more noteworthy qualities."

"On the contrary, that sounds like an impressive accomplishment," Rose said. "Depending on the size of your uncle's library, that is."

Louisa beamed. "It's enormous! I think he has at least five hundred books."

"Five hundred!" Rose could not imagine what it must be like to own that many books. It must be like heaven on earth. It was no wonder he'd had a copy of *The Pickwick Papers* to loan her. He probably owned all of Mr. Dickens's novels. "How did he happen to mention that I enjoy reading?"

"I was asking him all about you. Sophie and I were curious to learn more, especially since you are going with her to the ball tonight. He also told us you are related to a countess. Sophie was most interested to learn that."

Of course she was, Rose thought.

"Louisa, stop rambling and go find your sister."

"No need, here I am." Sophie glided into the room like a princess. "How do I look?" She came to Pearl's chair and twirled around to give her mother the full effect.

Pearl clapped her hands in delight. "You are stunning, my dear."

Rose had to agree. Sophie's gown was beautiful, and Rose would never have guessed they'd had trouble arranging her hair. It looked perfect to her. It was all gilding the lily, though, as Sophie was beautiful without any of those fine trappings.

Sophie stopped twirling and turned her attention toward Rose. "Good evening, Mrs. Finlay. I hope you are well?" Her greeting was cooler than Louisa's had been. Sophie was a natural beauty, but her manners were artificial and polished. Rose was beginning to prefer Louisa, whose manners were polite but unregulated by pretension.

"I am very well, thank you." Rose stood up. "Shall we get to that ball?"

"Yes, there's no time to delay," Pearl said enthusiastically.

182

"The carriage is waiting outside. How I wish I could go with you!"

"I do too," Sophie answered. Rose thought this might be a sideways attack on her, but she thought better of it when Sophie took her mother's hand and squeezed it, adding, "Mama, you've simply got to get better! There are so many wonderful events planned between now and Christmas, and I want you to be with me." The longing in her voice was undeniable.

Pearl gave her a misty smile. "I promise I will do my best." This was surely all she could say. From the things John had said, Rose had the impression that Pearl's physical problems were growing and not surmountable. Pearl gave her daughter's hand a comforting pat. "Now, be on your way. I've given you your instructions for this evening. I've done the same with Mrs. Finlay."

"Good." Sophie said this with an air of satisfaction. She and her mother nodded at one another, and Rose could tell something was passing between them that wasn't being said aloud.

She didn't have to wonder long about what that might be. By the time they were out the door, the flash of childlike vulnerability Sophie had displayed with her mother had been replaced by an air of haughty confidence. The carriage was barely underway when Sophie said, "Mrs. Finlay, I believe you and I should clarify exactly what our expectations are for this evening."

She said this in such a high-handed manner that Rose could make a fairly accurate guess about what was coming. "Suppose you go first."

Sophie looked taken aback by Rose's equally firm response, phrased almost like a direct order. Her chin lifted. "That was precisely my intention. I have several things to say to you. First of all, I'm not in need of a chaperone."

"Then why am I here? There are plenty of other things I could be doing this evening. If I'm not needed, you may instruct the driver to take me home right now. It's not too far out of our way." She made as if to signal the driver.

"Wait!" Sophie reached out to stop her. "You can't do that!"

Rose sat back. "Then you're saying you *do* need a chaperone."

Having been thus cornered, Sophie gave her a dark glare. "I'm sure you are well aware the rules of society dictate that I cannot arrive at an occasion like this on my own."

"Nor any occasion, for that matter."

"Nevertheless, it doesn't mean I need someone watching over me as though I were two years old. I cannot have you interfering or injecting yourself into my conversations. This evening is too important to risk it being ruined by an overbearing busybody."

"I can see you have every confidence in my ability to do my job properly."

Sophie easily read the sarcasm in Rose's voice. "Why should I have even an ounce of confidence in you, when I don't know the first thing about you?"

"I completely agree. You and I should have had time to get to know each other before your mother and uncle made such a momentous decision for you."

"That's right," Sophie said vehemently, then looked taken aback to realize she and Rose were on the same side—at least on this issue.

"Your mother told you *nothing* about me?" Rose pressed. She knew this could not be the case because Louisa had mentioned Rose's cousin.

"I'm aware you are related to the Countess of Bancroft. That is the most likely explanation for why Mama agreed to have you come. But just because you had one Season a long time ago doesn't mean you understand anything about how things are done now."

Rose raised a brow. "Pray tell, what, specifically, is different between how things are done now versus how they were done back in the Dark Ages when I attended my first ball?"

Sophie crossed her arms and frowned at Rose. "You are very impertinent."

"That's because I'm not your servant. I'm your chaperone." Rose paused to give this statement time to sink in. Sophie needed to understand who was in charge here. The girl only stared at her mutinously.

Not the least bit daunted, Rose continued. "I expect very little will have changed in the twelve years since my Season, except the fashions. There will be rules to adhere to and expectations to be met. People will be sizing up one another, trying to determine who is on the way up in society's opinion and who is on the way down. There will be debutantes seeking romance and husbands—two things those silly creatures think go hand in hand. There will be men seeking wives—the richer, the better. All these interactions will have a shiny polish, no matter how much ugliness lies underneath."

Sophie blew out a breath. "My mother has sent me to my first ball with a joyless crow."

"I want you to enjoy yourself. I want you to enjoy the sparkle and fun of the ball, and the excitement of meeting new people, the dances, and all the rest of it. My job as your chaperone is to help you navigate this maze without being led astray, falling prey to men who might see you not for your innate qualities but merely as a means to their own ends."

"As I said, I can take care of myself. I don't need your help."

Sophie turned her gaze out the window of the carriage, and Rose thought she saw a glimmer of a tear picked up by the light as they passed by a streetlamp.

Rose realized she had gone too far. It hadn't been her intention to crush the girl's dreams, only to temper them with some honest facts. What would eighteen-year-old Rose have made of such comments, if told to her by someone more than a decade older? The answer to that was easy. These things would have glanced off her.

"I want to help you, Sophie," Rose said kindly. "I don't wish to be overbearing or ruin your fun. I have no doubt you would have preferred to come out tonight with your aunt or your mother."

Sophie shook her head vigorously. "Mama doesn't care enough to come. She prefers to order us about from her chair, and it's clear she'd rather spend time with Louisa than with me."

The hurt evident in her words touched Rose. This girl had lost her father and was craving her mother's love. Rose had no doubt it was there, but Pearl was unable to physically demonstrate her love and care in the ways Sophie clearly yearned for.

Rose had a brief moment of doubt. She was in no position to be a surrogate mother for this girl. She had neither the ability nor the temperament for it. She had hoped to be a mentor of sorts, but she couldn't even do that unless Sophie was willing to listen to her.

"Let us reach a truce. I can see I've already put a damper on this evening, and it's not even underway yet. My apologies. This is an exciting time for you. I understand how much this means to you, and I will do my best to help. I can't guarantee you'll like everything I tell you, but I do hope that in time you will come to see it is for the best."

Sophie gave her a wary look. It wasn't exactly friendly, but at least the superciliousness was gone.

They spent the rest of the ride to Lady Randolph's home in silence. Rose searched her memories for anything that might be useful tonight, including names of people she'd met long ago who still populated the ballrooms today. She recalled the names of many dances, and even some of the steps.

Sophie's dour expression disappeared when their carriage pulled up to the Randolph mansion. As they joined the glittering throng entering the home, Sophie became cheerful to the point of giddiness.

Rose had been feeling some trepidation about attending a

high-society event again. Even though she was here as a chaperone, there were bound to be certain expectations about how
she conducted herself. Rose had no plans to be like Jane Eyre,
tucked away in a recessed window. Would they accept her presence as a guest and not a servant?

In the end, their entrance went smoothly. Rose recognized
Lady Randolph immediately. She was a tall, formidable-
looking woman, but her temperament was convivial. Although
engaged in conversation with two other ladies, Lady Randolph
turned toward Sophie and Rose as the footman announced
them.

She came directly over, bringing the two ladies with her.
"Welcome!" she said cheerily. Holding up a pair of spectacles,
she looked Sophie over. "Miss Cochrane, you are absolute perfection," she announced. She pointed toward the dance card
that Sophie had just accepted from one of the attendants. "I
can already foresee a battle among the gentlemen to be on that
coveted card."

"Thank you!" Sophie replied as she slipped the ribbon holding the card over her gloved wrist. She began eagerly scanning
the crowd while Lady Randolph turned her attention to Rose.

"And here is Miss Trent. But it's Mrs. Finlay now, I understand?"

Rose nodded. "It's lovely to see you again, Lady Randolph."

"I see my friends Jane and Mrs. Drayton," Sophie said, indicating the pair, who were halfway across the room. "I'll just
go and have a chat with them."

"That will be fine," Rose said, even though Sophie had not
asked permission. In fact, the girl was ten steps away before
Rose had time to respond.

Her clear refusal to acknowledge Rose's authority caused the
other ladies' eyebrows to lift in surprise. Then Lady Randolph
laughed and said, "Ah, the impetuousness of youth. And so
excited to be attending her first ball! I remember you at that

age, Mrs. Finlay." To her friends, Lady Randolph said, "Mrs. Finlay's first Season was the same as my Dorothea's. There were so many charming debutantes that year. Beautiful and clever. I doubt we'll see a cohort as talented as that one again." She pointed with her eyeglasses toward Rose. "You were one of the more clever ones, as I recall. And an excellent dancer—as was your cousin." She added for her friends, "Mrs. Finlay's cousin is the Countess of Bancroft."

There was an audible intake of breath from the ladies at this information. They looked at Rose with increased admiration.

"That was another excellent marriage made that year," Lady Randolph went on. "Along with my Dorothea, of course."

"Your daughter is doing well, I trust?" Rose asked.

"Yes, indeed. She and Lord Camden are very happy. And their family is growing! They've just welcomed their fifth child, so she cannot be here this evening."

"Five!" Rose said in astonishment.

"Is she trying to best Her Majesty's record of nine?" joked one of the ladies.

"I certainly hope not, for her sake," Lady Randolph said, joining in their laughter. "Lord knows I was worn out with just three."

During this conversation, Rose had done her best to keep an eye on Sophie. She and the Draytons seemed to be moving farther away, deeper into the crowd. Rose had no doubt Sophie was doing this on purpose, either to put distance between her and Rose or to hunt for Sandy. As long as she remained in sight, Rose didn't mind giving her some room. For now.

Lady Randolph introduced the other ladies, Mrs. Hanover and her sister, Miss Jessop, who'd never married. They all chatted for a few more minutes before Lady Randolph left them to greet other guests. Mrs. Hanover and Miss Jessop were first-rate gossips. They knew who everyone was, and they pointed out a few of the more illustrious guests to Rose.

They were still chatting when the doorman announced the latest arrival: "The honorable Mr. Sanderson Deveaux!"

Sandy knew how to make an entrance. All heads turned in his direction as he strolled in with the confidence of a king. He greeted his hosts with extravagant enthusiasm that seemed designed more for his wider audience. Lady Randolph greeted him with equal good humor and pretended to push him forward toward the ballroom with the admonition that he'd better do his duty and fill up the ladies' dance cards.

"Isn't he handsome?" said Miss Jessop after Sandy had breezed by them without a passing glance. She gave the kind of sigh that seemed more appropriate for a young lady than a woman of a certain age. "His father is Lord Ormond, you know. He'd be quite a catch, but he has thus far eluded the marriage knot."

"I wonder why that could be," said Mrs. Hanover with a dry edge to her tone that suggested she wasn't as impressed by Sandy's charms as her sister was.

Rose chuckled, thinking it served Sophie right that in her desire to separate herself from Rose, she'd placed herself at the exact opposite end of the room from the person she most wanted to see.

Sandy began to weave his way through the crowd, pausing to greet people he knew, but always with his gaze traveling around the room, as though making a mental catalog of everyone here. He didn't engage in any real conversation until he reached a sumptuously dressed woman. She was adorned in jewels, and Rose thought it likely her gown had threads of real gold. Sandy whispered in her ear, and the lady nodded and smiled.

"That's the Duchess of Sunderland," Miss Jessop told Rose. "Her husband is one of the richest dukes in the kingdom. They live like it too. They have a palatial mansion in Northumberland. I've heard they employ over one hundred servants."

"She's the duke's second wife and nearly thirty years younger," Mrs. Hanover said. As they watched the duchess murmur something back to Sandy, she added, "I've heard those two are *particular* friends."

Miss Jessop poked her sister with her fan. "Hush, Myra! You can't mean it."

Mrs. Hanover shrugged but gave a knowing smile. "Just look at them."

Rose was indeed looking at them, and with keen interest. She was remembering the telegram Sandy had sent to this woman just last week: *"Please keep Miss B at bay . . . Am pursuing another prospect."*

Who is Miss B?

Rose said, "I suppose there are many young ladies who wish to set their caps for Mr. Deveaux?"

"Yes, naturally," answered Miss Jessop. "I believe your Miss Cochrane is one of them, is she not?"

"Is she?" Rose affected a look of surprise. In truth, she was amazed that Sophie had already entered the gossip mill when this was only her first ball. "She has competition, no doubt."

"Most certainly. There's Miss Underwood, who came out last spring but is still unattached. . . ." She listed several others, along with some tidbit about them.

"Don't forget Adelaide Bryant," Mrs. Hanover said, cutting off her sister's stream of information. "She's positively smitten with him. Her father is a powerful man in Parliament, *and* he is very wealthy."

"Her looks are, however, unfortunate," Miss Jessop added with a sad shake of her head. "There she is, hovering at Mr. Deveaux's elbow."

Rose easily discerned who Mrs. Hanover was referring to. The poor girl was rather plain. She was doing her best to be artful and alluring anyway, trying to catch Sandy's eye while affecting to be unaware of him. Rose felt sorry for her, not least because she knew Miss Bryant was nothing more in Sandy's eyes than a pawn in a chess game.

Despite the request he'd wired to the duchess, Sandy clearly wasn't abandoning this pawn just yet. He pretended to fall for Miss Bryant's act. He allowed her to catch his eye, responded with pleased delight, and went over to talk with the girl. He opened their conversation with a bow and a kiss of her hand. However, he did keep their interaction brief. He signed her dance card, speaking the whole time in a way that, judging by the girl's reaction, was a stream of profuse compliments. Then he moved on.

Miss Bryant pouted at having lost his attention so quickly, but she was soon distracted by the Duchess of Sunderland, who engaged her in conversation. She was apparently doing exactly what Sandy had asked her to do, freeing him up to pursue other game.

"If you'll excuse me," Rose told her new companions, "I should see what has become of Sophie."

Surprisingly, Rose found Sophie before Sandy did. He was working the crowd, mingling with his admirers, while Rose skimmed the edge of the ballroom. Sophie was still with her friend, although the mother seemed to have gone off elsewhere. Sophie frowned as Rose approached.

Despite this, Rose said cheerfully, "Are you enjoying yourself?"

"I was."

Her friend tittered.

Rose fixed the girl with her most severe stare. "You are Miss Drayton, I presume?"

Miss Drayton's smirk faded. She looked surprised at Rose's take-charge attitude but nodded.

"Where is your mother?"

"Well, I . . ." Miss Drayton stuttered, now looking too frozen to answer.

"Who knows?" Sophie broke in. "She has her own friends, and we have ours. The dancing will begin soon, so I'd appreciate it if you didn't stand too close. My card isn't quite full yet. I don't need you spoiling everything."

Sophie's brazen attitude seemed to buck up her friend. Miss Drayton lifted her chin in the same defiant angle as Sophie's. "I believe my mother went to find some punch. Perhaps you'd like to go there too? That's generally where the old ladies spend their time while the rest of us are dancing."

This sudden, double-barreled attack took Rose aback. She was trying to decide how to address this deplorable lack of manners when Miss Drayton added, "It's over there," and pointed toward the refreshments room.

Rose automatically looked in the direction she was pointing, only to realize a moment later that as she'd done so, Sophie had slipped away. In a heartbeat, she was a full twenty paces away, meeting Sandy and chatting gaily with him.

The orchestra began the music for the first dance, and instantly, Sandy swept Sophie away to join the others on the dance floor. They must have decided before tonight to save the first dance for each other.

Rose expelled a breath in frustration. She could already see the evening would be even more challenging than she'd expected.

CHAPTER

Sixteen

Several dances in, Rose could see that Sophie had taken to this world as easily as a duck to water. Her first two dances had been reserved for Sandy, but after that, she had branched off to other admirers. Each of those men had been allotted one dance only. From what Rose could see, Sophie was flirting with all her partners with equal vigor.

Sophie participated in every type of dance with ease, from the lancers, which required knowledge of intricate steps and patterns in a group, to the two-person dances, such as the waltz or gallop. Rose had to acknowledge that, based on her comportment on the dance floor, Sophie was prepared and mature enough to enter society. Pearl had been correct on that point.

As to the girl's emotional maturity, Rose had her doubts. She was still stewing over the rude words tossed at her by Sophie and Jane Drayton. Her concerns swelled again when Sophie began a third dance with Sandy. He held her more familiarly now than he had during their second dance. He was beaming at her, revealing the full force of his admiration. Sophie was positively basking in it. They were a striking couple. Handsome, impeccably dressed, and moving together in perfect unison, they drew admiring looks from everyone around them. If the gossip mill had started up for Sophie before tonight, it was surely in full gear now.

As the couple twirled around the ballroom, Rose made up her mind about one thing. She could not allow this disrespect from the girls to continue. Jane Drayton was also dancing, so this could be a good time for Rose to get in a word with Mrs. Drayton about the girl's behavior toward her.

She found Mrs. Drayton, as Jane had so impudently predicted, near the punch table. She was chatting with another woman. They paused as Rose approached.

"Good evening, ladies," Rose said. "Might I join you? I hope I'm not intruding. It's Mrs. Drayton, isn't it? I'm Mrs. Finlay. I've come here tonight with Miss Cochrane."

"We have already heard all about you from Mrs. Cochrane," Mrs. Drayton said. Her voice held cool disdain, as though she'd already decided not to like Rose. Mother and daughter were very much alike, it seemed.

"And from Lady Randolph," chimed in the other lady. "I understand you are in some vague way connected to the Countess of Bancroft?" She sounded more dismissive than impressed.

"She's my second cousin." Seeing these women weren't inclined to be friendly, Rose decided to get to the point. "Mrs. Drayton, I met your daughter earlier this evening. She is a lovely girl." Rose paused after this slight exaggeration of Jane's charms, long enough to allow Mrs. Drayton to enjoy a moment of pride. "However, I'm afraid I must report that her behavior toward me was less than polite."

Mrs. Drayton's brow furrowed. "You must be mistaken. My daughter has excellent manners."

"Perhaps tonight's episode was an aberration. Nevertheless, she ought to be reprimanded for it and told such behavior toward an elder person is unacceptable. She will profit from the instruction."

"I will speak to her about it later." Mrs. Drayton said this in an offhand way that made it clear she would do no such thing.

"I'm quite serious about this," Rose persisted. "Both girls are still immature in many ways. There is a possibility they could bring dishonor to themselves and to you if they are not closely guided."

Mrs. Drayton drew herself up to her full height. "Mrs. Finlay, what makes you think you are in a position to order us about? You were engaged by Mrs. Cochrane to be Sophie's chaperone for this evening, that is all. You have no connection to the family. You have no authority over my daughter, nor over Sophie, for that matter."

"I beg to differ on that last point. Since I am Sophie's chaperone—"

"As to that point, I told her mother your presence here was completely unnecessary. We already offered to bring Sophie with us. I'm far better suited to watch over the two of them. In fact, given your own disagreeable behavior, I'll be sure to recommend that she not allow you to be involved with Sophie ever again."

"Quite right," the other lady chimed in with a sniff. "You attended a few dances some years ago—solely because of your better-placed relation. You are wrong to think that gives you an understanding of how things work in society. After all, you never advanced your social position, did you? You are a widow who works at the post office. What makes you think you can direct any of us as to what is proper?"

The vitriol in the woman's words, coupled with the fact that she already knew so much of Rose's background, hit Rose like a blow to the chest. She had underestimated how quickly gossip spread in these circles. These ladies had no other purpose than to humiliate her. Many others in this room might happily do the same. Rose thought she had thick skin, but hearing the accomplishments she was so proud of repeated as evidence she was not even worthy of notice stung more than a little.

Why was she even here, putting herself through this? It would appear that in this one thing, Rose was in full agreement with these two harridans. Not that she would admit it to them.

"I shall be making my own report to Mrs. Cochrane after this evening," she informed them. "I will express my opinion that both girls could benefit from a further lesson or two in etiquette."

Mrs. Drayton merely huffed. "She'll take your advice, I'm sure."

"In the meantime, I shall get back to my commission. Good evening."

Rose turned on her heel and began to stride away, only to run head-on into the Duchess of Sunderland.

"I beg your pardon, Your Grace," Rose murmured, moving aside and intending to continue on.

The duchess stepped back into her path. "Think nothing of it. I was, in fact, coming over to speak to you, Mrs. Finlay. I'm a good friend of your cousin, Lady Bancroft, or Livvy, as I like to call her. How is she? We did so miss having her in London this past spring."

Looking at the duchess close up, Rose could see the lady was as fond of cosmetics as she was of jewelry. Rose hadn't heard her cousin specifically mention the duchess by name, but then, she hadn't seen much of Lavinia these past few years. Unlike the women Rose had just spoken to, the duchess was addressing her with what appeared to be genuine friendliness.

"She is well. I thank you for your interest. Her third son was born last March, which is why she was unable to spend this past spring in London."

"Three sons now! My felicitations to them. Will you let Livvy know I was asking after her?"

"Thank you. I will."

"Shall we enjoy a glass of punch?" Without waiting for an answer, the duchess wrapped her arm through Rose's and began to walk toward the punch table. Rose enjoyed seeing the looks on the faces of Mrs. Drayton and her companion as they passed. Perhaps the duchess's positive demeaner toward Rose would lift her in their eyes. Not that it mattered. Rose no longer cared what they thought of her.

The duchess hadn't bothered to identify herself. She must assume everyone knew who she was. Rose thought back to Mrs. Hanover's comment about the duchess and Sandy being "particular" friends. Rose could half believe it. But if it was true, why should the duchess want to help Sandy capture other prey? Rose decided to ask her cousin Abby about it the next time she saw her.

"How long have you known Lavinia?" Rose asked the duchess as they walked.

"I suppose you could say I took Livvy under my wing after she married Lord Bancroft. I'd only been married a few years myself, and living so far out in the country, I was desperate for good company. Our estate is only a day's travel from theirs, and we used to enjoy frequent visits with one another. We see less of them now because we live most of the year in London."

"Is His Grace here this evening?"

The duchess shook her head. "He's home. Poor man, he's frequently troubled by gout. That's why we spend so much time in town. He can get better medical treatment here."

They reached the table, and the duchess handed her a glass of punch. "I remember very well the Season when Livvy came out. She was so popular, she might have had any of the gentlemen, but she and Lord Bancroft bonded over badminton, of all things!"

The duchess launched into a humorous story about how Lavinia and her future husband had met during an afternoon of lawn games. Rose was familiar with these facts, but the duchess was an adept storyteller and added many humorous details that were new to Rose.

"I remember you, as well, from that Season," the duchess added.

"Do you really?" Rose had a vague memory of the duchess, but she didn't think they'd ever been introduced.

"You also had a suitor, as I recall. Would that have been Mr. Finlay?"

"It was."

At the duchess's polite prodding, Rose gave a brief history of her marriage and what she'd done since Peter's death. It was the version she presented to everyone, which had the more unsavory elements removed. As she did so, she couldn't help but marvel at the woman's kind interest. It presented quite a contrast to Mrs. Drayton and her friend.

Rose began to notice more and more people moving toward the refreshment tables. She also realized the dancing band had been replaced by a string quartet. The guests who had been dancing were taking advantage of the break to partake of a cool beverage.

At the same time, another realization came to her. During their conversation, the duchess had not asked Rose why she was at tonight's ball. That was surely because she already knew. Sophie could easily have communicated the information to Sandy, who'd told the duchess. That was very likely why she'd taken time to talk with Rose. Perhaps she and Sandy had decided Sophie's chaperone was a greater hindrance to his plans with Sophie than Miss Bryant?

Rose set her glass aside. "If you'll excuse me, there is something I need to attend to. It's been lovely chatting with you."

The duchess looked ready to object, to find some other way to keep Rose engaged. But seeing Rose's determination, she must have decided it would be futile. She dipped her chin. "It's been a pleasure, Mrs. Finlay."

Rose spent the next several minutes threading through the crowd, trying to find Sophie. The girl was nowhere to be seen. Neither was Sandy. Where might they have gone? The garden seemed the most likely place for a couple seeking to be alone. Rose walked out a set of doors that opened to a terrace. There would be no privacy here. Several dozen people were taking advantage of the chilly night to cool down. Sandy and Sophie were not among them. Rose did see Miss Bryant. She was accompanied by a young man who was speaking earnestly to her. He seemed the happier of the two. Miss Bryant's gaze kept flitting to the people on the terrace and in the garden. Perhaps she, too, wondered where Sandy had gone.

The garden below had sparse foliage at this time of year, and the paths were wide. It was easy to see that Sandy and Sophie were not there either. Rose went back inside.

As she searched through the public areas again, Rose's worry increased. Nearly a half hour had passed since Rose had begun looking for Sophie. How long had she been gone before then? So many things could have happened in that space of time. Rose's worry threatened to blossom into panic. She had been given one simple task—to watch over Sophie—and she'd failed.

Finally, she caught sight of Jane Drayton coming out from one of the corridors near the cloakroom. She hurried up to the girl. "Where is Sophie? Do you know?"

Jane smirked. "Why, have you lost her? Tsk, tsk."

Rose bottled her frustration, figuring that pressing a girl like this harder for answers would not be productive. "Please tell me where she is."

Jane gave an annoying shrug. "It's not a secret. She's in the ladies' retiring room." She pointed her fan over her shoulder, toward the corridor she'd just exited. "You're welcome!" she added caustically as Rose rushed down the hallway without a further word.

Sure enough, Sophie was in the retiring room. She was seated in front of a mirror, watching as the attendant fussed with her hair, rearranging a few pins. "I'm afraid that's the best I can do, miss, without a hair iron," the maid said.

"Sophie, where have you been?" Rose demanded. "What have you been doing for the past half hour?"

Sophie shooed away the maid and turned to reply to Rose. "I've been here. I got a bit too energetic with the dancing and my hair was askew. I've been trying to get it presentable again."

Sophie's face was flushed, but Rose didn't think it was due to the exertion of dancing. "Is that *all* you've been doing—this entire time?"

Sophie's gaze flitted briefly to the mirror before returning to Rose. "You see that I am here and perfectly fine, except for this emergency with my hair." She stood up. "Now I must be getting back to the ballroom. I've promised the next dance to Mr. Young."

Rose took hold of Sophie's wrist as the girl attempted to brush past her.

"What are you doing?" Sophie protested.

Rose took hold of the dance card attached to Sophie's wrist, turning it so she could read the names. Sandy had been allotted the two dances before the break. Had they even danced them? Or had they used that as an excuse to sneak away?

Sophie was at least telling the truth about Mr. Young. Rose could see his name listed next. She let go of Sophie's wrist.

Sophie immediately began to rub the spot, as if Rose had bruised it. "I shall tell Mama you've been physically abusing me, as well as being rude to me and my friends."

"You may tell her what you like, but you won't be leaving my sight for the rest of the evening."

"You are an odious woman."

Sophie strode swiftly out to the corridor. Rose followed close on her heels. She was going to make good on her promise and not be distracted by anything or anyone.

The rest of the evening was more painful than Rose could have anticipated. After more dances, there was the midnight supper to endure. Unused to staying up so late, Rose was exhausted. But that wasn't the worst of it. Whatever good credentials Lady Randolph had tried to publicize for Rose at the beginning of the evening had been erased by negative gossip—undoubtedly promulgated by Mrs. Drayton and others. Even Mrs. Hanover and her sister were cooler toward Rose. The Duchess of Sunderland simply ignored her for the rest of the evening.

The pettiness of these people refreshed Rose's memories of the things she'd hated during her Season twelve years ago. The supper banter consisted mostly of gossip, snide or risqué comments, and inferences about people or situations that Rose knew nothing about. These were not directed at Rose, but not being in the know distanced her from the group, highlighting that she was an outsider. Seeing how others were reacting to Rose only emboldened Sophie to increase her insolence toward her.

By the time the evening was finally over and Rose had bundled Sophie into the carriage for the ride home, Rose knew what she had to do. She said firmly, "Sophie Cochrane, I've a few things to say to you."

Sophie plucked at her gloves with agitated energy. "You may save your breath, Mrs. Finlay. I already know what you're going to say, and you're going to be wrong about everything."

"Nevertheless, you will not leave this carriage until you hear it."

She let out an exasperated sigh. "It's not my fault no one at the ball wanted to talk to you."

"Is that what you think I'm upset about—that my feelings were hurt? I care nothing for that. I'll probably never see any of those people again, and I'm glad of it."

Sophie looked appalled. "How can you say that? The cream of London society was there! The very best people!"

"I suppose that depends on who is setting the criteria."

"You don't know anything about it. That's why you shouldn't have come."

"Here's something I do know, Miss Cochrane. Sandy Deveaux's charm endears him to the ladies, but there is a darker side. I've seen evidence that he picks up women for his own pleasure and discards them when he is done. He may well do the same with you."

Sophie's mouth dropped open in indignation. "That's vicious gossip. You can't possibly know what Sandy intends to do."

"Granted, no one knows the future. There is a chance Sandy could marry you. If he decides your dowry is high enough."

"You think he cares only about money?" Sophie sputtered. "Sandy has never tried to hide from me that he's had romantic inclinations toward other women. But those were passing fancies, nowhere near what he feels for me!"

"And how do you know this?"

"He told me so!" For a moment, Sophie looked embarrassed to have let this slip. But then, evidently, she decided to stand firm. "Tonight, as a matter of fact. We did have a private meeting, just before you saw me in the retiring room."

"So you lied to me earlier."

Sophie pushed back a stray bit of hair from her forehead as she met Rose's gaze. "I did not lie. I merely did not fully answer your question."

"What, exactly, did Sandy share with you during this meeting?"

"As I said, he admitted he's had lots of dalliances, but that none of them were serious. He told me that the moment we met, he knew I was different from any lady he's ever known. His father needles him constantly about settling down, but Sandy has been resisting the idea. Only now does he feel he's ready to seriously contemplate marriage."

"Surely he didn't propose to you!" Rose exclaimed. That

outcome was better than ruining Sophie's reputation, but it could end up in misery for the girl just the same.

"Not in so many words. We've only just begun courting, after all."

"He hasn't even met your mother. Why does he think he has permission to court you?"

Sophie let out a huff. "He *would* have met her under normal circumstances. It isn't Sandy's fault Mama never goes anywhere. He will visit our home when the time is right."

"In the meantime, he was bold enough to get you into a quiet corner, whisper tender endearments in your ear, and kiss you senseless. Am I right?"

"Mrs. Finlay!" Although Sophie feigned shock at Rose's frank question, Rose was sure of the answer. Peter and Sandy may have come from very different backgrounds, but they were cut from the same cloth.

"I have no doubt he kissed you," Rose said, more gently this time. "I also don't doubt that you found it wonderful. I was once in that position myself, years ago. I found nothing wrong with such behavior because I was certain I was in love and that the feeling was reciprocated. I'll wager you feel the same way."

"You . . . allowed a man to . . . ?"

"To kiss me," Rose finished for her. "Yes. Very privately, and very thoroughly. It was heaven. It was exhilarating. I don't blame you for having the same sort of reaction."

In the moment of silence that followed, Rose felt another shift in Sophie's attitude. She'd gone from belligerent to flustered to . . . what? Wondering? Listening?

"You won't tell Mama, will you? She won't understand."

Rose let out a breath in relief. Perhaps she'd gotten through. "Did Sandy press you for more than kisses?"

"No! He's a gentleman, despite what you may think."

This time, Rose felt the girl might be telling the truth. "Then perhaps we might keep your encounter confidential for now. Nevertheless, you should remain on your guard. If he should try to cajole or even force you into anything further, then you will know he's not sincerely interested in you."

"Is that what happened in your case?"

The question sounded sincere. Sophie was looking at her intently now.

Rose swallowed and decided to be honest. "He came close. He was very . . . *ardent*, shall we say. But no, that line was not crossed. Instead, we were married within three months."

"That's good!" Sophie gushed. "When you know it's true love, why delay? Perhaps that will happen with me and Sandy!"

"Unfortunately, marriage is not always the happy ending it's touted to be. I knew he'd loved and left more than a few women before he met me. But I was sure I was different. Turns out that, no, I wasn't."

This information doused Sophie's brief moment of excitement. "He married you, but he didn't love you?"

"I believe he cared for me—in the beginning. But the truth was that he cared mostly for himself. He could see I was devoted to him, and it fed his vanity. I was blinded by love, and the modest sum of money I brought with me—a gift from my great-uncle—served his purposes. As did my willingness to help his mother, who'd been a long time recovering from a nasty bout of influenza. However, it wasn't long before his eye wandered again. His work required him to live in York for an extended period of time. I wasn't able to go with him for a number of reasons. While he was there, he took up with another woman. Married her, in fact."

Sophie drew in a startled breath. "Your husband married someone else? But how could that be?"

"Neither of us knew about the other woman until my husband died."

Rose was sharing this primarily to startle the girl into awareness, to show her the need to tread carefully before leaping to lifetime commitments.

Instead, Sophie shook her head and held up both hands to stop her. "Please don't tell me anything more."

"I'm simply warning you to be careful," Rose persisted. "All men present the best image of themselves to the world. Too often, however, there are uglier truths beneath. Don't allow infatuation with a man to blind you to the truth. Find out who he really is before you make a decision you might truly regret."

Sophie pressed herself back against her seat, as though distancing herself from both the moral of this tale and from Rose herself. "Nothing like that is going to happen to me. I wish you hadn't even told me your ghastly little story. Your life may be a failure, but mine won't be. I was right in what I said earlier: you can't possibly understand anything about us."

Rose didn't flinch at Sophie's attempt to belittle her. After a long evening of such attacks, she was inured to it by now.

Neither of them spoke for the rest of the journey. Rose began to berate herself for having shared the details of her story. She had wanted to help Sophie gain clarity about her own life. All she'd accomplished was to put herself in a bad light and confirm Sophie's already low opinion of her.

Upon reaching the Cochranes' home, the driver alighted and opened the carriage door. Sophie gave him her hand, but before she descended, she turned back to Rose. "Don't bother coming inside. Mama will have gone to bed hours ago."

Rose was tempted to go inside anyway, just to prove she was still in charge for these last few minutes, but she knew it would be pointless. At this impossibly late hour, Pearl was surely in bed and sound asleep. Rose longed for nothing more than her own bed as well. She remained in the carriage while a footman escorted Sophie into the house.

Rose gave the driver directions to her home, then sagged against the seat as the carriage began rolling again. Her feet ached from standing for hours in tight shoes, and her ribs felt bruised from the stiff corset. One advantage of the mundane world she was returning to tomorrow was that her working clothes afforded greater comfort and ease of movement.

Why, oh why, had she agreed to come tonight?

It was probably a good thing she'd never had children. She had no idea what to say to get them to understand. Perhaps Sophie was right: Rose was in no position to lecture others.

Her biggest mistake had been sharing so much about her past. The blasted girl would probably blab it to her whole family. Including John. Once he learned about that, on top of the way she'd antagonized his family and failed to watch over Sophie properly, he'd know his trust in her had been misplaced. The friendship they'd been building would surely be ruined. That thought was the most devastating of all.

It was all water under the bridge now. She'd just have to put this night behind her—as she had done with so many previous catastrophes—and get on with her life.

Warm tears began to sting her cheeks as she watched the empty streets roll by, mirroring the bleak landscape of her thoughts.

CHAPTER

Seventeen

John paused before entering the post office. It wasn't so much a quick prayer that he sent heavenward as it was a reminder to the Lord of the longer prayers he'd already been offering for days.

He'd returned to London last night, after a rough business trip that was complicated by having Edward in tow. The ball had taken place several days ago, but his entire family was still up in arms about it.

Throwing his shoulders back, he feigned a calm and confident air as he went inside. He wasn't sure what kind of reception he'd be getting after having sent Rose into battle with all of the opposing forces arrayed against her. The account he received from Pearl, and from Sophie after much badgering, had not been good. He had to find a way to make amends.

Rose was nowhere in sight. There was another clerk at the counter. "May I help you?" she asked.

"I was wondering if I might speak with Mrs. Finlay."

The clerk appraised him for a moment, then offered a smile. "She's in the back. I'll go and fetch her."

John moved to the end of the counter, where he and Rose had spoken before, and stood awkwardly waiting, hat in hand.

Rose came out from the back. Catching sight of John, she hesitated for a moment, almost as if considering turning around, before she evidently made up her mind to continue forward. She looked like she was bracing herself as she approached him. "I can't talk long. I'm in the middle of an audit and my supervisor is waiting on me."

"I apologize for disturbing you at work. I'm here to offer my sincerest apologies for what happened at the ball." He spoke quietly but fervently. "I had hoped things would go better than they did. I underestimated how far Sophie and her friends would go in their efforts to set the general opinion against you."

Rose looked slightly disarmed by this introduction. "I think we both miscalculated a number of things. I did my best to help Sophie. She was too headstrong to listen to me. I sent my report via letter to your sister, although I assume it was dismissed in favor of whatever story Sophie gave her."

John winced. "You know Pearl has a blind spot in these matters."

Rose nodded. "A rather large one."

A quick glance around showed John that their low, earnest conversation had caught the attention of the clerk. Furthermore, a tall, portly man came out from a back office, evidently looking for Rose. John had mere seconds to obtain his goal. "If you would be so kind as to meet me at the tea shop later to discuss this, I would be eternally grateful." John didn't mind pleading. "I'm seeking only a few minutes of your time, and whatever you can offer me of your valuable insight."

Rose looked surprised at this request, but like John, she was aware her colleagues were watching them. "All right," she conceded as the tall man began to approach them. "But I can't stay long. I have other plans for tonight."

"Understood. I'll be waiting. Thank you."

Rose turned away and strode toward the man, who must surely be her supervisor. The two had a brief conversation before returning together to the private offices.

John stood where he was for several moments, thankful Rose had agreed to see him. Perhaps all was not lost. She had been cool toward him, and rightly so, but he'd found ways past her aloof exterior before. Perhaps he'd manage to do so again. He wasn't going to allow the misbehavior of his family members to derail his relationship with Rose. He'd make things up to her in any way he could. He beamed at the clerk, who'd been watching their conversation with undisguised interest even while she'd been interacting with a customer. She responded with a brief smile of her own. Replacing his hat with a cheerful tap, John left the post office.

Rose's version of events matched the guesses John had made after talking with Pearl and Sophie. She explained how things had started off well enough, but that eventually Sophie and others had managed to turn people against her. "I believe the Duchess of Sunderland helped with that as well. She initially went out of her way to talk to me. Later I pieced together that it was to provide a diversion for Sophie and Sandy."

"A diversion?" John said in surprise. "For what?"

Rose took a moment to stir her tea, although she hadn't added anything to it. As John watched her, he thought about how glad he was to be sitting in this cozy shop with her, drinking tea and talking, while blustery rain spattered against the windowpanes. He wished only that they could be discussing pleasant topics and not his troublesome family.

She set down her spoon and looked back at John. "Did Sophie tell you anything about our ride home from the ball?"

"She mentioned that you spoke about your husband."

"Did she go into the particulars of what I shared?"

John swallowed, growing uncomfortable under her steady gaze, not knowing if he should admit that he was now privy to some unpleasant things about her past. The facts were so shocking that he didn't think Sophie had been lying. She might have set the gossips on Rose for being "unworthy" to hobnob with them, but John didn't think the girl was cruel enough to make up a story as outrageous as that.

Rose took a sip of tea, calmly waiting for his answer.

"Yes," he admitted. "She said that your husband was . . . that he was a . . ." He couldn't finish the sentence.

"A bigamist?" Rose supplied.

"Yes." He shook his head, still disbelieving. "Is it true?"

"Let me clarify that he married me first. I was the legal wife." There was a hint of pride as well as pain in her eyes. "Nevertheless, his betrayal caused suffering that I've had to live with—or rather, try to put behind me. I discovered this after he died, so what else could I do?"

"But how could a man do such a thing—especially to you? It's unfathomable!" He blurted this out with such feeling that it brought a modest smile of thanks from her. It was the first time today that there had been a break in her reserved demeanor. John was heartened to see it.

He meant what he'd said. How could a man be married to Rose and desire someone else? Rose had such keen intelligence. She was honest, kind, and seemingly intrepid in any situation. She was pretty too. He hadn't really acknowledged to himself before now that it was one of the reasons he was drawn to her. It did not negate the many others.

He was glad she couldn't read his mind. His thoughts had skittered down a rabbit hole, thinking of all the ways she was so appealing. He certainly couldn't stay there. He dragged his thoughts back to the surface. He wanted to express in the harshest possible words his true opinion of the man who had hurt this woman. He forced himself to remain polite. "I am in awe of your fortitude in the wake of such terrible circumstances. I'm sure it was heartrending."

She nodded. "Not to mention mortifying. I've never told anyone, aside from one close family member. I wish I hadn't told Sophie, since my reason for doing so went entirely over her head."

"What was your reason?" He genuinely wanted to know. It must have been something serious to provoke Rose into revealing those awful facts about her life.

"To show her just how close she was treading to danger by brazenly encouraging Mr. Deveaux's attentions."

"What happened?" John asked in alarm. "If he seduced my niece, I will personally ensure he pays for it."

Hearing the murderous tone in his voice, Rose held up a placating hand. "I don't believe it got that far. However, they did manage to get away privately for a half hour, eluding my notice while the duchess deliberately engaged me in conversation. Sophie admitted he kissed her, but she insisted that it didn't go further."

"Even so, I imagine those were not chaste pecks on the cheek."

"I expect not."

Surprisingly, Rose's own cheeks tinged with pink. She must be feeling the same embarrassment he was at having this conversation, at picturing Deveaux and Sophie in a passionate embrace, quite possibly in a darkened room. . . .

John slammed a hand on the table, causing the teacups and silverware to jump, and Rose along with them.

He quickly reached out to stop the items from clattering. "My apologies. I overreacted."

"It was understandable. I'm angry too—at myself as well as them. I ought to have been more vigilant."

"Don't blame yourself. You were fighting on multiple fronts. You did as well as anyone in that position could have done. Besides, you said yourself there was no real harm done." He was trying for both their sakes to look on the brighter side.

"That's probably true, but it might have set the stage for some future attempt to compromise her."

"What can we do?"

She drew back. "I'm sure there's nothing more *I* can do for her."

"I'm not talking about chaperoning. Pearl has assigned that task to Mrs. Drayton. But—"

"*Oh!*" Rose drew in a sudden sharp breath. "Who else has Sophie told my story to? Do the Draytons know? If any of those gossips should get hold of it . . . Not that I care a whit about them, but they might be only too happy to spread the news to the wider world. Why didn't I think of that before?" She began to speak more rapidly as the fear took hold. "I can't imagine what might happen if my employer should somehow get wind of it. It would taint everything they know about me. Maybe even call my integrity into question—"

"I don't believe that will happen," John broke in. "Sophie told only Pearl and me. Pearl immediately ordered her not to breathe a word of it to anyone else, not even to Marjorie."

"Will she obey that order, do you think?"

Rose looked so pained that John once more berated himself for involving her in this mess. "I believe she will. I wish I could say it was altruism driving the decision to respect your privacy, but it's more likely self-preservation. They both know the family's image would be tarnished by association with you."

John tried to say the words as kindly as he could. The truth was unpleasant, but it could be reassuring to her just the same since it meant her story would remain secret.

"I hope you're right and those ladies keep their mouths firmly shut." Rose spoke fervently, but John thought she still looked rattled. As though she'd seen her entire life mere inches from a downward spiral. "All the more reason for me to stay far away from them, in hopes they'll soon forget me and get on with the life they've so happily chosen for themselves."

The bitterness in her voice cut John to the quick. His loathing for the bigamist and the "better people" were just about equal right now. John hated that Rose was determined to distance herself as though she were at fault and not them. She could not realize how much he would miss her help. He sighed. "So I am alone again on the watchtower. Let me say again how grateful I am for all you've done."

"I believe you're doing the best you can," she said, softening a little as she caught the forlorn note in his voice. "Honestly, you could try to keep watch over Sophie day and night, but in the end, she will be the one who makes the difference."

"How depressing." He rubbed his temples in a vain attempt to ward off a headache.

"As for Sandy Deveaux, you'll have to decide for yourself how to handle him."

It was not a pleasant thing to contemplate. "Do you suppose it should be rapiers or pistols at dawn?"

"I hope it shan't come to either."

John was pleased to see his wry joke had for a brief moment unearthed her smile again.

It quickly passed. Rose stood up. "I should go."

"Please, allow me to take you home. The weather is abominable, and I've brought a carriage."

"You've had a carriage standing outside this whole time?"

"The driver is a hardy soul, bless him. I had no idea a monsoon would be upon us."

"Even so, I couldn't possibly accept. I think it would be wiser for us to part here."

Was she really saying good-bye *forever*? John scrambled desperately to think of a way to keep from losing her. "I'm afraid I must insist on escorting you home. There's an important reason for it—aside from this brutal weather."

"Oh? What's that?"

"A famous French philosopher once said, 'Never loan anyone your books. They never get returned. The only books in my library are those I've borrowed from others.'"

"Wise words," Rose agreed, although she looked puzzled as to why he was mentioning this.

"If you're determined never to see me again, I'll have to ask for a return of my book. I couldn't bear to part with it permanently. It's a first edition."

"Is it? In that case, it was reckless of you to loan it out."

"I had trust in you, that you would take good care of it. Of course, if you aren't finished reading it, I can make arrangements to come by another day. It would be no trouble at all."

Was he being too obvious about his desire to keep spending time with her? Probably. He couldn't help it. She was too remarkable and fascinating to be allowed to simply walk away.

"I did finish the book last night, as it happens." Glancing out the window at the pouring rain, Rose shrugged, as if that was the reason she was giving in to his entreaties. "I shall accept your offer for a ride home."

"Excellent! Then we can discuss the book on the way." Inwardly, John was thanking God for the rain, and for the "problem" of how to return his book. How many wonderful things could turn on seemingly small details.

⌒⌒⌒

What am I doing? Rose thought as the carriage pulled away from the curb, one wheel skittering until it gained traction on the muddy street. *Merely taking advantage of a ride in a fine carriage to escape a soggy walk home. Besides, if he wants his book so badly, he can certainly have it.*

Rose had made it clear she'd expected this to be their last time together. In light of the way her attempts to help his family had only made things worse for everyone, this seemed the only reasonable course of action. She wasn't prepared for the misery she felt at the easy way John had accepted her decision. He'd even decided to wrap up the final loose end by reclaiming his book.

As the carriage rolled on, however, Rose began to get a different impression. John cheerfully steered the topic of conversation to *The Pickwick Papers*. He prodded Rose for details about what she liked or didn't like, drawing her into just the sort of lively conversation they'd enjoyed at other times when they'd chatted about books. John seemed wholly absorbed in the discussion, as though nothing else was on his mind. As though he'd forgotten the things they'd just talked about—Sophie and the ball and all the rest of it. As though he thought their friendship was continuing on just as it was, despite everything that had happened and all he'd learned about her. It left Rose with an odd feeling of mildly optimistic uncertainty.

When they arrived at Rose's building, John immediately got down to help Rose out of the carriage. The driver came down from his seat and brandished a large umbrella to give them both shelter from the rain, which had lessened from a torrent to a steady drizzle.

"I will get the book," Rose said. "You may think me rude for leaving you here, but I believe it's the best thing to do."

"I understand." He added with a smile, "I'll just wait here and take in a bit of sun."

The man really had a way of being so disarming and personable. It was too easy to enjoy his company. For a foolish moment, Rose wanted to stay here with him, to keep their pleasing conversation going. She reined in that idiotic thought. "I won't be long," she told him and hurried into the building.

When she reached her flat, she was surprised to find the door unlocked. She had a good idea what that meant. Instantly her mood darkened. She pushed open the door. Sure enough, her mother-in-law was sitting on the sofa, knitting as comfortably as if she were in her own home.

She looked up as Rose entered. "I was beginning to worry. Were you delayed by the bad weather?"

This wasn't the first time Rose had regretted giving her mother-in-law a key to her flat. "Mother Finlay, what are you doing here?"

"You invited me, of course. Did you forget?"

"No, we agreed I was coming to you tonight."

"Did we? I was sure we planned to meet here, especially when you didn't turn up at my house." The way she said this sounded like a censure, which it probably was. "Well, never mind." She set aside her knitting. "I've made a pot of tea. It's still hot. Just the thing to take off the chill."

"There is something I need to do first. I've promised to return a book to an acquaintance who is waiting downstairs." How thankful she was that she'd told John to wait outside! It would have been supremely awkward to explain a perfectly innocent situation to her mother-in-law.

"Why did you leave your friend outside in the rain?" Mother Finlay said as Rose retrieved the book from a nearby table. "Invite her up for tea."

"There's no time. I'll be right back."

Rose hurried out of the flat before Mother Finlay could stop her.

The rain had abated enough that the driver had put the umbrella away. He'd returned to the driver's box, out of earshot, or at least pretending to be. John was standing by the carriage door, looking at ease, apparently not minding that there were still enough misty droplets falling to leave a shimmer on his hat and coat.

Rose extended the book toward him. "Here you are." Too

late, Rose realized she ought to have wrapped it in paper first to give it some protection from the elements. She'd been in too much of a hurry to get back outside before Mother Finlay could ask more questions. "Oh dear, it's going to get wet."

"Quite all right." John took the book and quickly set it inside the carriage. "It will be safe enough there."

He turned back to Rose, his expression becoming somber for the first time since they'd left the tea shop. He gave Rose a searching look, as though he was trying to compose what to say next.

Rose thought it best not to delay their moment of parting. She didn't want to give Mrs. Riley more fodder for gossip. "Good-bye, thank you again for the loan of the book."

He shook his head. "I owe you the greater debt. Listen, I've been wanting to ask you something—"

Rose took a step back. "My heavens, I think the rain may be starting again. Please forgive me if I hurry back inside."

It was the flimsiest of excuses, but John accepted it. "Another time, then."

"Yes, another time, perhaps." Rose turned away and quickly went into her building.

When she reached her flat, her mother-in-law was in the kitchen. She came back to the sitting room with a cup of tea in hand. "I made it nice and strong, as you like it."

Rose accepted the cup with a word of thanks. She took a seat in the armchair, while Mother Finlay returned to the sofa. Rose fully expected her mother-in-law to nag her for more answers about the friend downstairs. Instead, she picked up her knitting and began work. "I had a wonderful dream about Peter last night. I dream of him a lot, you know. Sometimes I feel like these are visits from him, from heaven."

So the conversation was to be about Peter, rather than her friend. Rose didn't know which was worse. "What was the dream about?" she asked, knowing it was expected of her.

"Do you know, I can't really remember! It was just comforting to know he was there. Someday we will all be together in heaven. Won't that be wonderful? Rose, I wonder that you don't have such dreams."

Rose took a sip of tea to hide her grimace. "Peter fills my thoughts in other ways, I assure you."

"I'm sure he does," Mother Finlay said, still in a blissful frame of mind. "I'll see my Simon there too. How comforting it is to know that the bond of marriage is eternal, surpassing even this short earthly life."

Rose made a small noise, as if murmuring assent. She had heard variations of this speech countless times. She knew she could simply bide her time with noncommittal remarks until the old lady moved on to something else.

This time, however, Mother Finlay gave a cry, as if in pain. "Oh, it can be so hard sometimes to wait!" She turned a sorrowful gaze to Rose. "It can be lonely, but we must wait and bear that burden until the great moment of reconciliation."

Rose was surprised to see real tears in the lady's eyes. Mother Finlay sniffled and began to look around at her lap and the sofa, as if searching for something. Rose guessed she was looking for her handkerchief.

Rose got up to help with the search, ready to fetch another one if needed. She caught sight of the lost item on the windowsill. It would seem Mother Finlay had been standing there, watching Rose's interaction with John.

Heart sinking, Rose crossed the room back to her mother-in-law. As she gave the handkerchief back, Mother Finlay took hold of Rose's hand. "Remember, your husband is waiting for you." She actually looked terrified, as if watching Rose about to step off a cliff.

"Mother Finlay, I think you have the wrong idea. That man you saw me with outside is a mere acquaintance. He was kind enough to loan me a book, that's all."

"Is that truly all it was? Or is he trying to turn your head? You must be strong, my girl. For Peter's sake. And your own."

The last thing Rose wanted was to obey such a command. Yet hadn't she been thinking that parting ways with John was wise for other reasons? But that was before he'd shown up today and done all he could to keep their lovely friendship intact. And yet it could be dangerous to allow herself to care too much for him. If she'd learned anything from her own life, it was that such an emotional attachment couldn't end well. All these conflicting thoughts were at war within her, vying for preeminence. Until she could sort it out, she would leave things as they were, without a set plan or commitment for meeting him again. It was, if nothing else, surely the safest route.

"Yes, Mother Finlay. I will be strong."

CHAPTER

Eighteen

A promotion was surely on the horizon. Rose decided to act accordingly, redoubling her efforts around the office. She was finally rewarded one afternoon about two weeks later when Mr. Gordon invited her into his office for a private conference.

Now she sat opposite his desk, looking at the envelope he'd just handed her.

"Go ahead, read it," he prompted with a smile. "I expect you have a good idea what's in it. And did I mention the repairs on my home in Somerset are complete?" This had been the reason for his holidays from work. Rose knew he was making improvements to an old family home in the countryside so he could live there after he retired.

"That is good news," Rose said. "Will you be celebrating Christmas there?"

"I certainly will. It will be a pleasure to escape the Big Smoke and breathe sweet, fresh air. I might even decide to stay beyond Christmas, for an indefinite time."

Smiling, Rose opened the letter and began reading. It was

an offer from the assistant superintendent who oversaw the post office branches in London. Rose was being offered the manager's position at this branch, along with an associated raise in pay. She had been scrimping carefully in order to keep living where she was without a roommate. This new salary would be welcome indeed.

She looked back up at Mr. Gordon. "It says I'm to begin my new position on December thirteenth. That's just a few weeks away."

"Yes, I'm anxious to leave town. To be honest, my wife is doing poorly. She's the one most in need of healthy country air. I am sorry to leave you just as we get busy with piles of Christmas cards and a torrent of telegrams from last-minute holidaymakers. But I know you can handle it. A new clerk will be transferring from the post office in Bayswater next week. He's got plenty of experience. He'll take over your current position as assistant manager. This is well deserved, Mrs. Finlay. I congratulate you."

Rose took in a breath, allowing herself a moment to enjoy the satisfaction of attaining this goal. She felt vindicated as she remembered those people at the ball who had looked down their noses at her. Rose had a tangible achievement to be proud of. She didn't know if any of those pampered ladies could truly say the same.

"Yes, we shall manage it," she assured Mr. Gordon. "And may I say, sir, how grateful I am for your good opinion of me. I know you did some campaigning on my behalf at the main office."

She didn't need to say it, but she was referring specifically to the fact that she was a woman, yet he'd recommended her for the managerial position anyway. In this respect he'd gone out on a limb since most women weren't offered managerial positions unless it was to oversee groups of women only.

Mr. Gordon nodded to indicate he understood what she

meant. "I have always felt that promotion by merit is the best policy in the end. Common sense, intelligence, and dedication are critical. You possess a high degree of all these qualities." He pushed back his chair and stood up. "But that's enough with the compliments. Even the best people can suffer from too large a head if overly flattered." He tempered this warning with a good-natured grin. "It's nearly five o'clock. I shall ask everyone to stay for a few extra minutes once we've closed up, and I'll make the announcement."

As expected, everyone congratulated Rose warmly. No one was truly surprised by the news. Rose was gratified by their response. She made her first official speech as their future manager to let them know how much she valued everyone and that she would strive to ensure a good working environment.

A few minutes later, Rose began her walk home, still excited, the offer letter in her pocket. Her mind was buzzing with plans. She had several ideas for improving their processes at work. Once she was in charge, she would waste no time putting those plans into action.

When she reached the building where she lived, her thoughts were so filled with work that she hardly noticed the carriage parked nearby. She paused, however, when she heard a voice calling out to her. "Mrs. Finlay! Wait!"

Rose turned to see Sophie, of all people, exiting the carriage and running up to her. "Sophie! What are you doing here? Are you all right?" Rose blurted out the questions practically in one breath.

"I need to talk to you. I've been waiting here for ages."

"How did you know where I live?"

"Peter remembered."

"Peter?" Rose gasped the word.

"Yes, he brought you home after the ball." Sophie pointed back toward her carriage driver. Of course. Peter was a common enough name. Even so, the reference had been jarring.

"May I speak with you? I need help, and I don't know what else to do."

Rose's first thought was to point out the girl's impudence at thinking she could just come here and request a chat after all that had happened. She thought better of it after taking a good look at Sophie's expression and hearing a note of fear mixed in with the sense of urgency. Sophie had come to her, and she was requesting help. Rose would be an ogre to refuse.

"Would you like to come inside?"

"Yes, thank you."

When they reached her flat, Rose had barely closed the door when Sophie exclaimed, "Mrs. Finlay, you were right! And I was such a fool."

A nearly overwhelming dread welled up within Rose. She took hold of Sophie's arm. "Are you speaking of Sandy? Did he hurt you?" At the very thought, anger began to replace the dread.

"No! I mean, yes, but not in that way—oh, it's just so awful!" The girl had been holding up well enough in the street, but now she appeared ready to give in to her distress.

"Come and sit down," Rose urged. She helped Sophie remove her coat and hat, then gently pulled her over to a chair. "Shall I make us some tea?"

Sophie sank onto the chair and looked gratefully at Rose. "That would be lovely."

Rose put the kettle on to boil and prepared the tea. She was itching to know what had happened, but she'd find out soon enough. And besides, she also wanted a cup of tea. Tea would never solve a crisis, but it always made it more bearable.

Rose brought out the tray with the tea things and set it on a table near the sofa. She was happy to note that Sophie appeared to be calmer. Perhaps sitting for a few minutes in the quiet room had helped.

"This is a cozy place," Sophie observed as Rose poured the tea.

"It's humble, but I like it."

"You don't ever feel . . . well, confined?"

It wasn't too surprising that Sophie should ask this question, given that she lived in such a large house. "Not at all. In fact, I've got an entire bedroom that no one uses. It feels like a scandalous waste. Sugar?"

"Two, please. No milk."

Rose obliged. "Now, what's this about?"

Sophie suddenly looked hesitant to talk. After a moment, she said ruefully, "You're going to have a lovely time saying 'I told you so.'"

"Please, just tell me what happened," Rose said gently. "I promise to withhold judgment."

Sophie took a deep breath. "Several days after the ball, I saw Sandy again. It was at a tea party at Lady Blessington's home. She has a lovely conservatory filled with exotic plants and flowers. It was rather like an indoor garden party."

"At this time of year, that sounds ideal."

"Yes, it was very nice. Sandy and I were able to have a private conversation behind a large, leafy bush—heaven knows what it was. I believe it came from South America."

"And what did you talk about?"

"Sandy said he'd done nothing but think of me day and night since the ball and our magical kiss—" She cut herself off, looking embarrassed by this admission.

"I know he kissed you at the ball," Rose reminded her.

"Right," Sophie said with a sheepish smile.

Rose marveled at how Sophie's attitude toward her had changed since that night. Something had clearly woken this girl up. "Go on. What else happened at the tea party?"

"He said he wanted me to meet his parents. They keep a home here in London. Sandy said I should pay them a call, and he'd be there to make certain I wasn't turned away. He said he knew they would love me. He mentioned again that they've been after him to settle down. I took it to mean that he was starting to consider me for his future wife."

"Of course you did." Rose didn't mean this as a reproof so much as to express her belief that Sandy was a master at getting women to infer the wrong things from his words.

"So I went to His Lordship's home on the appointed day. I took Aileen with me."

"You took only your maid?"

"Well, I couldn't ask Mama to go. The continual rain has made her feel weaker than ever. I didn't want to involve the Draytons. I knew they'd be dripping with envy, and besides, they weren't invited. Sandy made it clear he doesn't like them."

Sophie said this last part with a superior air. Apparently, she had no qualms about setting aside her "dearest friend" if that friend might be detrimental to her plans. The girl still had a high opinion of herself, despite whatever had happened.

"Aileen has accompanied me on calls before," Sophie went on. "She waits in the servants' hall while I visit with the hostess. I didn't think there would be any problems. When we arrived, the butler led me to the parlor while a maid took Aileen belowstairs. When I got to the parlor, only Sandy was there. The butler left, closing the door, and the two of us were alone! Sandy apologized, saying he hadn't realized his parents had returned to their estate in Sussex because his father's rheumatism was troubling him."

"You ought to have left the house that very moment," Rose said.

"Yes, I know. But to be alone with Sandy was so delightful that I didn't want to leave! We sat together on the sofa, talking of the most interesting things. In time, he said he was beginning to care for me deeply. I admitted that I felt the same way about him. Then—it seemed so natural—he kissed me. At first, I wished he might keep kissing me forever."

She paused, closing her eyes, either remembering how

wonderful the kiss was, or steeling herself to continue her tale. Rose understood that both might be true. She waited silently until Sophie spoke again.

"Then things began to change. He became less gentleman-like, not at all like he was at the ball. He began to get very forward, urging me to allow things that I knew were wrong." Setting down her teacup, she put her hands to her face.

"You didn't allow him to continue?" Rose demanded. She was ready to find Sandy and strangle him, no matter the consequences.

"No!" Sophie answered vehemently. "I pushed him away and ran toward the door. He followed me and took hold of my arm, trying to stop me, to flatter and cajole me into staying. I resisted, telling him off in no uncertain terms. I think I was half hoping he would be a gentleman after all and offer an apology. Instead, my words must have angered him because he became quite ugly toward me. He warned me that if I told anyone about this, he'd ensure things did not go well for me or my family."

"Despicable man," Rose muttered.

Sophie nodded. "I was so horrified, I ran straight out of the house. I was nearly to the street corner before I stopped, shivering, not knowing what to do because my coat and hat were still at the house. And so was Aileen! But they must have fetched her up from the servants' hall because a minute or so later she came out of the house, carrying my things. We hailed a cab and went straight home."

"You do realize he had set up the entire situation just to seduce you?"

"Yes, and all I could think of was what a fool I was and how right you'd been."

"Have you told your mother about this?"

"How could I? I'm too ashamed. And besides, there are Sandy's threats—I don't want to hurt my family. We could be ruined! It's frightening to think one man could have such power over us."

"Welcome to reality," Rose said, though not unkindly. "I'm sorry you had to learn this lesson so young. What will you do now?"

"I need to find a way to get Mama to understand that Sandy is not the match for me—without her knowing what happened. I gave up a proper Season as a debutante to come out early, thinking he was interested in courting me. Mama will be crushed to discover we based our decision on deceptions and faulty assumptions. But now that I'm out, I've got to continue on." Sophie lifted her chin, perhaps seeing herself as an undaunted heroine overcoming adversity. "I'll just find someone else. A proper gentleman."

Rose couldn't deny she was gratified to hear Sophie talking about a sensible plan of action. She was ambivalent about the idea that Sophie should find another suitor posthaste, but she knew it was the expected thing for a girl in her position.

"That's why I've come today," Sophie continued. "I wanted to ask a favor, although I've no right to do so after I behaved so abominably at the ball."

"I accept your apology," Rose said. The girl had learned her lesson before it was too late, and Rose was thankful. "What did you want to ask me?"

"There is another dance in a few days. It's a charity ball, for a very good cause, and it's hosted by my uncle's club. He's one of the officials—stewards, they call them. Will you be my chaperone?"

Rose was awash in astonishment. There were so many problems with this request that she barely knew where to begin. "Do you really think your mother would allow me to resume that role, knowing what she does about me?"

Sophie's look grew wary—or was it guilty? "You've been talking with my uncle."

"I have. He gave me a comprehensive report of everything you said and did after the ball."

Sophie dropped her gaze. "Then you know I told them everything you told me. About your husband, I mean."

"Yes. That's a very big reason why I can't be your chaperone. I won't be subjected to further gossip. It was bad enough last time, but now—"

Sophie's head jerked up. "That won't happen! I haven't told a soul, other than Mama and Uncle John. Not even Louisa! It won't be like Lady Randolph's ball. You'll see hardly any of the same people. However, I do think Sandy might attend. I'm nervous about seeing him again. I think having you there would be my best defense."

"Your uncle will be at the dance, and he already knows to be on the watch," Rose hedged. "I told him about your private interlude with Sandy at Lady Randolph's ball."

"You did?" Sophie looked genuinely confused. "He never confronted me about it. Nor did he tell Mama. I'm sure I would have heard about it if he had."

"Perhaps that's because I told him it was pointless to watch over you day and night. I said that, in the end, you were going to have to make your own decisions and live with the results."

Sophie shook her head sadly. "Mrs. Finlay, you are so wise."

"It's the wisdom of experience, unfortunately."

"You can't tell my uncle about what happened at Lord Ormond's house! Who knows what he'd do—and then, what awful scandal! We might never recover!"

"I won't tell him," Rose assured her, remembering John's intense reaction upon learning the pair had snuck away for a kiss. That seemed an almost innocent act compared to Sandy's attempt to get the girl alone and pounce on her.

"But you will go to the dance and help me?" She looked at Rose with wide, pleading eyes.

Over the past few weeks, Rose had done everything she

could to return to the life she'd been living before becoming entangled with this family. Now Sophie was asking her to step once more into their affairs. The girl's entreaties were nearly irresistible, but could Rose truly help the situation? Was Sophie correct in her assertion that Rose would not face the same scorn and ill-use as at Lady Randolph's ball? It was possible. John would be there, and in an official capacity. Surely Rose could rely on him to keep matters from getting out of hand.

"Ask your uncle first. It sounds as though he'll have a good understanding of what might happen at the dance, in terms of attendees and how they might react to my presence. He also knows your mother's mind far better than I. If he thinks it's a good idea to have me there, then I will agree."

"Thank you!" Sophie jumped up and came over to where Rose was sitting, joining her on the sofa and giving her a hug.

"I never thought I'd see this day," Rose murmured, surprised at how touched she was by this display of warm regard and by the feel of the girl's arms around her neck.

Sophie laughed and bounded back to her feet. "I'll talk to Uncle John tonight. He promised to join us for dinner. I don't suppose you want to come too?"

"No," Rose said firmly. "Now, be off with you. I expect you're late enough as it is."

Rose walked with Sophie to her carriage. She was relieved to see Aileen sitting inside it. Having a maid along was good for propriety's sake, even if Rose was sorry the poor girl had been forced to wait outside in the cold, along with the driver.

Rather than make supper, Rose sat thinking over this surprising turn of events for a long time. What would John say about all this? How would Sophie be able to explain her reasons for her request without revealing what Sandy had done? Rose had no doubt the girl would find a way.

Perhaps the bigger question was why Rose was willing to

face those possible slings and arrows once again. Much as she wanted to help Sophie, she knew there was more to it. The answer was tied up in that confusing bundle of emotions she'd felt the last time she'd seen John. They seemed to have coalesced into a desire to see him again, come what may.

CHAPTER

Nineteen

John sat in the parlor next to Sophie, hardly able to believe what she was asking. After dinner she had pulled him to the far corner, opposite from where Louisa had engaged her mother in a game of backgammon. Here, in low tones, she'd asked if Rose could be her chaperone for the charity ball.

He shook his head, uncomprehending. "Would you mind explaining to me how you came to decide this was a good idea? I had the impression you did not get on with Mrs. Finlay."

"I've come to see that I was wrong about her, and that she was right in many of the things she told me."

"And how did you make this discovery?" A possible answer to that question made him very nervous. Sophie had proven she could find ways to slip away on her own.

Sophie gave a nonchalant shrug. "I've simply been thinking over what Mrs. Finlay told me that night. She warned me that I ought not to be in a hurry to give my heart to any man. I should be circumspect and not favor anyone too soon, no matter who he is. Nor should I assume that just because a gentleman fancies me the inevitable result will be marriage." Sophie gave him a smile. "Don't you think that's wise?"

While John appreciated hearing these sentiments from his niece, he couldn't help but suspect she was being more than a little disingenuous. "Sophie, if you plan to lure Mrs. Finlay to another party simply to belittle her and heap more social embarrassment on her, I shall be utterly disappointed in you— and likely disinherit you completely. You are better than that."

Sophie gasped. "I promise that's not the case at all! How could you think so?"

She did look truly shocked at the idea. Perhaps John had misjudged her and jumped to the wrong conclusion.

"I'm sincere in wanting Mrs. Finlay to be there," Sophie insisted.

"Persuading her may be harder than you think. I'm pretty sure she's ready to write off the whole lot of us." He'd been struggling with himself about whether to go and see her again, unsure what her final words and actions had implied.

"She has no objections, if you don't."

John started back in surprise. "How do you know that?"

"I went to see her."

"You did *what*?"

"Shh!" Sophie hissed, sending a worried glance toward her mother. "I had to apologize for my abysmal behavior, didn't I?"

Once again, John marveled. He didn't bother to ask when and where she'd spoken to Rose. This was simply more proof of Rose's caution that it was going to be impossible to keep watch over Sophie continually.

"What are you two whispering about?" Pearl called. "Why don't you come over here and share it with us?"

"In a moment, Mama," Sophie returned cheerfully. She dropped her voice again and addressed John. "I wanted to talk to you first, before telling Mama. If we all agree, then it will be easier to persuade her. You don't think Mrs. Finlay is unsuitable, do you, based simply on what happened to her in the past?"

"Certainly not, and I'm glad you're not holding it against her either. But we can't discount what happened last time. Even without knowing those aspects of Mrs. Finlay's background, most of the people at Lady Randolph's ball snubbed her. That's bound to worry your mother. She's highly concerned about avoiding scandal of any kind."

"I still think we might convince her it's all right. She'll rely on your opinion, especially with Aunt Marjorie out of town. Besides, this charity ball won't be quite as exclusive. More regular people will be there. I daresay they won't have any opinions on Mrs. Finlay one way or the other."

John took some amusement from that assessment. It was true that the charity ball, sponsored by his club to provide scholarships for poor boys to train in mechanics and industry, would have more "regular" people in attendance. Despite Sophie's designation, they were far from humble. They were merchants, bankers, and wealthy businessmen.

Even so, he took her point. Many of the aristocrats and others of the upper crust were off to the country at this time of year for hunting parties and the like. They returned for the more fashionable balls such as the one at Lady Randolph's home but skipped others they deemed less important. There were still a few on the list for this charity ball, however. Including Sandy Deveaux. That fact alone made him happy to have Rose there. Especially now that even Sophie seemed keen on the idea.

"So what do you think?" Sophie asked.

John still couldn't quite believe that Sophie was pressing for this. He was very interested to learn exactly what had transpired during her conversation with Rose. "I'll speak with Mrs. Finlay tomorrow."

"Thank you!" Sophie exclaimed, beaming with delight.

"I won again, Mama!" Louisa said, triumphantly removing

her last piece from the backgammon board. "Uncle John, will you play?"

Exhaling a deep breath, as though relieved the game was over, Pearl left the table where they were playing and returned to her chair. "Come and tell us what you've been whispering about all this time," she said, waving them over.

"Yes, tell us," Louisa said, swiftly arranging the backgammon pieces for a new game. "And you can play me while you're at it."

"I don't know if I'm brave enough to play you again," John teased, taking the chair Pearl had just vacated. "I haven't won a single game out of the last dozen we've played. I'm getting demoralized by all the losses."

"I was just asking Uncle John if Mrs. Finlay could be my chaperone for the charity ball," Sophie said.

Pearl stared at her daughter. "You did?"

"He thinks it's a good idea."

Pearl transferred her amazed look to John. "You do?"

"You have to admit she did a fine job at the ball. She watched over Sophie and brought her home safely. If the pompous ladies of Lady Randolph's set look down their noses at Mrs. Finlay for merely having an honest occupation, that says more about them than about her."

"Well said, Uncle," Louisa chimed in. "I think all those ladies are too full of themselves. I like Mrs. Finlay."

"But Sophie doesn't like Mrs. Finlay," Pearl said, still looking confounded by this unexpected change of plans.

"I believe I was wrong in some of the things I said about her," Sophie answered. "I'd like to make up for my unkindness. Be more charitable in my dealings."

"That's admirable, of course, but Mrs. Drayton is just as willing to take you with her."

"She and I have gone to several events over this past week. I don't want to continue being a burden to her."

"What about John? He could be your chaperone. I thought that was our original plan."

"My duties as a steward will require me to be at the assembly rooms hours in advance to help with last-minute preparations. That means Sophie will have to travel there with someone else. I think Mrs. Finlay is a good choice."

"Truly, John?" Pearl gave him a searching look. "Even knowing what we do about . . ." She didn't finish the obvious reference to Rose's past but rather sent a worried look toward Louisa. Pearl and Sophie must have kept to their plan of not telling her about it. Louisa had just rolled the dice and was busy moving a piece forward, too preoccupied to catch the undertone of their conversation.

"Yes," John answered Pearl quietly. "Even so."

"So it's settled," Sophie said gaily.

"If she'll agree to do it," John added.

Pearl threw up her hands. "Fine, if you think this is the best plan."

"Your turn, Uncle John," Louisa said, pressing the dice-roller box into his hand.

As it happened, John won that backgammon game. He was surprised, given that his thoughts had been entirely centered elsewhere. He now had a good reason to see Rose again. If Sophie was to be believed, she was not likely to turn down their request for her help.

This was his fourth year on the planning committee for the charity ball. It was another instance where he'd taken on a responsibility that his brother used to fulfill. Unlike Lionel, John had never enjoyed this work. It took up weeks of his time and felt more of a burden than anything else. But now, he was heartily looking forward to it.

Rose was not the least bit surprised to see John walking into the post office the following afternoon. She'd been anticipating his arrival. He had timed it at ten minutes before closing.

She had just handed a telegram to Stan for transmission when she caught sight of John entering. She walked up to the counter—the same place where they'd had their last conversation in here. It almost felt like it was becoming a habit. She wasn't going to allow him to think his task would be easy, however. She addressed him with businesslike formality, even if she couldn't help but smile a little. "Good afternoon, Mr. Milburn. What brings you here today?"

He wasn't fooled. He leaned in and used a confidential tone. "I think you know. I've learned my niece has been trying to persuade you to attend a certain upcoming charity ball."

"So she has."

"Are you really willing to go?"

"I am considering it, incredibly enough. Proof that I'm a glutton for punishment."

"I admire you, nonetheless. May we discuss it further over a cup of tea in, say, fifteen minutes?"

His voice always had a certain warmth to it that Rose could only describe as welcoming. And now as he gave her this compliment and paired it with a request, his eyes were twinkling. Rose couldn't deny she was happy to see him again, even if he'd been drawn here because of his niece, whose schemes were often ill-advised, to say the least. She took his cheerful mood to mean he must have confidence in the plan.

Rose pretended to think it over. "I believe I can spare the time."

Her spirits rose higher when she arrived at the tea shop and saw John seated at a table already laden with tea and sandwiches. If there was one thing that almost made up for that terrible evening she'd endured among the "better" folk, it was the simple luxury of having a steaming pot of tea waiting for her as soon as she left work.

"What exactly did you two discuss that Sophie would turn you around from your determination to keep away from us?" John asked once they were enjoying their tea.

"She apologized for her bad behavior the night of the ball. She confessed that she'd helped to turn the tide of opinion against me, and that she'd been wrong to do so."

John nodded thoughtfully. "That's what she told me as well. Yet I'm still having a difficult time understanding why she suddenly came to that conclusion. She seemed to gloss over that point. Did she give you any details?"

Rose looked down at her teacup, taking a moment before responding. Sophie had begged her to keep the disastrous encounter with Sandy confidential, and Rose had agreed. She didn't much like it, but she had to admit that for now, at least, it was probably for the best. "I think Sophie's conscience got the better of her." She met John's gaze again. "She's a good girl at heart, even if she's prone to acting impulsively at times."

"I agree, but I feel there must be more to the story. Do you really think that's all it is?"

"She told me she saw Mr. Deveaux at a tea party a few days later." Rose wasn't sharing a confidence to state this fact. Their attendance at the event would be public knowledge. "I think—based on some things she said—that she has grown disenchanted with him. She would like to distance herself from him."

"This makes me happy, if still somewhat baffled."

"Part of your duties as a steward involves making introductions, isn't that right? Sophie is amenable to meeting other young gentlemen. She's realized she ought to throw a wider net, so to speak. Perhaps she will find someone who is the right match for her, whether or not he comes from an aristocratic family."

"That's been my wish for her all along." He sighed. "It would be wonderful if all my family problems could be solved so easily. I do my best, but . . ."

Rose was surprised to see his suddenly dejected look. "Is Sophie not the only one giving you trouble?"

"Unfortunately, no. Marjorie's son Edward was expelled from his school. He's only fifteen, but he's determined to follow in his father's footsteps. That was the age when my brother began to work, ultimately building his own successful business. Edward thinks he can do the same and has rejected his father's wish that he should finish school and go on to university."

"If he wants to find gainful employment, is it really such a crime? Some young men are simply not interested in ivory towers. As for me, I'd give anything to be able to spend hours in those grand university libraries."

"I feel the same way. And so did Lionel. It was a privilege we never enjoyed. Edward's younger brother, Rupert, has an academic bent and excels in his studies. But Edward is a different story. I can't understand it."

"Perhaps it's not so terribly surprising. My father's brother had four sons. Our two houses were on the same street, so we saw a lot of each other growing up. Each of them took very different paths, despite being about as close in age as they could get."

"Yes, I see what you mean." He thought it over. "I suppose Sophie and Louisa are another case in point."

Rose nodded. "Exactly."

"Do you have any siblings?"

"A sister, born when I was five." Rose felt a twinge of sadness, remembering the playful little girl whom Rose had delighted to entertain and coddle. "We lost her very young to scarlet fever."

"I'm sorry to hear it."

"I still miss her, even though she died so long ago. I often wonder how my life might have been different if she'd lived."

"Losing a sibling is never easy, no matter the time of life. Lionel . . ." He shook his head sadly.

They shared a moment of understanding as they thought over the loved ones they'd lost.

"Will Edward take on his father's business, eventually?" Rose asked.

"He's mentioned it several times. But he's too young to take on any kind of responsible position. He'll need some practical experience, and to acquire some polish, before he could succeed at buttering up potential clients."

"I'm guessing that's a forte of yours."

"It's all in how you sell it. Show the novelty of the thing. Something that makes it unique, out of the ordinary." He shrugged. "Whether it is or not."

"Perhaps Edward might attend a training school like you did or apprentice somewhere."

"It would have to be the right sort of place. He's a clever lad with a high degree of intelligence. He just hasn't mastered the art of sitting still."

"What is he interested in?"

"He seems to prefer manual tasks rather than cerebral ones. He loves trains. He even has several models of locomotives. But we can't just send him off to be an engineer or fireman. That wouldn't be a proper career for a lad of his station. Our family has worked hard to get where we are."

"There's always telegraphy, if you don't think that's too humble. The schools start training boys at fourteen. It's not enough to live on at first, but perhaps he'd still be living at home?"

"Yes, that's another reason why he wants to give up school. With Lionel gone, he feels obligated to take care of his mother and siblings."

"That's quite noble, really."

"It's the best of intentions but not terribly helpful. He's with them in Ramsgate right now. There's not much he can do there but add to the cost of the hotel, but his mother and sister are glad for the company."

"Why don't you bring him by the post office one day after

239

they return? We can demonstrate the telegraph machine, maybe allow him to try it out. Our primary telegrapher, Stan, isn't so much older than Edward."

"That is a thought. It's definitely a manual occupation."

"And it requires a quick mind."

"Which I'm sure is why you mastered it." He said this with a sly smile, then picked up the teapot to refill their cups.

Rose blinked, the compliment seeming to come out of the blue.

"Would your manager object to this impromptu demonstration during work time?" John asked.

Now it was Rose's turn to smile. "I can pretty much guarantee she won't."

His brows lifted. "Care to elaborate?"

"I'll be taking over the manager's position in December." It gave Rose great satisfaction to be able to say those words aloud.

John looked equally pleased. "Congratulations! Advancing in the corporate ranks by day, chaperoning by night. Is there anything you can't do?"

She could not quell a certain thrumming in her veins just now, nor prevent the glow that seemed to be spreading through her. "I hope only one of those jobs is permanent," she quipped.

She'd been referring to her manager's position. Surprisingly, it seemed to take him a moment to work that out. He looked at her with an intensity that gave rise to another round of warm feelings.

Finally, John shrugged and gave her a relaxed smile. "I can only say I'm thankful that for now you have the energy to do both."

"I won't, if I don't get home soon," Rose joked. "I've a list of things to do before bedtime."

He looked sheepish. "I've taken up quite enough of your time with my family conundrums."

When they left the tea shop, Rose politely but firmly turned down his offer to take her home. She didn't need to add to Mother Finlay's worries about her seeing a gentleman, even though Rose was determined to live her life as she saw fit. She did finally give in to his insistence on paying for a cab for her.

When they reached the cab, John didn't help her in right away. They merely stood there, looking at one another. Rose felt the unspoken sentiment passing between them that neither was anxious to be going. She reminded herself that in her case, it was because she had promised to dine with Mother Finlay this evening. But there was nothing to be gained by putting it off. She turned resolutely toward the cab, and John helped her in.

"I will see you at the dance," John said. "As one of the organizers, I hope I can find a way to make it enjoyable for you, even if you are there to be a watchdog for Sophie."

"All I need are a few less harpies and I should be fine."

He laughed. It wasn't the first time Rose had heard him laugh. She loved that the sound always seemed to impart happiness to her as well.

During the cab ride home, Rose realized another reason she couldn't escort Sophie to endless dances. She had only one proper ball gown. She'd already worn it once. As with last time, she had no time or money to obtain another. The manager's pay was not in her pocket just yet. Her concerns dissipated when she remembered John hadn't seen that gown. Rose found herself thinking with some surprise that this was all that mattered.

Her meeting with John had set her behind the time when her mother-in-law would be expecting her. Rose had the cab driver let her off at a bakery near Mother Finlay's home and bought a Sally Lunn cake to bring as an offering for being late.

This gift of her favorite treat seemed to appease Mother Finlay's agitation, as did Rose's explanation that she'd been delayed at work. She shared the happy news of her promotion, allowing the old lady to think that taking on extra duties had been the cause for Rose's longer workday.

"I've invited the Reverend Dr. Purcell and his wife to dine with me on Tuesday," Mother Finlay said as they were finishing their dinner. "You'll come too, won't you? The Purcells are keen to see you again."

"I'm afraid I can't. I'll be dining with the Shaws that evening." This was true, although Rose was happy to forgo dinner with Mother Finlay's friends. Dr. Purcell was the minister at the church Mother Finlay attended. He had a number of religious views that Rose simply could not agree with.

Mother Finlay pursed her lips. "How inconvenient. I'll see if the Purcells can change to Wednesday."

"I'm sorry to say I have plans for that evening as well."

This comment drew a critical look from her mother-in-law. "You've suddenly become the social butterfly, it seems. What are you doing Wednesday?"

"I always have a busy schedule. You know that." Rose stood up and took their empty plates to the sink. "Shall I slice that cake for us now?"

"I can easily guess what you're doing Wednesday," Mother Finlay said. "I expect it has something to do with that liveried carriage that was standing outside your home for over an hour yesterday."

Rose blew out a breath, trying to remain calm as she sliced the cake. Silently cursing nosy old women, Rose brought out the dessert plates and set them on the table.

"Mrs. Riley is quite concerned," Mother Finlay persisted. "People may start to talk if you begin receiving gentlemen in your flat."

"If Mrs. Riley had been more perceptive, she might have noticed it was a young lady who visited me yesterday, not a gentleman. However, she may keep her wrong assumptions if it will make her happier. There's nothing that lady likes more than gossip."

Mother Finlay gave a little sniff. "You might be more charitable toward her. Don't forget she lowered the rent for you, when she might have got more from someone else."

This was true, and a good reminder to be careful with her words. Her sharp tongue had landed her in trouble more than once. If Mrs. Riley was to raise the rent now, Rose would be back where she was before her promotion.

"You're right, I should not have been so rude," Rose said. "Next Wednesday, I will be attending a charity dance at the Marlborough Rooms on Regent Street. I will be acting as a chaperone for the young lady I just mentioned. She is the niece of a friend."

"Would that be the *friend* you borrowed a book from?"

Rose sighed. Mother Finlay's dogged pursuit of this issue was beginning to wear on her. "Yes."

"'That man is a mere acquaintance. He was kind enough to loan me a book, that's all.'" Mother Finlay repeated almost verbatim Rose's remarks from their previous conversation about him.

Why was her mind so sharp on details like this when she couldn't remember simpler things, such as the name of the laundress who had taken her sheets for washing?

"Are you pursuing that man?" Mother Finlay demanded.

"Certainly not!"

"Well, then, is he pursuing you?" Her voice rose in righteous indignation before Rose could answer. "You must not allow it!"

"And why, pray tell, mustn't I?" Rose answered hotly.

"That man is nothing more than a devil, luring you with the pleasures of dances and liveried carriages and heaven knows what other fine things, so that you will break your marriage vows and dishonor Peter's memory."

This was the reason Rose disliked Dr. Purcell so intensely.

He was the one who had given Mother Finlay the outrageous idea about the sanctity of marriage lasting beyond the bounds of death. Rose simply couldn't believe this teaching to be true. It angered her that Mother Finlay should be gullible enough to accept it so completely.

Rose had been subjected to similar speeches from her mother-in-law countless times. She'd always borne them with what she considered remarkable restraint. Today, however, she was not going to suffer it. Her blood boiled at the remembrance of how Peter had done something far more reprehensible, breaking their marriage vows while they were both still very much alive. "Why are you so convinced that it's sinful for a widow to remarry? So far as I can see, Dr. Purcell does not hold the prevailing view on this subject. Widows and widowers remarry all the time."

"Just because it's done doesn't make it right. Why do you fight against the truth so vigorously? Especially now, when it just so happens you have a gentleman inviting you to dances? I warn you: there are men who find a certain allure in widows, knowing they may be easier to sway to give in to improper advances since they have known the sweet delights of love and are desperately lonely—"

"Stop!" Rose commanded, furious at hearing John disparaged so casually. He was a thousand times the man Peter had been. "You know nothing about this gentleman. He is an honorable man. His family is in a tight situation, and I have agreed to help. That's all."

"*That's all*," Mother Finlay echoed, rankling her once more over that phrase. "Will you promise me it will go no further?"

"No, I will not." Her own words amazed her, even as they came out of her mouth. "You may badger me to no end, but you will never convince me it's wrong for a widow to remarry."

"Impudent, faithless woman!" Mother Finlay took hold of Rose's hand—not to contemplate the mourning ring, as she often did, but to pull Rose closer. Her pale gray eyes fixed on Rose's face. "Did you ever really love my son?"

The question was hurled like an accusation. As though Rose was ever and always the person who fell short, the one without feelings, who didn't understand what was good for her.

Enraged, Rose broke free of the woman's hold and stood up. If Mother Finlay wanted an answer to her question, then by heaven she was going to get one.

"Once upon a time, I loved your son. With all my heart. I trusted that he loved me just as fully in return. But then he betrayed my trust in the most heinous way possible. He died before he could make it right—if indeed, he ever intended to. If I'm to be shackled with him for all eternity, then he'd better have the very best apology waiting on his lips the moment he sees me. And if groveling is allowed in heaven, so much the better!"

Leaving the stunned old woman behind her, Rose grabbed her things and stormed out. She didn't even bother to put on her coat and hat until she was out on the street, her heart racing.

Rose had never intended to blurt out the awful truth, and certainly not in such an ugly way. But that woman had finally pushed her to the brink.

Rose would pay for that little tirade, no doubt. One would think Rose had the upper hand. There was no formal connection between them. She could walk away, and prove she was as heartless as Mother Finlay implied. In truth, their relationship was an uneasy balancing act. Ultimately, Rose would probably have to be the one to make amends.

Not tonight, however. It would have to wait until both their heads had cooled.

CHAPTER
Twenty

"Are we finally done?" Pearl leaned heavily on John's arm as they left the office of their solicitor.

It had been a grueling afternoon for his sister. They'd had a final hearing with the judge of the chancery court, followed by an hour in their solicitor's chambers wrapping up the final details. He would guess it had been months since she'd been out of the house for such an extended period of time.

"We're on our way home now," John said, mostly to comfort her.

He led her to the curb where her carriage was waiting. John was glad that at least the day was sunny, despite the cold. That had helped keep Pearl from flagging. She was always happier in the sunshine, as though drawing strength from it.

Once they were in the carriage, she leaned back against the seat with a sigh of relief. John felt the same sentiment. He was glad to have the legal and financial issues surrounding Roger's estate settled at last. He would have preferred not to spend nearly a full day on this task when the charity ball was just two days away, but that couldn't be helped. When both this and the ball were behind him, he hoped his life could resume its normal routine.

John didn't think his sister was merely tired. He sensed an air of dejection in her slumped posture, as though they had lost their case. This was confirmed when she murmured, "What shall we do?"

"You've nothing to worry about," John assured her. "We got the greater part of what we were after. With careful oversight, you'll be able to live comfortably." John knew he would have to remain heavily involved in his sister's financial affairs, but those would be simpler now that they were done with the courts.

Pearl began to wring her hands. "I still don't understand—I thought Roger had set aside a larger amount for Sophie's dowry."

So that's what was troubling her. John should have realized that with two daughters nearing marriageable age, that would be foremost on her mind. "Roger had planned on providing a larger dowry. It was unavoidably reduced by unforeseen circumstances, including his untimely death. Had he lived, he would have been able to fund the dowries as he'd expected. Sophie's dowry will still be respectable—and adequate, I believe, for a good marriage."

"But will it be enough to make the *best* sort of marriage?" Pearl asked with dismay. "I had such high hopes for her."

"It won't be large enough to attract fortune hunters," John pointed out. "That's a good thing, surely? We want to find a man who cares for Sophie, not her money. She has quite enough good qualities to win a gentleman in her own right."

He thought he'd made a reasonable point, but Pearl only frowned. "I hope you're right. There is one tiny worry I have, though."

"What's that?"

"It's possible that the current, er, public understanding about Sophie's dowry is incorrect. I might have let slip the wrong information, which . . ." She stopped, looking embarrassed.

"Which is now gossip?" John suggested.

She nodded, giving him a worried look.

John could easily guess she was afraid of losing a suitor from the highest echelons. Someone like Sandy Deveaux, for example. John would be just as glad if that man turned his attentions elsewhere. Besides, if what Rose had said was true, Sophie was no longer as keen to make that connection. "If any gentleman wants to seriously court Sophie, we'll just have to set him straight on that point. I don't believe things are as dire as you fear."

Despite these exhortations, Pearl's anxious expression remained. "Do you think I made a mistake allowing Sophie to come out early?"

"I won't lie to you, Pearl. It might have been better to wait. But it's done now. Even so, there's no need for Sophie to rush into marriage. There's no reason why she can't enjoy the Season next spring, even if she's not officially a debutante. She was never going to be on the list to be presented at court. We're not important enough for that."

"I know all those things," Pearl said. "I still worry that I've allowed our affairs to get in such a muddle."

John was sorry to see Pearl's lofty dreams and expectations brought down to earth so soundly by today's events. At the same time, he was glad she had a better grasp on the reality of her financial situation. He just had to help her focus on how well off they were, especially compared to so many people who could not begin to afford the same luxuries his family enjoyed.

"You'll be happy to know I've done a thorough review of our roster of attendees for the charity ball. It includes a good number of eligible young bachelors who will find Sophie to be an attractive catch in all respects."

"Speaking of that ball, here's some good news I forgot to tell you earlier," Pearl said, brightening. "I received a note from Marjorie yesterday. She says Ellie is doing much better. Marjorie is bringing them all back to London, and she and Edward want to attend the charity ball."

"Wonderful," John said, albeit with more enthusiasm than he was feeling. He was thrilled to learn his little niece's health was improving, but he would have preferred to be free to execute his duties at the ball without the distraction of Marjorie's being there. She was bound to want to take up his time. And what would he do with Edward? "Edward is rather young for such an event, don't you think?"

"Marjorie thought he might be able to help the planning committee in some way. She says he's keen to be of use."

John frowned. "Yes, I imagine he's at loose ends now that he doesn't have proper schooling to fill his days."

"Don't be harsh on the lad," Pearl entreated. "Marjorie has been so happy to have him back. I think she missed him more than she'd let on. He does so look like his father, and he has his energy too. Surely you can help him find some useful work."

"We'll come up with something. Mrs. Finlay suggested he might do well in telegraphy. She even suggested I bring Edward to the post office so that he might try it out and get a taste of what's involved."

Pearl shot him an annoyed look. "You've been talking to Mrs. Finlay about Edward?"

"The subject came up. Do you object?"

"It seems we've brought her into so many of our family affairs. I don't feel entirely comfortable about that."

"There's nothing to be concerned about. We didn't discuss the topic in great detail. I simply mentioned Edward's situation because I thought she might have some insight about it. She has been a great help to us with Sophie, after all."

"Yes, about that." Pearl leaned forward, as if this topic had energized her. "Do you think it's necessary for Mrs. Finlay to attend the charity ball? Marjorie will be there to look after

Sophie. She and Edward will ride with her to the ball, so, you see, Mrs. Finlay's presence will be superfluous."

John would never describe Rose as superfluous. It seemed an insult even to think so. "I can't disinvite her, Pearl. That would be rude, not to mention unkind, especially since she was gracious enough to accept the request after what she endured at Lady Randolph's ball." He didn't add that Sophie was bound to fare better under Rose's oversight than Marjorie's. "I see no reason why they can't all go together."

"But the donation fee for her to attend—"

"I'll cover the donations for all their tickets." John refused to be talked out of this. "There are still plenty of advantages to having Mrs. Finlay there. For one thing, it will free up Marjorie to enjoy herself. She can mingle with her friends, perhaps even fill out her own dance card. She does love the dancing."

Marjorie was always pestering him to dance whenever they attended the same events. Personally, John would love to keep her busy so she wouldn't spend her time annoying him. "She can make new acquaintances with some of the gentlemen there. I'll ensure the introductions are made."

Pearl gaped at him in astonishment. "Are you speaking of introducing Marjorie to *single* gentlemen?"

"Why is that such an outlandish idea? She's been widowed for five years. There's no reason why she might not consider the idea of remarrying."

"I see." She crossed her arms in consternation, much like she used to do when they were having childhood squabbles. "Now you think it's all right for a widow to seek another husband."

"I never said it wasn't," John answered in surprise. Then he understood what she was getting at. "I merely told you not to try to pair *me* with Marjorie. You know all the reasons why. Don't ask me to explain it again."

"Yes, I understand. In fact, I understand quite a lot now."

John opened his mouth to ask what exactly she meant by that, but before he could, the carriage came to a halt. They had arrived at Pearl's home. In the ensuing bustle of getting Pearl inside, the moment was lost. It was probably just as well. It was a sore subject, and John had no desire to revisit it.

Dinner with the Shaws was just the medicine Rose needed. It brought back pleasant memories of the easy camaraderie she'd enjoyed with Alice and Emma during the years they'd lived together at the boardinghouse. The bonds of friendship they'd forged were still strong.

Rose hadn't had much time to get to know Alice's husband before the pair left on their long journey overseas. Tonight, she was getting a taste of his outgoing nature and sharp wit, always tempered with his charming Scottish accent. Best of all, it was clear to Rose that Alice was supremely happy. That was what mattered most.

With so many things to catch up on, they were far into the meal before Rose had been able to tell them about Lady Randolph's ball and the events that had led up to her going to it. By now she felt comfortable enough around Douglas that she did not mind including him in this conversation. In truth, he reminded her of John in several ways. They were both intelligent, self-made men with a hefty dose of common decency thrown in. That they had met already, however briefly, was an interesting coincidence as well.

"I don't think those ladies were sufficiently impressed that your cousin is married to an earl," Douglas observed, a hint of humor in his eyes. "Especially as he is a Scotsman."

"You would focus on that detail," Alice said, giving him a friendly poke in the ribs. "I think those women who maligned Rose were simply jealous of her."

Rose shook her head. "How on earth could they be jealous?"

"Because you are head and shoulders above them in all the ways that count. They sound petty and vain."

Rose grimaced. "I have to agree with you on that point."

"Or maybe it's something to do with your being a widow," Alice went on. "Do you remember in that spinster book where the author said that a widow has a greater draw on men than a single lady? It was phrased in such a humorous way, something about how a widow's allure is equal to twenty-five spinster power! And that a wise spinster knows that when a widow enters the game, the spinster may as well withdraw and leave the playing field to her."

Alice and Douglas laughed over these overblown observations, but Rose merely scoffed. "That lump of trouble belongs in the dust heap."

"You're probably right. I would put it there myself except it seems to have gone missing." She eyed Rose. "It's quite mystifying."

"Well, good riddance, I say." Rose still didn't want to reveal that she had it. She was going to make Emma sort out that mess.

"I find it ever so interesting you fell into this business of chaperoning," Alice mused. "I believe you're highly adept in the art of guiding young ladies, even if those society women didn't think so. You certainly did an excellent job with Emma."

"I'm glad I was able to help her. She was determined to find a husband and had no parents to help her navigate her way. You may be sure I thoroughly vetted the gentlemen vying for her hand."

"You did that with Douglas, too, in a way," Alice answered with a laugh. "If he'd walked into your post office and tried to send me any other telegram than the one he did, I have no doubt you would have set aside all business etiquette and roundly told him off."

"I didn't even realize what a close call it was," Douglas added.

He tugged at his collar in an exaggerated sign of relief. "Thank heavens I passed muster."

"So you see, Rose, it's obvious you have a penchant for helping others," Alice continued. "I believe there's a motherly streak in you."

Rose shifted in her seat at the use of the word *motherly*. "Stan, our young telegrapher, accused me of that recently too," she said, shaking her head. "Simply because he had a cold and I made him some tea."

"'Simply because . . .'" Alice repeated with a smile. "You know, sometimes I think we are more blind to our finer qualities than to our faults."

"Excellent insight as always, my dear," Douglas said.

The pair exchanged a smile that for some reason made Rose's heart ache. These two were on a good road, and there would be a baby soon to add to their joy. "There appears to be a motherly streak in you as well, Alice."

"I resisted the idea for years, as you know. It was only after I knew I was in love with Douglas that I could hear what my heart was telling me. And now, here I am." She placed a hand on her stomach and smiled.

Rose fought back tears as the memory of her own lost children brought a fresh round of pain. Even though Peter had been the worst sort of rat, Rose would have raised her children with fierce love and protection. She would have done anything to make their lives wonderful.

"Alice, shall I help you clear away?" Douglas said with extra bright cheerfulness. He seemed to have read her distress, even if he didn't know the source of it, and was working to change the mood. Rose was grateful for that.

"I'll help too," Rose offered.

After they'd moved the dishes to the kitchen, they settled into the parlor for coffee. Rose had not stopped thinking over what Alice had said. Perhaps she did harbor these urges to help young people. But when did her good intentions cross the line into meddling? And would Rose herself one day be worse off for her efforts? By the time they were all seated again, she'd made a decision.

"There's one other thing that happened on the night of the ball that I haven't told you about," Rose said. "Sophie and I were riding home, and even though I was furious about what she'd done, I still wanted to help her. I wanted to make her understand the dangers of giving one's heart away too soon, of trusting a man who had not proven himself worthy of that trust. I decided to use the experience of my own life as a cautionary tale."

There was a moment of silence. Then Alice asked tentatively, "Is this about your husband?"

"It is. I never spoke about him to you and Emma, even as dear as you two are to me. Yet for some reason I divulged everything to a misbehaving girl I barely knew."

Alice gave her a sympathetic smile. "Perhaps that simply means you're ready to tell the story."

"Perhaps." Rose couldn't entirely explain it. She'd revealed so much to Sophie in the heat of the moment. Despite John's assurances, there was always a possibility Sophie or Pearl would let the information slip—whether intentionally or on purpose. "I may as well tell you also, if you don't mind hearing it. If somehow these sordid details become public and ruin me, I wouldn't want my friends to be the last to know."

Alice's eyes opened wide. "With an introduction like that, you must tell us."

Rose shared with them what she'd told Sophie after the ball, broadening her account to add details about her family, her one grand Season, meeting Peter, and all that had happened afterward. She even included something she'd not told anyone before: by all accounts, Peter had been blind drunk on the night he'd died. He'd stumbled headlong into the street and fallen under the wheels of an oncoming carriage. Rose had always felt it would be degrading to admit that her husband's vice and stupidity had led to his demise. She thought if this embarrassing truth were known, it would make her widowhood somehow less honorable, and her along with it. But she had no fear that it would lower her in Alice's eyes. They knew each other too well by now.

Alice responded to her tale with all the compassion Rose had expected, offering her condolences. Douglas added a few words of sympathy and some deprecating remarks about Peter that Rose found immensely satisfying.

In the end, though, Rose held back the darkest and most painful facts—that she had suffered two miscarriages early in her marriage. She still couldn't bring herself to speak of them, to voice her agony aloud. And besides, how could she reveal such horrors to a friend who was eagerly anticipating her first child? One day they might discuss it, perhaps, but not now.

"What an extraordinary story," Alice said. "I understand now why visiting your mother-in-law has always been such a trial."

Rose nodded. "One day, she and I will have to finally reckon with all of this."

"I have no doubt it will be hard on you both, especially at first. But perhaps it will be better in the long run, even for her."

"I hope so," Rose replied glumly. However necessary it was, she was still dreading it. Their falling out hadn't done either of them any favors, unless it was to free up Rose's evenings. She couldn't help but feel guilty about it at times, but at least she knew Mrs. Riley had begun looking in on Mother Finlay regularly.

"How did Sophie react to everything you told her?" Alice asked. "Based on your earlier comment, you seem worried she might somehow use the information against you."

"That's always a possibility. I hope my fears are unfounded.

For the moment, I'm happy to report that Sophie seems to have taken my admonitions to heart. In fact, I've been invited to chaperone her to another ball."

"That's astounding!" Alice exclaimed gleefully. "I'm glad they were wise enough to understand what a boon you are to them. When and where is it to be?"

Rose filled them in on the details of the charity ball.

"I'm glad to hear Mr. Milburn will be at that dance, and that he will be so heavily involved," Alice said, nodding her approval. "Things are bound to go better—especially as you two have become such good friends. Do you suppose he knows how to dance?"

Douglas rolled his eyes. "He's in for it now, poor chap."

"You still haven't mastered the art?" Rose teased.

"Only when I'm dancing the waltz," Douglas replied. "And only with Alice. I hope for your sake that John Milburn is better at it than I."

His words irresistibly conjured up a picture in Rose's mind of her and John dancing. She didn't know whether he was a good dancer, but in the vision, he was as smooth and dashing as in any girl's best dreams. Rose quickly cleared her head of the vision before she began trying to imagine what it would feel like to have his arms around her as they waltzed.

"I haven't danced in ages, and I don't plan to start tomorrow. I'll be busy keeping a sharp eye on a young lady who still has a lot to learn."

"You never know what may happen," Alice insisted. "Especially if dancing is involved."

Rose didn't blame her friend for taking a romantic view of the situation, but she could not allow herself to contemplate going down such a road. She might find ways to harbor less bitterness about her past, but it wouldn't change her plans for the future.

CHAPTER

Twenty-One

On the afternoon of the ball, Marjorie had decided that Edward should go with John, rather than with her and Sophie, in order to help out. Although skeptical at first, John was pleasantly surprised that Edward had in fact been able to make himself useful.

He'd been primarily passing messages and information among the subcommittees overseeing the last-minute preparations in the various parts of the assembly rooms where the dance was being held. These rooms were spread out over a large area. There was a coat check and a greeting station near the main door, another great hall for socializing, the cavernous ballroom, and rooms for refreshments.

Finally, about thirty minutes before the official starting time, all was declared to be in readiness.

"Let's go sample that punch," John suggested to Edward. "I'm feeling parched, and once the people start arriving, there won't be a moment to spare for finding refreshments."

Edward readily agreed. "I wanted to try it earlier, but Mrs. McCall shooed me away. I don't think she'll do the same for you."

Sure enough, the plump matron who was in charge of the punch table was more than happy to offer a glass to each of them.

"I think she rather fancies you," Edward whispered after they'd moved to some chairs to sit and enjoy their beverages.

"She's the wife of Colonel McCall—the chief steward for this event," John reminded him with a smile.

Edward shrugged. "All the same. I think many women like you. You have a lot of charm, and it draws them to you."

John turned to look at him askance, wondering where in the world the boy got these ideas.

He grinned. "That's what Mother says."

"I see."

"Was my father like that too?"

Edward's earnest look as he asked the question raised a familiar pang of sorrow John had often felt for him. It pained him that Edward had lost his father so young. "He was very personable, that's for sure. Everybody liked him. He was very good at persuading people to take his side or do what he wanted. Our father once joked that Lionel could sweet-talk a miser out of his last farthing."

Edward smiled. John thought it likely the boy was picturing himself being like that someday. Maybe he would. He'd certainly returned from his trip to Ramsgate with a less surly attitude than he'd been displaying for months. Perhaps now that everybody had agreed he could stay in London, he was feeling less defensive.

"Mother said there is another lady accompanying them tonight."

"Mrs. Finlay. She helped us as a chaperone while your mother and Ellie were in Ramsgate."

Edward nodded. "Louisa wrote and told me all about it. She thinks Mrs. Finlay fancies you."

John raised his brows. "I beg your pardon?"

"And that you fancy her," Edward continued.

John shook his head. "I should have thought Louisa had more good sense than to run rampant with such theories."

"So it isn't true?"

No, of course not. John opened his mouth to say it, but nothing came out. His brain snagged on Louisa's assertion that Rose fancied him. The opinion of a fifteen-year-old—who despite her more sensible traits was as prone to romantic fantasies as her sister was—shouldn't make the least bit of difference to John. But somehow it did.

He stood up. "We'd better get back to the front entrance. Guests will be arriving soon."

Edward followed willingly. He didn't remark on the fact that John hadn't answered his question, but John was pretty sure the boy had noticed.

◦◦◦

Rose had been pleased to receive a note from Pearl saying she would send her carriage to pick up Rose and bring her to the Cochrane house before the ball. She thought this bit of kindness augured well, even if she suspected John had pressed the idea on his sister.

However, as Rose entered the carriage, she was surprised to discover that someone else was already inside. Light from a nearby streetlamp, as well as the lantern affixed near the driver's seat, softly illuminated the interior of the carriage. Rose saw immediately that the lady was unknown to her. She was quite striking, with dark hair, dark eyes, and a pale complexion. She wore a burgundy cape and hood over her gown that set off her features to great advantage.

The lady took a thorough review of Rose in one sweeping glance. Rose was glad she'd accepted Alice's loan of a fur-lined cape that she bought while in New York City, as well as a sapphire-studded comb for her hair.

"Good evening, Mrs. Finlay," the woman said as the carriage began to move. "My name is Marjorie Milburn. I'm John and Pearl's sister-in-law. I suppose they've mentioned me to you?"

"Yes, of course. How do you do?" This woman's chilly air of superiority, which she had amply established with a mere look and a few words, matched the impression Rose had formed from things Sophie and others had told her.

But why was she here? John had said Marjorie was out of town. That was the reason Rose was called upon to be here, after all.

"I just returned yesterday from Ramsgate, where I took my youngest child for some sea air," Marjorie explained. "She was doing poorly, but she is much better now."

"I'm glad to hear it."

"She is subject to these episodes, especially in the winter. Happily, she does recover fairly quickly. I am so glad to have returned in time to attend the ball. My oldest son, Edward, will be attending as well. He's just fifteen, but he's tall and mature for his age, so he'll have no trouble fitting in. He's already at the assembly rooms helping John. The boy truly looks up to him."

Rose nodded and murmured, "How nice." She gathered that nothing more was required of her. It was clear Marjorie planned to do most of the talking.

"I know you acted as chaperone for Sophie while I was out of town. We are all grateful to you. As Sophie's aunt, I have been the one to take on the oversight of her launch into society. Her mother is simply unable to do so, given her poor health."

"Yes, I know," Rose said. "I've been happy to help."

"It takes someone with skill and an understanding of how society works to secure the best possible match for her," Marjorie went on. "Now that I have returned, I will be taking on the role of Sophie's mentor once again. You will no longer need to concern yourself with this situation—although, as I said, we do thank you for rendering this service."

She was being sacked—from a position for which she was never hired! Had Marjorie come here to tell her she was not wanted at the ball? That was surely not the case, since the carriage was clearly on its way toward the Cochrane home. "In light of these facts, I'm surprised Mr. Milburn asked me to come out tonight."

"He didn't know I would be back in town," Marjorie replied. "Otherwise, he would not have invited you. Once he knew I'd returned, he considered telling you not to go, but I persuaded him it would be disrespectful to cancel at such a late date."

Marjorie was doing her best to portray herself as the nicer person, but Rose wasn't convinced. She didn't think John could be as callous as the woman implied. "How very kind of you."

"Think nothing of it. I was certain you'd be grateful for the opportunity to attend the event. John's club organizes this charity ball every year. It was headed for several years by my dear late husband." She paused, withdrawing a handkerchief to dab her eye. "You are a widow, too, I understand," she added, giving Rose a mournful look that was supposed to acknowledge this sad bond they shared.

"My husband died seven years ago," Rose said without a hint of emotion.

"For me, it's been five years. It seems like such a long time, and yet no time at all. Tell me, Mrs. Finlay, have you ever considered remarrying?"

"Never."

Marjorie seemed genuinely surprised by this response. "Truly? Well, I can understand that sentiment. I have felt it deeply myself. When Lionel died, I was sure I would never love again. And you know, having three young children, I felt at such a loss. Thank heavens I had John and Pearl to turn to. John has anchored us all, brought our two families together, and helped us through so many difficult hours."

261

"How fortunate for you." Rose's good manners kept her from wrinkling her nose at this theatrical speech.

Marjorie put her handkerchief away and glanced out the carriage window. "It appears we are nearly there." When she returned her gaze to Rose, all traces of a widow's melancholy and vulnerability were gone. "There is something else I'd like to share with you before we arrive. Just between you and me."

Rose dipped her chin in a display of diffidence. "As you wish."

"John has come to mean so much to me since Lionel died. They share many of the same admirable qualities. I suppose that's not surprising, since they were brothers. John and I have spent a lot of time together. He helped me sort out the financial affairs, and he even took on Lionel's business. It is thriving, which supports me and my children, whom John dearly loves. Since we are being honest, I'll tell you that he loves me too. And I love him."

Stunned, Rose could only sit speechless.

"We cannot let on to anyone about how we truly feel," Marjorie continued. "We can never marry, what with the laws being what they are. Such an act would make us outlaws and pariahs, and how could we ruin our family's reputation and our children's future? Therefore, we can only nurture our love in *private*." She gave a significant pause. "And we continue to pray that one day the laws will change."

Rose felt as though she'd had the wind knocked out of her. Why was Marjorie telling her this, just after she'd told Rose her interactions with the family would be finished after tonight?

The answer wasn't hard to deduce. She was worried Rose might be a competitor. She was warning Rose to stay away. Rose had always been aware of Pearl's distrust. Perhaps that had been for the same reason. John was involved in their lives more than most brothers would ordinarily be. He was a husband to them both, so to speak, in many of the duties he carried out for them.

Could this closeness have led to something more with Marjorie? Rose had heard of such things happening.

Yet somehow, Rose could not believe it. More to the point, she didn't want to believe it. After all that had happened with Peter, Rose had believed she could not be fooled by a man again. John had impressed her as being straightforward and honorable. He was so easy to like. Their times together when they had been able to talk about their own interests and not the troubles of his family had been pure pleasure. But then, John had purposely targeted two of Rose's favorite pastimes, with the book and the theater tickets. Rose reminded herself that if one was in the process of being fooled by someone, one didn't know it. How many times had she noticed John's easy charm and been reminded of Peter? John had agreed theirs was a friendship only. Could a man have a friendship with a woman while carrying on a romance with another? These questions and doubts made her queasy and heartsick.

The best thing she could do was, ironically, what this hateful woman was telling her to do—with one small twist. Tomorrow she would walk away from this entire family once and for all. But tonight, she would carry out her duties to the fullest. Sophie had specifically asked for her help. No matter what Marjorie might think about it, Rose was going to do all she could to keep Sandy Deveaux away from Sophie.

$$\backsim\!\infty\!\sim$$

John and several other stewards for this dance, including Colonel McCall, had been greeting guests at the door for nearly an hour. Their duties included checking people off a list of attendees, thanking them for their donations, and generally gathering information about the guests and what they were hoping to get out of the event. John was becoming perturbed that Rose and the others had not shown up yet. The number of guests mingling in the great hall was growing. John had garnered a list of prospective dance partners for Sophie, but she wouldn't be able to dance with any of them until she'd met them and got their names on her dance card. He wanted to ensure she had no time to spend with Deveaux, should he make an appearance tonight. His father's name was on the list as a donor, but Sandy often took his place at events like this.

Edward had spent most of his time in the coat-check area, making a show of helping out while in reality chatting with the three young ladies who were working there. They didn't seem to mind. Edward was a handsome lad. Perhaps he would turn out to be as appealing to ladies as his father had been.

"There's your party, I believe," Colonel McCall said.

Sure enough, Rose, Marjorie, and Sophie were entering the main door. John hadn't seen Marjorie since her return to town, but she wasn't the one who captivated his attention just now. He blinked in surprise when he saw Rose, who was resplendent in a fur-lined, hooded cape. An attendant helped the ladies remove their wraps, revealing Rose in a deep blue gown that looked as fine as anything John had seen tonight. Her hair was drawn up with a decorative comb that seemed to sparkle in the gaslight. This was so different from her simple workday attire, yet she wore it with ease. The entire effect was stunning.

While the other two ladies were checking their wraps, Sophie came over to John and gave him a peck on the cheek. "Good evening, Uncle. How is the ball progressing?"

"You nearly missed it," John said. "Don't blame me if there are no young men left to fill your dance card." He was trying to sound severe, but in reality he was still recovering from seeing Rose in such finery. How had she not been the toast of Lady Randolph's ball?

"We shall get right to it," Sophie said cheerily. "Where are the dance cards?"

"Here you are," said Edward, coming up to them and hand-ing her a dance card and a pencil. "I've got cards for Mother and Mrs. Finlay too."

"Thank you, Edward," Marjorie said proudly. "Do take one, Mrs. Finlay," she said when Rose shook her head at being offered a card. She plucked the card from Edward's grasp and forced it into Rose's hand. "You might change your mind later."

Rose frowned but kept the card. Although she had nodded a greeting at John, she said nothing to him now. She looked out of sorts. A carriage ride with Marjorie could easily bring that about, although he had the distinct impression she was angry with him as well. Even with a surly expression on her face, Rose was having the most alarming effect on him.

"I'd better get back to work," Edward said, and hurried back toward the coat-check girls.

"Good evening, John. I've missed you!" Marjorie gave him a kiss on the cheek as Sophie had done, but instead of pulling away, she lingered an extra moment with her cheek near his, filling his nose with the scent of her perfume. Then she drew back just enough to give him her most dazzling smile.

It was an ostentatious display that made John uncomfortable. He took a step back. "I'll walk with you all to the great hall and make some introductions."

"Sophie needn't be in too much of a hurry to fill her card," Marjorie said. "Unless a certain aristocrat has arrived?"

"He has not." John looked over at Sophie. Her lips soundlessly formed the word *help*. It was clear she hadn't found a way to tell Marjorie she wanted to distance herself from Deveaux.

"Perhaps you ought to wait here and be on the lookout for him, John?" Marjorie suggested. "I'll look after the introductions for Sophie. I know plenty of people here. There's Mrs. Montefiore waving at us now. Be sure to tell Mr. Deveaux we're standing along the east wall. That should make us easier to find in the crowd."

She didn't wait for an answer but took Sophie's hand and

sailed off in the direction of her friends. Sophie looked back at Rose and motioned her to stay with them. Rose complied, still frowning, and followed them without another glance at John.

He watched them go. More specifically, he watched Rose. The bodice of her gown made a modest V in the back, revealing a tantalizing portion of her neck and shoulders. He was exceedingly grateful that something had caused Sophie to invite her. He hoped Marjorie wouldn't make Rose regret coming.

About a quarter of an hour later, Sandy Deveaux made his entrance. He gave his name to Mr. Smith, the committee member at the door checking names. "I'm representing my father, the Earl of Ormond, this evening," Sandy told him.

Mr. Smith, who had the natural awe of the aristocracy found in many of the middle class, made an obsequious bow. "It was so very kind of His Lordship to make such a generous donation to our humble charity, sir. I trust you will have a pleasant evening."

John walked over to them. "Good evening, Mr. Deveaux. My name is John Milburn. I'm one of the stewards here this evening."

He waited for the recognition of his name to sink in. It didn't take long. Deveaux took a long moment to study John's face, as if sizing him up. There was a certain wariness in his expression that John found surprising. He couldn't think of anything to do but continue to return Deveaux's gaze in a friendly way. Sophie might no longer want to pursue the man, but it would probably be best for everyone not to antagonize him.

After another moment, Deveaux's wary look was replaced with a warm smile. "A pleasure to meet you. I believe I have met your sister-in-law, Mrs. Lionel Milburn? And of course, your charming niece, Miss Cochrane."

John dipped his chin. "They have told me they had the honor of making your acquaintance."

Whatever awkwardness John had sensed earlier had passed.

At ease and smiling, Deveaux rubbed his hands together with delight. "Are they here tonight?"

"They are."

"Excellent. I shall be sure to find them."

"They are somewhere along the west wall, I believe."

Deveaux sauntered into the crowd and was soon waylaid by a group of admirers. That would keep the man distracted for a while but not forever. John sighed as he watched Deveaux's interactions. The man was so confident and clearly pleased with himself. Every other guest would surely treat him with the same high opinion.

John had several things to wrap up here at the entrance, but as soon as he could, he would go in search of Sophie and the others. He was still worried about the tension between Marjorie and Rose. He needed to make sure it didn't erupt into something worse—especially since he knew the two ladies were here tonight with opposing goals.

CHAPTER

Twenty-Two

Marjorie was deep in conversation with two ladies whose names Rose hadn't bothered to remember when Sophie left her aunt's side and sidled over to Rose. "I need to visit the ladies' retiring room," she whispered. "Will you go with me?"

Despite her efforts, her request hadn't gone unnoticed by Marjorie. "I'll come along too," she said.

"I wouldn't dream of taking you from your friends," Sophie insisted. "It's just a problem with the hem of my petticoat. I'm sure Mrs. Finlay can help me fix it."

"All right, but don't be too long. The dancing will begin soon."

"Yes, ma'am." Sophie took Rose's hand and practically dragged her through the crowd until they were out of view of Marjorie and the others.

"Do you know where the retiring room is located?" Rose asked.

"I don't need to fix my hem. I just said that so we could get away. I thought I caught a glimpse of Sandy. I'm so nervous to face him again. Especially with Aunt Marjorie determined to push his attentions on me."

"I daresay she'd think differently if you told her what he'd done."

"No!" Sophie exclaimed. "You didn't tell Uncle John about it, did you?"

"You asked me not to, and I've kept my word."

"Thank heavens! Knowing my uncle, he'd challenge Sandy to a duel on the spot."

"I believe he would," Rose replied, remembering John's remark on that very subject.

She had been fighting so many mixed emotions all evening. Marjorie's words in the carriage were still stinging her ears and her heart, yet when she'd seen John tonight, her heart had started a battle in another direction. She couldn't square the two. Added to this was the worry over Sandy and how they might politely distance Sophie from him. Rose would rather have told him off to his face and revealed him publicly for the lothario he was.

"I have to fill my dance card before he sees me," Sophie said. "Aunt Marjorie has only allowed me to reserve half the dances, and none of the waltzes."

"Yes, I know." Rose had been forced to stand by and do nothing all evening while Marjorie had been directing everything. "Why haven't you told her you're no longer as interested in Sandy as you once were?"

"There wasn't time. She returned to London only yesterday. She was so busy settling everything at her home and preparing for this evening that she never stopped by." As Sophie spoke, she continued to send searching looks over the ballroom. "We need to see if Uncle John can help us. Perhaps we can find the retiring room, and then I'll stay there while you look for him."

"I'll do my best. I don't know if I'll be able to find him before the dancing begins."

Her concern was confirmed when the orchestra, which had been playing chamber music to supplement the mingling and conversation, now played a loud flourish to signal the beginning of the dancing.

"That's for the grand march," Sophie said. "I'm happy my aunt let me skip that one. It's so tedious. But I have to be ready for the next dance." She was scanning the crowd as she spoke, either in search of her uncle or in fear of seeing Sandy. Perhaps both. "There's Colonel McCall. I met him once at my aunt's home. He's a steward, so he can help us."

Colonel McCall was only too happy to fulfill Sophie's request. Before the grand march was done, he'd introduced Sophie to enough men to fill the first half of her card, including all the waltzes. He offered to do the same for Rose, who firmly declined.

They thanked him heartily and began working their way back to Marjorie. "My aunt will be put out with me, but I don't care," Sophie declared. "I'll just have to explain everything later and try to convince her it's for the best. I'll persuade Uncle John to dance with her. That will put her back in a good mood."

"Marjorie enjoys dancing with him?" Rose asked.

"Oh yes, I sometimes get the impression she's in love with him."

Sophie giggled, marking this comment as a jest. Nevertheless, it almost seemed to confirm Marjorie's words: *"We can only nurture our love in private."* It was a good thing Rose had not wasted any time hoping to dance with John herself. It would seem he already had a preferred partner.

Marjorie hurried up to them, followed by a shy-looking, gangly young man. Sophie was all smiles as the fellow led her to the dance floor, but Rose suspected this was primarily from happiness at having found a way to evade her aunt's plan—at least for now.

With the help of the steward who'd been appointed the dancing master, the couples grouped themselves in sets of four for the quadrille. Then the dance got underway.

As they watched the dancing, Marjorie sent a sideways look at Rose. "I presume you were able to repair Sophie's petticoat?"

"It's in fine shape now," Rose answered.

A moment later, she caught sight of Sandy. He stood on the other side of the room, watching the dancers. Rose actually saw the moment his gaze alighted on Sophie, who was still smiling, even though her partner was having trouble keeping up with the intricate dance steps.

Sandy's eyes were fixed on Sophie for a while. He watched with evident approval as she skillfully executed the dance patterns, weaving among the other couples, changing partners, and then returning to her own. Eventually, Sandy's gaze moved over all the dancers and finally to the people standing on Rose's side of the room. He clearly spotted Marjorie, because he began to move in their direction.

"There he is!" Marjorie said proudly as she became aware he was coming over to them. "I knew Sophie would be the girl he wanted to see most."

Was he worried about what kind of reception he'd receive after that disgusting trick he'd played on Sophie? Rose couldn't see any evidence of it. Sandy must have easily surmised that Sophie had kept quiet about it, since Marjorie was obviously encouraging him to approach them. She started fluttering her fan and beaming at him with all the subtlety of a debutante.

"Mrs. Milburn, how lovely to see you again," Sandy said, giving her a small bow. He took her hand and gave it a kiss. "Do you know, I have been searching for you and your charming niece all evening?"

"I'm so happy you found us," Marjorie burbled. "Sophie is dancing just over there."

"So I see, and quite beautifully too. I should like very much to have the opportunity to dance with her. Do you suppose she has any openings on her dance card?"

"Why, yes, I believe the next one is open. It's a waltz."

He gave a satisfied smile. "What luck!"

"I hate to interrupt," Rose said.

They both turned to look at her, as though surprised she was there. "Yes, what is it?" Marjorie asked with irritation.

"As we were returning from our little errand, it happened that Sophie ran across a group of gentlemen she'd met at a recent party. They quite pressed her to accept their requests to dance. Her card is full for the next six dances."

Marjorie received this information exactly as Sophie had predicted. "You might have persuaded her to not be so rash," she said through gritted teeth.

Sandy's reaction was the same. Stronger, even. Rose could see carefully banked anger in his eyes. He said with cutting frostiness, "I'm sorry, have we met?"

"You may have seen me at Lady Randolph's party," Rose answered. "I had the pleasure of escorting Miss Cochrane to that event."

He nodded. "I thought you looked familiar." He didn't bother to ask for her name. Effectively dismissing Rose like a servant, he turned back to Marjorie. "What a shame I was not able to find Miss Cochrane before those gentlemen did, but I shall bear the loss somehow." He was pretending to make a joke of it, but Rose caught the note of genuine displeasure in his voice.

Marjorie heard it too. "I'll talk to Sophie, and we'll get this straightened out. Perhaps you might look for her at the break? The first dance after that is a waltz, and I'll ensure she reserves it for you."

Sandy took a moment to consider this.

He must have decided Sophie was still worth pursuing, because he nodded. "I will look for her at the break. In the meantime, please excuse me. My thanks to you, madam."

"A pleasure, Mr. Deveaux," Marjorie said, sounding breathless, probably from relief.

After he was gone, Marjorie turned on Rose. "How could you allow Sophie to do that?" she hissed. "You know she was supposed to save the waltzes for Mr. Deveaux!"

"We didn't even know whether he was at the dance," Rose pointed out. "Besides, as you made clear to me earlier, it's no longer my place to direct her."

Marjorie's eyes narrowed. "I'll make sure Sophie knows it too. She answers only to me."

The quadrille ended. Sophie's partner escorted her back, thanked her profusely for the dance, then left to find his next partner.

"Thank heavens that dance is over," Sophie said. "I wasn't sure my toes were going to survive."

"Sophie, how could you reserve the next waltz for someone else?" Marjorie demanded. "You just missed the opportunity to dance with Mr. Deveaux!"

"Did I? Oh dear," Sophie said nonchalantly.

Marjorie took hold of the dance card on Sophie's wrist and turned it around to read it. "Good. The waltz after the break is open. Put Mr. Deveaux's name on it right now. He will find you beforehand. I expect you to be looking for him. Don't be foolish enough to pass up this opportunity."

"Yes, Aunt Marjorie, I will. But I've got to go—here's my next partner." She motioned toward a young man approaching them. "And here's Uncle John," she added. "Why don't you dance with him?"

John joined them in time to hear this suggestion. "I believe I'll sit this one out."

"Nonsense," Marjorie said. "As one of the stewards tonight, it's up to you to set a good example." She pulled him forward before he could object.

Rose watched, curious to discover what kind of dancer he

was. As she had imagined, he was a very good one. He led Marjorie faultlessly around the floor. They moved well together, which Rose took as evidence they'd danced together a lot. Both of them were so adept that they didn't seem to even think about what they were doing. That was a good thing since, at the moment, they were wholly absorbed in what seemed to be a heated discussion. As Rose watched the back-and-forth between them, she didn't have to guess what they were talking about. Marjorie's anger was evident. John's demeanor was cooler but just as serious.

This went on for a while, until John leaned in and whispered something in her ear. Almost immediately, Marjorie's expression softened into a smile. Rose realized she had been looking for a moment like this, some confirmation of the romantic link between them that Marjorie had described. She'd been half expecting, half dreading to see it. Here it was.

She turned away her gaze, unable to watch more. She focused instead on Sophie, who fortunately had a more proficient dance partner than she'd had for the quadrille. Sandy had found another partner for this waltz, but he cast his gaze often in Sophie's direction.

Rose sighed, giving in to discouragement. Their tactics had only delayed Sandy's attempts to get at Sophie, not prevented them. Rose didn't think Marjorie was going to let up unless someone gave her a clear understanding of the problem. Sophie had initially gotten herself into this complicated situation by not being completely honest with her family. Now it appeared that same tendency might prevent her from getting out.

However, a greater issue was troubling Rose. She had discovered a side to John that tainted everything else she knew about him. There wouldn't be any remedy for her disappointment over that.

"It was a mistake to bring that woman here tonight, John. Pearl and I tried to tell you she ought not to come, but you refused to listen to us." Marjorie's face was clouded with anger.

"Why, what's the problem?" John asked.

"Mrs. Finlay and Sophie snuck away on some pretext. By the time they'd returned, Sophie had filled her dance card with other names and nearly ruined her chances with Mr. Deveaux!"

John was glad to see his niece taking measures to avoid Deveaux. It appeared Rose was helping her with this, exactly as he'd hoped she would. Marjorie, however, was fuming at this development.

"Did you say Sophie *nearly* ruined her chances?" John asked.

"I saved the situation." Marjorie's eyes flashed with pride. "They will have the waltz after the break, despite that woman's efforts."

"What makes you think this was Mrs. Finlay's doing? Perhaps Sophie is no longer interested in Mr. Deveaux."

"Don't be ridiculous. She's positively enamored of him."

"Are you sure her feelings haven't changed during the weeks you've been away?"

Marjorie looked genuinely surprised. "Why would they?"

"It's not impossible. I think it's clear from her actions tonight that she does not wish to spend all her time with Deveaux."

"If that's true, it can only be because Mrs. Finlay has somehow poisoned her mind against him."

"To be honest, both Mrs. Finlay and I have reservations about Deveaux. He's known to be a rake. He might see Sophie as merely a temporary bit of fun and then move on to someone else."

"Yes, he's a ladies' man, but I have heard him say that he is at last looking to settle down. Tonight, he sought out Sophie directly. He was very upset that she practically rebuffed him. I believe he is serious about courting her."

"Even so, it can't hurt to be cautious."

"Do you think a man like that will wait around forever, regardless of how he feels? The insult could very well cool his attraction to her. And then we will have lost what may be the chance of a lifetime."

John thought that would not be the end of the world, but Marjorie continued on before he could reply.

"Furthermore, I do not share your good opinion of Mrs. Finlay. During the ride here, I gave her and Sophie specific instructions for this evening. And yet they deliberately disobeyed. I don't think it was Sophie's doing. I think Mrs. Finlay instigated it."

"Why would she do that?"

"Out of spite, of course! Perhaps she was thinking too well of herself after Lady Randolph's ball, especially after Sophie begged for her to come again. Perhaps she feels a sense of superiority in controlling a situation like this, thinking she knows what's best for our niece. The gall! But you know, childless widows can be like that. They crave what God has not given them, and so they grasp at other people's children."

"Stop right there, Marjorie," John commanded. "You will not speak so uncharitably about Mrs. Finlay. As a Christian woman, you ought to know better."

Marjorie gave a little humph and did not look the least bit chastened. "It matters not what I think of her. She'll be gone after this. I told her clearly that her services are no longer required."

"She's not a servant you can order around." John understood now why Rose had looked so angry when she'd arrived. Her hackles would have been raised at being treated like a scullery maid.

Marjorie gave him a defiant look. "Then what is she, exactly? And don't say she is a family friend because we barely know her and don't care to. I don't care in the least if her cousin is some Highland countess. What good has she made of that connection? She's a common clerk."

"She's *my* friend," John said vehemently.

"Don't allow her to poison your mind as well. Remember that we are your family. Everything was going perfectly well until she began meddling in our affairs."

When Marjorie went on the attack like this against anyone—and John had seen it before—her face took on a dark, ugly cast. It ruined an otherwise pretty face. Marjorie was only thirty-six years old, but at times like this she looked much older. Furthermore, their heated conversation was beginning to draw notice from those dancing nearest them.

John sent a bright smile at one lady, trying to appear completely at ease in order to assuage her concern. He drew Marjorie closer and whispered in her ear. "You might want to relax that frown, Marjorie. I'm telling you this out of kindness to you. Remember that we are on display to hundreds of people. Let's be sure to give our best appearance."

Marjorie softened against him. He didn't think this was entirely from his words, although his appeal to her vanity surely had some effect. More likely she was taking advantage of this opportunity to get closer to him, seeking physical contact. She did this often, especially when they danced. John did not try to pull away. He merely prayed that this would help calm her. She would never see reason otherwise. He had seen fear in her eyes, even as she was railing against Rose. He knew how Marjorie felt about him, and he knew there was little he could do about it. But he would always strive to do his best for her. She had truly loved his brother, of that he was sure. And she cherished her children.

"I always put our family first," John added soothingly. "You know that. We will all do our best for Sophie."

She sighed, taking obvious comfort from those words. She pulled back to look at him. "How is this?" she said, offering up a smile as an actor on a stage might do.

"Much better. Keep doing that."

Her smile became genuine. "You are a dear man, always putting up with my foibles, looking after me. Without you, my world would have unraveled completely."

John wasn't about to tell her that asking for Rose's help had been the best way he could think of to help Sophie. He believed Marjorie was misguided in her driving need to see the family rise in society. John could tolerate this to a point but not at the expense of the children.

Nor if it meant hurting the woman he cared about. "I'll have a chat with Mrs. Finlay," he said with cool authority, allowing Marjorie to draw her own conclusions about what he would say.

Twenty-Three

As soon as the waltz was over, John led Marjorie back to where Rose was standing. She was doing her best to appear as if she were so absorbed in watching Sophie that she hadn't even noticed their approach. John's only thought was that it was a crime for such a beautiful woman to be stoically standing alone, setting herself like a sentinel instead of properly enjoying the evening.

When she finally did meet his eye, it was with an impassive expression. There was no hint of what she might be feeling, whether angry, forlorn, or any other emotion. "Sophie has already met up with her next dance partner," she announced, indicating the girl's location with her fan. Sure enough, Sophie was just beginning the polka with a young man John didn't recognize.

"His uncle is a viscount," Marjorie said. "I was able to get us introductions earlier this evening."

"But is he rich?" Rose asked, affecting a wide-eyed earnestness that underscored her sarcasm.

Marjorie's only reply was a murderous stare.

"Mrs. Finlay, I wonder if I might have a word with you?" John said before Marjorie could get riled up again.

"Shall I come too?" Marjorie asked, seeming eager to be part of the setdown.

"I think you'd better stay here and keep an eye on Sophie. We wouldn't want to lose her again, would we?"

"Quite right," Marjorie agreed. "I'll keep a proper eye on her."

"She was never lost," Rose protested under her breath as John took gentle hold of her elbow and began to steer her away.

"I know that," John replied quietly.

Rose went along as John guided her through the crowd, although she was clearly bewildered. The evening was in full swing, and the guests were in high spirits. John and Rose were forced to stop a few times while he handled questions from another steward or responded to a greeting from someone he knew.

At last, they reached the room that had been John's goal. It was an office of sorts, although there was also a large table with a dozen chairs around it. The proprietor of these assembly rooms used the place to meet with potential clients. The room was locked, but John had the key tonight since they were storing their supplies for the charity ball here.

John let them in and turned on a small gas lamp, then closed and locked the door behind them.

Rose looked understandably alarmed. "John, what's this about?"

He liked that she had used his given name. Maybe it was a consequence of hearing Marjorie and Pearl refer to him that way, but John wanted to think it was for a different reason. He hoped she was growing in her regard for him. "I have to talk to you. It would be impossible out there, or anywhere else that I could think of. I hope you'll indulge me."

She eyed the closed door. "It looks like I don't have a choice."

John stepped away from the door, giving her clear access to it. He purposely left the key in the lock, so she could easily leave. "I'm asking you to stay," he said gently. "I have something important to say. I'd be honored if you would listen."

Upon hearing this entreaty, Rose must have realized this was not going to be a meeting to upbraid or belittle her, as Marjorie implied. He could see curiosity beginning to overcome her wariness. "All right."

"First and foremost, I must apologize to you for Marjorie's actions this evening. I told her she had no right to treat you disrespectfully or to imply in any way that you are not equals."

"Thank you."

Although she wasn't exactly smiling, it was the first friendly look he'd gotten from her all evening. John figured he was off to a good start. "I'm sorry I brought you into this mess of family affairs, not once but twice."

"I'm glad you did," Rose answered. "Sophie had good reason to seek help from someone who could shield her from that man. Marjorie isn't going to do it."

"Marjorie doesn't understand yet, although I did my best to get her to see reason. I believe she'll come around. In the meantime, Sophie is being very resourceful."

"Yes, it was her idea to sneak away and fill the dance card," Rose confirmed. "We didn't get it completely filled, though. There wasn't enough time."

"I wouldn't worry. Deveaux will claim a dance or two from her tonight, but that's as far as it goes. I'll ensure nothing else happens. Besides, Sophie herself doesn't want things to progress further."

Rose's mouth quirked. "I admire your confidence on that score. A girl her age can change her mind countless times in five minutes."

It was that small movement of her lips, unconsciously enticing, that set John's pulse thrumming. Together with her quick mind and strength of character, she was becoming irresistible to him. And her beauty too. It was subtle; perhaps not flashy or head-turning, but far better, because it was grounded in her own sense of worth. The gown she was wearing somehow accented all of it, as a setting for a fine gem.

His head was swimming, but even in that maelstrom of thoughts, he knew exactly what he wanted to say next—what he wanted to *do* next. But he didn't know if he had the courage to attempt it.

What had they been discussing before his thoughts had run away with him? Ah right. Sophie. He cleared his throat. "Sophie's opinions about things are variable, that is true. Her whims are legendary. I have no illusions that the months ahead as we navigate her establishment into adult society will be easy. I wish I was in a position to ask you to continue on, to keep doing what you're doing."

Rose lifted a brow. "I was under the impression you were eager to be rid of me."

"Why would you think that?" He knew the answer before he finished asking it. Marjorie had told her so. He shook his head. "You were misinformed."

"I see," Rose answered calmly. "Yet you are willing to allow Marjorie to have the final say regarding who attends to Sophie."

"The final decision will be her mother's. Yet I won't deny that Pearl depends heavily on Marjorie's knowledge in these matters. I am merely Sophie's uncle." He gave her an apologetic smile. "Our family setup is more complex than most."

"So I understand." She drew herself up and looked coolly at him. "In fact, I had not fully understood the nature of your relationship with Marjorie until tonight. You might have been more forthcoming with me about this, but I fully sympathize with your plight, and I respect your wish to keep it private. What happens in your family is your own personal affair. It's not my place to judge, and I won't."

John nearly got lost trying to follow Rose's implications. Then it all clicked into place with such terrible clarity that he was stunned speechless.

"And, in any case, it matters not to me," Rose went on. Although she spoke calmly, her voice cracked a little. "Since I've been sacked from this job, I may as well collect my things and look for a cab home."

"Rose, wait!" John finally found his voice, although Rose's hand was on the doorknob by the time he did.

She paused but did not turn around.

"Rose," he said again, fervently, "I beg you to hear me out. It's not what you think."

She turned to face him. "Just how is it, then?"

"Marjorie likes to think that I am in love with her. She feeds that fantasy in her mind. I think it's because I'm Lionel's brother. She desperately misses him. She longs for a husband, a protector. She transfers those longings to me. But I don't believe it's genuine love. I certainly am not in love with her. There are some lines that simply cannot be crossed. Even if there were no impediments at all, I could never love her. I've always been very clear with her on that subject. But sometimes people won't hear what they don't want to hear."

He paused, waiting for her response. He thought he could see her battling with herself to believe him, but something still held her back. He stretched out his hands in silent beseeching, praying for her to accept the truth of what he was saying.

She took a deep breath. "John Milburn, I am asking you to be completely and utterly and uncompromisingly honest with me."

She appeared to be trembling a little. This was so very important to her, as though she were staking her life on it. He knew why. She'd been devastated by a man's lies before. But he sensed she was trying to overcome that, to believe that this time was different.

This glimpse of a tiny crack in her armor gave John hope. "Every word is absolutely true." He took a tentative step toward her, afraid she might still bolt from the room. But she remained where she was, searching his eyes to find confirmation there. "Here is something else that is true. The woman I love is standing in this very room."

There. He'd said it. The words were out, never to be retrieved, but he had no wish to. He was glad to voice the feelings that had been growing and taking root in his soul, along with the certainty that this woman was in his life to stay.

John reached out and gently stroked her cheek. Her gaze dropped, but she leaned into his touch. He wished he could find a way to erase the pain she'd been through. He didn't know how to do that. All he knew to do was kiss her. Slowly, with deliberate care, he bent his head toward hers. She raised her lips to meet his. In that moment, he finally understood why a man would be willing to set aside an unfettered life and risk any number of troubles to pursue a woman, capture her heart, and hold on to her forever.

⌒⊙⌒

Rose was hardly able to believe she was again in a man's arms, willingly returning his kisses. The years since Peter's great betrayal seemed to stretch out behind her like a vast desert, parched and empty, and now here was water. Wonderful, refreshing, glorious water, hydrating her soul.

She ought not to accept his declaration of love so easily, and yet she did, clinging to it as she did to him. She had been thirsting for this, although she had tried to deny it. His arm came around her waist, and this, too, fed a deep need within her.

Just a little longer, she thought, as one delicious kiss led to another. *Just a little longer . . .*

When he finally broke away, it was to softly nuzzle her, placing his cheek next to hers, still holding her gently, a thumb sending tremors of delight through her as he caressed her neck. "Oh, Rose." It came out as a satisfied sigh. "I've wanted to do that for ages."

"Have you?" She could barely speak, breathless as she was with pleasure.

He drew back just enough to meet her gaze. "Haven't you?"

"Perhaps. I don't know." Even now, Rose found it hard to say the truth aloud.

"I'm just glad you want to kiss me now," he murmured, and pressed his lips to hers once more.

It was wonderful. And a wonder. Desires long buried arose and poured forth in the kisses that she returned with equal fervor.

In time, John's kisses moved down to her neck, causing more exquisite sensations. Rose heard the music from the dance, faintly audible through the door behind her. Her eyes fluttered open, and she surveyed the dimly lit room. She began to realize that the past was echoing. This was how it had been the first time Peter had kissed her.

"John," she said, gently pushing him away, "we have to stop."

He reluctantly complied, although as he stepped back, he took hold of both her hands and kissed them instead. "I want to marry you, Rose Finlay, if you'll have me."

Rose gasped.

John gave a little laugh, ardor burning in his eyes as he looked at her. "I'm surprised too! I never thought I'd propose marriage to any woman. But I'm sincere. Will you marry me?"

Rose extracted her hands, hugging herself as the heat from their embrace cooled. She reminded herself that the experience of pleasure was no sign she was on the right path. She'd made that mistake before. "No, John."

His surprise turned to pained confusion. "Do you love me, Rose?"

She turned her gaze away. "I'm feeling quite a lot of things right now. But feelings cannot be trusted. They will come and go, hot and cold, changeable as the wind."

"Perhaps not, if they stem from true love. Can you dismiss them so easily?"

He looked desperate to reach out for her again, but to her relief, he refrained. She might not have the strength to refuse.

"I can't get married again, John. I couldn't face it. I made my decision long ago. I have other plans for my life now, and they don't involve marriage."

"I assure you, I had no plans for it either. I've seen the heartache and troubles that can result from it. I live with them every day, as I help my family with their struggles. It has often led me to think, why should I desire to entangle myself even more?"

"Exactly."

"But I've changed my mind. Surely marriage can be a joy and not a burden."

"Stop talking about marriage!" Rose cried. "I can't abandon my independence. I suffered dearly for it last time. Subject to a man's cruel whims—"

"I'm not interested in having a meek lamb that I can order about," John insisted. "I love you precisely because you know your own mind. From the beginning, I've sought your viewpoints on many things. I want you by my *side*." He put special emphasis on the word. "We approach life together."

It was tempting to believe him. He probably meant every word. That was precisely why she loved him. But as she considered these things, a greater fear arose. She supposed it had been quietly at the back of her mind all along, a powerful reason why she'd resisted falling in love with him. Mixed with the loss of her autonomy, it would be too much to endure.

"You travel constantly. If I married you, I would be left alone for weeks on end, wondering what you are doing. And with *whom*."

"You think I would be unfaithful to you?" John looked as though she'd just physically slapped him. "How could you even imagine such a thing?"

"I'm sorry. You'd be right to hate me for suggesting you'd be so base. I know you have no intention of it now, but things happen, temptations arise. . . ."

"I have no intention of doing it now or ever! It's a good thing Peter Finlay is dead, or I'd kill him myself for what he did to you."

His fierce words, shocking as they were, touched a deep chord within her. But Rose's wounds ran deeper. "I know it's an unreasonable fear, but there it is. I cannot escape it." She placed her hands against her temples, although it was her heart that was in greater pain. Fear had overwhelmed her desires. "I beg of you—please, let it be."

The room fell silent except for the strains of a waltz playing dimly in her ear.

"I should not have tried to rush you," John said at last. He spoke quietly, his face now stricken with remorse. "I've only hurt you, and I apologize."

Rose lowered her hands, feeling exhausted more than anything. "I think it would be best if I leave. No one will mind. Marjorie will be ecstatic. She'll assume you sent me away."

"*I'll* mind very much if you go." John gave a resigned sigh. "But I can see why you feel it's necessary."

As they walked out of the room, Rose felt she was leaving something irreplaceable behind. She would not allow herself to regret it. Regrets could easily lie in any direction. Her life had been destroyed once; she would not risk it happening again.

John insisted on accompanying her to the door to help her find a cab. "I'll give the driver an extra tip to wait until you are safely inside your home," he told her.

Why was he acting so amiable and not sulking like a spurned lover? Perhaps some part of him was relieved to remain free, despite his professions of love. Whatever the reason, Rose was grateful for his kindness.

Edward was at the coat-check area. "Are you leaving already, Mrs. Finlay?" he asked as one of the attendants went in search of Rose's cape. To Rose's surprise, he seemed disappointed. Maybe his mother hadn't had time to turn his opinion against her.

"Yes, I . . ." Rose's voice faltered as she tried to come up with an excuse. Then she realized she didn't need one. She had a real reason, and stating it strengthened her resolve. "I can't stay late. I have an early day tomorrow."

Edward nodded eagerly. "I know you work at the post office, and I had been hoping to talk to you about it. Uncle John told me you'd offered to show me how the telegraph machine works and perhaps let me try it out. I'd love to have a look at it. Might I come by soon?"

John looked embarrassed that his nephew had bounded up with this request, even though Edward could have no idea of what had just happened. "That might not be possible after all, Edward. Mrs. Finlay is very busy."

He seemed as disappointed to be saying those words as Edward looked upon hearing them. Seeing them together, side by side, it was easy to discern the family resemblance. Rose remembered John's description of how Edward was anxious to get on in the world. She guessed that ambition and a willingness to work were shared traits of the Milburn men.

Even though so many things had changed since Rose had made her offer, she thought it would be unkind to the boy not to make good on it. "I'd be happy to have you come by. Perhaps early next week?"

"Thank you!" Edward grinned.

"You are very kind, Mrs. Finlay," John said. The way he looked at her brought back in a rush all the feelings Rose had been fighting to suppress.

She did all she could to present an untroubled appearance

as John led her out to a cab. It helped that Edward insisted on coming out, too, and waved at her cheerfully as the cab drove away. It saved Rose from the possibility of changing her mind, of surrendering her heart to John in spite of her better sense.

During the ride home, Rose cried like a foolish woman, telling herself over and over again that she had made the right decision.

⁓◌⁓

John went back to that private room for several minutes before returning to the festivities. He needed time to gather his thoughts and his wits. He'd bared his heart to Rose, and she had turned him down. There remained a barrier around her heart. It had been built, brick by brick, by the pain caused to her by another man. It was not going to be easily surmounted. He consoled himself with the belief that there must be a way, and that he would find it. Surely no woman could return his kisses as she had if she didn't care for him. Just thinking about it now brought a fresh round of longing, one that was hard to set aside.

He reminded himself there was nothing more he could do about it tonight. He had other responsibilities that he could not shirk. Finally, he pushed himself to leave the room and rejoin the fray.

He found Marjorie in the refreshments room. By now, the first half of the dancing was over.

"Where in the world have you been?" Marjorie demanded. "And where is Mrs. Finlay?"

"I had some business to attend to. Mrs. Finlay has gone home. We all felt it was best."

Marjorie smiled in triumph. "I'm sure it is."

"Where is Sophie?"

"She's over there, enjoying a bit of punch and conversation

with Mr. Deveaux. They are getting along swimmingly. I've decided Sophie must have been merely pretending her disinterest in him, knowing how much a man prefers to be the pursuer. It was a bold stroke, for she has entirely won him over, as you can see."

Yes, John could see. Sophie was in full flirtation mode. Deveaux was giving Sophie his undivided attention, as if there were no other women in the room. It would appear all of John's actions had led to the worst possible results. He had acted too rashly and scared Rose away, and meanwhile, Deveaux had made his move.

But John was not going to give in to despair. He'd never yet given up the belief that God was always with him, no matter the circumstances. Somehow, he'd find a way out of both predicaments. Sophie wasn't lost just yet, and Edward, bless him, had unwittingly provided him with the opportunity to see Rose again.

CHAPTER
Twenty-Four

The following days were very full, as Mr. Gordon had begun training Rose to take on the manager's role. Rose worked hard to keep her mind occupied with this work. It helped her push away the second thoughts and the agitated sorrow that came with them.

It was only when John came through the door on Monday that Rose's resolutions were tested. Seeing him walk up to the counter brought back irresistible memories of the other times he'd done the same. She missed their discussions over tea and gingerbread, feeling their loss afresh every time she walked by the tea shop.

Today, however, John was here on a different errand. Edward was with him, eager for the telegraphy demonstration. Surprisingly, Sophie had come along as well.

"Have we come at a good time?" John asked.

"We're not overly busy at the moment. However, we need to limit the visit to fifteen minutes, so the telegrapher does not get behind on his tasks."

She led them all to the recessed area behind the counter where the telegraph machine was located. Stan saw them coming and stood up. The moment he laid eyes on Sophie, he stood a little straighter and smoothed back his hair. Sophie seemed amused by this and favored him with an appreciative smile.

Rose introduced the family to Stan. "Mr. Reese is a first-class telegraph operator," Rose informed them. "He's been with us for about a year."

"I worked at a post office in Hackney for four years before that," Stan said. "I like it here much better." He seemed to be looking directly at Sophie as he added that last bit. "Are you interested in telegraphy, too, Miss Cochrane?"

"Goodness no," she exclaimed. "I came along because my sister is having a piano lesson today, and I was desperate to get out of the house."

Everyone laughed, but Rose wondered if Sophie might have come for another reason. Her surmising seemed correct when Sophie pulled her aside for a private conversation once Stan, Edward, and John were deep in conversation about telegraphy.

"I was sorry you had to leave the ball early," Sophie said. "Aunt Marjorie told me you had been let go, but I knew that was preposterous."

"Why do you say that?" Rose asked.

"It's obvious, isn't it? You were there as our friend. How could Mama have even hired you when you already work here?" She motioned around the post office. "Besides, Edward said the way you left was not at all like someone being thrown out on their ear."

"That's true," Rose conceded. "However, it is also true that your mother and aunt are not likely to invite me back any-more."

"I know, and I'm sorry for that," Sophie said. "They are a little bit jealous of you, I think."

"Jealous?"

Sophie nodded. "They are very protective of Uncle John, if

you haven't noticed. We've had so many upheavals over these past few years. They are fearful of any more changes."

"That's very perceptive of you."

"I wish you could have stayed at the ball."

"Did you have trouble with Sandy after I'd gone?" This had been worrying Rose.

"Not at all. Aunt Marjorie urged me to spend time with him, and I'm glad I did. Sandy apologized so eloquently for what had happened. Everything really had been a big mix-up. He was sure his parents had been planning to stay in town until after the charity ball. His father is a supporter of that charity and attends the ball every year. Once Sandy explained everything to me, he apologized for being too forward. He's so taken with me that he couldn't help himself!" She beamed with womanly vanity. This was followed by a dreamy sigh, as though a man forcing himself on a woman was somehow romantic. "So you see, we've quite made up. Isn't that wonderful?"

Rose could only stare at her in disbelief. Sandy had worked himself back into Sophie's good graces in record time. Then again, a man could easily get a woman to capitulate, if she was willing. Hadn't Rose herself been surprisingly willing to accept John's advances, despite having firsthand knowledge of how much heartache it could cause in the end? "Please, Sophie, just remember to use caution. You are very lucky there was no real harm done. You can't have any more mix-ups, or you might be ruined."

"I will be careful," Sophie assured her. "My aunt praised me for the way I handled Sandy at the ball, making him wait. She said it's good to leave a gentleman just a little bit uncertain as to his prospects. Even someone like Sandy. Perhaps especially so!"

"We'd best be getting back to the others," Rose said. She no longer had the stomach to discuss Sophie's amours. She had done her best, but the girl was still too wrapped up in her dreams to see reason.

They returned to the telegraph area. Edward was enthused at what he'd seen, and he'd written down information Stan gave him on how to apply to the telegraph school.

"Thank you for this," John said to Rose. "Who knows if this will pan out, but it won't hurt to pursue it a little further." Seeing that Edward and Sophie were still talking to Stan, he added softly, "I suppose she told you about Deveaux?"

"Yes. I'm worried for her, John."

"So am I. I will do my best to keep watch over her. I also remember the advice you gave me, that ultimately Sophie herself must make the choice to do the right thing. That's what we all must do in the end, isn't it?"

"Yes." It felt bittersweet, looking at him now. Rose knew she could be passionately and forever in love with this man if she allowed herself to be.

John said quietly, "Rose, I just want to tell you how much I . . ."

He paused, watching her face, perhaps looking for an opening to broach that tender, dangerous subject again.

Rose gave a tiny shake of her head, silently begging him to go no further.

He seemed to accept this, replying to her movement with a nod of acquiescence. He changed his stance and began again, this time speaking as though to any friendly acquaintance. "I just wanted to say that if you should ever want to borrow another book from my library, you have only to ask."

The words, beautiful and kind with just a tint of wry humor, actually made Rose feel light-headed. She looked into his eyes, as though holding to an anchor, until she felt sure her legs were still supporting her. "Thank you."

After they'd left the building, Rose watched as the three of them walked down the street, Sophie in the middle with one arm holding to each of the men. John laughed at something Edward said, and they all smiled at each other. The scene was so charming that Rose felt a pang of envy. But there was no time for gawking out of windows. She turned away and got back to work.

⚬◦⚬

The next day, Rose was minding the service counter while the other clerk was on her lunch break. She'd had a string of customers and hadn't noticed until she'd finished with the last one and had a moment to look around that a man had been watching her.

Sandy Deveaux was standing by the windows. His eyes met hers, and she could easily guess he'd been studying her while she'd been helping the customers.

Seeing she was now free, he sauntered toward her. He looked her over critically. "I knew I'd seen you before, someplace other than at Lady Randolph's party. How long have you been working here?"

He asked the question in such a commanding way that Rose automatically replied. "Eight years." She ought to have told him it was none of his business.

"How odd that I must have sent telegrams and bought stamps from you so many times, yet I didn't recognize you in another setting." He gave a little chuckle, as though amused with himself at his poor powers of observation. "In my defense, you did look quite different."

"Are you here to send a telegram, sir?" Rose asked in a businesslike tone.

He shrugged off her question. "I find myself wondering why you should have turned up as a chaperone for Miss Cochrane."

"With all due respect, sir, my private affairs are—"

"Private," he finished for her. "So are mine, as it happens. That's why I believe I'll go elsewhere with my business. For now." He gave her a hard, withering look. "Good afternoon, madam." He turned and walked out.

Stan came over to Rose. "What was that about?"

"Nothing to be concerned over," Rose said, but she had a terrible feeling that wasn't quite true.

~⌒⌒~

Rose did her best to put the disturbing encounter with Sandy out of her mind. His abrupt departure had left her dreading that something bad would come from that meeting. When two days passed without incident, she decided it was foolish to keep worrying about it.

The next afternoon, however, Mr. Gordon returned from a meeting at the main post office looking very unhappy. He called Rose into his office and shut the door.

When they were seated, he took a moment to clean his glasses and resettle them on his nose. Rose couldn't recall ever seeing him look this uncomfortable. He cleared his throat before speaking. "Mrs. Finlay, I've just spent an hour in the assistant superintendent's office. I received a troubling report. There was a complaint lodged against you recently. It has come to light that you have been sharing the confidential information of our clients with individuals outside the post office."

"That's not true!" Rose shot back.

He held up his hands. "I confess I had a difficult time believing it. I've always believed you to be above reproach in the way you carry out your duties. We handle a lot of sensitive information here, especially over the wires. Our clients include important men of business, as well as gentlemen and ladies of rank."

"I have never shared confidential information," Rose insisted. "Not to anyone."

"Based on your good reputation, I would have been glad to reject this accusation out of hand. Circumstances, however, will not allow me to do so. This complaint is from a certain highly placed gentleman who I am not at liberty to name."

"You don't need to," Rose muttered.

Mr. Gordon leaned over his desk. "You knew right away to whom I am referring? To anyone investigating this matter, that might imply some measure of guilt."

"I know who it is because I have had certain dealings with him outside of business."

"Dealings of a personal nature? That would seem to explain why this complaint alleges you have used confidential information for personal gain." He shook his head in disappointment.

"Don't believe it!" She did not want to lose Mr. Gordon's good opinion. It was one of the few she cared about. "He has no proof!"

He held up a hand again. "Please remain calm. This is not a court of law."

"I wish it were—then I might be able to face my accusers. We could lay out all the facts and prove that I am innocent of this charge."

"I understand your desire for justice. However, at the Royal Mail we must do things more circumspectly. I'm not in a position to prove or disprove the facts under dispute. I'm sorry to say, it wouldn't matter anyway. When we are dealing with a person of such high rank, there is only one choice, and that is to address their concerns until they are satisfied."

"You can't be sacking me!" Rose could barely suppress a rush of panic.

He readjusted his glasses and looked at her kindly. "No, not at this time."

Rose exhaled in relief.

Mr. Gordon cleared his throat again. "However, a compromise must be made. This personage conducts a lot of business at this branch. In order for him to feel confident that his correspondence is being securely guarded, we must ask you to move to another post office. There is an opening for a clerk at the Great Suffolk Street office in Southwark."

"Southwark?" Rose said, aghast. The industrial area south of the Thames, with its warehouses lining the river, was a far cry from Piccadilly.

Mr. Gordon kept speaking as though he did not notice her distress. "They need a good clerk who is accurate at the till and understands the parcel post system."

"But I'm set to be the manager here!"

He gave a long sigh. "Yes, that is unfortunate. I'm going to have to put off my retirement and train the clerk coming over from Bayswater. His current manager feels he would be up to the job."

The past two days, Rose had been growing confident that everything would be all right, while in truth, plans had already been set in motion to remove her. All because of Sandy Deveaux—and the whole lot of lords and ladies who destroyed people's lives on a whim without the tiniest scruple. She was powerless against such people, and she was growing to bitterly resent it.

"I'm very sorry," Mr. Gordon said. "I did my best for you. I knew it would be a travesty to let you go after you had given us years of stellar service. I'm aware it would be a severe hardship, too, to lose a position in this way, leaving under a cloud, so to speak. These were very hard decisions to make."

Rose believed he'd done what he could, but this was still a bitter pill to swallow. "I will always be grateful to you, sir. I appreciate that for all these years you've been willing to advocate for me."

She stood up, wanting to leave while she could still retain her composure.

"There is one more thing," Mr. Gordon said. He handed her a piece of paper. "Here is the information regarding your new assignment. Your supervisor will be Mr. Pettit. We have agreed that the reasons for your transfer will remain entirely confidential, so that you may get on better with your colleagues."

Rose went to her own tiny office and sat for several minutes, trying to come to terms with what had just happened. To be reduced to a mere clerk, after how hard she had worked! Anger and sorrow welled up in equal measure. Multiplying these troubles was the fact that Mrs. Riley had informed her just yesterday that her rent would be going up. The enmity between Rose and her mother-in-law was still festering, unresolved. Mother Finlay resolutely refused to speak with her. Mrs. Riley was acting as a liaison of sorts, but there was never a doubt whose side she was on.

The only "good" thing to come from this situation, if one could describe it that way, was that she was still employed. And thanks to the intervention of Mr. Gordon, there was no black mark next to her name. There was no reason why she could not eventually rise to being a manager somewhere else. It wasn't the first time she'd had to start over.

She arranged the papers and files as best she could, so that whoever followed her might have an easier time. Sandy and all the rest of his ilk could malign and belittle her as much as they chose, but Rose would never be anything less than professional.

Later, she told Stan what had happened. She felt he deserved a proper explanation for why she was leaving. Mr. Gordon would likely give the rest of the staff some vague reason that provided no real details. As the principal telegrapher here, Stan was familiar with Sandy Deveaux and knew what kind of man he was.

Stan reacted with the same indignation Rose was feeling. "It's ridiculous to think you would go blabbing someone else's business!" he exclaimed. "What's more, it's criminal to move you now. I mean no disrespect to Mr. Gordon, but you were poised to be the best manager we've had."

"It's kind of you to say so."

"I mean it." He gave her a grin. "Mr. Gordon never brought out tea or looked out so well for our messenger boys, did he?"

Rose was grateful for the little lift to her spirits. "I suppose not."

"Why do you think Mr. Deveaux is spreading these lies about you?"

"Do you remember Miss Sophie Cochrane, the young lady who came with her cousin to see the telegraph machine?"

"I certainly do," Stan said, clutching his heart with a grin. "I told Edward Milburn he was welcome to come and chat with me anytime—especially if she accompanied him."

Rose couldn't help but smile at this. She wished Sophie would consider men who were younger and more principled than Sandy Deveaux. Unfortunately, she'd been raised to seek men of wealth or rank, and preferably both, and that's just what she was doing. "Mr. Deveaux is currently among the active suitors for her hand."

"That lets me out, then. Not that someone like me could ever be in the running. Even so, I can't help but think she'd be better off with anyone but him."

"I agree, and I worry he might mislead her about his intentions."

"I hope he doesn't do anything to hurt her. Since you are friends with the family, do you think he decided to get you out of the way since you are privy to some of his correspondence?"

"I believe that's exactly what happened."

Stan let out a low whistle. "What a dirty dog."

"I couldn't agree more," Rose said.

It was hard, walking away from that post office for the last time. Rose had thought this would be her permanent workplace. She ought to have known that nothing in life can ever be permanent. She glanced into the window of the tea shop as she passed. The table where she'd first sat with John was empty. That seemed fitting, somehow.

Rose kept on, despite the miserable, murky fog that had settled on the city. She decided to start saving money now by walking home rather than going by omnibus. Cabs were definitely out. She was going to have to invest in good shoe leather from now on.

CHAPTER

Twenty-Five

John was beginning to regret coming to Marjorie's house for dinner. The whole family was gathered here, although Marjorie had just sent Ellie off with the nursery maid to prepare for bed. Even Pearl had found enough strength to come out tonight.

It wasn't that John didn't want to spend time with them. He'd been especially glad to see little Ellie, who was indeed looking stronger after her trip to the seaside. What was irking him was that as they sat in the parlor before dinner, the conversation had turned to a sensational robbery that had occurred at a post office in London's diamond district.

"The newspapers are calling it the crime of the century!" Edward held up the newspaper he was reading. "Listen to this: 'The clever thieves had a masterful plan. They turned off the tap at the gas meter just before closing time. They strolled into the panicked crowd under cover of darkness, slipped behind the counter, and stole the bag with the registered mail.' It was just hanging on a peg! And the value of the booty was eighty thousand pounds! There were diamonds, sapphires, emeralds—"

"That's enough for now, Edward," John said. "I don't think there's a person left in England who doesn't know all about it."

John had been traveling for the past week, and he'd heard the robbery spoken of everywhere. Every mention of the Royal Mail only highlighted in John's mind the way Rose was continually in his thoughts. He'd been thinking over their last conversation at the post office and wishing there was something he could have said or done to make her want to see him again. He knew he had to find a way to help her cross the chasm of fear that kept her from even considering the idea of marrying again. He had to prove she could trust him.

"It seems the staff there were shockingly lax," Louisa observed. "Imagine leaving thousands of pounds of fine gems so unprotected. Do you suppose all the post offices are so careless with their registered mail? I wonder what Mrs. Finlay would have to say about it. Isn't she a manager?"

"I was thinking the same thing," Edward said, as eager as Louisa to carry on with the subject despite John's admonition. "I was going to ask her about it when I went to the post office yesterday."

"Why did you go there?" Marjorie asked crossly. "We want nothing more to do with that woman. It's bad enough that you went there once already."

John and Edward had not told Marjorie about their visit to the post office until after the fact, knowing what her reaction would be. She had indeed been very angry—not that Edward was interested in telegraphy, but because they had spent time with Rose. Marjorie was still holding a grudge over what had happened at the charity ball.

John had smoothed over the situation by emphasizing that the telegraphy angle would be a good way to introduce Edward to business. He'd explained how telegraphy was one of the few viable opportunities open to someone his age. He'd emphasized how it could be a training ground and a stepping-stone for incorporating Edward into his company. It was something they could build on as he got older and John began to train him in the other aspects of the business. It had been hard at first for John, and even Marjorie, to accept that Edward was not going to advance to university. Now, spurred by his discussions with Rose, John was beginning to believe other options could be just as advantageous for the boy.

"I went there because Stan had offered to loan me his training manual and a practice set for tapping out Morse code," Edward said. "He's an excellent chap."

"What did Mrs. Finlay have to say about the robbery?" Louisa asked.

"She wasn't there. Stan said she'd been transferred to a different post office."

"She moved?" John interjected with surprise. "Where did she go?"

"Great Suffolk Street. Stan said it's in Southwark, not too far from the railway station."

John had been to Southwark on business at some of the warehouses and machine shops. The area wasn't nearly as pleasant as where Rose had been working. "Why on earth would she transfer down there?"

"Stan implied that it wasn't her choice. He said he couldn't give me any more information, but I got the impression she'd been forced out."

"Oh dear!"

This comment came from Sophie. She'd been glancing through a ladies' magazine and barely paying attention to the conversation. Now she looked up with a dismayed expression.

John thought he read guilt there as well. He began to get an inkling of what might have happened to Rose. "Sophie, did you by any chance talk with Mr. Deveaux about Mrs. Finlay?"

"Yes, but only because he brought it up. He said he'd walked into the post office and was surprised to recognize the person working there as the lady who'd been with me at the charity ball. He asked me how she'd come to be involved with our family. I told him she was a friend of yours, and we'd asked her to be my chaperone for a few events."

"I hope you told him that woman is no longer connected with us in any way," Marjorie put in sharply.

"Marjorie, please," John said, still trying to follow the thread of an idea. "Sophie, did you tell Mr. Deveaux about any of the conversations you'd had with Rose, specifically as regarded him?"

"Not at all!" Despite this strong denial, Sophie looked more confused than certain. "That is, I might have said she'd warned me to be cautious in my dealings with gentlemen who wish to court me."

"Did he seem angry at this?"

"I don't think so. He did ask me a few more questions, but finally he seemed to laugh it off."

"It's good for us that he did," Marjorie said. "Just look at how well they are getting along."

"Do you really think a marriage proposal could be imminent?" Pearl said. She'd been sitting quietly for much of their time together, but this subject had roused her.

Her question must have referred to some previous conversation between the two of them. "I told you it was merely my private opinion," Marjorie said, looking uncomfortable, as though she'd been caught spreading rumors. "But I won't deny all the signs look positive."

"They certainly do!" Sophie said with a breathless joy that seemed to have wiped away any thoughts or concerns about Rose.

John allowed the subject to drop and was glad no one else showed a desire to return to it, but that didn't mean he'd stopped thinking about Rose's situation.

After dinner, Sophie surprised him when she found a moment to come up to him privately and say, "I can't believe Sandy is connected with Mrs. Finlay leaving the Piccadilly post office. I'd feel terrible if it was somehow my fault. Aunt Marjorie blames her for trying to chase away Sandy, but in fact, she helped bring us together."

John didn't take any comfort from that remark. He still didn't trust the man, and he had a feeling Rose's transfer had something to do with him. She worked at Deveaux's primary post office, after all. He might very well have wanted to get her as far away from his affairs as possible. Moving her from the vibrant heart of the city to the grimy wharves and smokestacks south of the river would be just the way to do it.

"Please don't tell Aunt Marjorie I told you this," Sophie added. "I hope all may soon be forgiven and forgotten, but we know how hard it is to change her opinion when she's made up her mind on something."

"You may be certain I won't bring up the subject of Mrs. Finlay with her again," John said. He couldn't think of anything he was less inclined to do.

There was only one way to sort this out. He had to talk to Rose and find out what was going on.

Rose's first week at the Southwark post office had been grueling. It was just as busy as the Piccadilly office, but the pace felt more hectic because of the poorly trained staff.

Being reduced to a mere clerk had been difficult too. Rose was unused to being the recipient of orders barked out by a harried manager. She could see Mr. Pettit did not have the overall management well in hand. Any suggestions she tried to offer had been rebuffed, with both the workers and her new manager finding ways to remind her she was merely the new person here. Despite Mr. Gordon's assurance that the reason for Rose's transfer would be kept confidential, she could sense a general mistrust of her among the workers. She knew from the first hour that she was going to have to work hard to prove herself.

"I'm just not sure I have the energy for it," Rose admitted to her cousin Abby, as the two of them enjoyed a meal together at a little tavern near the estate in Sussex where Abby worked.

After the miserable week she'd endured, Rose had been over-joyed when Abby had invited her to come out and spend Sunday afternoon with her. The windows of the tavern had been thrown open, for the day was surprisingly mild. The clear air provided a respite after the smoke and fog of London.

Best of all, she'd been able to finally share her troubles with her cousin. She didn't hesitate to speak frankly of all that had transpired over the past weeks. Abby was ten years older than Rose. The two had not spent much time together in childhood, but the age gap seemed negligible now. They had grown espe-cially close in the years after Rose's disastrous marriage. Abby was often able to offer her wisdom and advice, much as an older sister might have done.

"It must be difficult to start over again at the bottom," Abby said. "Perhaps things will get better there with time as they get to know you. It sounds like you'll have to gain their trust. I've no doubt you will, for your excellent qualities cannot help but manifest themselves."

Rose gave her a grateful smile. "You always look on the bright side."

It was true. Abby's placid demeanor often felt like a balm when troubles arose. Her ability to remain calm in even the most trying circumstances probably explained why she'd been so successful as the head cook at Lord Ormond's country home.

Abby's expression grew serious. "Even though I believe you

will ultimately find your way at the new place, I must say I'm still quite put out by the way Sandy treated you. It was unconscionable."

"You assume he has a conscience," Rose remarked dryly.

"On the contrary, I'm well aware he does not." Abby shook her head. "When I came here at age fifteen to work as a scullery maid, he was a child. I watched him grow up, saw as he began to develop more and more unsavory traits. He became aware early on that his older brother would be taking on all the responsibilities of the earldom, and he must have decided this gave him license to become a libertine."

"Is it true his father is pressuring him to get married?" Rose asked.

"Oh yes, His Lordship has been actively seeking out suitable prospects. By suitable, I mean wealthy, primarily. The gossip belowstairs is that Sandy's profligate ways are putting stress on the family's finances."

Rose thought back to Sandy's telegram to the duchess before Lady Randolph's party: *"Pursuing another prospect. Everyone profits."*

"What can you tell me about the Duchess of Sunderland?" Rose asked. "I heard someone at Lady Randolph's party describe the duchess and Sandy as 'particular friends.'"

"Ah." Abby sent a look around the tavern, then lowered her voice. "It seems those two have been carrying on an affair. They've been doing their best to keep it secret. Somehow Lord Ormond caught wind of it. Maybe he heard quiet rumors passed along by those who know them well. We only know about it in the servants' hall because there was a frightful row between him and Sandy. His Lordship threatened all sorts of consequences if this should become public knowledge. That's why he's been badgering Sandy to get married. He thinks that will solve the problem."

"If that's true, would there be any reason the duchess would want to help Sandy find a wife?" Rose had not divulged Sandy's telegram to anyone, but its contents still troubled her.

"I'm sure she knows things cannot continue on as they are. They are both under pressure to maintain appearances, but the duchess has the most to lose if a scandal should erupt." Abby took a moment to give the question some thought. "If I were Sandy, I might try to find a wife who not only has a large dowry but is easily pliable to my wishes. Then I could continue to carry on with the duchess on the side. If I were the duchess, I would agree to this too, if only to keep up those all-important appearances." She gave a shiver of distaste. "I feel dirty putting myself into their ways of thinking for even one minute. If my guesses are correct, their actions would go against all common decency—especially when it comes to marriage, not to mention how one should treat other people."

"They certainly would," Rose agreed. Sandy had added many problems to her life, but he might well succeed in ruining Sophie's. That was far worse.

"I'm so glad I'll be leaving their world behind soon," Abby added.

Rose stared at her in surprise. "I beg your pardon?"

Abby gave her a happy smile. "I'm getting married, Rose. In the spring."

"How did that happen?" Rose asked, almost too astounded to speak.

"It's happened over time. I met Gerald Binghamton over a year ago at the local fair. I suppose I didn't think much of it at the time, but he began to write to me, asking to see me again. I agreed, thinking it would be nice to have a friend nearby who wasn't in any way involved with the Ormond house. He's a solicitor—can you believe it?"

Abby's branch of the family had been fairly prosperous at one time. But when her mother was still a child, her grandparents had been swindled out of their money—first by a man who had tricked them into making a disastrous investment, and then by the lawyers they'd hired to fight him. In the end, they'd lost everything and struggled with debt for the rest of their lives.

Seeing Rose's horrified expression, Abby laughed. "Not everyone in the legal profession is terrible. Gerald truly wants to help people. His clients are local townspeople—shopkeepers and the like. They benefit from his services."

"But why now? You take such pride in your work. You've even prepared a feast for the Prince of Wales!"

"I shall consider that my crowning achievement—if I may make such a terrible pun! But after twenty-five years, it's time for a change. I've dedicated my life to that family, but I can't work there forever. Now I can spend the rest of my life with a good man, knowing my future is provided for."

Rose was happy for her cousin, but she knew Abby's marriage would change the nature of their relationship, just as it had with Alice and Emma. "It seems everyone I love has been getting married," she murmured.

"A little romance can be a fine thing when it's between two good people who are right for each other. I've been content with my life all these years, but falling in love with Gerald has changed my outlook."

"This was what you were referring to in your letter, wasn't it, when you talked about the seasons turning rapidly?"

Abby nodded. "It appears the same is happening for you."

"Too rapidly, in my case," Rose said ruefully, thinking of how she'd lost all she'd worked for, seemingly in a heartbeat.

"Change does not always have to be for the worse. Not even in your case. With change might come a new vantage point or new opportunities." Abby reached out to give Rose's hand a squeeze. "I could see you wanted to center this conversation on other things, and I've been obliging you. But I believe there is something important left to discuss: your future with John Milburn."

Rose shook her head. "I'm not going to marry him."

"Not even after the way you so resolutely stood up to Mrs. Finlay on the subject?"

"It does appear ironic, I suppose," Rose conceded. "But just because I disagree with her on principle doesn't mean I'm ready to leap into marriage."

"I understand your hesitation after all you went through with Peter. But maybe this is your chance to finally leave those old sorrows behind and move on."

"I'll be moving on, but not in that direction. It's just too big of a leap for me."

Abby crossed her arms and pretended to give Rose a skeptical look. "I can't recall too many times over the years when I've heard you declaring that something was too hard."

"I'm always ready to strive for what I believe is right. But in this case, I just can't settle my heart on it. For one thing, it would look like I'm coming to him because I can no longer support myself."

"So it's pride that's fueling your decision?"

Rose didn't even blink at this admonishment. The need to stand on her own two feet was too deeply embedded within her.

"Perhaps it isn't really pride but fear," Abby said. "Perhaps those two things are linked. The reasons you gave me for turning him down all seem rooted in fear."

"I'm well aware of the problem, however it's labeled." Rose added miserably, "How does one ever get past that?"

"You might think it's impossible. But is it? Perhaps not, if you seek God's help. The Scripture says, 'perfect love casteth out fear: because fear hath torment.'"

Rose had definitely been experiencing the torment her fears had caused. She had not sought God's help. Abby had touched a tender spot, one Rose wasn't ready to explore.

"It seems clear to me that you love John, and yet you're not *allowing* yourself to love him." Abby smiled at this apparent contradiction. "If that makes any sense."

"It does," Rose admitted, remembering how she'd thought the same thing herself.

"With all you've told me, it seems John loves you just as deeply. So the problem must not be insurmountable."

Rose would never dismiss her cousin's guidance out of hand. Abby had sustained Rose through her worst trials over these past years with her steadiness, wisdom, and kindness. She was immovable in her faith and her belief that things could work out for the best. But Rose still had questions.

"Abby, there are so many complications. There are the problems with his family, and if Sandy should by some miracle truly want to marry Sophie, what then? Would I be his in-law?"

Just saying that aloud made both of them gasp. It was truly impossible to conceive of such a thing.

"These are hard questions," Abby agreed. "I still believe that if you proceed with the willingness to find the answers, you will."

As she rode the train home, Rose continued to turn over in her mind the things Abby had said. Her cousin always had a way of leaving her with a spark of hope, even in the darkest times. Rose didn't know when or how or even if she would find the answers she sought. But she decided she would look for them nonetheless.

CHAPTER
Twenty-Six

A couple of days after her visit with Abby, Rose was busy at work when she was startled to see Stan Reese coming through the door. He rushed up to the counter, where Rose was waiting on another woman. "Mrs. Finlay! I've got to speak to you. It's very important—it may be an emergency!"

The lady Rose had been waiting on eyed Stan with annoyance. "Wait your turn, young man."

Rose finished up with her as soon as she could, while Stan bounced nervously from toe to toe. Ignoring the glares from the other clerks, she stepped outside with Stan. She immediately started shivering, for the day was foggy and cold. "What's the emergency?"

"A telegram came through this morning for Sandy Deveaux. I think it was from Miss Cochrane."

"Stan, you can't be telling me this!" Much as she was intrigued, she couldn't allow Stan to risk his job.

"I've seen them together outside of work. I can tell you that much, right? They were at the tea shop twice last week and then again yesterday afternoon. I watched them through the window, but I made sure they didn't see me. They were looking very cozy together, if you know what I mean. And then, this morning, the telegram—"

"Stan!" Rose stopped him again, torn between what was right and what she desperately wanted to know. She could see Stan struggling with this too, trying to decide what to say.

His eyes widened, as though the answer had come to him. "Mrs. Finlay, would you by any chance like to go to Victoria Station today? Perhaps for luncheon? There's a restaurant in the terminal, and I understand it's very good."

Heavens! It was worse than she had imagined. "Wait here. I'll get my things."

She hurried inside to collect her coat and reticule. "It's a family emergency," she explained to one of the clerks. She didn't have time to try to explain herself to Mr. Pettit before she dashed back out the door.

⁘

"Stan Reese, is that you?" John was surprised to see the young telegrapher standing outside the Southwark post office.

"Good morning, sir. I came to see Mrs. Finlay. She—"

Rose burst out the door at that moment. "John! Oh, thank heavens you're here. We're just on our way to Victoria Station. You've got to come with us!" She looked up at him breathlessly. The icy cold was already tingeing her cheeks pink.

"What's this about?" John looked uneasily between the two of them.

It didn't take long for them to explain, even though they had to use tortured and roundabout language to do it. A vision of Sophie running off with Deveaux awoke a fierce anger in John that he hadn't known he possessed. It was fed by the need to protect his niece at all costs.

They began walking toward the cab rank on the corner. "Stan, return to work," John directed. "We're not going to put your employment in jeopardy."

Stan objected vigorously, but by the time they'd reached the cabs, John had prevailed. He gave Stan money for his fare, then helped Rose into a cab.

They asked the driver to hurry. He was doing his best to oblige, despite the fog. It swirled around them, stinging their faces as the cab sped forward. Rose didn't seem to mind getting closer to John for warmth, her arm touching his. He was fully aware of this contact, even if Rose seemed too absorbed in the current crisis to notice. It felt natural to have her by his side.

"You arrived just at the right moment," Rose said. "If Sandy and Sophie are indeed at the railway station, I don't know how Stan and I would have been able to stop them."

"I know you would have given it your best effort," John said with feeling. "As will I." He looked out at the city street moving past them in a blur, his anxiety rising. "What is Deveaux's game? To elope? Or simply to run away with her and ruin her?"

"I think I can guess the answer to that question. There was a day when he got Sophie alone in a house and attempted to seduce her."

"What? When did this happen?"

"Before the charity ball." Rose quickly described the incident. "That was the real reason Sophie was trying to avoid him. She had seen what Sandy is capable of. She begged me to keep it a secret. I agreed because at the time I thought it was best for the family to keep this under wraps. Sophie knew how you'd react if you found out what happened."

"Yes," John spat out, his anger increasing. He jammed a fist into his palm. That was going to be Deveaux's face if John found him with Sophie.

"I've discovered the limits of my secret-keeping abilities

today," Rose said ruefully. "And I allowed Stan to break confidentiality rules, although we're trying to pretend he didn't."

"Do you regret it, if we can help Sophie? Where is the moral high ground?"

"It's shrouded in fog, as surely as we are."

"We see through a glass, darkly." It was strange to be reminded of a Bible verse while anger and murderous intent were making his blood hot. *God, help me*, he prayed. He surely needed the help to get through this situation.

"I feel remorse but not regret, if that makes any sense," Rose said.

She shivered as another blast of cold air hit them. John wanted nothing more than to put his arm around her, to offer comfort as well as warmth. He settled for wrapping his arm through hers, patting her gloved hand with his own. What if Rose lost her position over this incident? John's anger surged again. Somehow, he would find a way to make that right as well.

When the cab pulled into the busy railway yard, John was ready. He leapt down and turned to help Rose. She took hold of his hand and jumped down nimbly, her face set with grim determination. John overpaid the driver, not waiting for change. He and Rose rushed into the terminal.

They paused inside the door, confronted by a daunting scene. There were hundreds of people milling about. If Sophie and Deveaux were here, how were they going to find them? He tried to scan the crowd for familiar faces, but it was a sea of bonnets and top hats. "Do we have any idea of their destination?" John asked. "That might at least help us narrow down which track."

"No," Rose answered with dismay. "Stan mentioned the restaurant, but I think he made up that part in his effort not to tell me what he was telling me."

John looked up at the face of a giant clock, which seemed to be taunting him with a reminder that time was of the essence.

It was all he could do not to rush off in the first direction that struck him.

"They must be headed south or east, if they're leaving from this station," Rose mused. She stared at the large board that listed destinations and departure times. "I have an idea. Last time, Sandy lured Sophie to his father's house in town. What if today, they're going to his house in the country? Then they'd want the train to Crawley. It leaves from track three."

"Do you think they are really going to see his parents this time?" That possibility was at least better than outright seduction. John felt a vague flicker of hope.

"No," Rose answered confidently. "The earl and countess have left the country to escape the bad weather. They are in Nice."

"How do you know that?"

She turned to look at him. "Because my cousin Abby is the head cook at their estate."

John stared at her in shock. Here was another piece of information she had never told him. She was very good at keeping secrets, whatever she might think. No wonder she'd known so much about Deveaux and had taken such an interest in Sophie's situation. Her knowledge must be deeper than anything she'd picked up from his telegrams.

All these realizations coursed through his mind in a moment of time. He took hold of Rose's arm, and they began pressing their way through the crowd.

The waiting area by track three was even more compressed than the main hall had been. It was evident the boarding would begin soon. Mercifully, the gates were not yet open. If the couple had been on the train, there would have been no hope of finding them.

John spotted them first. His eye was drawn to Sophie's hat, a pink one that was one of her favorites. She was seated on a bench next to Deveaux, who was holding her hand, leaning in to speak with her, and she was smiling as she listened. The pair looked as intimate as a married couple, and this alone brought John's rage to full boil.

He strode over to them. "What's going on here? Deveaux, how dare you take advantage of my niece like this!"

Sophie shrieked in surprise. "Uncle John!"

Deveaux stood up, looking maddeningly unruffled. "It won't do to make a scene, and I advise you not to."

"This is what I think of your advice," John roared, tearing off his right glove. He landed a solid fist on the man's jaw before either of them had time to blink.

❦

Sandy was out cold on the ground. John stood over him like a victor in battle, staring down everyone in the crowd now encircling the scene, warning them all to stay back.

Sophie had risen from the bench, overcome with panic. "Is he dead? Somebody help him!" She began tugging at John's arm. "How could you do this? It's not what you think!"

Rose took hold of her, forcefully detaching her from her uncle and pulling her away. "It's exactly what he thinks, Sophie," she said fiercely, trying to still the girl's movements. "Be quiet and listen to reason."

"But . . . Sandy!" She pointed down at the prone man, her face contorted with horror.

He was in bad shape, his face already darkening and swelling from John's punch. But Rose could see his mouth was open, taking in air, even as he lay unconscious. "Hush!" she ordered, holding Sophie tightly. "He's not dead."

John's command of the scene had kept any onlookers from advancing, but Rose could see two policemen and a station official pushing their way through the gathering crowd.

John saw them too. "Rose, will you take Sophie home? We've got to get her away from this."

It was more of an order than a request, but Rose was fully willing to comply. Rose had no idea how John intended to deal with the police. There wasn't time to ask. She pulled Sophie away, despite the girl's continuing protestations, and steered her toward the main entrance. To keep the girl moving, Rose kept reiterating that this was for the best and that she'd explain everything once they were outside.

By the time they reached the station yard, Sophie's hysteria had calmed, although she was crying. Rose quickly got them into a cab.

"You told Uncle John about the time I went to the earl's townhouse, didn't you?" Sophie accused. "Even after I explained to you that it was an honest mistake! That's how he got the wrong idea about what we were doing today."

"When a young woman boards a train with a known philanderer, the obvious conclusion is always the accurate one," Rose said. "You have to understand that Sandy has no intention of ever marrying you."

"He was taking me to meet his parents! We were only going to be gone for the day."

"His parents are not in Sussex, Sophie. They are in France."

"I don't believe you!" She began to fidget, tugging at her gloves and pulling her cape tighter. "How could you possibly know? Perhaps Aunt Marjorie was right when she said you're always trying to butt in and ruin things."

When Rose had raced off after Sophie, she had no idea what she'd expected the girl's response to be, but this belligerent ingratitude wasn't it. Sophie was desperate to cling to her dreams, despite the evidence they were collapsing around her. But Rose couldn't excuse it. She had her own serious troubles to face.

Today she had risked her professional reputation and, most probably, her livelihood. She would probably have to beg to keep her position, to save whatever remained of all she had worked for. The problems of the pampered girl sitting next to her seemed very small in comparison.

"Perhaps I was wrong about everything," Rose said. She spoke calmly, having no desire to quarrel with the girl but rather looking for a way to get through to her. "But perhaps you ought to spend a moment considering what would have happened if I'm right."

Sophie didn't reply, but Rose could almost hear the girl's thoughts as she struggled against Rose's words, not wanting to believe the awful truth.

Neither of them spoke again until the cab had reached Sophie's house. Rose instructed the driver to wait. She walked Sophie up the steps and pressed firmly on the bell. Sophie began to look fearful. "What are you going to tell Mama?" she asked Rose, as the butler opened the door for them.

"I'm not going in," Rose said. "This is a family matter. You must decide for yourself what to tell your mother. I advise you to be completely honest with her."

Sophie gave her a look of distress, as though silently beseeching her to stay. It was almost enough to make Rose change her mind. But she truly felt it was better to leave now.

"Sophie, I've done all I can for you. It's time for you to learn how to take responsibility for your actions, including how to deal with the results. Your best course is to tell your mother everything. Leave nothing out. It will be hard to do, but you will be better off for it." She stepped back, motioning the girl inside.

Rose waited until Sophie was in the house and the door was firmly shut before returning to the cab. It was going to take the last bit of money in her pocket to return to Southwark, but she had to get there as soon as possible to have any hope of keeping her position.

During the ride, Rose could well imagine what was unfolding in the Cochrane household. They would have a tough time of it, but Rose thought it was likely they would recover, especially with John's help. For all the men in the world like Sandy and Peter, there were men like John. His actions had been the model of selflessness today. Rose had seen the ferocity with which he fought for those he loved. It made her love him all the more and regret that she'd ever spent a moment thinking such a man would ever be tempted toward infidelity.

If she could relive that moment when John had proposed to her, would she decide differently? It was tempting to think so. But the answer was not that simple. There were still so many things at stake.

It was much more difficult to guess what might be happening at the railway station. Rose had been able to pull Sophie from the dangerous situation, but John was still in the thick of it. What legal penalties might he face or, worse, what retribution from the powerful Ormond family? For the first time in longer than she could remember, Rose found herself praying.

CHAPTER
Twenty-Seven

John, there you are at last!" Marjorie met him at the front door and practically dragged him into the parlor.

Even Pearl was on her feet. She threw her arms around his neck, clinging to him. "Thank heavens you're safe! We were worried sick. Is Mr. Deveaux all right? Sophie thought you might have killed him! We thought you'd been arrested! Then what would we have done? Everything would have been lost!" There was genuine terror in her voice.

John gently disengaged her grip. "I'm here now, as you see. Mr. Deveaux is very much alive."

"Thank heavens!" Sophie exclaimed.

She was seated on the sofa, looking rumpled and her face tearstained. John was thankful that was the worst she'd suffered.

"Where is Mrs. Finlay?" he asked. He had expected her to be here too. Now that he thought back on it, he realized he hadn't specifically told her so. There hadn't been time.

"She said she couldn't stay and that this was a family matter," Sophie answered.

"Good riddance," Marjorie put in. "She's caused us enough harm."

"Such as saving your niece from disgrace?" John had just passed the most disagreeable afternoon of his life, and he was too worn out to mince words.

"They were going to visit his parents!" Marjorie insisted. "It was highly unusual, I'll grant you, but it needn't have been the catastrophe you've made it to be."

"His parents are currently in France," John said flatly.

"Are you saying Mr. Deveaux intended nothing more than a fling with Sophie?" Pearl asked in horror.

"No!" Sophie protested dolefully. She was clinging to her hopes to the last, it seemed.

"Surely that can't be true!" Marjorie exclaimed.

As John surveyed the three of them, the anger he'd been feeling all day finally cooled. He had every right to rail on them for their pride, willful blindness, and the bad decisions that had brought on this calamity. But looking at them now, he knew that simply presenting the hard truth would be punishment enough.

He took a deep breath. "It's time for all of you to finally let go of your illusions. I will tell you what happened, and we will discuss where to go from here."

Pearl sank down on the sofa next to her daughter. "Yes, John, please tell us everything."

"How did you know to look for Sophie and Mr. Deveaux at the railway station?" Marjorie asked. The note of defiance in her voice was subdued, but still noticeable. "Was it because of Mrs. Finlay? Is that why she was with you?"

John shook his head. "I'm not at liberty to tell you how we found out about it. On that point, you'll simply have to be thankful that we did. Mrs. Finlay wanted to come along, and I'm grateful she was able to help us. Why wasn't Aileen with Sophie?"

"She's been ill since yesterday," Pearl said. "Some kind of stomach trouble. She can't even get out of bed."

"It's true," Sophie insisted, seeing John's skeptical expression. "You may go and interview her yourself if you don't believe me."

John could accept the truth of what she was saying. He could also see how Sophie might have taken advantage of that to slip out of the house unaccompanied.

Sophie continued looking earnestly at John. "Are you quite sure that what you said earlier about Sandy's parents is correct?"

John didn't want to crush her spirit, but he knew he had to be truthful. "Yes, I knew before reaching the station that Lord Ormond was in France. When we found you waiting to board the train with Deveaux, I was furious. Perhaps I ought not to have let my anger get the better of me. But, Sophie, I knew he was out to hurt you, and I could not allow it."

Sophie dipped her chin, miserably accepting his words.

"After Sophie and Mrs. Finlay left the scene, we moved Deveaux to the stationmaster's office," John continued. "He was already gaining consciousness. There was a medic who stayed with us until Deveaux was fully alert and it was clear he'd suffered no lasting harm. A constable arrived and wanted to question us both, but Deveaux asked if everyone could leave the room for a few minutes first, so that he and I might talk privately. Naturally, they obliged him." John couldn't keep the rancor out of his voice as he added that last comment.

"Thank heavens there was no lasting harm, or he might well have called for you to be arrested," Pearl said.

"He could have had me arrested anyway," John answered. "He wasted no time pointing that out to me. But he had a different plan in mind. It seems he was prepared to marry Sophie, thinking he could force a quick marriage to her before his father could catch wind of it and stop it. The earl is dead set on his son marrying a young woman with better connections but whom Deveaux loathes."

"He wants to marry me?" A gleam of hope returned to Sophie's eyes.

John hated to have to disappoint her again. He shook his head. "Deveaux thanked me for having stopped the plan once he learned your dowry isn't as large as it had been rumored to be."

For once, Marjorie was speechless. Pearl was in shock as well. Pressing a hand to her chest, she looked pale as death.

"Deveaux said he's not interested in raising a fuss. He'd like to keep everything quiet, so that our reputations are not tainted. To accomplish this, our solicitors will be meeting tomorrow to discuss terms."

"We have to give him *money*?" Pearl asked, aghast. "We are ruined." She leaned her head against the sofa and wiped her brow with her handkerchief.

"We are not ruined," John said firmly. "It's a setback, but we'll manage. The most important thing to understand is that we must never speak of this to anyone outside the family. In fact, I recommend we talk of it as little as possible among ourselves, too, lest something should be overheard and spread."

"We are putting money into the pocket of an aristocrat." Pearl shook her head. "I can't believe it."

"That's why they're always rich, I suppose. And we are not." This observation came from Marjorie. It was a rare moment of clarity for a woman who was typically too starry-eyed about the highest classes. John hoped this was a sign that she was learning to see the world as it was, not as she wished it to be.

Tears began to fall once more down Sophie's cheeks. Although they had all been hurt by these events, John felt most sorry for her. Her dreams had been the loftiest, rising effortlessly with the naïveté of youth, and they'd had the farthest to fall. "You will recover from this, Sophie," John assured her.

Eyes lowered, Sophie murmured, "Mrs. Finlay was right."

"Let's not talk of that woman anymore," Marjorie said.

"Actually, I believe we should talk of her," John said. "She's proven herself to be a great friend to this family. We should all be grateful to her. Anyone who denigrated her should be heartily ashamed of themselves."

"A friend? Are you sure that's all she is?"

John wasn't going to allow her to keep needling him about this. He'd been giving them the unvarnished truth today, and he wasn't going to stop now. "I hope that in time she'll be more."

Sophie's head jerked up, and all the women stared at him. John found that he didn't mind. He was happy to lay this out in the open, just as he planned to do with Rose as soon as he could see her again.

"John, you can't be serious," Pearl said, panic rising again in her voice.

"Let me assure you all that whatever happens, I have no plans to abandon this family. Not under any conditions. I will provide oversight as I have done, and I will continue striving to do my best for you. We'll all be happier if you can set aside your fears on that issue."

"You say that now—" Marjorie began.

"Why shouldn't Uncle John get married if he wants to?" Sophie broke in. "He has a right to be happy too."

John was rather pleased to see the other women had no answer to that.

His pleasure was tempered, however, when he saw the way Marjorie slumped, her eyes squeezing together as if she were in pain. He knew she'd been lying to herself about many things. It may have been her way of assuaging the devastating heartbreak of having lost a beloved husband. John prayed she could finally come to terms with this and find the peace she needed.

By the time he'd left them, several things about the family dynamics had shifted in ways that John felt were for the better.

Despite her physical weakness, Pearl's determination to be more involved with family issues and make decisions for herself had been reignited. Marjorie was going to have to accept that she no longer had the last word on everything. John was glad to think that Pearl would have a greater influence over her daughter again. Perhaps it meant Rose would have an easier time of it, if he could ever persuade her to join this family.

Early the next morning, Rose walked out of her lodgings.

She had just raised her umbrella against the misty rain, preparing for another cold and wet walk to work, when she noticed a carriage parked at the curb. The carriage door opened, and John jumped down to the pavement. He was smiling, which seemed a miracle after the last time she'd seen him.

"Fine weather we're having," John said as Rose instinctively lifted her umbrella higher so that he could stand under it.

Her joy at seeing him safe and sound after the debacle at the railway station was overshadowed by more immediate concerns. "I'm afraid I've no time to chat. I must get to work. I can't afford to be even one minute late."

She wasn't exaggerating. She'd had to grovel to Mr. Pettit to retain her position. This she'd just barely accomplished and under threat that even the slightest infraction in the future would get her sacked without question.

"That's why I've brought the carriage," John said. "You'll get there early—and somewhat less damp. Thank you for taking Sophie home yesterday. I was sorry you didn't stay, but I don't blame you. I thought you'd want to hear how things turned out."

"I certainly do," Rose agreed. She allowed him to help her into the carriage. He took the seat opposite, smiling at her as the carriage got underway. "What a luxury this is," she murmured, thankful to be riding to work rather than trudging through the muddy streets.

"I'm relieved to know you didn't lose your position over Sophie," he said. "I was worried, trying to think of some way I might help you if you had."

"You were?" Rose ought not to have been surprised. John was too good a man to allow someone else to suffer for his family's sake. She didn't ask what ideas he'd been mulling over in this regard, just on the chance, slim though it was, that marrying her was one of them. It was a topic she wasn't ready to broach again. "I saved it by the skin of my teeth, but I'm still there. So tell me, how is Sophie? And what happened with you and Mr. Deveaux after we left the station?"

"Sophie is heartsick, as you might imagine. She understands the enormity of what she did. It may take time for her to recover, but I truly believe she'll ultimately be better for it."

"So there will be no public scandal?"

John shook his head. "It seems we've managed to avoid that, thank God. The train began boarding, dispersing the crowd just as we hurried to move Deveaux to the station office where a medic could attend to him. He came to nearly right away and immediately took charge of the situation, despite his swollen jaw." He flexed his right hand with a smile of satisfaction at the mention of that, then filled her in on the rest of the details.

Rose was highly offended on John's behalf that he should be forced to pay for this outcome, since Deveaux had been the instigator of the scandal. There were plenty of things she could say about it, but she knew she'd be wasting her breath. She gave a resigned sigh. "It was the best course, I suppose, since it will protect Sophie."

"I'm glad to hear you still have some sympathy for the girl," John said with a smile. "Let me assure you, she has learned her lesson well."

"Let us hope it lasts this time."

"I think it will. She is grateful now for all you did. Her relationship with her mother has actually improved, hard as that may be to believe. Sophie said you had instructed her to be totally honest with her mother, and she's followed your advice."

Rose was pleasantly astounded. Maybe her attempts to help Sophie had worked after all. Maybe Rose had been too hard on herself to think she had been unqualified to offer any guidance that could be of real value.

"I hate that Deveaux ruined your chance to be a manager," John said, as the carriage came to a halt in front of the post office. "That's probably another reason I was so ready to punch him."

"Was it?" Rose felt guiltily flattered. "While I can't approve of violence, I thank you for the sentiment all the same. I have every intention of moving forward and regaining what I lost."

"That's what I love about you, Rose. You are indomitable."

Love. The word resonated in her ears.

Much as she wanted to stay here with him, it was time to go. She moved forward in the seat, preparing to leave the carriage. "Thank you for the ride. I do wish you and your family well, in spite of everything."

"Wait." John took her hand. "I wonder if we might meet again. Over tea, perhaps?"

Rose shook her head. "There's no ABC depot near this post office."

"I'll meet you anywhere. You have only to name the place."

It felt so good, having him hold her hand. The way he was looking at her, much as he had on the night of the charity ball, told her he was not speaking only of renewing a friendship. She thought of Abby's remark, *"a little romance can be a fine thing."*

For Abby, it had been an easy choice to give up the occupation she'd once reveled in but which was now tedious and burdensome. She was setting aside the way of life she'd known for years and walking away without a backward glance.

Rose's work had become burdensome, too, and downright awful. Yet the idea of simply abandoning it did not feel right. She kept thinking there was still something she wanted to do in life. Something she'd been called to accomplish. Even if she wasn't entirely sure what it was.

"John, there are many things in my life that are unsettled. And in your life too. It can't be an easy time for your family right now. They need you. I feel it would be best if we refrain from seeing each other."

She hated to say the words, knowing what she was putting at risk. She did love this man. But there were still pieces of her life's puzzle to work out, and most importantly, some remaining fears to put to rest.

John appeared to be having equal trouble accepting her words. He seemed to chew on them a bit. Then he said, "Are you saying never again, or simply until the conflagration burns itself out and the ashes cool?"

Rose couldn't help but let out a little laugh, refreshed once more by his wonderful, wry humor. "The uproar these events have caused your family must be worse than I thought."

"It will pass. It may take time for their battered pride to heal. They are already coming to accept that mistakes have been made but all is not lost." He continued to cradle her hand between both of his. "I understand your desire to take some time. I will wait until you are sure. You know how I feel. Waiting a while won't change that."

She allowed John to help her down from the carriage. When he let go of her hand for the last time, she felt as though a rush of cold that he'd been temporarily holding back was now surrounding her once again.

It wasn't easy, standing on the gloomy street and watching as the carriage rode away. Was she on the right road?

CHAPTER
Twenty-Eight

John immersed himself in his work, looking for ways to increase his client list and reduce expenses. In addition, he'd gone on daily visits to his family to keep up their morale. It all kept him busy, but never prevented him from being intensely aware of each new day that passed without hearing from Rose. After a few days of this, John had been happy to receive an unexpected offer that could afford him a pleasant break. He'd been invited to join a member of his club for luncheon.

As he sat opposite Douglas Shaw, he was glad he'd accepted. They had met a few times before Shaw had left the country on a long business trip. Now that he was back in London, it seemed he was actively renewing his acquaintances.

As they dined, they both shared details about their companies and found plenty of common ground. Shaw was an engaging fellow with many interesting stories to tell. At one point, when John had been discussing the necessity of incorporating his nephew into the business, Shaw had related to him about how he had risen from being a young telegraph operator to a partner at his company. It increased John's confidence in the choices he'd been making for Edward.

"Did I mention that my wife was also a telegraph operator?" Shaw said. "Speaking of which, I believe we share a mutual acquaintance—Mrs. Rose Finlay."

"You know Rose?" John was so taken by surprise that he used Rose's given name without thinking.

Shaw smiled. "She and my wife, Alice, are good friends. They lived in the same boardinghouse a few years back."

"I imagine she's told you a lot about me—and my family." John was beginning to feel uneasy at the thought.

"Rose is not a gossip, as I'm sure you're aware," Shaw answered. "She's a private person. Sometimes even my wife has difficulty getting her to talk about what's going on in her life. She has not discussed your family, other than to say she was a chaperone for your niece a few times."

This information lessened John's concerns. He was still smarting from the solicitor's bill, and he didn't want the money he'd spent to avoid scandal to have been in vain. Then again, he should have known Rose could be trusted. "When was the last time you spoke to her?"

"We haven't seen her for a few weeks. We've been out of town visiting my in-laws, and when we returned, we found a letter from Rose telling us she had transferred to a different post office. From the sound of it, she's been demoted too. She didn't give us any reasons for this drastic change, but as you can imagine, my wife and I are concerned."

"You're perhaps wondering if I know more about her situation?"

He nodded. "As we have established, Rose can be tight-lipped. But Alice and I got the impression that you and Rose are friends, especially as you had trusted her to be a chaperone for your niece."

"Yes," John answered, feeling the twinge of longing that had grown familiar over the past week. "We are friends."

Shaw was looking at him in a way that seemed to signal he understood the meaning behind John's words. Had they seen the same kind of feeling when Rose had spoken of him? John hoped so.

He gave Shaw the best answer he could. "Rose was forced out of the manager's position at Piccadilly. The person responsible for it wanted to get Rose away from that post office. I can't tell you anything more, except to state categorically that Rose did nothing wrong. There were circumstances beyond her control."

"I see. It was as we imagined, then. My wife plans to visit her tomorrow, but we thought it might be helpful for me to talk to you first."

"Oh? Why is that?"

Shaw gave him a diffident smile. "I don't want to intrude on your personal affairs, but since we are speaking of Rose, who is a dear friend, I thought I could be a little bolder. Please don't hesitate to tell me if I'm overstepping."

"Ask what you like," John said, more than happy to discuss the situation with someone who knew Rose and could lend a sympathetic ear.

"Is Rose still acting as a chaperone for your niece?"

"Not at the moment, although I hope she will consider it in the future." He gave it barely a moment's thought before adding, "In fact, I've asked Rose to be much more involved in my family."

They'd just been discussing telegraphy, and now here they were, speaking in code. Shaw's quirk of a smile showed he was decoding the message just fine. "Have you? Splendid!"

John shook his head. "Nothing is settled yet." He deliberately phrased his response this way because he wasn't going to accept the idea that Rose would keep refusing him forever.

"Is that because she's determined to keep working, by any chance?"

It was an arresting question. "To be honest, I hadn't really considered that possibility." On the night she had refused John's proposal, they'd discussed many things but not her work. "I can only say that for whatever reason, she's doggedly determined to stick with the Royal Mail, despite the contemptible way they treated her. As if she has something to prove, either to herself or to those who demeaned her."

"She has spent years dedicated to her profession," Shaw said. "She had made a plan for herself and pursued it with such determination that she can't imagine doing anything else. And she values her independence and guards it just as fiercely as she pursues her goals."

John nodded. Perhaps it had been on Rose's mind that night, after all, bound up with her fear of becoming too dependent on someone else. "That's very insightful."

"Most of that insight is from my wife, who went through something of the same challenge herself. But she continues to find ways to pursue the work she loves. I'm proud of her for that."

"She sounds like an accomplished woman. I can understand why she and Rose are such good friends."

"I hope to introduce you to her someday." He sat back and studied John for a moment. "There are some men who believe women should give up their professions when they marry. Do you have an opinion on the subject?"

"I can only speak for myself. If Rose should want to continue on at the post office—and I personally couldn't fathom why—I wouldn't stop her. My biggest regret would be that her talents are being wasted there."

"Perhaps she'll find something better," Shaw suggested.

"I hope she will," John said.

He'd found this entire conversation quite illuminating. Best of all, it had raised his spirits to spend time envisioning life with Rose, speaking of it aloud. It made him feel as though the reality of it was that much closer. God must somehow be working in the situation. John felt sure he'd done all he could. He must wait; Rose would come to him when she was ready. And when she did, he'd be ready for her.

⁓⊙⊙⁓

Rose had not been surprised when she received a note from Alice asking if they could meet. She knew her friend would want to learn more about why Rose had been so unceremoniously sent down to Southwark. What had surprised her was the location Alice had suggested. It was an address on Leadenhall Street that Rose didn't recognize.

As she approached the building, she noticed it wasn't too far from Alice's former workplace, where Douglas was still a partner. This was a busy street located in the City, London's financial and business district. Rose's interest was piqued when she saw the ground floor of the building had a telephone exchange. She knew there were only two or three of these in London, although this newest invention for communication was catching on, and the number of subscribers was growing.

She watched through the window as a group of very young men—Edward's age or younger—were hard at work. They sat in front of large boards, moving wires around, plugging and unplugging them. This was done seemingly at random, although Rose knew there must be a method to it.

She turned away to greet Alice, who was just approaching her.

"How are you, Rose?" Alice asked, smiling with her unique brand of warmth and compassion that was as potent as any effusive hug could be.

Rose took a step back, afraid this kind greeting might actually make her teary-eyed. "As you see," she replied, putting on a cheerful expression. Although when she was around Alice, it wasn't difficult to feel happy. She was thankful to have such a friend.

Alice turned to peer through the window of the exchange. "This is fascinating, isn't it? And so appropriate that it should be here, in this building. Douglas says his company will likely install a telephone in the next few months. He thinks there will soon be enough other businesses with telephones to make it worth the expense. There is even talk of installing them at post offices for public use."

"Is that why you wanted to meet here—to show me this?" Rose did find it interesting, and she was amused at her friend's enthusiasm, but any mention of the post office these days only brought down her spirits.

"Actually, we're going up to the fifth floor." Alice went to the building's main door and opened it for her. "This building has a lift, which will make things easier for me in the coming months, I must say."

Alice spoke with cheerful pride, as if she owned the building. Rose knew that couldn't be true, although it was clear when the lift operator greeted her by name that Alice was no stranger here.

When they reached the fifth floor, they exited the lift and walked a short way down the corridor. They paused at a door marked *Mrs. Shaw's School of Business*.

"You've opened your school already?" Rose asked, thoroughly overtaken by surprise.

"Not yet. We're still setting it up." She unlocked the door and ushered Rose through. They were standing in an empty room that had several doors leading off it. "This will be the reception area. Then we branch into larger rooms. . . ."

Alice led Rose through the space, pointing out the rooms for instruction in telegraphy, typewriting, and shorthand. "Eventually I'd like to add more classes to cover bookkeeping and other forms of clerical work, but I think this is ambitious enough for now."

"It certainly is!" Rose was astonished at the scale of the undertaking—and at Alice for launching the project when she had a baby on the way. "How are you managing this?" she asked, genuinely awed.

"Douglas helped me write up the business plan, and we have some investors who are helping us to get it going by purchasing the equipment and the lease. We have the money for all expenses and salaries for the first year. We have notices and advertisements ready to go, once we have settled on a start date."

"But when did you find time to do all this?"

Alice laughed. "There was a lot of time to think and plan on those long ocean voyages."

Rose looked out the window of the room where they were standing, the one Alice had designated as being for telegraphy training. Traffic bustled along the street below. Pedestrians hurried up and down both sides of the street, all looking purposeful and intent on their destinations. For Rose, the very air of the place was charged with the energy of commerce. It was a world that was looking ahead and full of plans. Was this world going to leave her behind, stuck as she was in a position that held faint hope of advancement?

Behind her, Alice said, "The most important thing I have left to do is to hire staff. I've already engaged two people. They will be my receptionist and a clerk for handling the bookkeeping and student records. Now all I need are teachers."

Rose turned to look at her, excitement beginning to bubble in her heart.

"They must be the right sort of people, naturally," Alice continued. She began to tick things off on her fingers. "Skilled, experienced in the field they are teaching, clever, organized, and able to take on a multitude of tasks and work with a wide variety of people. They must have compassion for their students and yet be able to drive them to excellence."

"I see you have high standards. It may be difficult to find such people." Rose did her best to match Alice's matter-of-fact tone, but inside she was leaping for joy.

"I've got my eye on a few."

"I suppose you will teach telegraphy?"

"That had been my plan, but sometimes plans change." Alice laid a hand on her stomach and smiled, not looking the least bit perturbed at the interruption this future arrival would be causing. "I will still have the general oversight of the school, but I need someone who can be my primary assistant, to watch over things and report to me when I can't be there. Someone with managerial experience, for example. If such a person could also teach the telegraphy classes, that would be a huge plus. I had wanted to ask you from the start, but you'd just been promoted to manager at Piccadilly and were perfectly content there. But then—"

"My plans changed," Rose finished for her.

Her change of circumstances had not been happy, as Alice's had been. Then again, hadn't Abby insisted that change needn't always be bad? *"With change might come a new vantage point or new opportunities."*

This was a momentous decision. Many people with business acumen would point out how risky it was to give up steady work for a business that had not yet earned its first shilling. Rose could not afford to be cavalier about the money she depended on for survival. Alice had said they had money to pay their staff for the first year. And then? The school would surely be a success. Rose was prepared to expend every effort to ensure it was.

"When do I start?"

After they'd finished discussing the details, Rose walked home. She felt lighter than air, as though her feet weren't quite touching the ground. Yet she was very grounded indeed.

She realized Alice had never even broached the subject of her demotion. That was old news now. There was only a better future to look forward to. She could begin again to live her life as she saw fit. It was as though the last piece of the puzzle had fallen into place.

Or very nearly. There was one last, very important thing she had left to do, before she would really be at peace.

At the next post office she passed, Rose popped in to look up an address in the city directory.

CHAPTER

Twenty-Nine

The houses lining the street where John lived were stately and elegant but not ostentatious. Mayfair had resonated elegance and respectability for over a hundred years. Rose walked past the line of homes, all neatly kept, their steps scrubbed clean. There were iron railings painted in gleaming black in front of each set of steps that led down to the servants' entrances. There was little to distinguish one from another, aside from minor details such as a window box, a display of statuary, or plants on the front steps.

The treelined street was quiet but not sleepy. People walked at an unhurried pace. Several gave a polite smile or nod to Rose as they passed. Every now and then, a private carriage or a cab passed by. Everything about the neighborhood had a peaceful air. Rose could understand why John would want to live here.

She checked the house numbers as she walked. At last, she got to the address she was seeking. The four-story house with its neat façade was nearly identical to all the others on the street.

As Rose walked up the steps to the front door, she realized there was one very interesting difference between this house and the others. The door had a large and ornate brass knocker. It was oval and about the size of a man's face. It had an intricate design that did not exactly look like a face, but still, it suggested one. It brought to Rose's mind the door knocker on Scrooge's home in *A Christmas Carol*. That door knocker had briefly turned into the face of Marley's ghost as Scrooge approached it, giving the old fellow quite a fright. Once Scrooge was inside, he turned to look at the back side of it, half expecting to see the pigtail on the back of Marley's head. Had the knocker reminded John of the same thing? If so, it was a charming bit of whimsy.

The knocker was probably more for decoration than for use, as most people rang the bell these days. The house had one of those too. But Rose opted for the knocker just to hear what it sounded like. The handle was heavy and made a satisfying rap on the door. The noise was certainly loud enough to be heard inside the house.

Rose began to grow nervous as she waited for someone to answer. She'd kept her nervousness at bay during the long walk to Mayfair, but now she began to wonder if she was doing the right thing. There were other ways she might have contacted him that were wiser. What if he was out of town? She would feel heartily embarrassed for having come here.

It was too late for second thoughts. The door was opened by a butler, who regarded her with an affable expression. Rose had no reason to suppose all butlers were old, but this one looked not too much older than John. "May I help you?" he asked politely.

"My name is Mrs. Finlay. I apologize for coming unannounced. I wonder if you could tell me whether Mr. Milburn is at home?"

Without a moment's hesitation, the butler opened the door wider. "Yes, ma'am. Won't you come in?"

Heart racing, Rose walked into a well-lit entryway with a polished wood floor and a long mirror on the right wall. At a glance she could see everything here was of the first quality, while not being pretentious or showy. Just like the home's owner.

Rose couldn't resist turning around to look at the back side of the door as the butler closed it.

"You're not leaving so soon, I hope?" John said.

Rose turned back. He was standing at the far end of the corridor, looking at her with evident surprise, although he also smiled.

"I was merely curious to see the back of the door knocker."

This sounded completely foolish, of course. She opened her mouth to explain, but she was cut off by John's robust laughter. "Were you looking for Marley's pigtail, by any chance?"

"Yes!" she returned with a grin.

"I knew it." He clapped his hands together with delight. "Rest assured, there are no ghosts in this house."

"I'm glad to hear it." Her words came out a little breathlessly. He was standing not two feet away from her now, his presence filling her senses. It was all she could do to remind herself that there were still many things to discuss, important issues to be made plain. She could not assume she knew for sure how John would respond to what she'd come to say.

"Might I take your coat, ma'am?" the butler offered.

While the butler was collecting her coat and gloves, John said, "I happened to mention to Bryant here that if a Mrs. Finlay should ever call, to bring her in right away. I'm happy to see that comment has borne fruit."

"You expected me to come?" Rose asked in amazement.

"Well, there was that standing offer that you might come and borrow any book from my library."

"Ah, right."

A plump lady whom Rose guessed to be the housekeeper came out from a back room and approached John. "Would you be wanting some tea for you and your guest, sir?"

"Yes, thank you, Mrs. Drake. Earl Grey, if you please. We'll take it in my study."

"Very good, sir," she said. Even as she addressed John, she was looking at Rose with the same friendly curiosity as the butler had.

"I thought we'd be more comfortable in the study," John explained to Rose as he led her down the corridor. "The parlor makes a good show for guests, but it's too formal for my taste."

The study was, in fact, his library. Two walls were lined with books. A large desk and chair took up a good portion of the room, leaving just enough space for a small leather sofa. The third wall had a large sash window that looked out onto a small garden.

"This is delightful," Rose said. She ached to peruse the shelves, to see what treasures they contained.

"I'm glad you like it. It's my favorite room in the house."

"I can see why."

"I get some of my best work done in here. Especially when I'm working through a thorny problem or trying to come up with new ideas for my company. My hope is that by surrounding myself with the work of geniuses, some of it might rub off on me."

"I have no doubt it has." This entire house spoke of the successful life he had built for himself. Through the window, Rose could see two workers tidying up the garden. One was clearing dead leaves out from the bushes while a second raked the gravel path. Although much of the garden was dormant for winter, it still looked like it would be a pleasant place to sit on a mild day.

Rose could not have envisioned a more perfect place to live if she'd tried. Everything about it spoke to her, drew her in. Perhaps it was only because of the man who lived here. Or perhaps because it was an extension of the man himself. They had been like-minded on so many things. Why should she be surprised that his home would seem so perfect as well?

"I shall make good on my promise to loan you any book you

like," John said. "Although perhaps you might first indulge me in a bit of conversation?"

"I'd like that," Rose said.

John led her over to the sofa. Once she was seated, he joined her on it.

His closeness felt so good. Flooding her mind with memories of when he'd held her. Kissed her. Offered her his heart . . .

First things first, Rose. She cleared her throat. "I have some very good news to share. I felt sure you'd want to know about it since we are friends and I know you've been concerned about my welfare."

If he was taken aback by her attempt to change the mood that was so obviously settling over them, a slightly lifted brow and a small movement to readjust himself on the sofa were the only indications of it. "Wonderful! I'm all ears."

"I have been hired to work as a manager and telegraphy instructor at a new business school."

"That's brilliant! Which school? When do you start?"

"We'll open in January, but I'll start work right away to prepare the lesson plans and handle other details." Rose was gratified by his easy, instant expression of happiness. "The school has been started by a friend of mine. It's called Mrs. Shaw's School of Business."

"Mrs. Shaw's . . ." John repeated, his voice trailing off. He looked, if Rose were to try to describe it, thunderstruck.

"Her husband, Douglas Shaw, is a member of your club, I believe. He says he remembers meeting you."

"Yes," said John, smiling. "He's a capital fellow."

Mrs. Drake arrived with the tea tray. As the aroma of the Earl Grey tea wafted from the teapot, mingling with the scent of books and leather, Rose decided she couldn't think of a more perfect bouquet.

"This is cozier than the ABC depot, isn't it?" John said, noticing how she'd inhaled and smiled in delight.

"Indeed."

"Tell me all about the school," John said, once they were settled with their tea. "I want to hear everything."

She happily obliged, and John's enthusiasm for the project was unmistakable.

"I'll sign Edward up for that school," he said after they'd talked at some length. "Perhaps he'll be the first student to matriculate. I already know he'll get on well with his teacher."

He said this with a look of such tender regard that Rose, who was long unused to being the breathless sort, thought her rapidly beating heart might keep her from breathing altogether.

He took her now-empty teacup and set it aside. "If you'll indulge me, there is another topic I'd like to discuss." He gently took hold of her hand. "We touched on it at the charity ball."

"There is one other thing I neglected to tell you about that school," Rose said, before he could proceed further.

He paused, waiting for her to continue.

She took a breath, preparing for the final hurdle. If John wanted to marry her, she had to be completely honest with him, revealing her deepest heartache, one she had not even shared with her dearest friends. As a widow, she could keep it locked away. But not as a wife.

"Alice will have a great need for my managerial abilities in a few months because she is going to have a baby, and this will likely keep her at home for a month or more."

"You did mention that," John said.

"What I did not mention is that I accepted that important role because . . ." She gulped and plunged in. "Because I will never be in her position. What I mean is that no matter my circumstances, I cannot have children."

She closed her eyes, ashamed that she'd had to admit this awful truth. But she could not in good conscience marry a man who desired children. For years she had harbored debilitating guilt that this was perhaps why Peter had sought another wife.

In the silence that followed, she could feel John looking at her. She could imagine him reconsidering everything, trying to decide how best to step back from this awkward situation, to pretend that he hadn't really intended to propose to her again. She steeled herself to go along with such a charade, for both their sakes.

"Rose," he said quietly, "I love you." He began gently caressing her hand, and she dared to open her eyes. "I love *you*," he repeated. The slight change of emphasis, and the way he looked at her, made her heart trip over itself once again. She had laid down her greatest burden, and he had accepted it.

"I would never make light of this situation," John continued. "I can see you feel it deeply. But we must also reflect on the fact that God has blessed us abundantly in other ways. You will soon have an entire brood of students to look after. You will be able to make an important difference in their lives. As for me, I'm involved almost daily with the care of five nieces and nephews. That seems like plenty. Three of them are already quite enamored of you—"

"Even if their mothers are not," Rose could not help but say.

"They'll come around. They have been truly chastened by everything that has happened. In any case, I've already told them that if you were ever to agree to be my wife that they would simply have to accept it."

Rose gasped. "You did?"

"I most certainly did."

"Now that I think on it, I had a similar situation with my mother-in-law. She is dead set against my getting married again."

"Is that so?" John's surprise turned quickly to amusement. "It seems we have been wrestling with similar issues."

"Yes. Although . . ." Rose thought back to her argument with Mother Finlay on the night she'd agreed to escort Sophie to the charity ball. "There was one occasion when I categorically told her I would get married again if I chose to. At the time, I had no intention of marrying anyone. I think more than anything I was simply cross about her meddling in my affairs."

"And now what are your intentions?"

After all they'd discussed, and all they'd been through, he may have expected her to reply easily, without hesitation. But Rose couldn't bring herself to give an answer. Her heart was too full.

John ran a finger lightly over her mourning ring. "Why do you wear this? I have to say I've been wondering about it, especially after you told me about Peter."

"It was given to me by my mother-in-law. I wear it to appease her. She grieves for her son so deeply that I've never been able to tell her the truth about him. I believe it is long past time I did."

"It is probably for the best," John agreed. "I think it's admirable that you've wanted to protect her, but holding this secret for so long must have been a terrible hardship for you."

Rose looked down at the ring, which for the past seven years had been a symbol of all that had been awful in her life. "There is another reason I've worn this ring."

"Oh?"

"It was to remind myself that men are selfish, conniving, traitorous creatures who are driven by vanity and pride and who are never to be trusted."

Rose was only being honest, but she could see that John was taken aback by this unexpected torrent of abuse against men. She wanted to laugh, but also to cry at the knowledge that she'd held those destructive beliefs in her heart for so long.

"Not all men, surely?" John said at last. "Granted, I can name a few that fit your description—"

"Not you, John Milburn." She tugged at the ring. "You have shown me just how wrong I was." Indeed, there would never be another man like him. She had truly found the very best one. As the ring came off her finger, Rose felt free of the bitterness that she'd been harboring for years.

"I will admit I was remiss on one important thing, however," John said.

Rose dropped the ring into her reticule. "What's that?"

"You had every right to reject me before. I did not propose to you properly the first time." He dropped to one knee in front of her and took hold of her newly bared hand. "Rose Finlay, will you do me the very great honor of becoming my wife?"

Rose was embarrassed to find herself blushing at this unabashed display. Never had she thought to find herself in this position again. She took a breath, preparing to answer, when an object on John's desk happened to catch her eye.

It was a leather portfolio, the kind used to carry papers while traveling. Rose had seen it while making her initial review of the room, but she hadn't stopped to consider what it signified. Looking at it now, it was a symbol to her of just how far she'd come. She loved this man, and she was ready to trust him with her whole heart. She would keep this house while he was away and never doubt she was secure in his love.

She turned her gaze back to John and saw with amused mortification that he was beginning to look worried by her silence. Rose had never been one to delay action once she'd made a decision. She wasn't going to begin now.

"Yes, John," she said. "I will marry you."

In an instant, John was back at her side on the sofa, kissing her to seal the deal. Then he paused, pulling back to look at her. "My dear Rose, I ask only that, in the midst of the busy life you plan to lead after we are married, you'll find plenty of time to be with me. Do you think you can manage it?"

Rose placed a loving hand on his cheek and smiled. "I promise you that will be my first priority."

EPILOGUE

Everyone was together again, and Rose couldn't be happier. John and Rose had invited Emma and Mitchell, along with Alice and Douglas, for a reunion gathering. Although their own wedding was still weeks away, John had insisted that Rose was the official hostess for this party. It had seemed quite natural, especially as the servants treated Rose with cheerful deference, as though she were already the mistress of the household. Every time she visited John's house, it felt more like home. Very soon it would be, and the anticipation was sweet indeed.

Tomorrow was Christmas, and Rose would be joining John's family celebration. Louisa, spurred on by hearing Rose describe her childhood Christmases, was preparing to read *A Christmas Carol* out loud after the holiday dinner. Edward also wanted to join in the performance. Rose was heartened to think one of her family's traditions would belong to her new family as well.

Mother Finlay had declined the invitation to join them, but that had not been from malice. She was recovering from a massive shake-up of her world. Rose's first honest conversation with her had been as difficult as expected. The lady was being asked to give up many false notions about her son. Change was going to take time. John, bless him, had been doing his best to win her over and convince her she wasn't being abandoned. In truth, that had been her greatest fear. She was also mollified when they'd made it clear they would never do anything to shame her publicly. The few people who knew the details would never speak of it again.

As Rose and her friends enjoyed coffee in the parlor after dinner, the topic turned to the future. In January, John and Rose would host an elaborate Twelfth Night party, to which all of their friends and relations had been invited. Their wedding would follow two days later. Their honeymoon trip would be delayed until summer, owing to the rough winter weather and the impending opening of Alice's school, but Rose didn't mind. She couldn't think of anything better than spending long evenings by the fire in that book-lined study with her new husband, where they could read and chat and plan the rest of their lives together.

Everyone cheered the news that the student roster at Alice's school was filling up. As John had predicted, one of the students was Edward. The lad was more than eager to begin.

"I'm surprised his mother allowed it, to be honest," Rose said. Even though John's nieces and nephews were happy about the upcoming nuptials, Pearl and Marjorie had been more grudging in their acceptance.

"I believe Edward will be the bridge," John told everyone. "He loves his mother, and he wants fervently to take good care of her. Yet he also thinks the world of Rose and will allow nothing bad to be said about her."

"They will all come to love Rose in time," Emma declared. "Who wouldn't?"

"Indeed, who wouldn't?" John echoed, placing a gentle hand over Rose's.

His touch always sent her into breathless fancies, the sort she thought she'd left behind years ago. Rose was learning not to ignore or suppress such feelings and simply enjoy them instead, although she did wish she could at least stop blushing like a schoolgirl.

"To think, it all started with this book," Emma said, smiling. She motioned toward the spinster book, which was lying on a small table in front of the sofa. Rose had brought it along tonight and confessed how the book had been "borrowed" by Emma, who had then thrust it into Rose's keeping. It was now officially returned to Alice, but she showed no great enthusiasm for taking it back.

Rose gave Emma a critical look. "What would you describe as the *all* that started with this book?"

"Why, our marriages, of course!" Emma replied without hesitation. "First, it brought Alice and Douglas together."

Alice rolled her eyes. "With as much trouble as that book caused me, I'm inclined to think my marriage happened despite it."

"There were some bumps in the road," Emma conceded. "However, 'the course of true love never did run smooth,' as the spinster book says."

"Actually, my love, I believe Shakespeare said it first," Mitchell put in with a smile.

"And then there was you and me" was Emma's response, and she beamed adoringly at him.

Alice cleared her throat. "Again, I think there could be an argument made as to whether your success was because of or in spite of that book." But a smile playing around her lips belied her serious tone.

"And lastly, there is Rose and John," Emma finished triumphantly, not swayed by these interruptions.

"Do not associate that book with me," Rose said firmly. The book might have amused her friends, but Rose had found its contents grating. "I got as far as the section describing how heartbroken the fair widow is—" she placed a hand to her forehead and heaved a melodramatic sigh—"and that this is the reason why the gentleman must work so hard to win her. Let me assure you that nothing could be more off the mark."

There was a pause. Emma looked taken aback at the bitterness that had risen suddenly in Rose's voice, even though by now she knew the unhappy story of Rose's first marriage.

"And yet I did have to work very hard to win you, my dear," John said, gently breaking the awkward silence.

"Did you?" Rose said in surprise. Although John had made the first overtures toward a friendship, Rose had supposed their love had grown naturally, as a seed planted in good soil, and that her own nosiness into Sophie's life had been the catalyst for all of it.

"Oh yes." John gave a wry chuckle. "Once you were in my sights, I extended every effort to capture your heart. A woman like you—honest, intelligent, proud, independent, and with an excellent taste in fiction—why, any man would be a fool to pass up such a rare and perfect gem." The warm and welcoming eyes that had drawn her from the beginning looked once more into hers. "And don't let me forget to add beautiful."

His boldly stated admiration gave rise once more to the effervescent happiness that had been so foreign to Rose for years. She found herself unable to answer, her heart too full to express itself in words. She could only return his gaze with love and thankfulness.

"It's clear to me you didn't read far enough," Emma said, pulling Rose out of her gauzy feelings. "This is the passage you ought to have read." She popped up from her chair and grabbed the book from the table.

Rose emitted a groan and tried to stop her, but she was too late. Emma returned to her chair and opened the book to the precise page with so little effort that she might well have had the entire thing memorized.

She began to read aloud. "'The woman who has lost a husband with whom she had never known true love is harder to win than any other. If she is persuaded to enter the marriage bond again, it must be on her terms. She will be clear-eyed, knowing from bitter experience every sort of trouble that may arise. Yet she is willing to plunge ahead with the confidence that this time she has made the right decision. Old things have passed away and all has become new. Her soul has truly bonded with another's for the first time. Then, at last, may she say without hesitation, "I am my beloved's, and my beloved is mine."' There, you see?" Emma turned the book so that the pages were facing Rose, even though Rose was sitting too far away to read them.

Rose was speechless. She had to admit the passage described her pretty well.

John, too, was nodding in agreement. "I think that is accurate, about it being on your terms. You showed up at my house to give it a thorough looking over, to see if it would be adequate for you—"

"That's not what I was doing!" Rose sputtered in indignation.

"—and to inspect the door knocker to ensure it was worthy of a true lover of Dickens's works," John continued, grinning. "It seems to have won your approval."

"It certainly did," Rose agreed, laughing at the memory.

"I believe the author moved from Shakespeare to the Bible in her quotations," Douglas said. "Perhaps that is a better reference book for life?"

"Although I am a devotee of the Bard, I must agree with you on that point," Mitchell said.

Rose wasn't surprised to hear the two men concurring on this. Over dinner, she'd learned more about the childhood hardships they had both endured, and how they had ultimately come to trust in God's loving-kindness to overcome their bitterness. John had faced his share of troubles as well, but his faith had never wavered.

All of them were inspiring examples to Rose. She found

herself being drawn back with gentle care to the sturdy, simple faith that had been her parents', and that she knew still guided the lives of her cousins every day.

"I still say this book is valuable, notwithstanding," Emma said, undeterred. "Alice, if you don't want it, I'll be happy to keep it in my collection."

"I shall take it home and give it some thought," Alice answered. "However, I think we may all agree that for us, at any rate, that chapter of our lives has closed."

Emma looked about to object, but Mitchell distracted her by murmuring a line in her ear that caused her to smile and brought a sparkle to her eye. Alice took advantage of the moment to gently pry the book from Emma's hands and place it back in the protective brown wrapper that Rose had brought it in.

Rose had just barely made out what Mitchell said: "Perhaps we might do our own research on the subject instead?"

John must have also overheard this remark. He gave Rose a sly wink and whispered, "I like that idea." It set off a fresh round of jubilant fireworks in Rose's soul. *Yes*, she thought, *a little romance can be a fine thing.* But it was just the beginning, and she was joyfully looking forward to all that was to come.

AUTHOR'S NOTE

I hope you enjoyed visiting 1880s London in LOVE ALONG THE WIRES. In case a few passages from this book raised some questions, I've attempted to answer them here.

Was that post office robbery real?
The robbery of jewels and other valuables from the Hatton Garden post office in November 1881 actually happened as described in this book. The perpetrators were never found, although a prisoner in a Belgian jail confessed to the crime years later.

Why were young men working as operators in the telephone exchange?
The telephone exchange on Leadenhall Street is based on a description from the time. Early on, young men were used as the telephone operators until it was decided that women, with their melodious voices and polite manner, would be more effective at that task.

What finally happens to the spinster book?
Personally, I suspect it somehow found its way once more to a quaint little bookshop in a friendly corner of London, where it fell into the hands of another lady wishing to learn how to navigate the mysteries of love. Whether that's the case, and what the results were, is impossible to say for sure.

ACKNOWLEDGMENTS

The goal of a historical novelist is to escape into the past for some length of time and bring an earlier world alive so that the reader can one day take that same exciting journey. Too often, though, the present world does its best to interfere with making that happen. To that end, I'm grateful for everyone who provided the support I needed at critical times to help make this series the best it could be. My thanks to my editors, Jessica Sharpe, Dave Long, and Charlene Patterson, the marketing and publicity team at Bethany House, and to Elaine Klonicki for reading my manuscript and providing valuable feedback. Thanks and love to my always-supportive husband and to my dear friends who supported me in prayer and never failed to believe that my books would be wonderful. I also remember with great thanksgiving Claudia Welch, whose mentorship and friendship meant more to me than words can express. She has left this world, but the impact of her life continues to resound. Most especially, I thank God daily for His love that never fails through any trial and for His abundant grace and blessings.

Jennifer Delamere writes tales of the past . . . and new beginnings. Her novels set in Victorian England have won numerous accolades, including a starred review from *Publishers Weekly* and a nomination for the Romance Writers of America's RITA Award. Jennifer holds a BA in English from McGill University in Montreal, Canada, and has been an editor of educational materials for two decades. She loves reading classics and histories, which she mines for vivid details that bring to life the people and places in her books. Jennifer lives in North Carolina with her husband, and when not writing, she is usually scouting out good day hikes or planning their next travel adventure.

Sign Up for Jennifer's Newsletter

Keep up to date with Jennifer's news on book releases and events by signing up for her email list at jenniferdelamere.com.

More from Jennifer Delamere

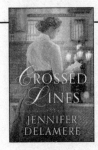

Mitchell Harris is captivated by Emma Sutton, but when his best friend also falls in love with her and asks for help writing her letters, he's torn between desire and loyalty. Longing for a family, Emma is elated when she receives a love note from a handsome engineer but must decide between the writer of the letters and her growing affection for Mitchell.

Crossed Lines • LOVE ALONG THE WIRES #2

You May Also Like . . .

Years of hard work enabled Douglas Shaw to escape a life of desperate poverty—and now he's determined to marry into high society to prevent reliving his old circumstances. But when Alice McNeil, an unconventional telegrapher at his firm, raises the ire of a vindictive coworker, he must choose between rescuing her reputation and the future he's always planned.

Line by Line by Jennifer Delamere
LOVE ALONG THE WIRES #1 • jenniferdelamere.com

At loose ends in 1881, Cara Bernay befriends a carefree artist, the brother of the handsome but infuriating Henry Burke, the Earl of Morestowe. Recognizing the positive influence she has on his brother, Henry invites her to accompany them back to their estate. When secrets on both sides come out, Cara devises a bold plan with consequences for her heart.

The Artful Match by Jennifer Delamere
LONDON BEGINNINGS #3 • jenniferdelamere.com

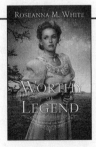

After uncovering a diary that leads to a secret artifact, Lady Emily Scofield and Bram Sinclair must piece together the mystifying legends while dodging a team of archaeologists. In a race against time, they must decide what makes a hero. Is it fighting valiantly to claim the treasure or sacrificing everything in the name of selfless love?

Worthy of Legend by Roseanna M. White
THE SECRETS OF THE ISLES #3 • roseannamwhite.com

◊BETHANYHOUSE

More from Bethany House

When their father's death leaves them impoverished, the Summers sisters open their home to guests to provide for their ailing mother. But instead of the elderly invalids they expect, they find themselves hosting eligible gentlemen. Sarah must confront her growing attraction to a mysterious widower, and Viola learns to heal her deep-hidden scars.

The Sisters of Sea View by Julie Klassen
ON DEVONSHIRE SHORES #1 • julieklassen.com

In 1942, a promise to her brother before he goes off to war puts Avis Montgomery in the unlikely position of head librarian and book club organizer in small-town Maine. The women of her club band together as the war comes dangerously close, but their friendships are tested by secrets, and they must decide whether depending on each other is worth the cost.

The Blackout Book Club by Amy Lynn Green
amygreenbooks.com

Captain Marcus Weatherford arrives in Russia on a secret mission with a ballerina posing as his fiancée, but his sense of duty battles his desire to return home to Clare. Clare Danner fears losing her daughter to the father's heartless family, but only Marcus can provide the proof to save her. Can she trust Marcus, or will he shatter her world yet again?

In Love's Time by Kate Breslin
katebreslin.com

◊ BETHANYHOUSE